LAST GENTLEMAN IN THE
MIDDLE DISTANCE

Last Gentleman In The Middle Distance

A novel by
JEAN E. VERTHEIN

Adelaide Books
New York / Lisbon
2020

LAST GENTLEMAN IN THE MIDDLE DISTANCE
A novel
By Jean E. Verthein

Published by Adelaide Books, New York / Lisbon adelaidebooks.org
Editor-in-Chief
Stevan V. Nikolic

For any information, please address Adelaide Books
at info@adelaidebooks.org or write to:
Adelaide Books
244 Fifth Ave. Suite D27
New York, NY, 10001

ISBN: 978-1-951896-25-6

Printed in the United States of America

1.

Denial copes with life and death. Anon.

Grabbing the door, the leather-jacketed man nodded to another one exiting, as the outer, winter air collided with the inner fireplace heat, pipe smoke, and breath that steamed onto the cold glass. He also nodded to Meta.

Meta, seated, was watching people come in the main door. She did not beckon back to him. She was mulling over whether to continuing to wait for Katia or slip away.

Her great-uncle Heinrich's allowing her friend's visits became Meta's lifeline, especially as he'd changed from gentry upholder toward countryside folklife supporter. He warned her. "Berlin is Gomorrah."

Outside the entrance, people were lining up or crowding though not entering. They were making noise grew louder

Here she was inside this Berlin coffee house and restaurant. A dragon, medieval-like, painted by an unknown artist in photo detail on the wall, could almost spit fire, laugh at her and leap off. The creature was not expressionist with bright colors but linear and precise.

Finally, through Meta was distracted from studying the creature by the arrival of her friend Katia. The outer glass door shook. Her longtime friend Katia waved and entered.

"I'd almost given up on you," Meta said. At their three-table cluster within the usual North German wooden framework corner. They chatted about their hats, over their hair and removed them. Others appeared to savor their late afternoon coffee and pastry. Still others were reading their newspapers from a rack along the wall opposite the dragonet.

"That man over there in the military jacket is staring at me," Meta said, in a topic-change. She meant the one who had nodded at her a half an hour earlier. When speaking, she dug her heel into the rug beneath the table and by accident caught Katia's foot. "Sorry."

"So, do others? Does it matter?"

"I must get away." At that moment, the din outside the coffee house-restaurant grew into a racket and interrupted Meta. The restaurant's entry door fanned open, so its manager and waiters had to slam it shut against men in khaki still squashing against it.

Their red crest arm bands seemed to whirl. Black on red bladed swastikas, the men's armbands above their elbows bumped, rattled and crushed against the windows. Also, like farm tools in flight toward customers inside, the marchers turned into attackers drummed and shouted. Customers inside gripped their hands or the tables' edges. Some kept heads down, not watching. Some peeked at the uproar. The crowd outside seemed about to burst through the door, until it was locked.

Meta froze, unable to see whether her friend ducked or even noticed the ruckus. Meta watched her hands, tipped with fresh vermillion nail polish, clutched each other. She glanced up to see any words inscribed in the wooden canopy and paneling. She looked for gilded runic like letters or old Germanic, like guidance found on old rural houses. None were there. Afterall here she was in flamboyant Berlin.

She tried praying. But could she neither mouth words or mumble them, except some from the Lord's prayer. Katia would be silent, maybe blank-minded or worried about her man, said to be her fiancé.

Meta opened her eyes to tight skirt that revealed her calves, shaking slightly above her silk covered pumps, heels round like smaller calves. The shoes were stained in blue, rose and white, merging into each other color.

Toward the door, the men with swastika armbands were, as seen through or gleaned

At, were moving away from the heavy door they'd been unable to break through

"We're here for a feast," noted Katia. "Let's enjoy it. We'll move and eat at the big table?" She'd wriggled out of her red coat, which contrasted with her waved platinum hair.

"I'm hungry; I'll sit right here, not move and eat roast duck." Meta half-twisted her leg around her chair leg. "Who's there now?"

"Youngish, thin, hair-pomaded to his head? "If my Alf's late getting here to meet us," asked Katia. "How will he get in?" Dizzying window images suggested that would-be entrants, now blobs pressed against windows, could not whoosh in past quasi-soldiers. Presumably, Meta worried about the Stahlhelm paramilitaries were bumping there against the windows. The manager or one in charge locked the door.

"No," said Meta, trying to ignore the scuffle. "I'd like to get out of here. Fast. Besides that fellow over there is there?"

"No one's there. You're getting carried away." said Katia.

"Don't stare, just glance," Meta said. "Dark bearded with dark glasses?

"Look sideways."

"How can I see, except by looking? Only a thin nondescript man's there. Don't bother about him. He looks harmless enough. Sip your wine, sit back. Stay calm. Oh, the other one in the jacket came back."

"Every few days at work," said Meta, "the phones work, someone calls me."

"Of course, phones ring. Then trace the calls. Trace him." Katia tapped the tabletop with her knuckles.

"The authorities would refuse my report as useless. After three months, he still whispers."

"How's your training going?" asked Katia.

"This is lifework. Don't mock my treatment for my therapeutic training. He's not the one, but one like him." Didn't Katia see? Cold anxiety was swamping Meta, unsure about the events at this moment. Shaken, she was relieved to see her longtime friend.

Katia looked unconcerned, nonchalant. "Your dream, you must know him.

"Eat your roast duck." Katia glanced at the door and at him. "That fellow won't eat you. "His bomber jacket must be military with no insignia."

"Flight jacket," Meta replied. "American style?"

At least, Grete might understand. Wretched, Meta asked herself. "Is my Todi still alive in the countryside?"

Worse, Grete herself had not been seen for months neither here in Berlin. Todi was seen. "Come in, come in," Meta had once said to her, when allowed to visit her own granduncle's domain. With a delicate and distant Berlin magic, Grete'd brushed in, sat within her spread-out pleated skirt, smiled, and kick-bounced her crossed leg to her inner music.

"Don't laugh," Meta said to Katia. "No one understands." Her throat swelled, and her head felt heavy. "Two people I've talked to about this kind of fellow with the military jacket have died.

Her friends meant leeway to come and go. Katharina von Weser, not the ones on bicycles on the roadway, were welcome at Cherusche Haupthaus and broadened experience of the world. Nevertheless, introducing Katia, her then new friend, to Uncle Heinrich's vulgar side and opinions embarrassed Meta, wishing for ordinary daily lives, like othermothers, fathers and siblings.

Wherever were hers, Meta wondered and why were they away?

"Say no more." Katia, whose white-blonde waves seemed like wires to register far-off data, was relieved, when Alf, her fiancé, pried his way through the demonstrators at the main door.

"I'm not sitting around waiting to die. Not me." Katia said, turning to welcome and kiss Alf.

"But what can I do, or we do?" asked Meta. "Todi is his grandfather's captive, as I used to be. Now so, a strange man calls me, and Grete is missing."

2.

Trees long uprooted for ground salt, farming and furniture left the moors semi-barren and heathery in rosy purple during August. Breezes crossed these moors through clumps of high pine, soothing the skin and nose with their aroma.

After the 1918 Great War armistice, if some were joyful in peace, most turned furious. True, its battles had spared the sandy and sour heath earth where Katia, Grete, and Meta grew up. "Hamburg and Berlin uprisings," about 200 kilometers away from the farms on the heath, "are too distant for worry," said Meta's great-uncle. The arc of watch and wait was beginning.

At age ten, Meta sped outside to catch up with her cousin, running alongside Hansi. At this point, her Granduncle Heinrich did not call her back in, while the children explored the loamy moraines with blue flax, cannabis, and sugar beets. They plucked blueberries for old cook's tortes, which would mellow Granduncle's wrath.

They also picked currants from the plant, raspberries and blackberries, treasured for good time's food or expectations of hard times' hunger. Sometimes while moving, they snagged themselves on holly or thistle spines, while searching for nut morsels, other berries, and safe mushrooms they'd learned to find.

As Meta rushed to claim them, low upright or flat stones, unseen within grasses, sometimes tripped her. Racing to catch up with little Hansi, she almost bumped into a rock, bush-camouflaged.

Observing her through his binoculars, Granduncle gave orders to his sister, Lore, Meta's aunt. "Don't let Meta drift across the heath. Lock the door, if you must. Hook the gate to keep her inside."

In tight periods, Heinrich v. Cherusch beckoned toward his neighbors to assist the area sufferers. He stood erect and twisted his short beard below his chin, bent slightly and re-erected his stature. To a passer-by half kilometer afar, he grinned, waved and shook his fist as a shout for success, as the fellow was leading a stallion, known for its powerhouse plowing thrust to prepare land for planting. The whole region was stoked to obtain the finest harvest five months or so later.

He rotated toward the youngest one in his household and called out to her, "Smell the fire!" Head down, Meta heard his calls and scooted ahead of the flames licking the land. Granduncle saw her roam the northwest German heathland, and yelled, "Come back. Watch out."

"How do we feed and protect you in this time of trial without plenty after the war, when you run about?

During these po war years, the house watchtower was off-limits to children, though forbidden, it lured them upward.

Hair blossoming around her face, the young girl's mother, was present one day and gone the next, in post-Great War years. Thus, Nanna began protecting Meta at nighttime. By seven, Meta slept alone upstairs in the room off the landing.

Against Granduncle's wishes, Meta now climbed up the watchtower near her room and begged for to look through his binoculars. "The fire's not spreading. Let me see."

"No." Fire was creeping more than expected toward his lands, fire that fellow large-farm-holders set and monitored was seen crossing the common ancient stone boundaries and smoldered on the old Plaggan woodiness. Inhospitable as food for lambs, its tender woody shoots, when cut, benefited humans. In time, Granduncle Heinrich reassured her, "This fire should burn out."

Inside the big house, Haupthaus, Meta, a fledgling whose childhood waned and adulthood waxed, slipped into the closet abutting her uncle's study. He'd say, "Listen: mice or chipmunks are rummaging inside the walls." Nanna urged him not to bother about them and return to his books; other householders would follow up on rodent noises.

At first, Meta held her breath against being found playing in there with her happy-sad doll.

The wall hole, bluish tapestry-covered, between the study and closet, so went family tales, might have served ancient confessors or entrapped viewers. Through the worn tapestry, Meta exerted her curiosity and began shadowing her granduncle's circle. He'd been educating it beginning followers.

"Arminius," Granduncle reminded his group, "is the Saxon turncoat soldier with Varus won the war against Caesar Augusts and his Roman legions. Meta the child understood this Arminius' victory.

His Saxon warriors in Saxonia also happened to be in the far away Holy Land, just as Jesus' parents sought a room in the inn. Finding none, they wound up in its animal manger, while traveling to pay taxes to Caesar Augustus.

In battle sanctity around bonfire councils in winter or his study in summertime, Uncle Heinrich's imagined warriors near his farm had crouched with battle-axes and swords. With his cronies, squires, lesser nobility, local merchants, and extended family, Heinrich reminisced about this marshland battleground area within bogs and fog. Heinrich's study's fire clicked, echoing the tribal restlessness alongside with the Saxanus smith myth. By 1923, Heinrich's protégés put their minds to old texts and the Rosenberg texts, other scholars and a stranger called Hitler.

Upstairs, the woman's master bedroom with ark-like bedstead, carved with bas-relief masks, intrigued Meta. Not a protégé, she peeked into the forbidden upstairs room. Her favorite doll in red sashed white shirtwaist carried upstairs with her was two-faced, happy front and sad back. Below, the fading mint silken bed dust ruffle puffed onto the floor. This room was more locked against her than the closet of Granduncle's study. On the floor next to the ruffle, Meta fanned out her other bisque dolls, who smiled with eyes closed and listened to her tell of fairy tales.

Since his wife's putative death, Heinrich, or Tante Lore if visiting, hiss-whispered to Meta, "Avoid that room. If found in there, you'll disturb everyone." Once a daytime housekeeper had left the door unlocked. So others took to saying, "No one's trustworthy these days."

Opening drawers, by age ten, Meta discovered mascara, lipstick, and rouge to tint her cheeks. Scented from a pale green

Parisian crystal atomizer, she intoxicated herself on her own skin with frankincense. Next, dolled up in a flowery, gauzy shirt-waist; she danced and shimmied in big red pumps with heels curvy like her calves in the tri-partite armoire mirror. One side angled just so toward the wall mirror. Infinite Metas appeared.

A true friend, she'd bring to this stable wall and the mobile wing mirrors. For now, her multiple images befriended her.

She jumped. Heinrich's gait pounded the floor, muted slightly by two layers: the valued Persian hall runner, safeguarded by a crocheted ragtop rug. Meta yanked off the fancy clothes and slid beneath the bed springs. Nerves exploded.

"Meta! Your scent belongs to one woman." Who? Bending down, Granduncle managed to grab her ankle against her resistance. Hooking her fingers around the springs and bracing her free leg against a bedstead leg, she countered his yanking her out from under and horsewhipping her. Still he ratcheted up the stings to thirteen, intolerable and bitter.

"This room's off-limits. You know who's in charge. Tell no one what's happened here. Otherwise, you'll be sorry." He locked her in.

The horsewhip was less painful than his tree branches, his switches, which hung downstairs on a rack in the back entryway and barn, a bit like a silver object in the front entry that warranted her wary curiosity—an iron catapult bolt point. Like most area gentry and small farmers, Granduncle accrued weapons, for sport, hunting and security and hung them on certain of his walls.

Six hours later, Meta was still locked with in the forbidden room. She heard Nanna plead. "Heinrich, please, set Meta free." But Nanna was forbidden to do so.

Meta kicked the door and spat out words. "Why is he so cruel?" The door seemed warped and moved but did not open. In the forbidden bedroom, she'd also hid other stuffed animals and breakable dolls, when she was younger. One by one, she removed them from the armoire drawers below the stored dresses. Meta smashed their heads on the floor. If still unbroken, she threw them against the mirror, which cracked.

A floorboard creaked. Nothing more happened.

She looked out and plotted. Through the bedroom windows, finger-shaped leaves glistened on giant oaks would shelter her and cover her escape, while she crawled out. As a kid, she'd climbed many trees.

Haw, gum, and birch trees spaced throughout the moor. Some clustered in an old grove, once called Alah, and had been worshipped in ancient times. On the rare inclines on the moor, lush foliage in salty, gritty air, along with giant oak domes and furry-wooly-prickly evergreens floated westward to the sea.

From Lower Saxony, low by the Atlantic, rivers launched multitudes. Thousands daydreamed of pushing out across the sea. In words no one else heard, she told her world: "I will go too."

Three hours later, Granduncle Heinrich still refused to allow Nanna to unlatch the master female-bedroom. Outside with Mrs. von Handler, they whispered and c, Meta thought. Mrs. von Handler said, "Keeping her in there gives us opportunity together without her that nuisance. She won't miss you."

By early dusk, the door's clicking by an unknown and unseen hand in the darkening awakened Meta. She held her breath. The door was still unopen. For once, she ruminated without tears.

Dazed while stricken there and thinking back, she darted from the kitchen down into the cellar. Wooden columns there braced the inner passages and ceiling of the semi-developed cellar. Pressed dirt walls had revealed root hairs to her, and other cellar parts, bricked, mortared, and plastered, snagged her tousled dark red-gold hair.

On some cellar walls, household cupboards, closed for years, enticed her into treasure hunting. So vintage wines, vinegar with mother froth, tasty-looking peppers, pickled pigs' feet and cucumbers lined the shelves.

Below in the sub-cellar, Ol' Christoph, family doyen, had reminded her, "Not a place here for you to play." In the wine cellar vat, southern wine by the liters had been able and still could fill decanters to satisfy family needs. How much wine remained since the war no one knew. Many now preferred ale.

After her nightmare or day dreaming for survival, here and now the door to the master female bedroom clicked again, as someone was trying out keys to fit the keyhole. Meta ruminated, stewed, and looked out in the early dusk across to the infinity of the new dawn.

If escaping from the house, including its upper bedrooms and subcellar with certain individuals like, Nanna, Christoph the farm manager, or Lore, Meta, if freed, would follow monarch butterflies, hovering on certain blossoms or "horrible Blues," loathed moths. She was a blue she was certain. Hummingbirds, like musical notes, were swinging around the trumpet morning glories, seen from above their fence. Meta's thoughts whirled.

Like down-turned baskets, beehives farther on pegged the heath's earth with bees producing honey, bites and endless beeswax. Rose hedges massed nearby on this sour earth in August, while the heath, called Saxum was as enchanting travelers in August.

Ancient markers—Measur (Judgment or divisibility), Metod (know-how and system) and Wurd (forename and praise)—hid like forceful though silent commanders.

Nowadays, her aunt, whenever present, saw to her breakfast and household tasks. "Sweep the ground floor. Dust furniture with the feather dusters." When sneezing overcame Meta, Nanna said, "Polish the silver instead." Both older women declared and chorused that her work capacity would strengthen by the time she became a housewife and mother. But if Granduncle and Frau von Handler again locked her in the master female bedroom, how could she do housework?

Still gazing outside after her ordeal, she observed that during late summer, the heathery dream-froth moor was visible outside every window. Below on the ground, upright and flat rocks tripped horseback riders or wanderers. Along the riverbank, horses glistened like silver, copper, or gold.

These words also kept replaying in Meta's head along with visits from Katharina Helene von Weser, oddly approved by Granduncle, though he'd disapprove of Katia's urban exposure. Certainly, he would scorn Grete.

Any furry creature dog, cow, horse, or sheep consoled Meta, their furry hug replacing parents no one spoke about. She'd confided in elder Nanna, "Animals are kinder than people."

Meta's thoughts raced. Worldlier than many, Aunt Lore, had reminded her of fears. "Berlinism is creeping into our rural life." Her cigarette and holder had been held upright with sparkles.

Both loved sleek horses. Breeding was revitalizing local farming by 1923; each foal cheered farm communities. The stock dealer who sold cattle, sheep, and an occasional horse to Heinrich came by with his daughter, Grete.

Heinrich made rounds with him for hours regarding sheep for his farm. Theodore van M. and Heinrich von C. also discoursed on headlines: past risings and putdowns in the cities and other connectors between them.

So, the afternoon belonged to the men. Hunting, fishing for trout or carp from the Elbe or Weser, crop failures and old war stories now consumed the men. Katia's father dropped her off when about to visit nearby cousins and instead stayed with the other two men.

The younger female threesome watched the fathers going on their way. Outside on the ground, Katia the art-lover pointed out the carved Gothic doors into the v. Cherusche household. If the three were blurring their eyes, the decorative scrolls above two windows looked like eyebrows wrinkly from laughing. This house they likened to a face on the countryside.

Thereafter, Meta eyed the house anew: a live red brick mass, layered above their sheltered, would-be princess lives. Katia noted, "Without the war, my mother says, we'd have been ladies."

Because these respected visitors had newly arrived, Meta had been let out after many hours in the previously locked master woman's bedroom.

Minutes later, Nanna urged Grete in at the front door. Waved in, Grete picked a rocker in the corner near the corner furnace, covered by the chessboard-style tile, for warmth. Her bright chestnut eyes, beneath her fair natural curls, observed Katia and Meta in their playful made-up dance to gramophone music. "Look!" She demonstrated still newer steps.

Breathless, after trying to follow Grete's dance steps, they sat down to speculate on their lives with laughter, though Grete was quiet. First, they wrote in each other's autograph books. Books they'd imbibed in they also sang out about, as if characters were real, known friends.

Suddenly, Lili's brothers popped up at the back door, while Granduncle Heinrich was off with the other fathers. The brothers and father were sent off.

Meta signaled, NO to Nanna about Lili. Nanna seemed not to see the point. The original threesome was dumbfounded at Lili's thrusting herself into their group.

3.

Area men sought out other men and horses, both conscripted for the Great War, later called World War I. Both were lost to the community in wartime, sources of personal grief thereafter and woes from shortages. The mournful sounding trains and mourning doves seemed to announce these losses faced by Heinrich and neighboring farmers across the countryside. Rivers Ems over to the Elbe juiced this land mass and floated along. Of trees long uprooted for ground salt access and farming, some clumped on the semi-barren moor with rosy-purple heather in late August. Breezes over the moor, soothed the skin and carried a piney aroma.

Granduncle Heinrich had long approved of Katharina Helene von Weser. Through the open window, Meta heard Katia down at the front door. Her urban exposure has been helping Meta range out into the countryside. Otherwise, she only mentally escaped from her circumstances.

The heathery dream-froth moor disguised upright and unseen flat rocks that could trip horseback riders or wanderers on foot. Over along the river bank, horses shimmered.

Area men sought out other men and horses. Both of were conscripted for the Great War, later called World War I. As sources of personal grief thereafter and woes from shortages to overcome, both were lost to community in wartime and peace time, Tension built up within persons and communities.

Heinrich, younger than his sister by ten months, both in their late fifties, stroked his grey and black goatee. "Berlin's corrupting the countryside. Better off people complain the most. The poor don't appreciate what we high agriculturalists do for them."

"Yes, they do," she said.

"Not much, so we all must," he said, "work together against the enemies."

Lore mourned. "The country's sliding away from democracy into decay with dozens of parties. I wish for the social kind, not the political kind!" Meta also favored a jolly good time.

As breeding horses began to revitalize along with farming, each new foal cheered the farmers. The stock dealer who sold cattle, horses and sheep to Heinrich also came by with his daughter Grete.

"What's the idea of Holland sending so much butter here?" Heinrich asked.

"It's the best there is."

"But this onslaught of cheap butter drives out quality here."

Meta tired of churning milk into butter and was relieved when Grete's father replied, "Business is business.

"It takes years to nurture a good bull and cow for milk for butter."

Heinrich, dressed in an old shirt from military service under his grubby dinner jacket, used for work, said, "From now on, we'll put all the attackers, bulls, politicians or practical Jewish businessmen, surveying our farms back in their place."

Grete's father kicked the dust with his right heel. "We'll see."

Watching the fathers go on their way, the younger three-some was on its own like daughters, in their Brudervolk. Katia's hair waved like wires seeming to receive signals from afar.

They were talking, first in the hall inside the front door and, then, in granduncle's study, someone turned a key in the door keyhole to the latter, locking or unlocking the door? The friends stood up at once.

4.

By thirteen, because she and the others were too old for hide-and-seek or play with porcelain dolls and too young for full, all out adventures, they talked books, invented dances and stole vile old ale, from the subcellar. Pretending to dance to gramophone music, Meta called, "Look!" Clumsily, she made up new steps. One—Two—Thee!

Breathless, the three sat on the side porch and wrote in each others' autograph books, popular in America, and read what each wrote. Other long books read and imbibed in sang out to them. Lili sat taking in their antics.

Interrupting their chitchat and self-made cachet on the porch, the original girl threesome was now still aghast toward Lili's pushing herself into their Kultur Kunst Klub, a little intellectual club for art and culture. Common enough, they crisscrossed books heard about and read. Formerly, Katia read Tacitus in Greek, German classics and English ones, learned and loved, such as, Jane Austin, the Bröntes, and Trollopes.

"No," Meta read Heidi, the Fontane classics, less Greek and Latin.

"No." Grete favored French naturalists, Tolstoy and lately Vickie Baum.

From the Romans about the German tribes, "Chatti, Cimbri, Cherusci, Anglii or Alemanni," Katia reeled off this singsong that Grete repeated.

"More than his own," Katia said, "Tacitus loved the Teutons. Next Katia asked Grete, "How long has your tribe been here?"

"About 1600 years."

"You're sure? About when did our tribes join up as Saxons," Meta added from hearing Granduncle.

"No," said Katia, "they kept separate longer. Know also that in Jesus' childhood, the Romans," Tacitus wrote, "lost out to the Saxons." She whirled on one right foot.

"Right afterward, the Romans crushed the Jerusalem temple." Meta chimed in.

"How so?" Katia stopped twirling.

"We came here about then," added Grete, tapping her feet, about to dance.

"The Franks battled us Saxons and forced us into being Christians, Granduncle said. "God-believers, not gods. Now Uncle urges us backward rather than forward to rid us of that Christianity, Aunt Lore says. We Saxons were also the first pirates, some say, backed by their gods. Saxons had to get out of the way, hide or listen in. Watch out!" Meta snapped, while she whispered.

Grete listened. Katia spoke. "Be careful. Watch out."

Moving inside the back door through the hall toward his study they plucked items for use, just as they dramatized pirates. Meta wound a red scarf around her forehead and put on an earring of Frau von Handler from within Uncle's couch pillows and covered her right eye socket with a black bottle cap like an eye patch.

High stepping around them, Lili wielded a broom like a long sword. Grete waved a long white scarf's two ends like flags. Lili, quiet until now, marched around.

Katia found a dustpan for a shield and ruler-sword. Meta pilfered a sax, a stone knife and shield, from her uncle's study, off-limits. They both jabbed the air and jousted with each other without horses. Jumping on the old elephant hide couch, Meta defended it from attack. Lili still followed. With a measuring stick, Katia pretended to hijack this long boat.

Meta smirked. Uncle Heinrich would trust her new friends, except maybe Grete. She imitated his rumbling voice. "Saints knocked down Wodan's altar and high, great holy tree."

"But it was the soldiers of Charlemagne the tall Great King, Meta said, "who chopped down the Saxons' Tree of Life, Saxon Temple called the Irminsul.

Katia noted. "Sounds like the human soul."

Much later, the Prussians lost this battle much though won the war to conquer Lower Saxony and Hanover," Meta continued. "No more battles, since before the Great War, 'to end all wars.' We're going backward."

"No," said Grete, out there with her father the cattle dealer. "On the heath, life's quiet as can be, at this moment." Girls of the time were not meant to think, only to play, so they did so.

The girls were prancing down the hall and following her into the study, where tall Katia knocked her head against the iron right angle brace between wooden column and library ceiling. Suppressing a cry, she patted her head.

From a shelf, Meta removed a box: bandanna and stuffed raven inside, "Memory." Meta shouldered it and strutted around in the unlit, semi-gloom. Falling, its claws she grabbed to break its fall gripped her white cotton shirt.

"Ravens are smart," noted Katia.

"One's Memory, its partner's Thought. Uncle says it's missing." Steps made her shove them back up, re-shelving them. Meta hooked her uncle's huge black umbrella on her arm, stomping to "Bravo, Bravo!" Their acts never stopped, unendingly.

Her Tante Lore's sister Annike was said to have been shipped off before the Great War from Hamburg to New York. Also on the shelf were Heinrich's carved Indian head and velour cowboy hat, which "the defector Annike supposedly gave him." To mend fences against straying Holsteiner, Jersey or Guernsey cattle, he'd wear it, though not to talk business with the fathers.

"Someday, I'll wear a cowgirl hat like that," said Grete, humming the Charleston, as they caught on to one another, hop-moving right feet backward and left arms ahead and following her in an instant. Next, they kicked their left foot backward, as their right arms were swinging forward. After several reversals, they moved their knees sideways and their hands across their knees. At the end of several rehearsals, they hooted. "Yippee, we're flappers, now we're Flappers!"

Their hoopla in the hall and granduncle's study might filter through closed doors. Heavy steps approached.

Grete, breathless, sat on a maroon armchair. The steps passed.

Katia clicked open her compact to rouge her cheeks and handed it to Meta, who pouted in front of the mirror. "Dull." She snapped the compact shut.

From a dangling pouch, Katia rolled tobacco into tubes from tissues. Turkish clove cigarettes or regular nicotine ones from America with the stately camel before an Egyptian pyramid, Meta caught one tossed to her without matches. Emboldened by smoking, she next inched open Heinrich's drawers for tobacco used in his meerschaum pipe.

Instead, an opalescent handled knife and revolver the length of her hand lay there. She dropped them into her big work dress pockets. She slammed the drawer shut within the drawer and the study door. "No one will know."

Kati grew confidential. "Did I see you snuggling up to that good-looking stable boy?" Finger to her lips shushed Katia and protected quiet Grete.

Grete's dress styled with a pleated white skirt with aqua skirt panels and white top was much filmier than Meta's dark brown corduroy jodhpurs and high boots. Her dark red-blonde curls and Katia's unruly white curls were untamed by hot irons. Quiet on the sidelines, Lili sat in her blue work over-dress setting off her vivid cloisonné features and sometimes wild demeanor.

Meta hoped for new flaring skirts with an English style cap to race across the green moors, while bi-planes whizzed overhead. Infatuated with the elevated beauty of horses, she'd inadvertently spotted a nude, a showering male laborer on the ground. Rarely yet were horses seen in the world war aftermath on the roads these days in Lower Saxony.

"No, you did not see me with him." Meta shushed Katia.

Clomping in, Nanna implored them, "Quiet down. Here one does not smoke, risk fires. Or talk about risqué subjects. Heinrich forbids you in his study, don't you know?

"The fathers will be back here from the fields anytime.

"Settle down where you belong or go outside. The air's healthier there rather than in here by fireplace and with stale pipe smokiness."

Life was increasingly unsettled in Lower Saxony with postwar soldiers, and labourers, like caterpillars, which were moving with disjointed legs.

Granduncle Heinrich designated the older peasants "Look at what little stock is left for agricultural work." He'd meant to urge others to hand over land to younger ones north and west of where Meta grew up.

Once outside, the girls and their fathers gazed across the land.

Also, red-brown timberwork farmlands were sheared into "Ever smaller allotments would never do." He continued, "Too many family members collapse productivity." Thus, his complaints were cranked out.

Closer by, her granduncle's hundreds of Hektars, an old brick factory and unused kiln, barns and Haupthaus, hall house, once long ago from one grand tree now comprised his "estate." Its hall house was mostly brick walled in with some diamond shapes.

"Why do you have brick factory?" asked Meta.

"Too many questions!"

"But your buildings have all their bricks."

"Some might crack and fall, and we'll need more."

At two flattened roof end points of the main house, two horse heads crisscrossed. Seen as predators in unclear mental states, serpentine figures, zoomorphs or protectors, they were also protectors. Inward heads of horses toward each other meant ongoing family proprietorship; outward heads indicated new ownership. Some folks thought they also guarded their domains. Others deciphered magic from these Hengst and Horsa.

Before the war, farmers had bred horses; workers shined their coats. To enhance these glorious creatures, whose hoofs below elegant fetlocks pranced, while overall they were curry-combed and groomed to outglitter their riders.

One day, Katia, whose father was just able to afford new horses outside old battle zones, invited Meta to ride a young horse. Doubting her ability to prance cross-country and dodge high burial marking stones, Hugelgraben, hill graves, and smaller Hemengraben, she dared ride there? Without camouflage by bushes, she could see the occasional dolmen that would stop or stymie the young horse.

Her half ball newly cut silky hair bounced into her eyes and matched her reddish-brown polished boots. To acquaint the off-white horse Rolando or thoroughbred amber Rodolpho with her, Meta let them smell her hand. Rolando nipped it when offered hay though allowed rubbing between his eyes and patting his back. To mount this tony almost pure white bronco, jumpy like a Pferd, she, too short, threw on his reins, held tackles on pulleys and attached them to the big oak tree within the large fenced in area. To hoist herself up to mount, she climbed on an upended water barrel and threw her right leg over him.

Grabbing the bronco's flowing mane with the rein was easy but stretching her legs over the horse, a Zaurieter, breaker-in, or Pferd, vaulting horse, without a saddle hurt. Rolando needed some nudging and controlling. Guided by Katia, holding Rolando's reins, Meta rode on the worn earth path within the fenced area. Enthralled with this go-round, she clutched the reins and bounced along. Abruptly, Katia, running alongside, let go. The horse tore off. When safely riding, she and the horse jogged and jockeyed. Synchronizing with the young velour horse, Meta rose and lowered herself on this glorious creature.

"Hold on!" The horse reared and heaved her to the ground. She was unable to lift herself up.

Her back and legs ached from the fall. Pulled by wild horse, her palms were burned from gripping the reins in the fall, and her legs scraped on sharp pebbles.

Katia could do little. Heinrich ran up. "I warned you to be careful. I yelled to you. 'Hold on.'"

Refusing to hold onto him, she tried suppressing her pain. In spite of herself, tears squeezed out of her eyes.

"I better not lift you—never know my back—with your injury." Granduncle said.

"I can't move. My tail bone's cracked, must be."

Katia and her father must have dashed up, when the horse bucked and threw her to the ground. They assisted Heinrich lifting and dragging her to a pump. There she gripped the spout and its handle to pull herself up to a nearby bench. No one blamed her at the moment for recklessness and injuries. Her back though felt bolted off-center, rigid and heavy, as she limped to sit. Her torso felt too dead-weighted to move.

Throbbing, she'd oppose Uncle Heinrich's expected "I-told-you-so" by saying nothing. He patted her face to check her consciousness. Stinging and half-sitting, propping her right leg on a stump and half-sliding off the bench, she was dazed.

"That horse should have been broken in before you rode it." He offered his arm to her. "Didn't I tell you'd hurt yourself around young horses? Take an old nag the next time for practice."

She turned her head away, as they hobbled to Uncle Heinrich's cart and workhorse, where he tried to assist her climbing in. In the cart, she agonized with each bump into unreality. In passing horses on houses, they turned down at her or away in disgust from her.

Once at her uncle's property, Heinrich and Christoph helped her limp up to the porch couch below windows open at noon. Nanna examined her. "No blood, just bruises and scratches, aren't they? No blood, gut." Broken bones we'll see about? Calendula, arnica and capsicum and other salves and hot and cold compresses were applied on Meta's back ache and burning neck, arms and palms.

While applying the compresses and salves, Nanna's white crown's and bun's filaments dangled and burnished around her face in the late afternoon back sunlight. She was keeper of the family health. Meta prayed to Nanna's Virgin Mary, Mutt Gottis, to appease the horses' spell, uncle's orders, and her back pain. Which way evil, which way good?

At thumps on the front door, her head wrenched in turning to see new arrivals. Heinrich answered it, rather than wait for two elder women to do so. Inside came his fellow countrymen in country work clothes or Sunday best. He closed the doors behind them, swallowing the words Meta strained to hear. "We all shall combine on the land now into one solid community."

5.

Once Uncle Heinrich had slyly allowed Nanna several weeks earlier to unlock the door to let Meta out, her back pain began lessening. Without Frau v. Handler, he pressed Meta to ride a repaired bicycle with old leather side bags, rather than a horse with saddle bags. That that bicycle might, if some parts unscrewed and break apart worried Meta. Never mind, she'd figure out what to do, and do what she must not do while relenting and giving into him and other unknown forces.

He goaded her into delivering tied and knotted stacks of bulletins to local stop-offs, the farthest two kilometers away at another Haupthaus. It would resemble the one she lived in, though without visible bricks because of its stucco covering and without a tower. Changes might cause outer changes in its structure and words he spoke, so Heinrich instructed her. After all, bricks fall apart without tuck pointing and do melt, though do not burn—they are made by hand—and consolidate structures. He emphasized such possibilities.

"This other big house, you will see, possesses a tree falling onto its roof, like the bent stone Irminsul. Meta knew little of what he spoke about. "He doesn't fix it. Also, there'll be no carved horse heads for ownership or proprietorship that preside from the flattened roof corners. Pshaw, once they did. The devil, he removed them. She would pride herself in finding new ones for freedom, horse heads rearing up with heads upward."

Good for him, Meta thought to herself. But when she arrived at this big house, if in the right place, it was made of stones, not bricks, stacked and arranged to balance themselves while cemented, as the rare solid stone house from late middle ages were.

An old servant met her at the stone house entrance. "Come in, dear, sit down and wait."

A portrait slanted and stood on the parquet floor by the staircase. "Beautiful Mala," the tiny metal plaque said on the lower frame. Long satin hair rippled around her dark eyes, long-lashed, that if alive, would swat men's glances at her bosom that reveled in itself. Elevated portraits of Hanoverian red uniform soldiers, like the British, and Prussian blue on the wall interspersed with bosomy ladies in gauzy dresses with faintly smiling bright-eyed children.

The old servant shuffled into another room behind a door, too warped from humidity to shut. He announced Meta. "Sir, a bold young woman awaits you."

Finally, he managed to reach Meta, shivery from the draft from the door ajar between the front entrance and invite her into the living area, the Stube or parlor. He waved her in. Behind him, she dragged in from the cart a bundle of small, local newspapers left outside this doorway, though she could have dropped them at the side entrance or in the Stube. But her granduncle had insisted she convey them only inside the front door, and she tried to do as she was told but was uncertain about what to do next.

The manservant drew her inside, what turned out not to be the stub or parlor but instead was the ancient haus part, where a fire was crackling in the room center. Above it, from within the squared-off scaffold around the fireplace large enough to walk into, sausages dangled with five loaves of bread just baked; smoke rose from slow-baking haddock and salmon. The smells made her wistful for some prior golden time Nanna talked about when hungry.

With the proprietor's back to her, she surveyed his hall. He was speaking aloud about his plan like a recitative from music she little knew of, as if his hall house was a festive operatic space. He kept speaking. "Rough wood entices me. A wall torn down here leads me to tear another down there to restore the whole inner-place to its original open wooded manger.

"Oh. You must be Heinrich's daughter! Sorry, I thought you were someone else or still coming." He laughed. Meta laughed to fit into his mood and said, "No, his niece."

"Trumpets could usher in the evening joys." He laughed again, she giggled.

True, at some medieval time or even in the last century, his hall embraced animals and people together, warming each other, during the winter, as in their haupthaus was enlarged from a manger farmhouse.

In other seasons, Georg told her what she already knew that sheep and cattle were pastured in the soft open hay dirt-floored area inside though near crunchy woodlots to silence their ba-a-aing, mooing or snorting to minimize their life sounds.

"Then gradually, windows were installed against nature. Vivid ruby crystal and emerald stained glass could much later on dazzle like the Ottonian New Jerusalem times and much later with similar Expressionist colors from art in the teens and nineteen-twenties and earlier from. . . ." This lively fellow with a slit through his mustache above his sandy-gray beard lost her with his words.

Stone mica glittered from around the fireplace. Children she'd played when little liked smudging themselves with ashes and blackened stones to annoy their elders.

"Ja, well, not here much, not many children around. I wish there were."

"We used to swing from hooks," said Meta. Balanced cauldrons on them were tenderizing rabbit over low fires. She remembered them and still saw them in some places.

"I'll remove the tree crushing the roof and fix up this beautiful place." He whispered. "Like you."

She shrank.

"Do you dance?"

"Only the minuet," she said. Safer than the shimmy. He grinned.

"Wait and see," he continued, "Roof will be fixed and walls more colored, like the Rathaus in Lüneburg, this house will soon be ready for a party."

Scratching his wispy bearded chin, he pondered "a dome over hall," Ottonian. She laughed at his 'syzygy,' without understanding his word. Heinrich would use such a word and loathe the idea of celestial bodies united in a universe. She remembered the word only many years later. Syzygy, a straight line between sun, moon and stars,

Every piece would fit together.

It bewildered Meta, saying it quietly over and over, as Georg continued, "Modern curved chairs and stark tables are loathsome Bauhaus nonsense, without our country romanticism."

His voice echoed rather than spoke "Pretend to hear lute, mandolin and maybe lur music with Meistersingers' songs played and danced? I'd sing them to you.

"Biffs and graces will astonish my guests." He seemed older, and she felt younger, a miniaturized person from a distant land.

In ancient days, Vikings pounded their oars upriver and landed nearby. "My hair and my deceased sister's was true child-blonde that darkened over time; hers forever pure white blonde in her premature death and grave. Mine now will turn white in life.

"And you, Meta, lovely dark reddish-haired girl, sit down. Br-r-r, you must be chilled in this drafty room or cold. We'll make you tea or hot grog. I can give you a doll, we have bisque ones here." He sounded like someone else other than whoever he was.

"I don't play with dolls anymore."

"No." He stood over her, until his father's old servant entered. "The young lady must leave."

Waved out by the servant, Meta pulled the newspapers farther, as granduncle instructed her to, inside the door of the old house's oldest section.

Georg dashed out.

"I'm ordered back home right away," she replied, as he handed her wildflowers by reaching for her palm to open it to squeeze and receive his bouquet.

As she was departing, the woman whose portrait in the entrance stood on the floor alighted from a long white sedan. Meta climbed into her horse cart.

6.

Two weeks later, Meta squinted up two human lengths of brickwork in quatrefoil design with its green and yellow bricks fit into earthen red brick diamonds. Great Uncle Heinrich fretted about his buildings needing pointing. Without mortar, bricks would drop on their heads; one had just missed Ol' Christoph.

"No mason's around here to fix loose wall bricks. No thatchers for roof leaks. No sweeps to clean chimneys." Great Uncle cited problems to care for. "Holes mean black insects fall through the roofs into the household. No one around here works anymore." War had taken its toll.

Their trusty mason had gone off to war and left sand dunes to sprout weeds and grasses, where sandpipers flew in to peck for mites. He never came back. Meta watched and waited for the family wagon to be ready to go. Trips anywhere relieved dullness or checked her urgency to get away.

Voices beckoned, and people waved from the road at the drive up to the house. A tall rangy, though bent late middle-aged man, white hair poking out below his work cap, walked up the drive with a skinny much younger woman and two younger men in work clothes, one in military brown shirt.

A dark blue smock outfitted the nervy girl, Lili, who'd visited earlier. Vivid dark eyes and high-relief lips, naturally red, greeted Meta. "I'm Lili."

"I know."

"That Pferd, bronco, I saw, threw you." She'd enjoyed seeing the accident, evidently.

"My folks with me do brickwork, pointing." They relied on her speaking for them.

Meta was anxious to rush her away, lest Uncle see her with them. He hated surprise visits. "Return later."

While meeting with his cattle dealer by appointment was a rare time he allowed Meta to play with Grete. But what should Meta do about Lili?

Neighbors grouped around Erbhof, the farm community or farm court inheritance, and were griped issue by issue. "Apportioning land to one farmer from the larger family, so as not to splinter it, thereby unifying it, cuts off siblings and children from ownership. "Ownership hereabouts bars the colored, of course, and the Jews, but they don't matter out here in the countryside. "Agreed?" Farmer Heinrich asked Cattle Dealer van Melke. The latter nodded.

Meta, overhearing her great uncle, blushed.

"How can we run the country," he asked back, "if family members are cut out of inheriting land? Only the trustworthy become chosen heirs." Uncle so declared. "Negotiate, winnow the best."

They shook hands, and the cattle dealer and his lovely daughter (even Heinrich said so) left.

As Meta watched, her uncle did not wave to her in the wagon for travel.

Besides, his trusty Ol' Christoph, thick wood marking pencil behind his ear, was pouring liquid dynamite to split stumps and remove them to free the land for pasturing and growing. An axe to this project would take days; dynamite to the stumps fragmented them quickly.

The restless and striking Lili intruded again, coming back up the road from her father and brothers. "I promise to walk over tomorrow." They were bunking near Draganatandorf or Barum, in the circle of farm villages between Lüneberg and Uelzen and were looking for agricultural work.

"Too soon." Meta vowed. "I'll meet you halfway." Grand-uncle's mood could indicate his readiness to meet them.

Within his mysterious schedule, the Cherusche were to make rounds to cottagers' and agricultural laborers' huts. Her aunt lamented their rarity and sought to circle farther out. "In this time without war, peace interferes."

"Hungry people," Lore continued and carried the chunky pug dog, Mopsi, said, "must see Heinrich's loyalty to them and willingness to alleviate heartsickness," rather than heartlessness.

"We also need order around here." He always said. She said this all to appease her brother.

After finishing his blasting stumps, Ol' Christoph helped Tante Lore, her daughter Liesl with her baby, Hansi, Meta and her Mopsi into their oldest, scratched wagon. Fritz the aging workhorse was linked to the whiffletree. Now harnessed, he moved in one place: tail flapped away flies and flank muscles ground and legs paced. Strapping him up, Christoph praised Fritz. "Lucky we have such a horse fit for army and carriage."

Because the family hid their Fritz during the war, he, quiet and gentle, survived the army draft of other draft horses to pull military equipment. On the tamped down dirt back roads, he still pulled their wagon.

Aunt Lore, looking down and around, as they rode along, noted with Meta and Hansi. "See, those children on the ground don't glow. Hunger's in lank hair, dull eyes."

Next, Great Uncle stopped the wagon to see about the well. The cover over the artesian well and its tank were cracked. Stones were breaking away from mortar. What could be done about this?

"If you're ever without water," Tante Lore said to anyone who would listen, "look for animal tracks to water sources. Carry iodine tablets to improve water in troughs, or else sip drops from leaves."

Meta asked, "Why?"

"Mist benefits you like dew."

"Like fog?"

Suddenly, ragamuffins buzzed around the wagon and nettled her brother. Lore said, "An indignity: houseless people without water must steal or beg for it."

"They can prop themselves up for shelter by the megaliths, Hunengraben, and add tree branches for roofs." Human-sized stones were also placed in a circle of seats to sit on and talk from.

"Who are the Huns?" asked Hansi.

"Strangers, invaders, who knows? People roundabout say they rode all over us here.

"But you ask too many questions. Study the great rocks," Lore said.

Heinrich came over and continued. "It's said that Huns overran our Heide in the 500s. Our folks mated with the Unknowns, East or West, who knows. Study Eurasia to the North Sea and its metal, timber and amber trade."

"We're special, you mean." Aunt Lore's husky voice lowered. "You're deluded. They're us."

Meta, confused, knew neither invaders, or her mother or father were absent.

"Protect what's best," granduncle said, "ours by right. We're here. Now real strangers, Sorbs, Wend, Czechs, Poles, Jews and other unacceptable types buy up our land at a steal."

"Evil overflows rapidly, don't you know?" Nanna asked.

Half-heartedly, Liesl, was visiting from Berlin, listened with ears holding back waved reddish hair and fastened with ivory barrettes, agreed. "Terrible about water."

The marsh dehydrated; only the mist remained. Heinrich was selling his marshland to cover annual expenses, taxes and new cow purchase to pasture in his rearranged field pattern.

Humble in their wagon, the party trundled along to deliver leftovers, clothes, bottled pickled cucumbers and peppers, sausages for hut dwellers the wagoners tried assisting. Or they gave foodstuffs to those hibernating in postwar makeshift shacks or crude ground holes.

"Don't stare." Lore swatted Meta's arm to halt her jumping off the wagon.

On the ground, Heinrich was poking around rocks or markers to re-tabulate his field sizes and borders to fence in cattle he was purchasing from Cattle Dealer van M.

"We're the natives here. Study geography," he told Meta. "Count and map the megaliths here." To decipher them, his map in his study required his magnifying glass. "Our people also worshipped them and trees–Tiwaz, trees for truth." Tree pillars rooted in the earth, into the universe and unto heaven.

Meta jumped off the wagon. Down in the streamlet, spiky animals, and longish flat-tailed, pieced roots and sticks and muddied them into their dam and kept patting them. Beaver energy cheered her along, as she fantasied the god smith Saxanus and fishing goddess Seaxnet, silver-scaled mermaid."

"Charlemagne, 'the Cur.'" Heinrich intoned over her beavers with talk about tree pillars, "chopped down in Verden and Geismar. World Trees downed, he next ordered thousands of born Saxon tree worshipers baptized."

Uncle expounded; Aunt Lore sighed. "Know the gods by tools and weapons–Celts for stones and *Saxons* for oaks and rocks, *Sax*."

"We were never the civilized Romans with Rome, Greeks with Athens or Hebrews with Jerusalem or Arabs with Mecca. We dwell in Hamburg or Hannover and maybe Berlin?"

"Ah so, Heinrich." His sister Lore injected. "But one's a lively harbor city-state, the other's a beautiful kingly court the Prussians grabbed. And Berlin's Berlin after Paris."

"Ah so, Greeks and Jews," he said, "lost out to corrupt and bankrupt Romans. We kept our Saxonia free, until now. To save it, we'll pull it together again. "

"You should have pursued your university studies," she said, "instead of squandering productive land by selling it off."

"Lore, our Saxons, led others across to Britannia, America and Australia for more fertile land."

"Others were already there, according to your history from a blowhard. Too nice a day for battle. Who knows who's getting ready for one, or when another's coming?"

Snapping his suspenders over his off-white shirt while his forehead temples were pulsating, he leaped back on the wagon and slapped the reins against Ol' Fritz's rump to get him going.

Meta's black puppy "Mopsi" jumped from her lap to Lore's and back. Other black pugs, Meta had heard, were killed off from the mother's litter; the neutral, lighter beige ones were given or sold. Her lap skirt cradled Mopsi.

"Births and deaths are cheap, but lives are dear. Many fled our shore, took the long trip out
. . . ." Standing, Lore projected a stage voice. "How can you go backward to go forward?"

"Party of Volk conscience." He retorted, when an arrow whizzed by his nose, while standing his ground, next to the wagon. It struck the wagon side and stuck there.

Her maroon skirt cut on the bias was caught on a splinter at their first actual stop in their local geo-circle. "These people will get our pumpernickel or buckwheat and survive," she said. In raggedy clothes, torn or moth eaten, they held out their hands.

"You're daft, a true social democrat at heart," so Heinrich said.

She handed produce over the wagon side: bread flour, carrots.

Suddenly, more arrows whished by, slicing the air. "Stop that bow," Granduncle Heinrich, shouted, "and keep that arrow from hunting us, until we pass. Use it on deer and wild birds!"

"Homemade arrows not molded new ones. Don't worry about them."

The riders ducked in the wagon, as it wobbled along, and Granduncle Heinrich drove Fritz faster onward. Abruptly, he stopped. He would not move. Heinrich jumped off the wagon to study the problem.

In the meantime, to prepare for future crises Lore urged the children to study Girl Guides or Wander Vogel, should they ever need temporary shelter, like lean-tos, branches tied at tops and spread into circles. "We children bent tiny branch huts with mud to crawl under or tied hemp ropes between the trees with old blankets or canvas over for tents. Prepare yourself. Alas, our tutor and governess ran off together, we lost our pretend villages."

Another arrow whisked by, as Hansi was awakening. "We made tents last summer in your garden, Grossmutter, grandmother?"

"Oh, not Grossmutter. Grande Maman."

"Grossmutter, watch out for attackers."

"They're practicing by missing us," Heinrich said. "Harmless traditional hunters."

Head, aglow blonde-silvery from sun through the forest canopy, Lore stepped off their wagon to swirl out their red and white tablecloth, flag-like, on moss. White cheese, pumpernickel and cold meats abounded from her basket.

"Be careful." Nanna reached in for an unlabelled wine bottle from Heinrich's wine cellar, and homemade ale.

Thereafter, he dozed and snoozed under the wagon, as did Lore by the tablecloth.

Meta and Liesl on alert played with her baby and Mopsi and sat watch. Noises rustled in the woods. A bird cawed. A cat ran into the clearing. Racket was booming.

War-ripped strangers from cities were returning to rural areas to scrounge for food and crowd in with relatives. "To menace the countryside," said Heinrich, awakening. With pans, cups and spoons tied to their belts, they skulked next to mutts. If better off, they carried prized items to sell to still better off farmers.

"Old soldiers die off," Lore, groggy, said. Heinrich was still out to move Fritz.

"Get back in the wagon," he said. "Not so old, those outsiders will assist us in the coming struggle.

"As for other monstrosities," Heinrich, lowering his voice, said, "Wipe out mad cripples and animals. Old soldiers in the forest are dangerous, if not recruited.

"Heinrich! You're one."

"Magicians, enchantresses, see?" Meta bit her cheek with her fantasy from old fairy tales. Elves, gods, smiths, kobolds from old tales were skipping and dancing, as mermaids were floating in streams and rivers, and tree deities squirreling around. Hudeken or Till Eulenspeigel behaved like tricksters, such as Loki, in the forest.

"Troublemakers now will save us later," Uncle said from the ground. "Duck down. Ignore them." Acting with the hunter's alacrity, he raised his forearm for peace to ex-soldiers. He saluted.

Strangemass, correct conduct, toward this felt menace, "Houseless veterans. Watch out for their tracks. Avoid their diseases."

Meta stood.

"Sit down."

Silence reigned, while the wagon was oscillating and inducing sleepiness. Lore inhaled and lamented. "Smell this free air. Unfortunately, no longer do green uniformed foresters select trees to cut down—and check on behavior. In the old days, we counted on them. When young before the war, our hammocks swung between the trees. We rested. We trusted."

Their wagon parked on a knoll, where Meta gazed at a hutment. "Who're they?"

"We're just fine," Heinrich said. "These are your forebears, living ones."

Meta sat up. Modest house timbers bore scripture, runic style, carved and gilded: Every plant, which my Heavenly Father hath planted, shall be uprooted.

7.

Meta called out to wagon travelers paused on the roadside. "Do you want turnips and potatoes?

A pretty girl greeted them with a Knicks, curtsy. "You grew them?" Her indigo jumper dangled like a scarecrow's garb over sticks.

"We've enough for you."

"Is this what they call your communism?"

"God, no," Aunty Lore said, "don't let my brother, Heinrich, get wind of your words.

For him, our giveaways of extra vegetables are communism. He'll be agitated.

"My grandmother's bedridden. Angela's my name." At fifteen, she was caring for the older woman. Her farm had been farther east and was sold to pay taxes.

"Monstrosities," Uncle Heinrich said, impatient to start up again, and was approaching the porch of Meta's good acquaintance. He was adding "to wipe out."

Meta, startled, asked. "Who? Folks, like these who survived in one rented farmhouse room or departed for America?

Angela grabbed the carrots. "I love 'em." Chewing, her gaunt face seemed to fill in and face turned orangey in the sun.

"Wash them," Lore said, "They're straight out of the earth and will make sweet soup for you: chop potatoes and onions with pepper." Lore lugged all the potatoes she could over to the girl.

Angela raced to the garden for a marigold (Targetas) bouquet for Lore. "Thank you. War's coming again, folks here say so."

"Hard times, worse times, bad times, until better times soon, my great-uncle says so," Meta said.

Her granduncle's sleepy head rolled puppet-like, as he waited for Lore and Meta.

Awakened, he snorted. "Stop!" Granduncle was brandishing his driving whip.

Trundling away, Meta craned her neck back at the Wendisch octagonal siding designs, unlike squared ones in Saxon areas.

Farther along, Ol' Fritz finally clipped along behind a man and girl on foot. "Stop," said Meta.

At the reins, Lore paused to gather up more potatoes.

"No, no handouts for these people." Meta said. "These days, people might assume you're communists who give or share?"

"But everyone welcomes fresh produce." Lore wanted to assist a father and daughter stuck by their lorry at the roadside.

Granduncle offered them a wagon ride to find a mechanic. He helped Grete up in with her narrow tan skirt and fine leather button shoes.

Moving along, the men discussed local herd market losses. "Cheap Polish frozen pork," Cattle Dealer van Relke identified with Farmer von Cherusche.

Grete and Meta chattered about friends and butterflies, netted and mounted, until they passed a Schweinhaus, piggery with curly tailed piglets, delighting them.

"We're a conquered province with more farm auctions than sales." Herr van Relke nodded. "Five years after the war," Heinrich said, "land's worthless; so city people grab it and food."

"Ex-soldiers steal animals," said Grete's father.

"This socialist government's worse than the Prussian Kaisers', worse than the King of Hanover's doing nothing for us."

Alongside the wagon, a cycling youth distracted Meta, who poked Grete. "I don't understand him."

Tossing his forelock from his eyes, he winked.

"Who's that?" Heinrich asked.

"I don't know." Meta said.

"Then don't signal to him."

"I do not."

Reaching the van Relke lorry, the men jumped off the wagon to investigate the breakdown. Heinrich decided to go on ahead and send Christoph back with repair gear.

Meta asked Grete in to see her mounted butterflies. They took nets out and searched for live ones.

Weeks later, after Heinrich's lorry repair favor, the Dutchman, Grete's father, stopped by with news on deals about new breeds for Heinrich. They guffawed on the porch.

Grete's sea blue eyes animated her manner. Beneath her thick dark blondish cap-style hair, she was grateful for sweets offered. She'd attended private school in the nearest town, unlike Meta tutored haphazardly at home, and, later on, attended a new Country Boarding School.

"I shear our sheep for Nanna's wool spinning." Meta demonstrated the spindle to Grete and began winding in wool fiber from raw soft off-white tuft. This wool puff, yellowish distaff she threw to Grete, who touched the lush wool to her cheek.

"Don't get rouge on it."

Grete asked, "You make yarn for tweed suits?"

"No-no, we design rugs, like the hall runner, a rug hooked on tarp, in damascene wave, lengthwise. Nanna taught me spinning, hooking and crocheting, and some weaving." Old wool lengths were folded and braided into odd combos of Renaissance colors (maroon-orange and chartreuse-teal-blue) whirling into circular rugs. They covered "oriental carpets" to preserve them, if the house was ever attacked, or the ancient carpets were stolen. Meta thought she'd made up a new Metod project, while telling how at first Uncle Heinrich disdained home-crafted upper rugs as modern childlike ones in brilliant Otto colors. But these hard times were changing his mind toward volkishness, folk-like.

"My mother," Grete noted, "styles gowns in her shop near here expanded to her Berlin atelier."

"Oh-h-h, I never knew my mother. I'm searching for her, I think, her gravestone. No one tells me where to look and never my father at all."

Wide-eyed, long-lashed, Grete asked, "You don't know your mother or father?"

Meta heard Fate. "I've known both," Grete said, "my whole life, even Mama though we go by train to see her, or she comes home."

At the wraparound porch's far end, Granduncle and Grete's father mulled over their battlefield stories, the bad treaty and shifting economy. The glory of failure and failure of glory focused on hyper-inflation in 1922. Unemployed veterans were troublemakers everywhere.

"It's truth." Heinrich spoke. "Hell, goods disappear."

"But livestock's picking up here, for sure," Grete's father said.

The men shook hands, and Grete hugged Meta, gesture unused to, and Grete left with her father.

The following Sunday, in black vest and high-necked white shirt with pressed black trousers, granduncle donned his suit coat, and Meta brushed off his beard's calico hairs on it. Waiting for her, he pleased himself with his new Strzygowski book, surprising Meta, because Heinrich distrusted Poles.

The Cherushes would go forth to church. During such a drive, he tried drilling knowledge into Meta. As they bumped long, he asked, "What are these flowers?"

"Loosestrife, St. John's Wort, Lobelia," she reeled off the primrose or Johnswort families and counted on his not knowing them. "Kingfisher and perch."

"Keep categories straight."

"You're driving the horses so fast, I cannot see the flowers, but they're there."

"Last conquered, the first to conquer?" he asked. "Saxons."

At one of the Lüneberg North Gothic churches, theirs, Lore rode up on horseback; her brother summed up his reading. "In the beginning, old pagans lined up wood staves for their ships and turned them upside down for temples."

"That's ridiculous." Aunt Lore said, while they walked toward the church entrance.

"It's so." Next, reaching the long table, before the sanctuary, Heinrich pursed his lips, while examining the labels on full wine bottle to be opened for the event.

Inside, Meta eyed the inside's glorious high peak, as if a boat upended. Light breathed air within the rafters. Her eyes scupted the Gothic terra cotta brick ceiling, reddening as the sun splashed through the glass medieval colored panels.

When she was swinging one leg across the other, when her Granduncle huffed. "For Heaven's sake, be quiet, count the bricks."

"703." A great coral dragon, cartilage and skin tautened its serpentine tail wagging the whole. Ribs through walls into buttresses extended legs outside.

Back on a beam, she deciphered Gothic script: I am the light of the world, golden verse heard but not understood.

"Two hundred thousand bricks." She announced. The magnificent pipe organ began pumping. All stood to sing.

Going back outside, out of pocket his compass' magnetic needle quivered. "Point out the angle of the Elbe, Weser, Ems, and the Atlantic." He corrected her on the angle toward the distant peaks of Swiss Saxony like clouds.

At the same time, Lore stayed behind to revel with friends, second and third cousins and planned for a sing-along. Clip-clopping up on her regal aging Urania, Lore rode up next to the small cart going through rows of beeches, oaks, birches and high conifers.

When she caught up with her brother in his paneled lair, she said, "You live in the Middle Ages."

"Knock before entering." All household women knew he meant if he'd been sipping ale, or entertaining his Mrs. von Handler? "Reading. Don't disturb me."

In post-war years, horse drawn carriages, gas or electric-ity-driven cars brought women over to see Lore. "After the wife's death," they visited in the parlor, Stube, or closed in porch, where woodsy green plush upholstered chairs and sofa embraced them, to glimpse and size up Heinrich.

Without Lore, Heinrich ate when he chose, bothered little about guests unless he invited them and preferred his old scripted parchments magnified to read by his Leica glass. He speculated "European Wodan or Odin drew on African Votun," according to Christoph who connived with him.

Lore, when present, directed the cooking. Marinade beef shoulder for sauerbraten, with fatty strips and garlic across. Meta's potato dumpling love brought her from her bedroom suite through underground passages to the kitchen to make them.

With dinner companions, heated embarrassment crawled over Meta. Grete, her father were invited, if the lorry was fixed and Katia, if she arrived. Hopefully, her uncle would not inflict his topics on ones who might become best friends.

On this occasion, Heinrich came out of his study to introduce a new figure—Harald in herringbone jacket nodded. Taciturnity prevailed over Nanna's chattiness. He starred at Meta.

Afterward, the men reentered his study, while the women strolled to Nanna's little upstairs sitting room. Lore sniffed. "Sour up here and down there, unless aired."

Nanna replied. "Watch for fleas, ticks, rabies from rodents and bedbugs from wrongheaded boys and girls, don't you know!"

Of the three, including Lore and Heinrich, only Nanna comforted her, like the runt in a mystery—her bloodline sprang from these people. No beauty with her portrait on the wall, Nanna was her elder angel with luminous white hair above her glasses slouching on her nose upturned like her chin. After eight decades, she was affiliated with another firmament, like a hag on Walpurgis Nacht, May Day eve, some joked, with a firepot to drop sins in.

"As for that nice girl Angela, Lore and Nanna chatted. Lore noted, "Saxonish and Wendisch, cares for her grandmother, while her mother and lives in America. Check their eggs dyed at Easter.

"Like sword handles." After that Harald left, Great-uncle Heinrich came upstairs. "The design's the test."

"Gut. Find their gods." Tante Lore mimicked him.

A shadow, just suggested, emboldened Meta. "Where's my mother?"

Nanna replied, "Died in war or assassinated in Berlin," scared Meta off from further enquiry. At the window, she squeezed back against her furies.

The next day on her way to town for supplies, Meta pouted at herself in a rough-hewn oaken rain water trough, where Holsteiner cows drank. On the ground, Sanddorn and early nightshade blazed red-orange.

In the town garden pool, her face rippled and broke apart from dogs lapping or wind blowing, instead of her mother revealing herself in the water. Meta's ardor might amplify and mirror her mother, but her portrait never existed, unlike in Katia's home, where her grandmothers and grandfathers on the wall of the stairwell looked down.

A girl came up to splash her sweating face. The two of them freshened up and paused. Martine was her name. A tiny gold star on a chain slipped down from her neck over the trough–a swastika or a Star of David? Meta could not tell.

Another youth with a rucksack arrived from their Turner Verein. Next to each other, both stood tall in blue striped over-blouse above muscular thighs with knickers and brown running shoes.

Like Wander Vogel, birds of passage, Meta began trekking across the heath to Katia's. Trains discharged honeymooners. Lovers on a tandem double axle cycled along, and another couple rode Arabian stallions on the bridle path. Some visitors waved.

Once Grete waved back to her friend Martine with her parents "from a famous family." Meta forgot to ask which family. Such holidayers grated on her in solitude. Most couples meandered without seeing her. Rage overwhelmed her.

On such a glory day, blue flowers, Blumengarten, "Harvest without Time" and "Men of Troy" splotched in rural area rills.

Occasionally, houseless ones in clothes like filthy bandages around skeletal bodies also rattled alongside stray animals into the holiday atmosphere of this part of the Heide.

Characteristically, Meta parked her bicycle by their timber-work merchant house in town and rapped its door knocker. New Swing reverberated through an open window. They two bounced to the music, as the needle scratched out on "Louis" records Katia's father purchased in Berlin.

"Aren't they forbidden to play?" asked Meta.

"Why not so?"

Next, she and Meta later walked in the great parkland. Katia returned home, and Meta cycled on.

Interrupting her reverie, an unknown halted his lorry and rolled down a smoky window. Her eyes blurred at the driver's stare and wave. Gaze averted, she recognized his split mustache as belonging to one of uncle's former cronies now held in contempt as a nationalist. Formerly a monarchist, Granduncle was sanctioning only absolutists and loyalists.

To her relief, a cow nibbled grasses nearby and ambled toward her above the Ilmenau River. The lorry drove off. Better to be befriended by a cow than cowed. Black and white mud-matted, her body flapped around her bones. No one on holiday noticed the poor cow, flagged her down and much less prodded this creature along. Who drove the mysterious lorry?

As dusk fell, the cow's tail fastened to one leg to prevent swishing, while stroking the cow's udder for milk, if overfull. She refused to comply. They two entered the red brick farming village, brown-gold maroon. As the village clock struck six, a bull reared his head out of his stall and roared.

While cajoled through the gate, the skinny cow moaned. "You're here." Meta posted her in an overgrown kitchen garden with hay. She knew to make friends with available persons to evade loneliness.

Next day, her new cow friend was missing. At the same time, Kathe Kollwitz drawing Katia sent Meta also haunted her with hungry, yearning children, eyes sunken into their skulls, and skinny arms with empty bowls. Meta dragged herself around.

In late summer, the moor aura deepened reddish-deep purple, bluing into the horizon and flowers and trees disassembled and floated and mesmerized her away, for the moment, from bothering about the cow. Pine needles or iodine hot springs brine or whey baths could soothe anyone. Through the Luneburger Heide on the Ilmenau, the river of Goethe river into the Elbe, barges once and still did carry amber, salt, iron, tools, and weapons through Saxonia, Dresden to Hamburg on the Atlantic.

Nearby, small Protestant and Catholic Churches angled toward each other, marking the plaza hub before the spa was fully opened for visitors. No one entered or left the church sanctuaries at the moment. Only breezes swirled over protruding rocks, like her body, near the lily pond.

Two hours later, a lorry swung again toward her, its singed brown ominous side scraped into planar tree-like bark. The voice deep within the car appealed. "Lost, little one?"

"No."

On this surprisingly cool late August day, she was in her soft dark vermilion wool cape, not her ratty blue one, against the coming fall chill; she'd veered away from Visbeck by bike.

From the twenty-third Psalm from her Bible, Meta fantasized about fleeing into a pastoral family, where skinny sheep grazed around the shepherd and shepherdess.

Wearing forest green wool great coats, the elder couple sat on the rocks their whole lives.

Everything fit. Mornings, they ate groats. Easing back after the war into their actual lives, on rocks their knitting needles clacked in purls and knits. "In vigilance, we spent the war years," Frau Shepherd said, "in care as big house servants, instead of outside with sheep, our place."

"We're back." The shepherdess, pulling white cheese and black bread from her sack, asked. "Where do you hail from?"

"Nearby. No thank you."

"Lost?"

"Hope not." Meta wiped her forehead uncertain about her whereabouts.

"Where's your mother?" Frau Shepherd stood with her crook to pull in a lamb against straying and guided other sheep into a hold for the entire herd with one large gate. Sheep in, poachers out."

"In heaven or hell," Meta said. "Nobody tells me where my parents are, so my great-uncle and aunt try caring for me.

"Maybe your parents are buried in that cemetery over there with high rocks and crosses."

"Oh, they wouldn't be that old."

Out of the sea of black-faced sheep, soft and woolly, a pair closed in, to stare at Meta and baa. The Herr Shepherd in local Plattdeutsch, incomprehensible, asked, "What's your name?"

"Von Cherusche, not my surname."

"Gut. Many like you without fathers or mothers look to work. Or they fall in with bad types without work. Careful, little beauty with the alpine red-streaked hair, watch out for errant knights with nothing to live on. They maraud.

"Stay a few days in the hutment with us. When it's cold, we rent a farmhouse room. You could too."

"No, I am supposed to belong in my uncle's house, I think."

Distant beyond, bark huts clung to the moor. Poking along with her gingko branch crook and sack and pulling her dangling sun-bleached curls out of her eyes, a human prow, she charged up the highest flattop rock to scan the horizon.

A dappled pony was pulling an enclosed cart was less menacing than the lorry, pulled up. "Little one, do you recognize me?"

Now fifteen, she felt six or seven. "I'll walk." Her crook pocked the earth.

Gently, the voice spoke, his head blurred out the window. She denied knowing him though eventually acquiesced. "Your voice's familiar."

Out of the cart, he stood below her. His scar like a minute lightening on his lip jabbed through his mustache, the feature

Lore called "his harelip." Could he know Lore from the front of the tapestry and Meta? His shoulders yoked his spreading muscular arms, and his solid legs spread below his powerful torso further lessening his full height. Shortening himself, still he soared above her. Yes, though seen through the rose and blue tapestry web, she was sure in granduncle's library; this man also had at one time presided over war meetings, until Uncle decided to unify all country folk. And, yes, she'd dragged papers into this man's hall. He'd continued to stop her.

"Georg Klaus?"

"Yes. Little one, always on the path." Others awaited her. If he returned her to great-uncle, who'd be gruff if he knew she was giving in. Still for a change, a ride would help one as isolated as she who guessed Georg's voice echoed within his red-flecked beard. Unsure, she hesitated, then, refused to sit in his car. For minutes, he hovered, then, left.

Discomforted, she discovered two sheep straying from Frau and Herr Shepherd's flock they oversaw. Their black Heideschucke masks were exposed as if charred; such fuzzy roamers needed fattening and removing of burrs from their curly buff wool, usable to spin into yarn. Her crook could help her to hide the sheep, and she would care for them. She'd do more than she had for the lean cow in the snarled garden hedge. Farther on, they'd be safe and hidden and munch grass. Better to lead these sheep.

Three days later, they too were missing.

Most bicycles had been drafted into the war effort for transport or for parts, so any cyclist on the road, other than holiday-makers, jarred her. Most bicycles never came back One cyclist behind her unnerved her.

"Seen any sheep?" he asked.

"I'm looking for lost sheep."

"I've seen you stealing lambs."

Her words throat-locked. "What?!?" He flipped out a bulletin and divulged his incomprehensible aim. His pale blue eyes narrowed under heavy-lids, almost non-existent, rolled back into his sockets, opened and fluttered.

"What's this?" She read German, some English, French or Danish phrases. It was in the local tongue written down she did not read.

The pale-eyed fellow with blond forelock he tossed back against the wind and patted her shoulder. She jumped back. Without knowing why, she grabbed leather bag on her bicycle for the small pickaxe and looked for a pitchfork stuck in dirt. "I don't understand you."

"You will." The cyclist rode away.

Friends widened her freedom. Katharina von Weser, not the odd cyclist, was welcome at Cherusche dinners and enlarged Meta's world. Nevertheless, exposing Katia, her new friend, to Uncle Heinrich's cur side and worldviews embarrassed Meta, wishing for normality with daily lives, mothers, fathers and siblings.

8.

Friends widened her freedom. Katharina von Weser, not the odd cyclist, was welcome at Cherusche dinners and enlarged Meta's world. Nevertheless, exposing Katia, her new friend, to Uncle Heinrich's cur side and worldviews embarrassed Meta, wishing for normality with daily lives, mothers, fathers and siblings.

Tante Lore preferred that Meta not be alone or beset by her brother, Heinrich. "You girls with Grete," Lore said, "please me."

Katia marceled her white blonde hair around her deep-set blue eyes and high round cheekbones, shaped like her breasts. "Comely," said Nanna. "She smoothes over upsets, don't you see?"

Great-uncle held out his hand without fingernail dirt from his fieldwork, this time to shake hers. "Sorry, your mother's on holiday," known from who knew what source.

"What?" Did he know?

All the same, belle Katia in a summertime pale greenish dress enchanted him. Her von Weser family name elevated her. During the post-Great War scarcity, her family managed Sunday dinners, which was all she knew, when produce was commandeered from small farms or bought from beleaguered farmers.

Currently, they were banding together. Granduncle Heinrich minded this process.

So far though, the girls were the first of their families like friends, Katia favored her maternal grandmother in the local countryside, where the Cherusche resided, over her parents in Celle or on their voyages.

On this day, less casual than on the Heide, Meta asked, "How did your family get its surname?"

"Not so long ago, it given to my grandfather. Yours is older." The Bismarck name means far end of the marsh or frontier.

"Great-uncle despised Bismarck," Meta said, "until deciding recently the Prussian leader had preserved Uncle Heinrich's way of life. Says now we could use him again, if we'd figure out our troubles from their beginnings."

"At least, neither your uncle nor my father," Katia replied, "has lost their land so far."

"Uncle Heinrich fears losing his estate, I can tell." Meta poured out hearsay gained from behind the tapestry. "Says he must sell some before losing all for massive, excessive taxes.

"And he's hurrying to sell me off! He'll wed me off, while young, to save on my costly upkeep. I'm nervous. His favorite niece, my mother, failed to marry well. I'm his grandniece. Still, the war destroyed records and my chance to survive on inheritance."

Katia whisked such topics aside for, "Do you like Georg. He watches you."

Katia's boldness astonished Meta. "Since he held me, he's forbidden here." Meta prevaricated and imagined.

"You're a Berlin girl, at heart," Katia said. "We'll go there soon. Cigarettes and Riesling go with the journey."

Nanna and Lore would never approve.

"Your dress," Katia noted, "becomes you. You say no one buys you anything." Kati could interest herself in someone else, beyond her own tunnel view, thought Meta.

Her only dressy dress, filmy near-mauve rayon with a minutely gathered ruffle at her knees, came from Lore. After her daughter's pregnancy, it no longer fit her but matched her skin. Meta said, "I feel naked in it."

"I plan to show who I am and be what I want to be," Katia said, "a book or gown designer, like Grete's mother in Berlin or New York. Money's poor now in Berlin, worse than the worst storm. One hundred pfennigs equal a mark, in New York 25 cents. Marks float in gutters."

"I'll teach children to protect themselves," Meta said, "like Liesl's. Or learn animal care."

"Veterinary work?" Katia asked, "To protect themselves?"

"Now the war's over, for sure, so you'd better re-enroll in the gymnasium, not that Country Boarding School you went to. Pursue chemistry and biology for your Arbitur, school leaving exam."

Meta replied, "I have. Who gets more fun–ladies or caretakers of creatures? I favor creatures."

Whiling away time, Katia capered with a maroon lampshade on her head. They hooted with the gramophone music. Next to the turnstile, Schottische music and other polkas lay with Bach and Beethoven. Meta laughed at Granduncle's friend's and Mrs. von Handler's musical choices. Meta favored the Louis "Satchmo" Armstrong discs Katia pulled from her bag.

"Careful around granduncle with music; bad for young girls, he says, too raunchy."

Meta pranced around in her pale yellow short dress setting off her dark amber hair, and Katia opened her bag to display her dark red drapery to make into knee-length dress.

Granduncle entered, watched. Pointedly he re-introduced, "Meta, here's Harald." Only lately did he, tall and dark, regularize his visits to the house. His somberness grew little into enthusiasm.

Unlike him, Georg, tall and red-blond hair, bounded forth, heartily and lustily. Like Katia, he posed the possibility of escape. "See?" she whispered to Katia. "Granduncle loathes him and favors Harald." In his more heroic aura, Georg was beardless mustached.

When Meta and Katia sauntered into the dining room, Georg was stooping, his posture sheltering others.

Bowing slightly, Harald eyed Meta, her cutwork bodice and skirt billowing above her knees drew him. She blushed and recoiled.

Brought to show Heinrich the collector a polished dagger, a Handsel, was prized more than his long-bladed sword, his Seax. Its handle and blade glittered. Heinrich had taken his down and polished it. With this golden dagger, shaped like Ol' Christoph's knife, Uncle Heinrich said he planned to carve the roast. "Imagine we are in the last century's charisma times. Georg will leave now."

Meta gasped.

"Know folks by their weapons," Uncle stated after dismissing Georg, "the Franks by barbarity, (frakki): Saxons their Seax, Celts by their Celts or Georg by hatchets."

At the dinner, Heinrich expounded. West against East: warriors fought Slavs across the Elbe and won. "We brought out the best in them. Some make good Saxons."

Meanwhile the cook's helper appeared. "Should I dismiss the bricklayers?"

Meta ran ahead to the door, pretending to greet Lili, as Georg's right had caught hers to squeeze and gave her a wild-flower bouquet. She knew it would soon wilt.

She also sought to treat Lili and her family like old friends. "On Sunday?" Uncle Heinrich was roaring behind her. "*Nein, nein,* I'll finish them, for God's sake. Stop meddling." He ejected her and spoke Serb-like or Polish words to Lili's brothers and Georg.

Back at the table, Meta daydreamed of Georg, Lili, Grete and Katia gallivanting off to Berlin, while Heinrich cranked out farm problems: weeds threatening their Garden of Eden; outbuildings' bricks were falling out, and the secret garden pasturing stray animals. He thundered away serenity.

"A skinny cow," Heinrich said, "wandered in and now a lost sheep, which means a pasture fence is down or cut." He wrote these items in his black notebook.

Silence reigned at his table. Should Meta say grace he'd taught her?

With the golden Handsel, he cut the crossties binding the roast. He sliced the first serving of lamb, dark and crunchy, for Lore, and a third from the center, rare, for Frau von Handler. Each visitor received servings of other dishes from the cook's assistant.

The old cook's layering of veal, pork and turkey yielded praise. "You've outdone yourself." Saying this to the assistant to let the cook know, Heinrich sliced the Turkey Galantine on the gold-edged platter and passed it around.

Meta, sleepy from eating too much, remembered the strutting turkey days before, and began fading into oblivion. Hoping for invisibility, she bent from her corner perch at her uncle's chair right. His toe was angling toward Frau von Handler's pointed toe. Meta was prying secrets under the table and noticed the dining table leg claws that gripped clear globes.

Below, Mopsi lay in wait, his snout flat. As he sprawled out to disguise his goal or sat, he lurked. Never full, tidbits falling off laps he snapped up. One thrown to him quieted his low whining for more, and he began snorting in happiness over a slice of Turkey. His bubbly eyes whirled toward any gift, as his tail curled up like a question mark. When Frau von Handler next dropped a turkey bit, he wagged his tail. Women's laps like bowls from skirts promised more than men's without such capacity to hold morsels that might slip off. He squeaked for more. "Shush, Sh-sh-shush."

By contrast, Harald, if cold-shouldered, would lose interest in her. During dinner, she glimpsed the balanced facets that marked off his face.

Between goblets of wine, Granduncle drew Harald into talk about metal. Before the compote, Meta resolved to thwart any projected tie with Harald.

9.

In a cerulean marquisette dress surprise from Lore, Meta twirled before the hall mirror. Usually, if warmish, she wore brown for the gardening. If cool out, a once-new indigo merino shawl worn for racing over the heath made her feel ready to soar by flapping.

Marveling here over her blue dress, the mirror stared back. Low-necked, it peeked at her armoire. From the last century, the dress style favored cover-ups, gauzy, chiffon or dotted Swiss, this wardrobe might bestow treasures upon her. One white rayon flared bell sleeves to shape its x-neckline of cutwork columns above a lotus appliquéd over the belly.

Her uncle loomed behind her in the mercuric glass. "Lovely, almost like your mother at your age. Can you see beyond yourself in the mirror long enough to listen? She never could."

Meta was startled. Was an old servant or cousin poised behind them?

"Yes, sir." Edge away, like Katharina and Frau von Handler.

"Unlike others taken in by you, I am not." Since the last war, while dealing with atrocities and dilapidated farmstead, his black-brown hair had whitened on top, though dark and graying at his temples. "To suit your scheming, first, take a package to Harald."

"I did."

"At 15 almost 16, you're headstrong enough to drive the cart with Ol' Fritz for longer distances than earlier. Your aunt tells me you wander. Georg notices. Drive to Georg's gate-house with packages entrusted for him and leave them outside, not inside." Heinrich turned on his heel and left.

Dare she demand, humbly of course, his allowing her back into school? To comply with him, could she angle toward him or plead for more school?

He'd referred to her mother. She'd skittered past this painful subject. It lumped in her belly and stayed put.

Could his odd trust in her delivering packages enable going to Berlin? To start her journey, she'd regale Aunt Lore's surprise gift dress by modeling it through double doors.

Strolling down the hall, Meta examined the hand-painted English hunt scene, hounds and red-coated and green-coated hunters on horseback ranged across four metres of mural to-wards the actual doors, one ajar. Out of sight, she remained silent within earshot and measured her breath...

"What about our Marianne?" Agog within the older women's gossip, she grew restless, and wretched.

"She lingers near Georg," Lore continued. "He tantalizes her. Watch them watch each other. The truth is clear. She cocks her head, smiles and laughs. He stretches to captivate her: the lure of wild romance."

Her ears burned. Meta was flogging herself internally with honor impugned, and Meta wished to jump on a silvery black steed to flee away forever into her self-made future.

"When her mother left her for Hamburg, I became Meta's guardian. But can I guard her, when she slips away all day and relieves us of responsibility for her? We forgive and forget her. Here in residence, if I accuse her of leaving without fore-warning, she denies everything, looks coquettish and impish with huge eyes under self-cut bangs. If she's late for my curfew, I lack energy to comfort or confront her.

"I bother too much and should go home. She plays our weaknesses off each other. Everyone here hobbles around, as if on peg legs. Because my Thomas and Johann died in the war, she's the light of my life. Since my Liesl married, Meta's playfulness cheers me. Then came attacks on Hansi . . . upset me."

Nanna asked, "What?"

"Lumpenpack threaten him in the school yard. A gang of bullies. . . ." She faltered. "Liesl's husband, the chemist, re-searched germs for Kruss on germs, where the money was; in time, he bettered himself into management. Abruptly, he died, you know, from war injuries or germs. I worry so."

Bewildered, Nanna sounded out. "Ya, ya, a lumberjack."

"No Lumpenpack." Lore fretted over her audience of memories. "My daughter and grandsons will be all right, won't they?

"After my husband Willi's death from war injuries or germs, my Liesl's husband died. She tried hanging on to their home." With her lace hankie, Lore dabbed her eyes. "But the small company death benefit necessitated leaving their good neighborhood for rundown Wedding in Berlin.

"I beg my Liesl to move back here. But Liesl says living there allows them enough food money and the boys' travel back to their good schools.

"Hits on the boys have happened more than once. Surprisingly, Liesl excuses such incidents, as toughening our little boys."

"Sometimes the young are old, don't you know?" Nanna said.

"I can't bear their danger." Mascara running under her eyes gave her a hairy clownish look. "I try sending a small allowance." Her cone of graying hair was falling.

Blued in ancientness, Nanna's eyes attuned to Lore. "Isn't it the truth—hellions go after gentle children—the tough gangs, despise them, don't you see? They're more of them every day." In her late eighties, still in her household right hand, a substitute granny, they assumed, whether she was Heinrich and Lore's mother or Annike's little known mother or aunt, always there, she chided others. "I know death. I've seen death in many others. But why attack our Hansi!?"

Age and missing teeth squashed her face, nose toward her chin. Welcome in Lore's suite, Nanna crouched in her chair. Her white hair bright like a lantern around her blue eyes, she was backlit from the lit-up fireplace. "The good suffer in silence."

"Look at Heinrich's meetings," Nanna continued, "with both thugs and gentleman types in here and in the barns. I know, I scout around picking up nuts and fruit.

"Sh-h-h, look and see."

Or see too much, thought Meta to herself.

She and the other children nicknamed Nanna, "Elf-Woman" and "Good-Witch," because of her sage care. Meta was gleaning Nanna and Lore keyhole insights, even if she disliked them.

"Caring for Liesl's children," Lore continued, "I followed a pack once in Berlin. If children tattle on gangs, the hellions go haywire. Older ones slip into gangs and bigger gangs more grisly in attacks than ever."

"That could happen to Meta, headstrong and high-strung; her mind's set on her path. If opposed, she bolts, steals time and stays put but could get assaulted on the road. Newspapers say so. I warn her, but she doesn't listen.

"The other day she insisted on attending a funeral for a woman never heard of, 'Lili's mother from the East. War or no, refugee types."

Lore said, "I told you not to let her go."

"Heinrich says, 'Meta's our responsibility and Lore's when here. But she's alone with us. So I speak for her most of the time.'"

"He won't listen to us. Most people don't bother to listen.

"Anyway, Marianne's cheeks naturally rouge," Lore said, "those bright dark green eyes and fair skin create a devilishly premature beauty."

Nanna's old body rose up and down and agreed. "No society's left for beauty, don't you know? War changes old ways. Would she meet anyone except by chance, don't you know?"

"Society's leftovers look gaga at this Saxon beauty." Lore responded, "Celt, fancy that auburn hair. Shall we send her to Reinhardt, the Berlin director in Muenchen or Berlin to create a star?"

"You can't. Sending her into decadent Berlin would backfire, don't you see?"

"Into a row with Heinrich, for sure. We must adapt."

"Can she enter society through Katharina?" asked Nanna.

"Little of it's left. So, Heinrich's matching her with Harald without his parents."

"Whoever does that nowadays?"

"He says his plan will do," noted Lore, "to observe ancient custom. Harald's the old Kaiser's hunting lodge steward. But the lodge is useless without a monarchy. Harald's a catch, who conjures money by selling battlefield scrap. He talks up productive land use around the lodge and profits by arranging for guests. He longs for the turn of the century a century ago."

"He gets away with all this. How so? His money's from hunting too?"

"Who knows? His crest bore a lion salient in olden days. He lives on that rump Hohenzollern estate, and he profits from used metal and wood, without taxes."

"Ah so, he's prowling," said Nanna, "for a 'castle bride,' don't you think?"

Lore sighed. "Meta's no castle bride. He's got no schooling, no Bilding, learning or cultural growth, integrity. . . Bland, he says little at the table with focus. His wandering eye should have been operated on in Berlin." She chuckled at her quip.

For sure, he's no castle groom," added Nanna.

"Well, anyway, his eye landed on Marianne, though she intrigues willy-nilly toward Georg. Others ignore George's tiny, harelip. Harald though must prove his worthy. His eyes pink from too much ale."

"Who doesn't these days? Better than dueling like in the old days," Nanna chuckled like one who liked her Riesling. "Ale or beer's for war, but wine's for peace."

"Harald's no soldier, Heinrich says, but Georg is. So Harald will be solid for Meta's home life." Lore continued. "He sees around the edge, never smiles and gets sullen or angry behind his wire glasses.

"Well, maybe. Maybe if we could arrange a duel behind the scenes between these two men, they'd wound each other unto death."

Then, Meta could determine what is best and next. Between the double door crack, Meta shivered. If Uncle foists Harald on her, the living Hell controls her. Rage projects on the hall mural—hunters pursuing the fox to the kill.

"Few call." Nanna thrived on visitors. Before the War, neighbors or servants strolled over with notes or cards to invite others to chat and laugh, like "'Blue' Bregganberg and his "Tootsi."

Nanna asked, "Hear noises?

"Why smile, Lore?"

"Meta! Are you there?" Lore called out. "Shame on you, listening to us at the keyhole."

"Nanna, I thought you were losing your hearing?" Meta replied.

Jarred, Meta twirled in to display the blue dress. "Lock the door against me or any listeners."

Nanna said, "You're like a 'blue' moth." Meta fluttered her arms.

Meanwhile, after the war ended, her uncle had ordered soldiers not to poach on his lands. Outside the double open windows, where Lore sat, he was slapping his horsewhip against a rock. In the upstairs Stube, he arrived from supervising feral cats, dogs and homeless soldiers and weeding porcelain berry and buckthorn brought over from England to Hanover that choked native trees. Dead branches needed clipping. After surveying his lands, he oversaw bundles of packaged tracts to distribute.

His sister stayed away from where they'd grown up, except when lonesome. He'd pried her from her Celle or Bremen homes to tend Meta and see Nanna whose hearing loss brought on degrees of loneliness.

To keep Lore around, he sometimes bit his tongue. Separating their solitudes pleased them Meta could tell and do what she wanted at times. He brooded in his library. Such was the method by which the family dwelled in this household.

Family indifference to Heinrich though disturbed him, he told them, as did their mockery of his old methods and odd-balls. So the women mulled over rejecting the old style match between Harald and Meta, even in these dire times. Instead of more listening, Meta ran off to the cows for milking.

"Change your dress," they called after her. She was confused.

When back, Nanna alone sat Meta down. "End this childhood wandering, becoming a half-virgin.

"I milked the cows."

"Christoph will do that. Someone will steal you, don't you see? Stomachs need food. You are fed and clothed. Someone desiring a child-woman, beautiful, healthy, will abduct you." She'd prepare Meta for life within old Saxon Metod.

"Care for yourself. If Heinrich pries on you and your comings and goings, don't you know his wrath? He's like an angry doctor with a knife?

"The time's now for you to launch your family. No sisters or brothers, no one rich will look after you for life. You'll fend for yourself like women nowadays after the war. And work, like me."

"I do for myself. I'll run the farm. You think like someone 100 years ago. Katia's Berlin her aunt taught her that. And Grete's mother."

"You'll do well with Harald."

"I have a secret."

"What?"

"I'm Meta, not Marianne."

"Call yourself Marianne. Silly wearing breeches. Times are improving now after the 1923 Depression. Dress up, wear dresses now?"

"You just said times are bad, so I must wed. Without pants, I'd be too girlish with cows and sheep."

"Dress like a lady to appeal to gentlemen."

"There are none." Hands propped at her waist, Meta divulged: "Granduncle sends me on secret missions."

Nanna rarely double-checked. "He's so much involved with politics, he almost ignores you."

So, Meta said, "Good for him, but not enough. And I have no parents! So I take care of myself."

"A dearth of boys, true. Many died." Nanna sighed. "War ended lives, two million, they say. The living are half-dead anyway. So, attract live ones. Luckily, the war left a man alive for you. Look at your breasts."

"I see them every day."

"A boy's?"

"I flatten them." Meta raised her skirts. Breeches under her skirts, she discarded at will to dodge older people. Her stiff lederhosen, a gift from the south to a now deceased soldier cousin, beneath her loose over-blouse she lifted to display her fallen breasts.

Having tried to conciliate with Meta, Nanna began treadling her wooden spinning wheel, as Lore pedaled at the piano. But tufted wool yarn emerged on the spinning wheel, but no sound from the piano.

Treadle, treadle. "No one's like you, Marianne. In olden days, they sent girls like you to a Beguinage, here in our Lüneburg. Your type's increasing, don't you see?"

"I do. But we're not polliwogs, preserved in amber. Besides, do you remember your perfect girlhood?"

Evidently, Nanna intended her to comply with the catch, Harald. Agitatedly, others must put Nanna up to hash the plan out with Meta, as Nanna treadled faster than in her usual rural way.

"Where do useful women or useless go?" Nanna asked. "Katharina von Bora left a convent hundreds of years ago to marry Luther. Convents emptied. Some women still go. Go see ones with an original world map and fine red wall hangings. The protestant sisters also make fine preserves from strawberries, apples. Head Mother, remember her upswept gold-brown hair and gold dust over her face, met us." In her convent, wood and gold Saxon filigree surround the organ, the Twelve Apostles reign on the high wall right and twelve holy women the left. Romanesque domes the roof.

"Remember the Holy Fools?" Meta said. "I do. I am going to be one of them. On wooden enclosures, zoo morphs swirled. Deer, rabbits and elk were telepathic from when the earth was new. A lean artistic youth played Bach for hours on the pipe organ, accompanied by Lore at the piano. His fire-haired girlfriend turned the music pages.

"You want me to enter a convent in this day and age?" asked Meta.

Nanna chuckled.

"Men escape women as warriors, don't you know? Link up with Harald, or go into the convent. Or stay on your own and drill with these new backward folk. Or get out."

Foreboding met fortitude in Nanna, who held forth. "See the trains, their sides with big black axed stamps on red. They're from the south, they're invading."

Unable to win details about her parentage or disapproval of Harald, Meta clunked away in her mother's old boots clunked down from Nanna's small clean upstairs quarters. Past the old woman's statue of Mary in blue, the Bevensen insignia, and past the foxhunt mural, Meta bent her course.

Tante Lore's daughter's bicycle or perhaps her mother's she rolled through the gateway. On the road, she pedaled over kilometres of marshland. Greenery was billowing into an opaque atmosphere. Only the road below was visible. Her basket held tracts.

Within this sea weather swathe, Meta's spunk lagged behind the goal she loathed—delivering tracts to Georg or Harald.

On the ground, sweet cicely and myrrh fringed the earth. New filaments grew, like chamomile. She pedaled quickly on-ward.

The eye-less blond ghosted out of the mist. He shook his shock of hair off his forehead. This gesture thrilled her, for he was taller than ever with measured linear features; limbs and muscles sculpted like the planar tree. From time to time, it shed its gray-green bark in patches. He did not.

"Oh, you're bicycling too, instead of trekking or driving a horse cart?" In the fog, he was the last creature in the world.

10.

Back half-dozing on his old couch, Heinrich's mind rolled into Marike. Tante Lore said so to her friend, interested in Heinrich. Two agricultural labourers said the same within earshot of Meta that his loose pants became a tent for Marike. Secreted in his office. She sank over him, as caught once through Meta's tapestry-covered the wall hole she was already outgrowing.

Local newspapers, authorities and pastors ranted about loose youthful morals after the war. Bringing Morike over, while Tante Lore was traveling, was intended to guard Meta from skipping off. Among the high stones and low-land fog, Meta had seen him pluck a pink bud for Marike's hair, his crown glory or hers.

Everything makeshift, Meta traded seeds and borrowed trowels from neighbors to break free. Between fatality and free will, Meta would forbid this foisting of Harald onto to her. She pined for the blond-red-haired Georg whose laughter rumbled. His eyes widened to slits; his joviality enveloped her. His strange exuberance was lustful? She'd tease Katia but not bother Grete? Lili with her carousing might. Gorgeous Mala and for that matter, so would younger Martine be in the know.

The youth Granduncle Heinrich picked for her, a second son, dark-haired and owlish, sapped Meta of life, and the tie little appealed to him. His lot linked to war materiél deals, along with a solid estate post, rendered him like a future 1923 prize.

"Ad infinitum," granduncle said, "in disorderly times, 1922 inflated currency serves as toilet paper." Still his Thing on his rock circle for a talkfest, his renowned outside seats or chairs inside, where they harped on money's high cost.

"Choose, I must, between pasture fencing and false teeth for Nanna."

The Measurer ticked away life, as Meta would succumb to her fate, Metod, or resist.

Meanwhile, Tante Lore glided over from her Celle home into this household of old daydreams. Her soft gray-green finery surpassed any social tatters. She would supervise dinner to celebrate 1923, better times. "Tante Lore's here," Meta called to Nanna, limping down the hallway. Within her rose scent, Lore rustled in. Meandering to a warmed greenhouse room, her closest friends enthused over her marine blue crepe dress and granduncle's jeweled old globe.

The women hugged one another or shook hands, according to degrees of friendship, sipped May wine, sighed over Meta's yellow net dress and Lore's atrium plants.

Next, they sorted rags, gauze, sticky tape and material for slings or plaster casts. Utilitarian, they ripped, stitched and folded for the poor, as done years back, and for the soldiers, they stored bandages and slings for future emergencies.

Phrases reverberated. "Peter died, and Hansi was attacked. I'm uneasy. Georg's better," said Lore.

Meta sat attuned.

"No May Day festivities this year. Maypole reminds us of better times in the town square," continued Lore. "Or worse in city squares.

"We don't need May Day," an unknown said. "Waste of town monies. Besides the lefties have taken it over in big cities. We could still have need fires, like bonfires."

On May 1, children, they reminisced, carried May baskets to neighbors until a grouch scared them off from hanging baskets on doorknobs to honor spring. They'd rush to the Maypole to grab colored ribbons and dance throughout the 100-metre circumference. Onlookers held hands, drank wine or ale within merrymaking and hugged.

"They can't steal our fun!"

"Yes, they can. No money for it."

"But we need fun."

"Saxon women," Lore said, "make do and thrive on Godsib, gossip, about men, babies, war, love, battle, hate, sex, greed, lust and lies. Unaware of his magnetism, my nephew Georg attracts many and dallies just enough with each girl or woman for hope."

Why announce this? Meta was crestfallen over thwarted Maypole joys and Georg. Lore kept up fantasies as hopes and discarded them.

"Saxon women dissect personality, like our Ol' Christoph cleans out the inside of fish." Lore continued. "He grew larger than life during tense wartime, stood apart and humored others. But Heinrich hates Georg's independence and refusal of deference toward himself."

"Joking's rare in men, don't you know?" Nanna chuckled. Her old garnet ring, bought for her in Prague sparkled, as her big dark red dress bounced with her body's laughter.

"What?" asked Meta?

"Meta, cat's got your tongue and handed it back to you?" Lore went on, "He's within himself. And women pursue him with as much fervor, just as his views on war disturb Heinrich."

"Nevertheless," a woman said, "war's misery, arrogance. He's not the only one who's lost his Sarah love called Mala, clouding his mind."

Meta blinked and bit her upper lip.

"True," another woman replied, "Others invite him everywhere; he goes but never reciprocates. A young oak in the wind bashed in his roof during the hectic war years. He could haul that dead tree away and fix his roof."

"He's not the only one; few entertain anyone these days. Everyone stays home without 'at homes.'" Bergitta, wearing a sapphire pendant, spoke often. "Many know how to live their lives, so pass Godsib along, weed outside, and polish the silver, but they don't invite anyone."

"Don't count on anyone," Rose said, coifed in a French roll and scarfed in wild roses twitching over her bosom and flashing her citrine topaz ring in the sunlight. "Men find little work to do. So why aren't women like aviatrixes? Women lost men in wartime, so they can soar and must take up new challenges."

"Why Waldemar," an Ursula named woman noted, "the big farmer, set up that pretty woman up the road, maybe Jewish, in the new condiments shop.

"In the store, one blonde, and the other dark curly older boy, belong to them. I'm sure. My children take my grandchildren there, though I don't approve. They should take their business to the good German shops farther down the road."

Unconvinced of her own perceptiveness, like insecurity, Meta nevertheless guessed they were carrying out their scenario for her sake.

"Oh, that's Mala," the woman in the back said.

"No," Another said, "the shop woman and Mala aren't related."

"But it's a good German shop," Lore continued. "Georg still mediates among peasants who object to such *Mittlestand* shops buying up land."

"True, true." Several chorused.

"Also, Georg objects to high war repayments?" Lore said. "My blood curdles that our country fades away, as war debt mounts up.

"Mine boils," one named Anna said.

"The costs top the war dead statistics. Some thrive on both debt and battle. Those who deny it nowadays will admit it someday.

"Everyone lost someone and mourns. How do we know we're not heading into a period worse than wartime? With no money to spend, we must hide what we have." Lore rolled a large bandage.

"Men love war," the rose-bosomed and finger citrine-ringed woman said. "My two sons were mad for it. Now their war's called the Great War, and they're gone. Thank Gott, my daughters live nearby."

"My one lives in Berlin. But never do I hear from Georg." Lore said, "my nephew by marriage, Georg, yes."

After the women left for home, Nanna and Tante Lore sat digesting the Godsib, while the fire in the fireplace was clapping. Meta perked up, when Nanna asked, "You told her about him and her parents didn't you?"

"I can't. Facts annoy us. Cemeteries draw her to search for her parents' stones, pastors tell me so."

"Bones?" asked Nanna.

"She even wandered, "Lore said, "into a Hebrew cemetery with signs, and she asked what they were, and if her mother was underground there."

"She won't find her mother there," said Nanna. "No parental gravestones either to find, poor dear.

"She fantasizes," said Lore, "about them like great people, as parents expect their children to accomplish greatness. Look at us living in the past; it's all we do. Tradition or Wurd or whatever stays put. The future's guessed at.

"She ought not to go out alone and, then," Nanna said, "find only Georg, I fear."

"Better not." Heinrich grabbed Meta's arm, as he clomped into the room. "Diseases and attacks are rampant in this country. The papers are filled with accounts. We Saxons specialize in death risks. Meta could go oversea with missionaries to Argentina. We pushed out the ne'er-do-wells, drunkards, busybodies, political cranks. Damn Utopian Sponge of the North absorbs the rest who leave.

"The sponge is like an animal that just grows. The hand that squeezes the sponge gets pricked from the prickles inside."

They were still talking, as if she were not there, when Meta began slipping back.

"The war spoiled us for future war," Heinrich commented.

"Joy's gone," Nanna said. "Everyone's jumpy. Feel it?"

Heinrich stepped out.

"Meta's a live-wire, rambunctious, for sure," Lore noted, "No wonder Georg's taken with her, fifteen years or younger than he? The scamp we indulged has changed.

"Her personality animates her dark beauty. Dinner candles light up her flawless rosy cheeks and that dark reddish-blonde hair. Who can resist her?

"Too late," said Nanna, "to clamp her down into a lady. In Berlin, the day of the lady's gone. Send her to that Swiss finishing school or one for gourmet art to learn wines and china. We used to marry off girls, like Meta, before they dishonored their families. Now she wholly fascinates this older man, your nephew."

"Sorry, not if I have anything to say about him," Heinrich galumphed back farther into the hallway, as his sister as Lore pounced with words and leaped to grab Meta inside the doorway and hug Meta who squawked.

"Dinner time: Go watch Old Cook bake the fish. See how salmon's laid on the platter. Learn to feed yourself later. If offered a kitchen job, take it. You must care for yourself. These days, everyone must grab any job offered, hard to find."

An hour later, having sprinkled parsley on the salmon with lemon slices, Meta tasted by aroma and carried it on the gold-rimmed platter to the table. Harald's presence threw her, as everyone admired the salmon with sauce beneath the Viennese Swarovski crystal lamp over the glaringly white linen tablecloth. Meta almost dropped the salmon simulate the finest cooking to please Georg, not Harald. Devotedly, she'd love him forever and please him sexually, as discovered from a manual hidden in Heinrich's library. To quell anxiety, she held her breath. Something was afoot.

To call the dinner to disorder, Great-uncle Heinrich lifted a crystal wine goblet. "To my daughter Marianne and her fiance Harald." Everyone clinked each other's glasses.

Dumbfounded and faint, she prayed that her slightest courtesy would not bind her to Harald in others' minds.

Her cousin, a rare visitor, Liesl, tall and fair like her mother, and Lore stood erect, their noses like sails in the wind, swept into song. Hoch soll sie leben drei-mal Hoch! Sie le-he Hoch, sie le-be Hoch. "Long may she live?" According to Heinrich, "Saxons love singing the latest news of the heart."

11.

The big old house brickwork was no sooner pointed, then, the chimney exhaled smoke with accumulated grit into the air. People inside the house were panting from smoke, even old cook's lay-about daughter ran for help.

The fire rose from the second back kitchen stove, which had featured cooking for long gone feasts required three ovens, one outdoors.

First, Ol' Christoph, atop the ladder, dropped rock salt down the chimney to stomp out the fire. But it continued, so he climbed down and ran toward a shed.

Inside the house, Heinrich, smelling smoke with his canny sense, leaped from his study and rushed outside. "Find Ol Christ."

Again, Christoph climbed the ladder, leaned on the chimney and dropped chains to loosen the gunk to clean it. The fire subsided.

"Get the creosote!" Heinrich ordered. Like an old fire-fighting hand, he changed places with Christoph and clanged the chains down the chimney sides.

"The flues broke," Christoph yelled. "Keep going and you'll have fires on the main floor."

Heinrich called back. "For God's sake, get a chimney sweep, some Till Eulenspiel, to root out grit." Swaying down the ladder, he touched his panting chest. "Any bird nest's tinder for chimney fires. Lucky this flame missed our house."

The ruckus, viewed from afar spared Meta, who still called him "Granduncle" to free herself of him. Only some God could rename him "father" and halt her escape.

As dreamed, the friends would go off on their spree. With steam enough, they'd contrive to reach Berlin; its modern gala of the arts lured them.

"The stinkpot of the Germans." Heinrich opposed her drifting toward Berlin.

Her friends would connive to reach Berlin, modern gala of the arts. Katia was ready. Angela had snuck over to see Meta, only to race back like a stretched rubber band to her grandmother's bedside, days later, Meta listened.

"In private, we speak Wendisch or maybe Sorbisch sometimes," Angela said, "and in public German, though I know little about Bautzen, our home city in the Toepferstrasse, in the business and residential area. From the mansion with the mansard roof there, Angela's grandmother, in their tiny borrowed farmhouse, had fled west away from revolutionaries' battles and family impoverishment.

"Her grandfather organized fieldwork and wedding carriage rental and four horses. And some festivals. Eventually, he died, so her grandmother took over, in her times, few could afford horses and carriage."

"My grandmother was devout, re-marriageable. Instead, she devoted herself to work and family.

One daughter left for the convent. Others of us stayed home without money. To hire out as cooks, we other sisters trekked on roads to farms to learn German specialties. Another drew and made wood models to become an architect.

While Meta now coaxed her into traveling, Angela fretted. "How can you leave your Nanna alone?"

"Others care for her." Cancer and hunger weren't Nanna's problems.

At this point, Meta's efforts pointed toward rounding up any friend for the trip on the bus and train to Berlin on the River Spree. Angela hesitated, and Katia was enthusiastic along with Meta. The later would bolt, not so Angela. Unlike the others Grete needed little pretext for visiting Berlin, for her mother was there.

As for Katia, rail travel, reminded Meta, was long and lonely. At age 10, she'd ridden from Dessau to Berlin. Her aunt met her and immediately removed Katia's hairpiece, feathers and bustle to surge toward freedom. Now enthusiasm for the trip aroused her.

The Berlin Zoo Garden exhibited Africans wearing grass skirts in from the colonies.

"You'll see everyone here," In the zoo and new department stores on the Freidrichstrasse, Leipzigerstrasse, Alexanderplatz and Pottsdammerplatz. With the new Rentenmark, we'll shop." Meta worried about spending money there.

Grete, the cattle dealer's chic daughter knew Meta and Katia better than Angela and Lili, the mason's daughter who'd evidently known better times, better life. They plotted to stay with Grete's mother or at a nearby Gasthaus.

Granduncle could hardly oppose Bildung in their "Kultur Kunst Klub journey." Her Klub was his Thing.

Meet at the crossroads for the rickety gray bus to the railroad they agreed to do. By dawn, race to the Berlin train station. Meta and Katia jiggled; hugged Grete and Angela and introduce each other. They'd discover Martine in the city. A troop en route to Berlin, they cheered 1923.

Never there before, Meta was agog. Nothing could derail her. The buildings grew higher and spread more than those at home. Crowds hurried. Forest and moor rhythms ill-prepared her for bustling women, tall big-breasted or petite, and slouch-shouldered men in crown-waved hair and shaved sideburns. Fabric-covered or suede pumps with pointy toes and calf-shaped shoe heels clicked the pavement below knee-length skirts, jouncing like mesmerists for watchers.

Youths swaggered, heads squared off above set shoulders. Businessmen and office workers sauntered at noon. Youngish women cooed over boys. Some many hung their heads below their shoulder blades.

Unter den Linden, the wide boulevard grew high lime trees above cherry maples and expanded into open greenery. From trees, old-time farmers once braided fibers into bridles, shoes, baskets, and rope fibers that once dangled the damned unto death.

Linden trees, Meta's old guidebook said, marked the city's Ritz quarter and backbone. The tree leaves now romanticized the avenue like chartreuse umbrellas.

Looking backward, Meta bumped an unshaven youth, going forward heads low. His ruddy hair bristled, and dirt stuck in his fingernails, as he gripped her white arms and mocked her. Their indents stayed on in soft arms. "Nice girl, sexy, eh, want to dance?"

High jacking her, he whirled her. "Toot, toot, toot tootsie," shook her. They bubbled and high-stepped, as if unstoppable. He threw her over his head toward the glittering ceiling.

Her friends sought to protect her. "Nein, nein, ya, ya, ya." To rid him, quiet Grete was flashing her fringed yellow boa. Katia waved hers. They looped their boas in opposed ways around his neck and yanked. Lili tried involving the manager in evicting these unwanted partners, like him.

When the original dancer gagged, he threw Meta around and pinched her arm, as she bolted toward the café interior toilet. She was shaking. The other three joined her.

After the strings tuned up came pizzicato. The violins startled and soared. A waiter whispered that Willi Stanke conducted them. "He'll be great someday. But look for the gypsy Ab Reinhardt! He's the greatest artist!"

"No, Bo Djangles is."

The troop of Meta, Grete, Katia and Martine and Lili bounced in their seats. Lili raised her arms with a fork and knife. The blade was sparking from the global crystal above. Its glass diamond facets splashed the dancers and foursome with tetrahedrons. The girls shimmied, did the hoochie-koochie and tangoed with each other.

Jazz, a secret lingo was zinging in and out of cafés, as they bounced past. Glass doors were ajar to the inner courtyard with outdoor tables, where waiters lit candles in the dusk. Imbibers' forefingers and thumbs balanced glasses and goblets with wine or held steins with ale. Others licked ices or bit tortes. One patron lay back in his white summer suit, colors a-whirl overhead, while his female partner swayed with her chin on her palms.

Meta's purse of tiny metal squares clinked to a kitschy foreign Paul Whiteman tune. In it, she'd hoarded rolls of Marks and filched coins that slid out of Heinrich's pockets between sofa cushions. Converting her find to Rentenmarks enabled buying foamy Schaum tortes with lingenberries. Each girl savored one Linzertorte.

Leaving the last café entered, they lifted stinky cheese on black rye to eat on the sly to avoid the ire of passers-by and park scouts.

They pointed ahead to the Wilhelm-Heinrich Universitat and Humboldt University they vowed to attend. Berlin intimidated Angela beyond her village, school and church choir.

By contrast, Berlin emboldened Katia, Lili and Grete; the latter probably came from some maternal birthright. Meta saw herself freer in the city, than she before.

Raven-haired Lili relished street feistiness between political groups and gangs on a side street. Swastikas on flags, grim black on white on red patches. To scrutinize this turbulence, Lili raced toward them. Punches thumped among the men. The others distanced themselves.

12.

On the Avenue of the Lime trees, they wandered toward the Brandenburger Tor, where the Goddess of Victory stood on her column. Into the Tiergarten, they took the long flat walk to explore the park.

They huddled and ate leftover dark bread and pale stinky cheese. Meta approached a public bench carved with "No Jews here." She gasped; it can't be so bad, and put her jacket over the words and sat down. They were planning to meet a friend of Grete, Martine.

From the gardens, they hobnobbed amid style-pacers, go-getters and slackers. Stores and specialty shops enticed the girls. Svelte deep-blue dresses on eerie, pale-faced heads and mannequin torsos lay like bodies and beaded tops hung in windows dressing. Strange, separate arms piled up were ready for screwing into armpit holes. Still, scenarios that progressed beyond the street granted the young women dreams of future lives.

Ada, the photographer known to Greta's mother's salon, came by with her Rolliflex and Graphex. She snapped them, smiled and waved them away.

Hours later, by the starless navy midnight, the girls plopped on their cots and talked. To confuse them and disguise her feelings, lest someone tell the truth on her, Meta told her friends, "I prefer Harald. True, Georg sends me lieder and jazz for the Victrola. He picks white violets, heather and beautiful castor flowers for me." The dread of returning to the farm home encased and even squeezed her.

"War comes again?" Katia asked, husky-voiced. The others shrugged.

Angela sighed. "We can guess. We're not over the first one yet."

At their third-rate hotel, their marks paid for a room wallpapered over cracks with dark paisley. Lili sneezed from the dust and urged them out early the next day for Schliemann's re-discovery of Troy.

The bright moon heightened city allure, neon and Lili awakened them to Berlin, while conducting an unseen orchestra with a pencil for a wand and whispered that Bach, Chopin, Brahms and the incomparable Wagner, remained her intimate friends. "Hear them and salute their works" The others sighed and objected to her trilling, bellowing and screeching.

Lili impressed them as surpassing their Kultur Kunst Klub level. Meta cowered within her inadequacy. Such unknown music Lili hummed and broke off. "I've had a not so happy life," and conducted her pretend sad orchestra.

"I prefer art museums," Katia said, waving her make-believe palette. "Or jazz."

"What about those boys?" Lili demanded.

That a shy person like Grete knew Verde and Rossini in two Berlin opera houses impressed them, but she knew nothing about boys. "Darlings!" Katia shrieked. "We heard live café music without boys. We must find some real boys." She joined Grete in easy dance steps and hummed.

Enough, Meta's Saxonist great-uncle claimed the Saxons opposed the Slavs, like Angela a Slavic and German Saxon on the Elbe's opposite bank. With a fishbone backbone and mousiness save for roseola cheeks, big-eyed Angela looked incapable of mounting a black steed to defend her Wendish-Germans in their glory. They could syncopate across the moor; hoof-beats kicking land, dry as dust.

During their semi-cloudy late evening, Grete rode an imaginary gold steed, and Katia cultivated high horses for culture, paintings and textiles. Lili with her pencil wand again was conducting with humming, as Grete with her boa stood down from her steed to waltz around the room.

"Grete," Lili asked, "do you read the Haggadah?" Limber, Grete instead tapped out from America, the Lindy, tango, shimmy or fox trot, hardly polkas or the schottische from America.

Her dance ingenuity stalled over the Haggadah. She blinked. "Oh, the religious text? Once a year at a Passover Seder, we read parts. My Dutch Protestant father tells us to celebrate and me to be a good little Jewish girl."

Like a drama, Lili, thought smart, had browsed the ancient Hebrew wisdom texts, in German, to spar with her brothers. For them, ancient scripts were preferable reading, and modern life was anathema, declassing their family into poverty.

"Did you go to school?" Grete whispered. "You survive in a hut, right? That's exciting,"

"They're driving us out too," added Grete.

"We were pushed west," continued Lili, "by the reds. Better-off houses though offered us hospitality along the way. So we spent a year in the grand Jewish merchant house in Konigs-berg." Suddenly, Lili screamed. "We were driven out!"

Katia, dozing, awakened. Moonlight also enflamed Meta's natural hair color. She propped herself until fully awake with carbon-haired Lili's prickly tale. Katia awakened and reached out to hold Lili's shoulders to calm her.

In the aftermath of war, Kaiser's overthrow and city uprisings especially in Saxony, Lili's family was driven from its West Polish home beyond Berlin. Anguished, her father was stricken with "a stroke." Her brothers lived in one hut, where Lili cared for their lank father, onetime patrician and engineer, whispered about by Great-uncle Heinrich. Lili's father spoke little but could do a ma-son's work and fix Heinrich's buildings. So his Lili interpreted.

"Must be Jewish," Katia guessed softly with Meta, "or dark-haired, intense Pole?"

"German intensity—from the East." Meta's voice lowered. "Not German from the West. She's flamboyant and stern." Ev-erybody like her is going westward.

"German." Lili shivered and snapped.

"We don't often light the Sabbath candles," Grete con-tinued. Her fair coif also glistened in the moonlight. "On Fri-days, we hardly read holy texts, like you on Sundays. My father looks then for cattle sales. There are few now, so mother aug-ments the family income in Berlin. My older uncle lost a job. For the younger, authorities made it verboten to finish school. Tomorrow we'll see my mother and Martine."

Katia sat on the window seat, where the moon was sil-vering her profile, hair and her pale chartreuse nightgown. Styling herself a flapper, she smoked her American cigarette and handed one to Lili, who rejected it.

"Ach!" Lili announced, "Mother's just dead, I plan to fly away."

In their second full day in Berlin, they set out to swig drafts of beer and visit Grete's mother's atelier and museums and gaze upon the boys. They delighted in jersey silk or fabrics clinging to the shapeless bodies, shaped in the store windows. Without the shirtwaist, structured by torsos with bosoms, Grete quoted her mother on flapper styles; her mother, Renate, was beginning to promote maternal authority. "Women, critics say, are losing their femininity by discarding our past elegance for risqué, brief dresses. These body tubes flattened curves, though some allow bosom décolleté and calves short hemlines." She smiled. "Which: maternal or sexual?"

The friends entered in the back door with less glass than the front to see in. Grete's mother hugged her and gave each a white feather. Martine showed them the way in and way out the back door.

At Grete's mother's atelier in the Hausvogteiplatz, less glamorous than Katia expected was more a pattern-making seamstresses' workshop than a couturier's salon, where they draped yardage and demonstrated Renate's livelihood. Grete glad to see Martine, her mother's aide, who served them tea and tortes, as she prodded models to parade gown designs in a long room and criticized their long curvy strides. Custom-made dresses were preferred for retail and displayed in the front windows in Renate's triangular building with corner entryway.

The style pacesetter for Berlin, Parisian gowns, the latest, appeared in the grand store Wertheim's, drawing the flossiest women. In 83 elevators, rising and falling tubes, the foursome giggled, as they rode them to don new lives, so a floor manager said, "Girls, girls, quiet down."

Ka De We, short for the Department Store of the West, also enthralled the foursome. The salesgirls were ultra-pretty and well mannered with patience while displaying specialties, such as lingerie, silken scarves and the like, lens-like store windows enlarged the minutiae of magical lives they could wiggle into via these clothes. In their postwar styles, blank pale mannequins forever sixteen to twenty-year old women, like Nefertiti or Nefartary, modeled.

Inside the store, the crystal chandelier lit up the aisles. The thrilled foursome crept around these opulent department stores. In one of its cafés, they licked strawberry and blueberry ices.

Outside, arm in arm, laughed, they sang and danced the hooch and Charleston and cavorted down the promenade. They loved their Charleston. Martine, let out for lunch, did lead them at first, and the rest followed. People gazed at their buoyant silliness, as if to say, "How can you in such rough times?" One couple applauded. Exhausted, the dancers plopped on a park bench and sang.

Meta again noticed the next bench's graffiti: "No Jews here." Why had she seen them? She cringed and jumped up tangoing in imagined drama away from the words.

Martine said. "Don't bother. These signs are everywhere. You just haven't noticed them."

They all began shimmying. As taught by Martine, they tried kicking like Admiral Girl lines, though clothed, not all naked, without sailor hats, in the park. In their free cabaret, they hooted and shrieked. Again, Lili stood out, ahead of the others, zigzagging to stir their march onward. Some others on the street joined in. Martine returned to Grete's mother's salon.

In their second night in the guest house, Grete suggested that by coming to Berlin Lili had left her mother to die.

A floorboard squeaked. "How dare you say such words?" Lili paced and conducted her invisible orchestra, wielding a long pen expressively like the small primitive warrior from the Lüneburg Rathaus, city hall.

"What happened?" asked Meta.

"She'd applied mud or feces to warm father's hut with an extra layer, when he was off working." Katia covered her mouth.

Meta said, "Don't gag."

"What am I talking about?" Lili challenged them. "She insulated walls against the cold. We stayed there, until we found a brick house cellar.

"We hunt berries, shoot rabbits and pheasants and gather nuts for pastries for nut cakes, like what old cook in our old house stove created; mother baked them in a big old tin over an open fire.

"When my father departed to scout our future, mother got sick. We decided to trek back East to our grandfather's house in Polish territory. We tried pulling her in a wagon to the doctor but could barely drag her dead weight.

"My brothers pleaded with her not to fight us. We'd grab the train bar to hoist her into a cattle car for help somewhere. We waited with the pigs for market for the train to stop."

"Not in Germany," Grete said. Meta tried muffling her laugh.

"The engineer passed by and waved to us. Mother broke loose and threw herself in front of the next train. It roared to a stop."

After a sob, Lili regained her composure. "Every train whistle's sound is my mother's cry."

13.

"You protect no one by clinging to your honor." Tante Lore so debated Heinrich.

"With anarchy around here, you grow less food. Everything's fallen apart," he said. "You fail to protect Meta. She's in crisis. I hear her cries from her nook in her room. Otherwise, she wanders, and God knows where, maybe Berlin or New York. Next, she'll sleepwalk on the estate wall that's crumbling. If the gate's locked, she'll pull out the stones and climb through.

"You and your need to marry her off to Harald! You blame everyone else. Contact me before doing anything I'd object to. She's headstrong. You can't go head to head with everyone you damn."

They seemed not to notice her return. Meta expected their wrath toward her, not between them.

"They'll play out," Lore continued, "little secrets, hidden from you. We all 'yes' you to death. So, you won't find the truth."

"You're carried away!" Heinrich bellowed. "You're my sister. Not her mother. On a working phone line, I'd hang up on you."

"The girl's not yours to marry her off? I'm your elder sister. When our mother died, I cared for you growing up, though you weren't much younger. I did, as others told me to do."

"When Meta wanted to study veterinary science, we spoke. No vets here treat animals, big or small, you said, big men vets only handle big animals. She's too small."

"Women go to school now. I could have finished. She could!

"In wartime, women run families and farms. Your mother did, remember? She handled animals, big or small. Your mother, ours, did so in the last war. Shall we wait for the next one? Look at her with Ol' Christoph, that old tinkerer, up hill and dale with the animals. She cleans chickens, milks cows and cleans their barns. Next, he'll teach her to shoot ducks and pheasants." Lore paused for this point to sink in that Meta was hardening. "Don't belittle her.

"Besides, her mother disappeared. You banished her—that fact alone—could pull you or Meta apart inside."

"By free will, she left for political reasons."

"You could be kind," Lore went on, "and hold off her betrothal to Harald. His family would object to her background, if known."

"That religious monkey business surrounds one's private little hell that obsesses no one else, but you."

Heinrich and Lore argued throughout the day about war, hope or conflict over the match between Meta and Harald. Tante Lore disliked him, and Granduncle Heinrich opposed George. Lore believed the war had affected them all.

"Untrue. War exposes every nerve. Every deceit, every lust." Tante Lore knocked the table. No religion.

"Private hells combine. You and your circle thrive on war forever.

"No wonder, she cuts loose with Georg. Separating them drains me. Nor had I the energy to pry apart her mother and you. Remember? You hypocrite!"

"Me?"

"Have you told Harald's her father or mother Meta's parental truth?" Lore asked.

"Harald needs no family permit to marry. He's a man searching for his own truth."

"They know nothing. Unite them in an old-style arrangement, and she will fight. We don't know his parents either. Anyway, she'll rebel." Lore palms drummed her thighs.

"Lore, you're failing in your mission. I'm dismissing you."

Lore laughed. "I grew up here, remember. I'm the eldest. Remember?"

"You have two or three homes; you don't need this one."

Back from Berlin, Meta sat perplexed and downhearted; they no longer bothered about whether she overheard their animosity. Withdrawing into her elfin shell to dodge her great-uncle, she lingered for clarity over former uncertainty. Evading turmoil from his control, she was dealing with her tizzies, like a child seeking to reassure oneself.

Not be clawed by a vulture, could she mount up on the wings of an eagle? But flight happens only at death.

From the couch, she moved outside on the heath, half-walked man-like with big steps and half-dragging bat-like. If her breastbone stayed put, her rib cage would loosen and ribs would launch her gliding above treetops. Nevertheless from such brooding came reverie.

For weeks, Meta forgot cold fear by plotting her exit from the house, she'd live in the woods; eat morels, black raspberries and greens. Maybe a vengeful woodman or a robber knight could kill a rabbit for her. Ol' Christoph would help her on the sly to fire up the roasting of meat.

Heinrich knew Meta's habits. She knew his. He saw through her and expected her to slip pro-Nazi Plattdeutsch leaflets within daily newspapers distributed throughout the district. Done twice before, she was nonetheless confused by the mishmash of ideas; letters and alphabets mixed up. When he found her mixing up town papers, he thrashed her elbows. The bundles were corrected the next, third time.

He followed her or ordered Christoph to do so, while she was flying on the heath, free, out of sight in independence.

Nanna, guardian angel, grinned at her pluck, while reproving her. Better people did not use their guts, especially area first families. "Find courage." Nanna laughed and encouraged her to nail down her flyaway world. She, Meta, would.

Something was stirring up Heinrich, whose untrimmed whiskers flared and eyes popped out when seeing her. He snapped his whip on the floor, though rarely on her or the horse's back. Jumping away from his whip or switches, she grew swifter than earlier. She feared him. His aged horse, palomino-colored, must have tired and died from hind whippings.

Meta resisted, taunting fate, and feigned indifference. "Why bother me? Who cares? Leave me to peace and quiet."

She mimicked her elders, rehearsing parts, especially Nanna's. Also, she warred inside without or with great-uncle and tried to learn how to play others off him.

Granduncle Heinrich shouted again over her thoughts. "You're like your mother!"

She'd rehearsed. "You're like my father."

Surprised at her voice out loud, she asked, "You knew my mother well. How so?"

His whip spat the floor, like a snake's hiss. Ol' Christoph had taught her to scrape the guts from carp, turkey and rabbits. She puzzled over his slip knotted nets that caught them.

From the pinewood siding panels, eyes watched her thoughts. Her eyes watered over escaping on the canal to the river, through Bevensen, a town recognized in 1920. Instead, she might go now in 1924 to the harbors of Hamburg or Bremen for America.

Instead, with bags of bulletins, she climbed on her rickety bike. Katia, better schooled of the two, gloried in galleries and orchestras, self-created as Bildung. Why not she, instead of this hell? On her scratched silvery bike, hell-bent, she swooped down the drive between poplars and birches, white bark lit, until clouds blinded the sun or the sun obliterated all.

In the fall of '25, fires in fireplaces scorched birch logs for warmth. This summer was cruel.

At Harald's doorway, farthest of her stops, she dumped the pack and raced out of the marsh estate of the ex-Kaiser.

Because her mother had left her and her father too, she could depart. She belonged to no one. True, Aunt Lore and Nanna might unite to confine her.

Georg was her last hope. At the hall gate, she knew not what to do. At the right gate? Or wrong one? Confused, had she taken the wrong turn? The last gift remembered was a castor bouquet with milkweed, narcissus and lupines. Or were they with beauty converting to toxic acid.

To escape, she could ride the moat on an inner tube from a wagon wheel or automobile. She pressed ahead. Aquatic, rodent and feline beings could squeeze through crevices and swim or rampage through the property. Instead she deposited the package at the door.

Unable to pass through the ironwork or unlock the gate and ride through, she leaned her bike on a post, found an opening between rusted parts, crawled under it and over a fake dirt moat, lined with glittering mica. If an old castle, not a Haupthaus, had been on piles, a bridge would have been lowered for crossing and drawn up after her. The fairy tales said so.

Tempted to spite her uncle, she spun back along on her bike and saw the eyeless youth again cycling toward her. Up close, he leaned over his handlebars. This time, hair, close-cropped made his eyes pale blue-gray, angling away, never quite toward her.

His local accent eluded her, whether Frisian or British-tinged. She concentrated so hard on his accent, but grasped no words. So too, the gathering fog permitted only the slight visibility of one's feet.

"I want a job to pay for my trip to visit my mother in Rugen," the tall youth was insinuating an unfamiliar charm. "Do you know that island?"

He was magnetic. Why. "You're the type to find me work." His eyes fluttered and rolled back. A chain was fastened to his wide dark leather belt with its holster missing its gun though a knife pointed down through its leather holder.

His eyes wavered over her belly. "You're with us?" He asked before he biked away.

Uncle had ordered her to stay away from him. Everyone conspired against her, Nanna and Lore included.

Even the black and white Holstein cow had died on her? Could the eyeless cyclist shoot her? Events funneled through periscope, kaleidoscope, telescope, and spectroscope: if only she could see. So dizzy was she that she worried she'd faint. Warnings from the old shepherdess warned about poor ex-soldiers, Raubritter or robber knights, swam in her head. Lightheaded, she lost consciousness.

Hours later, she awakened. Laced cutwork flowery white curtains bloused at the open windows, as the heat smelled. Her eyes blurred in the lit-up surrounding and rolled over to the body of someone thought to be Harald asleep, facing the wall. She lay back and edged back toward the free side near the door. His head was turned away; he lay rapt and slowly wrapped around her. Or did he? Was she? She could not disengage.

Again, she stole a look. A spiral faced the west window and his lower the east. A stilled writhing, white feathery, lay over her. She tried gauging his nerves and moves.

A tube arose between her buttocks. Did she pass out trying to remove it from her thighs? Breathing in slow heaves, she was hoping to ease away. When she tried, Harald or someone grabbed her. Quietly though she gripped the bedpost. Time and tempo were eons. From below, the chin and nose sculpted at the bedstead highpoint encouraged Meta to stick her leg into the cool air and touch the floor.

Slowly, a millimeter by eighth of a millimeter, she eased out. Not breathing, she could not look back.

14.

Later, Nanna divulged the proof that Harald had claimed her virginity, an odd bride-price for a misbegotten bride. This ancient and future bride-to-be, her great many greats back grandmother, according to Nanna, eloped.

Before the church banns and vows, even if they'd tried out their sexuality, their forefathers had urged for future harmony, loyalty, childbearing and food growing. As in the old territory, before life's demands overwhelmed them.

Hours later, Nanna accepted custom, even if half-known, informed Lore about Meta's status. Lore reacted. "I'm screaming inside over the worst: Heinrich sees the forcing child Meta a sign of our times, proven to him, that country life is falling apart and requiring ancient restorative customs. It's the opposite thought Meta.

"Although some farms are dismantled, he'll say, Berlin's artsy worldliness seeps in here to replace them. Too much freedom and cosmopolitan knockdowns—the old ways are rebuilding."

"But old ways like the new offer little hope?" She sneezed to stop tears and her topknot loosened. Was this a quarrel, Nanna wondered aloud, over old bridal methods? Had Meta's bedding stain proven her period or loss of virginity? With females abounding, males hardly required old ways of wooing.

Lore argued with her own daughter who argued with Nanna, who may have heard the tearing and moaning of Meta, and, in turn, argued with Frau von Handler who argued with her estranged farmer husband.

Nanna grumped. "Perhaps Meta spilled her monthly blood anyway. Other factors preyed on Nanna, alert in spite of age. Warriors, as culled from ancient sage texts, were allowed to abduct their brides. Christians did not bother little, nor did Harald, nor Georg. Nor the eyeless one?

"Such foolishness takes its toll," Nanna said to Lore. "Beauteous Meta is developing early frown lines, like footprints on a rose garden, and she's quieter than before."

Thereafter, Meta carried the opal-sided knife everywhere. Rarely, did she use it to open letters. Nor did mail carriers.

Maybe Harald was qualified to claim Meta into wifehood, as some old expedient marriages did, Heinrich implied and Nanna speculated, but not like the new-old marriage from sex among the young anytime. "Morality has decayed now," she reminded anyone who listened. Nanna and Heinrich agreed on this point, though Lore disagreed. Meta cared not at all what anyone said and began to withdraw.

Apparently, Harald abducted her before Heinrich's plan could work itself out. Bewildered Meta grew isolated, as everyone noticed and pretended nothing had been happening. No one minded her. She herself lost confidence in seeing what she tried to see.

Meanwhile, blood spots on the feather pad sprinkled like a blotchy galaxy. Harald's capturing was binding Meta. "This situation might lead her to oppose the marriage altogether, don't you know." Nanna predicted, knowing Meta's temperament.

Meta felt glass-covered or glassine; everyone slid past her. Heinrich did. Left in a lurch, Meta sensed her great-aunt's reluctance to comfort her or confront her brother.

Nanna pitied Meta, patted and tried to hug her. "This too passes, if allowed to." Under these circumstances, Nanna could do little. Nor could Liesl. To preserve her own life, she interfered not at all in Meta's life, and holed up in Berlin in Berlin. Mostly, they assured themselves that if Meta said nothing, then nothing must be happening to her. She must be recuperating. All would soon be normal.

Burning inside, Meta tried saying little. In fury, she once told Nanna, "You say life moves faster, as you grow older, so much so that your past joins your future. Or your future is your past. Mine separates!"

All who saw Meta whispered she was fine. If she hinted otherwise darkly, they ignored her. She lived in her tube gripped by threats from the unknown.

Meta dodged her great-uncle's flashing his riding whip. She magnified its details. Clenching and unclenching of his right hand, he asked, "Have you delivered the packet yet?"

"I-I tried in last week's fog but couldn't see."

"That bothers you?"

To know her habits, he did have her followed. From his stomping and whip snapping, Meta knew what to expect. He enclosed her by whirling it around her, binding her within a tube of anger, marked off from others. What if this damaged her baby?

His acts marked off finishing his plan for Harald's capture of Meta.

She: knock down everyone within hearing on the ground. Ward off anger and hostility. Stride on every heath path toward health and pray for strength. All you can do. Somehow her small hand knife pocketed or placed in her thoughts a small bow and arrow like Diana's, beside a deer pursuing Orion into the heavens. Cyclists and holiday-makers passed on by there.

Two months after her spree with her friends in Berlin, entrapment and dashes on the heath, she half-cheered herself through blanched trunks of birches. Fallen leaves crackled under her feet like crumpled messages. Still the darkest hours before winter matched her mood.

Externals distracted her. Nearby, the grounds dipped into a shallow bowl. There rocks leaned against each other in a matrix, resembling labia minor and major, the strange centerpiece in a tiny fountain splashed from a stream.

Nearby, small Catholic and Protestant chapels, smaller than arching grand brick Lüneberg churches, surprised her, especially as Nanna, a Catholic, warned her into silence within their Protestant family about Catholics. Both chapels were locked until Sunday worship or Angelus.

Genuflecting and reflecting on the ground, she recognized in the pool hair red-blonde from the sun rippling. A thought hit. Harald's attack flattened her into avoiding thoughts of it.

For months, neither Katia nor Georg appeared. But Grete did, to Meta's relief. She still counted on one friend with capacity for candor and wonder.

Twenty weeks after the attack, the old household servant shuffled to announce Grete. They hugged and chatted to catch up with loves, political fights, vet poverty, animals and pets, n newfangled cars and best of all, airplanes. Because of five lambs her uncle-father allocated to her in a weak moment, Meta remained determined to keep watch over a little flock and vouch for her right to study veterinary science. Resistance meant strategy with persistence. Was that the same as their heart throbs, not Georg, were little talked about? Harald was unknown to Grete. Grete planned to study art in London at Slade. Viewing Berlin, a hub for wayward youth who knocked adults and children off and "smutty arty folk, except maybe Kathe Kollwitz," meant her parents opposed her studying there. They yearned for a life higher than life, above and beyond.

"Oh, the sleazy ones?" Abruptly, fear drenched Meta. By age seventeen, she might be one. "Ah yah, in the city you can be bad, and in the countryside not so."

With, they could laugh over their elders' worries about their dances, virginity, smoking, games and imitate them. "Worry about those mad bohemians in Berlin." She mocked herself by telling what she'd said to Nanna, "Girls our age go on their own to pubs, and thousands go to thousands of pubs. We've done that?"

"They thrive on squalor," Grete replied. "But they intrigue me. I say, lighten up." Father tells me that our futures might turn us inside out. That's why your uncle loathes bohemians so much."

"He hates Berliner Expressionists," Meta continued, "and Viennese Secessionists, though less so. Anything new is apt to scorn German Saxons. Your father, I mean, your uncle, says so to my father."

Grete reached into the coal furnace, unlit in summer for some coal and with a compact mirror from her bag to smudge her eyelids and add mascara. "I'll do you. See how smutty we look."

Meta led her upstairs to the forbidden bedroom and armoire mirror looked in from four angles. At the special angle, they multiplied. They daubed on rouge and lipstick. The armoire opened, they tore into its clothes, lame, shimmering and net frothy nightwear. They giggled and danced more steps, creating their new lines of selves, kicking their legs like a dance chorus. Meta squirted her with frankincense.

Back downstairs to the gramophone for dance music. Exhausted, they hugged and fell onto the sofa. "You studied what at the country school you went to? Animal science?" They giggled

"I'm going to New York," said Grete. Her tapered painted fingers like detached musical keys twiddled.

"Can I come?" Meta expected a refusal.

"I'd so love you to." In her cryptic-talk, skip-racing, Grete observed, "But everything's planned for you here."

"Friends are free spirits. No Holy Spirit's to enter into us. Everything will shift, even for the farmers here, Ol Christoph complains, can't harvest their crops or bale hay, if need be, on Sundays, not on a day of rest."

Grete summed up. "We'll go to New York. You study horticulture, animal husbandry or veterinary science, and I'll study painting." She giggled and threw her head up. "I could go to Paris or Berlin or to America, where I have cousins." These words rang out as an era, felt eerily like a future bygone, a seen and unseen play distancing the two, as Brecht did. She'd been allowed to go to see the playwright's work that distanced audiences for clarity.

"Every step is planned for you and more or less for me," Grete said again. "Father with mother's consent demands I stay home. He hasn't met my boy friend. We sneak off dancing. They think I'm at my science tutor for my Arbitur."

"Maybe. Be careful. I might be with child."

"Oh, no."

15.

After Grete's papa fetched her, Meta sat licking and chewing her dry lips. Papa he was to Grete; Heinrich was simply grumpy. Off the hallway settle, she popped up because of the door knocker. The old servant though refused to answer it, knowing that the man of the house would.

For months, she'd not seen Georg, who now entered with an odd lordliness. Duty-bound, the old servant announced him. He waited in the foyer, for Meta. "By the way, I removed the tree and repaired the roof."

"I know. I saw."

Meta tensed. His tall presence spread throughout the small space, as he sat on the edge of the heavy table with carved legs. His loden jacket was odd in such a non-Alpine area like their lush heathland between Celle and Lüneburg. His arms braced his torso at his sides on the tabletop below which his legs spread.

She thought: hug him. If this tall and stocky man bound me to him, the table might tip. In front of everyone unseen, he shook hands with her. Stroke his fingers up, she wished, and down her spine.

Instead, he was formal. "My friends arrived late last night from Gotland. We ate without entertainment, except for the usual tales we tell each other. I was up early, but the others are resting. Because your uncle implored me to see him, I'm here to haggle with him."

"What about?"

With no answer, Georg disappointed her. His blue eyes gleamed within his reddish brown hair, burnished through the bubble glass. No chance to be with him. Nonplussed, she mumbled and gestured where to scout Heinrich. Neither man, both her seniors, cared she existed.

He acknowledged not seeing her for months. Faintly smiling, he smelled like an overgrown shag of a sheepdog. Alone, if too close, only three weeks before her small wedding, she'd breech expected conduct. Nanna and Lore claimed that good manners these days boiled up and vaporized like tea kettle water on the fire.

Minutes later, he glanced down at her from leaning against the nearest table. She moved closer, as her breeches stretched and tightened against her flanks. This son of her great-uncle's deceased best friend or Lore's husband's deceased nephew, or anyone who could volunteer his warmth to someone else. But she dared not ask and tried to forget the rapture.

He moved from the foyer table to the hallway, and she followed toward a window, diamantine in deep red and royal blue. Glinting in the noon sunlight, red, blue and gold tinged his hair and beard with patina slivers. His features magnified—older than hers were. His eyes were tired, sad or wary. She felt remote.

In silence, she noticed her dirndl country drab and the wood paneling and floor needing polishing beneath the Persian carpets with rich colors, temporarily uncovered by the usual rag rugs. Sent to hang them outside, she'd beat out the hell dust with a rug beater and hung on a coat hook its wire outlining a human back.

"Trouble? Are you all right?" She tried to divert his mind. His back to her, he glanced outside a lower clear window substituting for original stained, opaque ones. He rotated and embraced her and called her the slim, though "rounded beauty," city-acceptable.

"Your sinuosity numbs me," he said and smiled. The bare tiny line from his nose to lip marked his face through his mustache, dark red blond, with grayish. Could she nestle onto his shoulder and he lift her off forever?

"Are you all right?" He stroked her.

She should not want to touch him. Because Nanna had drilled in her that she as a young woman or lady, if such existed now even after the war, avoids wantonness. His eyes grazed her and narrowed toward hers and encroached upon her. "No."

His focus wholly on her emboldened her. Abruptly, she grabbed him to her for life and he her.

"What happened to my father?" she asked. Georg released her.

Ignoring her first query about his own state of mind, he pieced together the second. "This much—your uncle loathed your supposed mother and sent her off. "Heinrich is your father. He told you so."

"How?" Her hands on her hips sought to quell her excitement and fury. She backed away to

Seeing him beyond a blur.

"Well, he'll tell you the truth again. Your mother involved herself with your father and ill-suited him. She was daughter of Nanna and her husband, deceased in the first war in our era.

"Heinrich despises Berlin and Weimar, the cities and democrats she sided with. But it's more complicated."

"Thank you!!! We know all that. Take me; take me away with you forever." Again, she rushed across the inches between them and hugged him.

His matter-of-fact way kept Meta bereft. Her pace accelerated after him. Asked whether he knew she'd watched him from behind the tapestry's medieval scenes, while leading the gentry's meetings, he scrutinized her and said nothing.

Suddenly, after scanning her, he reached out, hooked his arms around her, squeezed and kissed her. "Be careful and wise." He turned on his heel. She could have wound herself around him, leaned into the small of his back and dipped her head between his shoulder blade muscles. He left probably to go to Mala.

Morosity oozed through her. Shying away from her thoughts to maintain her composure, she turned and collided with her uncle. He too said nothing more.

Back in the sitting room before Heinrich could object, Georg on his way out noted, "I am congratulating Meta on her forthcoming wedding."

Her insides sank. As Georg had embraced her, her uncle and Harald had been watching. She sank too fast into a hole and deep to fathom her own whereabouts.

Meta's wedding was inevitable. Lore's gift of a long white silk crepe dress with a peplum, collar-like at the waist in fancy lotus appliqué cutwork marked ceremonial necessity.

Nanna implored her to cooperate. "Receive the semen of Harald, and all will be taken care of. Georg cannot. Besides you'll have all the animals and flowers in gardens you wish for at Harald's place."

"I cannot." She tickled Nanna's standout lantern chin and nose.

"What you feel won't matter. True, it's hard to kill passion. What you do matters. Beliefs keep you going. Along comes war. But faith lights your way through fear.

"Harald's more afraid of you, than you are of him. Men fear some women. That's why your great-uncle so-called father sent your mother away. At best, women bond with others. Men stay fancy free. Stick to your match, you two can still be fond of each other, don't you see?"

Meta's shoulders drooped. Was this what mothers told daughters before marriage? Her chest sank.

"Sit up. You'll cope. Mary goes on beyond Joseph. So can you. What's the matter?"

"Already Harald's seed's in me, not all the way. I don't think so, anyway. I will create a baby but not with that bull-boy."

"Listen to the old songs. Look what happened to your mother and father. They adored you! Your mother disappeared. Your father slipped away to Hamburg, Paris or London and returned. Heinrich is here."

Meta left. On her way to her room, a sound came, the cow she'd led to her enclave here moaned she'd heard. High and low Meta scanned for her lost cow. En route through the small dormer window on the house wing, wooden horse heads writhed in the sunset on the roof points.

To see, she groped back toward a cupboard with candles and long wood matches for fireplaces or ceramic heaters. One match struck a flame and blew out in the breeze, and finally another lit the large wick. Her fingers within a thick oily rag were protected against dripping hot wax. She'd like to set fire to this place.

Who hung the carcass of the cow: hanging like meat in the tunnel, not in a locker or smoke house? This effigy dangled from rough-hewn rafter, once a tree trunk. Surely her uncle or Harald hooked there to swing from a beam over her frequented path to her suite. Few used it; in the old better days, servants might have hurried through. Now, few used the stairs and tunnel down here.

The carcass pendulum swung and knocked out time. As a child, she'd pretended to fearlessness; as a young adult, she rolled her cape around her fear, when haze and chill crossed the great northern moor. Light flickered. A reflected lantern was enabling her to see someone hanging!?

Coming to, faint but alert to the smell of baking and scurrying. Rats? Nanna stood over her disembodied. "Get up, dear; you can't sleep on the ground." Obedient in weakness, Meta rubbed her eyes.

Coughing, she was being smoked out of the tunnel and covering her mouth. Smoke and vapors from some vein of earth consumed her.

Voices like dreams were evaporating. Her candle still lit but wavered and nearly blew out. She slipped along and came back upon the figure from the rafter. When the candle died, a bat neared her. Improbable bats entered attics and barns.

Eventually, she re-lit the candle, climbed the stairs after Nanna to the kitchen. Good, she would not go through the open door. Instead she would sneak back down, across and up to her room and stay there. Diners, led by her uncle, could scour this corridor for her.

From the stairwell to her tower room, she heard a door thud behind her. When a draft blew out her candle again and she stubbed her toe in the dark, and she limped to her rooms to hide out.

Her hand around the candle squeezed its wax. She fortified herself inside against her outer door with a chest in her rooms. House carpenters built the sitting and bedroom long ago with a niche bed, walls in blue near a small blue and white tile heater. Chests carved with whirling flowers, sun symbols, held clothing and bedding. The heavy furniture was never moved. Here she intended to avoid Harald and Heinrich still in the house.

Meta fled under her featherbed and comforter. Prayers took in wounds, not words, against terror sluicing over her. Through the window, the full moon awakened her—the fog cleared—moonlight was blinding.

A voice seemed to call her from the stars. "Meta, I'm at peace."

Minutes or hours earlier, she'd shivered before the half-image of the effigy. If she'd hurried past it, nothing would have happened. Did she imagine and invent the effigy? She left her room to find out, Nearing the kitchen stairs, she'd feared being locked out, until she complied. In the big house, upper corridor, the clock struck seven, and her footsteps, sounding like boots, echoed. Her uncle had sacrificed the cow, which justified her removing herself from the upcoming dinner. Dreading beef for dinner, she'd returned to her room.

Now for a second time, her steps raced back to her room, and she fell on her bed. She got up from her bed and again stepped into the underground corridor. Clomping toward her, there he was. Risking his wrath, she said, "Uncle, why did you kill the cow and hang it up to ferment," she changed to, "'rot.'"

After casting around for words to describe her experience, she was still unsure of what had happened.

"The gardener Ol' Christoph took your sheep to the shepherd who tends our flock.

"As for your cow, she was emaciated, half-dead on her feet. Lately, there's no Jewish cattle buyer for her, either."

Meta cringed. He meant Grete's father, not Jewish, but Meta refused to reveal this fact.

"One used to buy and sell herds or singles here. You know the father of your so-called friend."

Meta shrank. Did Heinrich know all there was to know? When with her father, Grete had slipped her a note that a cow, maybe hers, had been seen. Her father pointed out the problem of loose cows in fields needing herding.

He spoke over her thoughts. "Someone found your cow. Understand, much is stolen around here these days. You are just one more thief, my dear, apt to be stolen yourself." All she could see in the dim light were his odd spats.

"Get this straight: The newspaper says crime has increased here 50 per cent recently.

Your meandering a pregnant cow bothers us, disturbs us.

"So we slaughtered her, salted and hung her by the locker door.

"Stick to pigs and piglets, if you must. We have plenty, more than anywhere else in North Niedersachsen."

He opened his fist. "Stop kidding yourself that you'll find your mother! She's dead.

"And stay home!

"One more thing, Harald will arrive back soon to share our dinner. And no more tomfoolery with Georg."

Upstairs her cousins were cheering each other. Mrs. von Handler's voice rang out. Was an actual betrothal party being enacted before an unacceptable oath?

Coerced into dressing in an outfit better than her ruddy cape and blue farm work shirt, for a young woman intended in better times to be a lady; Meta pulled on a black slinky number from the upstairs forbidden armoire closet and donned Wien crystals, a Berlin style to thwart Heinrich's and Harald's volkishness and entice Georg. She'd stage her entrance into the dining room.

Beforehand, she snuck into her old favored niche behind the tapestry to test herself and gauge what was going on. Captivate Georg? Trying to catch her breath, she was listening to find out what they were talking about. Where once she'd stood on tiptoes to do so, now tall, she bent over to look through the worn tapestry.

Talk encompassed drama: words got tossed from corner to corner. "Not only is the government allowing in foreign produce, like pigs, it supports the foreclosure of farms."

"Hog farmers are losing out," another agreed. "This Weimar government must go."

"Fifty or more farmers a month go." A certain man appeared to direct the agenda over others.

"Order," another cried out. "The NDSAP attacks the Guelphs. . . "

A tall man was blocking her view through the hole. Details heard would fit later on into a whole. The attack, for all she knew about history from her brief Country Boarding School near Berlin, the Guelphs opposed the emperor and supported the pope. What did the letters, boomed out, mean? Farther back in time, Dante was a Guelph; the Ghibellines hated him and cast him out as known from his Inferno and Purgatory. . . . He'd opposed he biggest landowners and supported peasants?

Truth or myth, one white-haired man held forth on "turmoil in Hamburg." Granduncle-father signaled to another dignitary whose hand crossed his mouth.

"But this matters," a high-pitched male voice said, "little now in 1923 after the Muenchen putsch and Hamburg revolt." For sure, Great-uncle opposed the revolt?

He grunted back. "The NSDAP attracts vets and one-time revolutionaries, ones in the woods here, because of our Volkishness. . . and the Freicorps. . .

Nonsense words to Meta.

Another speaker lingered on how no one deferred to rank anymore. He was sending his children one by one to America. Katia's father? Meta registered sounds without comprehending them. Peasants, another said, were riled up over low prices. Or was it high prices?

"Someone's listening?" This short dark-haired man said.

"So, what," Great-uncle Heinrich replied. "Small groups, like ours, strengthen our structure. Monoliths weaken and crack. Many small blocks together help. Look at the Saxon counties, ducal states and princedoms, built piece by piece, until they thrived. It's high time to fortify national conscious-ness, ah, the Volk in all of them."

"We here fought off the Romans." Another voice boomed, "We here fought off the French. We'll fight off the Jews. We'll fight off the leftists. We'll do in the Christians. We'll plan."

"Nein, nein," the white-haired man invoked this view. "Better a natural buildup. Better a natural disaster, rather than a man-made one. Your tight recruitment leads to a man-made disaster. Human disasters are worse than the natural ones, mark my words."

Without a periscope, Meta could not see who spoke, "True, true."

"Without recruitment, men on the loose spread their dis-ease, rags and dung everywhere. Give them more to do."

The man with spun glass white hair disagreed. A dapper man with a black mustache and meerschaum pipe smoked and leapt up to prowl along the wall for a hollow area for spies.

Her Grand-uncle countered, "Bah, no one's listening in on us, no opponent. Why would anyone bother? We're not yet important enough. We shall be. Let's break for dinner."

Meta shivered. Did her uncle still not know her hiding place? Of course, he did—from her childhood with her dolls. If caught, she wouldn't have to worry about being discovered. Spying, or knowing or not knowing what she was not sup-posed to hear, to see, to know. But they'd chosen to ignore her, denying what she'd live for. What did she live for?

As some men walked out into the waiting area, Uncle Heinrich came out of his library office and she exited from her long-time downstairs nook. He spotted her, as she slithered out from behind the tapestry. He brightened. She would have to do his bidding. "Good for you. Here's an errand for you," he beckoned with an envelope. He and Tante Lore had not planned a betrothal party after all.

Schooled for animals, as I am, O soul, for death, I must call on my mother and reassure her I am alive, she invoked.

The next day on the Heide, she kept walking to think. The heath calmed her, as she walked fast, whirled her arms, turned her head and strolled back toward the farm. She'd delivered her uncle's tracts by bike. She tried ignoring the eye-less one. "Frölein," he addressed her. He might help her. Probably not. They didn't talk. She did not stop.

From place to place, upside down baskets, clustered near sheds, where few people visited. Country people had used these baskets, marking old and modern times, since the 18th century, so it was told, to create honey. Everyone relished its sweetness in the countryside.

To maintain honey making, certain people must clean the extractors and all must follow the swarm.

Not far away and now, men's voices rang out. Creeping in closer to look in through a woody hole, once a knot and without understanding their words, she slipped along the small building wall unpainted, weather-beaten and splintery. Pulling a sliver from her thumb, she listened in through the split warped boards and a woody hole, near an outside door ajar.

One man in farm clothes stood and spoke inaudibly. But in this peep show man naked, half-stood with pants down visibly.

Still words spiked an argument. Before she understood them, a chair flew toward the rudimentary podium. Another slammed the wall. Next, a bearded man punched another. A stocky bearded fellow wielded a rug beater against the hind end of a man with knickers down. On a chair, a guy stood with a sword he whirled over the others.

They were growling epithets and swinging numchuks, metal finger covers for fighting to lacerate a thin guy.

She'd tell her uncle. Being a tattletale would lead him to blame her for seeing the melee. The underbelly was becoming showy.

16.

Upon her return, in the hallway Georg was bending toward Katia in her blue silk and touching her arm. The word, Beschmutzen, soiled or dirty, applied here. Katia was bending toward him. Was he disengaging from herself? Sadness webbed inside Meta, as she hurried to hide.

Her entrapment with Harald had been whispered about. Foolhardiness leads her to dash on the heath on its seasonally bleak flats in late gray winter, to seek our honeycomb. Georg had found her there in her childhood. Not now.

In the house, Harald, apt to be around, limited her activities, except her running up and down, back and forth through the underground passage, where old logs or tree trunks bolstered the house rafters. Logs as legs could bolster her legs.

With an orange cloche over her ears, she drifted on the land. No one missed her or welcomed her. Whether absent or present, hugged or hated, she counted on warmth tiding her over her anguish in her forthcoming marriage? Sleepwalk, she told herself. Keep distant from self, a practice she had repeated, ever since her latest attack experience.

Searching for her mother also sapped her energy. This inertia exposed her aching. The loss landed on her sternum. Leaden, it dropped to the pit of her stomach, allowing little joy from food. Her family chided her that she was too thin for formal dress.

Georg, she heard said, had lost everyone he ever loved. So, he was making up for possible losses of Mala and Meta with Katharina?

Aimlessly, wandering and poking around, she scouted around for Nanna. "You'll overcome your hurt," Nanna said. "Katia's befriending him does help him overcome losing you, more than you ever can."

"Besides," said Lore, just entering in her flowing iridescent maroon and dark green dress and newly tinted hair, "he's Everywoman's Everyman. Such a man every woman falls for—you have since childhood." Meta tried to listen and winced.

"Marrying Harald will please you," Nanna said and chuckled. "No human thrives without flaws, don't you know? Georg's look and sensitivity belie his anger. Ask what your flaw is that ties you to others." Meta shrugged. "Grace will improve your flaw," said Nanna

"Who's Grace?"

"The Gift from God."

"I don't want that gift. I thought she was a woman's name somewhere. Where is she, when I need her?"

Now too, Nanna, aged beyond the ancients, the uuarsago, wise one in Old Saxon, lowered her voice. "Marianna, if in life, two or three gifts come to you, good health, children, work; abide in them. You are blessed.

"When you were six years old at Christmastime, the special glittering pickle was hid for the cousins and local children to search for. Who found it? Don't you know? You were declared,

'The most observant child of the year, the most aware.' The glittery pickle was your prize for the year."

Days later, Georg continued ignoring her, whereas once he'd followed her, fetched her, plucked her, from the road. Now Georg passed over her for Katia, rapturous in her deep blue dress.

Hopelessness from Katia's latching onto Meta's not-so-secret-love botched their friendship. Nicknamed "Kater," tomcat, how could Katia veer toward Georg and stay her friend? Was Meta losing two friends?

The old woman, often chuckling, preached on: Losses collapse into each other and reinforce one another. The adage of one finger forward and three backward was never heard by Meta before. Others had. Thumbs up at blame or down succumbed to doubt.

To Georg, who'd left, she'd never shown off her slinky dress, silky in dark red satin with girlish lace, along with modernized Viennese crystals. How to slip up to him or win him to her room? But he'd never come to her. She's even changed the pillows, the sheet and featherbed cover for him. Harald never came for dinner either, as her uncle insinuated and bellowed he would.

Growing up in a place others called home, Meta had often U-turned toward the city statue of Diana at Lüneberg. From time unknown, this trading city-state had displayed this miniature virgin moon goddess of the hunt and marriage. The Diana, some declared, originated from a tree for worship in antiquity. She thwarted Acteon.

On the other hand, Heinrich had long admired nearby late Gothic churches for their terra cotta brick simplicity. "Travelers from Spain and Italy study these wonders. Still the south mocks us as barbarians.

"You'd be fortunate," he'd said, "to marry in one of them here."

"No," she'd said under her breath.

"You shall," he'd said.

"Southerners said we dragged out our axes to chop ice and our swords, sweeping northward, only to go south again to fight. We'd flocked to certain posts, stood our ground and fought. Or we'd rowed boats upriver."

She'd block him.

With the war long passed, the Rathaus, city hall authorities unlocked in 1925 its opulent Ottonian interior with Renaissance colors to the public. A small primitive warrior stature, like a child in a folded paper hat, and his sword swung like an orchestra conductor, Lili's. Now in this hall they toured. The bas-relief mural women interspersed with angels, graces who wore gossamer stoles like wings. Now tall, Meta eyed their profiles within gorgeous reds, blues and greens of murals inside a heady kaleidoscope.

Weeks after their first postwar trip into the city, another ensued. "Uncle, tell me," she asked, and, then, stopped. High stepping, the horse rode on to the church, and she risked his bluntness or silence. From the back seat, his dark hair topped the white at his temples.

Also meeting Harald for the marriage license, Lore gray-blue wool, setting off her upswept blonde-gray hair, and Nanna. She ignored the little nude goddess outside and nude Soest figures within the frieze and probably never saw them. Meta loathed asking, "What are these sculptures about?"

The elegant church near the Sand contrasted with their humbler neighborhood church they attended near their farming estate. "Think," Lore had said, "how many years we came into town here, then, stopped."

Here and now, between war and honeymoon journey, Harald and Meta visited an extinct monk's village, where. Green and rust-colored pine needles softened their footsteps. Harald might humor her urge to walk stocking-footed on the spongy ground.

Gray stone walls surrounded cells the size of beds with stone pillows. Shelterless, these monk cells, lacking racks for thatched roofs, from which Celtic monks had converted West Saxons.

Evergreens and ash trees soared above, though an old forester commented on elms dying out faster than the ash. Intertwisting in the wind, such trees darkened against the dusky sky, until the moonlight reflected on the birches for gliding through fantasy Alba.

On earth, birch light, pine aroma and oak strength marked the land. These Schottenkloster tucked new ideas back into this continental homeland.

Like their ancestors fanning through northwestern European estuaries: Ems, Weser, Elbe and Oder, Meta and Harald examined Deusche-Schiff-und Mashinenbau A.-G., Atlas-Werke shipyards geared to "Venture and Win," the Chamber of Commerce pamphlet informed them. The two of them, Harald and Meta, now gazed at the great harbor.

Farther on, passengers were boarding the Lloyd-Bremen ship ramp to sail to America. A group of nine trooped on, along and boarded, as Meta and Harald were leaving. All these women and one man, noisy laughing Americans curved in their coats, muffy fur collared, around them. Flickering in her, Meta was to set from Bremerhaven for the edge of the world to follow Cotton Exchange bales heading for America.

Instead across the North and Irish Seas, they lined up for Viking Dublin church crypt. In height, she reached Harald's mid-breast bone, which blocked his heart. Over it, his navy lapels arrowed toward his jacket's bone-colored buttons. On tiptoe, she made contact with his green cobalt eyes, with his dark mid-lock almost over his right eye. "Stop being impatient with me," he said.

Consigned to him, she conjured bravery to avoid deriding him, as Nanna had told to do. "Ah, sorry."

Back in Germany, narrow Bremen streets little fit all the pedestrians' movement. He held her hand passing the North German Lloyd shipping line offices, and Atlantic Club, near the artists' quarter by Lore's atelier, if she had one.

Down the riverbank, warehouses and medieval tenements gripped the landscape, where overcrowded, poorly aired flats dirtied it. When an old lady opened her apartment to visit, Harald tipped her 50 Pfennig.

Blocks away in the square to eat food wagon pasties and pastries, like the foreigners or the poor, would appall Heinrich. Never mind, he'd approve the Ottonian Saxon cathedral, prickly and spired. Here prone wooden medieval sculpture or a preserved knight of the garter? "Have you met big-headed Elkhart and Uta, sculpted monarchs?" compared with big knight Rolland outside, stories high, nude under his armaments, sword and shield.

Cheerier, Saxon Otto I and Anglo-Saxon Edith sat in the Magdeburg's Cathedral, near the Wise and Foolish Virgins. Meta suppressed laughter. "You've met them?"

Their sightseeing continued. Harald smiled. "Want to? How about the Holy Fools? Be one? So let's see the Lead Room." Bodies there had turned into mummies: Swedish general, Lady, English Major and Saxon carpenter. "The air here preserves the dead knight's skin and ours."

Ahead stood a couple, the woman in raven-cropped hair, like Meta's, and the man in helter-skelter fair hair like Georg's chuckled at Harald's remark.

In the crypt, Meta and Harald shook hands with one un-corrupted knight. "See his fine wrinkles," Harald noted, "We'll resemble him in our nineties, if preserved."

"If pickled in brine, we'll last." For living qualities, she tried snuggling up to Harald but found him rigid like the knight's arm.

"Underground so long, you'll wrinkle too from the Dark Ages."

"From the Middle Ages, buried." She bit her tongue. Be-ginning to show, she'd acknowledge her pregnancy soon. Ev-erything would be all right. To scrutinize the knight, she bent over her slight bulge.

The air enlivened them; this knight's preservative en-hanced themselves.

The one she craved, Georg, was far away. Great-uncle having finagled and boxed her into marrying Harald cleaved inward like a dagger in merriment. Surprisingly better treated than expected, she was unable to fake feeling for him though caved in, bided her time and imagined he was Georg.

Later on, they sipped pub ale and joked about wooden and preserved knights. Silence reigned. We're but strangers here, heaven's our home. She recited to herself and aloud to prompt his pique.

Harald was cross at her wish to dash into galleries of fu-ture: Modersohn, Kollwitz, Grossman, Grosz. Uncle detested them all—the past clashing with the future. Harald grumped at her musings, as they rushed up the street. Favoring glory red and wood, they both disliked the Bremen Rathaus' gold colored council rooms. She'd promised herself she would enter the land that took for its own flag, the guidebook said, "Bremen colors, red and white" in checkered and striped flag design, like brick Saxon building sides.

Next, in the Bremen Ratskellar, sepulchral with curved archways, the waiter offered tortes and cognac. Ongoing "war shortages," he claimed ah, except for ale." Harald ordered ale, and she cognac. Had the next war started? Sipping their drinks and admiring Slevogt's mural, they leaned back in oval caned-back chairs. Instantly, cognac too much tart bit her tongue.

Harald bit his over the vintage wine cost, unused to it during wartime. It was stored in the Rat cellar. They preferred Liebfraumilch. He drank her cognac.

Thus warmed, they hugged and momentarily, they stopped at the Memorial to the Fallen Soldiers inside the Church of the Dear Lady. Emma's walkway around the old city relaxed them. With his tongue, he licked Meta's ear. She laughed.

Back in their hotel, Harald lifted off her tube dress to knead and mold her breasts, loose now within his hands and tongue-tickle the nape of her neck. He swept his wife onto the bed. She la-laed and embraced him. Rubbing his buttocks, she felt him bolt up and remove her silky stockings and panties. Like a boat on waves, they rocked into the night.

On in their pilgrimage north with fewer dire knights, they remained on the lookout. From grand offshore islands, Ireland and England, to the continent via Bremen and back, they traveled north toward Denmark, where he'd longed to visit. Late at night, they determined to walk down the road.

There are many "temporaries in life," she guessed, in weariness. He was a man of the night; she was a woman of the day in the midnight sun. Farther South, the sun would sun flush their faces though little tan. Aggressive hot water, a Mutspell began blushing in their skin in erotic mud, so their flesh blended with the terra cotta.

After glowing from the baths, an event startled them on the continental shore. They stumbled upon a long band of figures, burnished scarecrows, were crowding the pathway.

As if lightening dazed them, figures straggled along, held shields over their torsos and hearts and rattled their metal. "Who are they?" Otherworldly bygones, Vikings, were marching by. Without personalities, faces wore gas masks, par-folded for a snout and built-in goggles for eyes at the top. "Flyers, Luftwaffe?" Two or three fool swore helms with horns

"Freicorps." Harald corrected. "See them."

"You know them?"

"Of course. Not your father's type he'd welcome into his house."

"He's my father?" She drifted. "I'd forgotten."

"You'll get used to him."

The metal layered these straggling Freicorps with extra hide, like warriors' armor in silvery sheen, reflecting Artic light that made discerning the metallic leaf design difficult. This armor lacked the medieval fluting, like pleating, to allow an old-young knight, a Saxon Thein to bend his joints.

A dagger could pierce it with or without metal. Like a crux or cross, a Misericorde dagger could thrust through the fluted elbow. The daggers puzzled her. The metal armor squares, about nine by nine millimeters, hinged on these strange pass-ers-by and flexed.

One soldier passed by, his vest dangled below his gas mask, like a bib from the war. But the type in a museum from the armory with upturned pocket for an erect penis was missing.

"Some ripped their pants on thorns or the razor wire in prison camp." Harald said, as Freicorps passers-by released from the army now lived with Mother Nertha. Nanna had warned her about them. Exposed, they were tender though rigid. Meta smiled and kept her own counsel at a familiar sight. Was he or wasn't he?

One resembled Georg, "Someone we know." Harald ig-nored her. That man, taller than Harald, twisted his neck, like a brass torque, to glimpse her. In fact, Georgs and Haralds were everywhere.

In gas masks, other phantoms electroplated in faint night sun, were foot soldiers retreating from some havoc toward the end of the world.

Harald disapproved of this parade she admired. "Is that Georg?" She writhed to see. "Let's speak to him."

"Who cares?" He, leaner and bonier than Georg, shot back. Georg, thickset in the torso, had grown extra graying dark blond waves of hair.

17.

Nine months later, Meta bounced her baby, mugged with him, adored and hugged him, dubbed Todi or "Tody" in English. Harald heard "Toby" from his formal Christian name, Teodor. She exulted in motherhood with less time for Harald, who was overseeing the estate lodge. Earlier, she'd not known about giving birth, except it was done to her. This baby was good-natured.

Country folk brought Torf to help newborns, by absorbing urine without causing a rash for tiny ones without cloth diapers in hard times. Uncle Heinrich would appreciate Torf or Plaggan from his Volk necessity. All were thanked for their earth gifts; especially one elder couple's handcrafted rocking willow crib.

In all, people did praise her re-peopling the postwar countryside. Carrying him everywhere, she sang acceptance of this baby, who thrilled her.

With Todi, she reentered the forest at age 17. Blooming above memory and riding in the iron-wheeled cart behind an old nag's bottom, reins in hands, Meta circled about for neighboring folks see her baby she'd never let go of. If only she drove a white horse or two dark horses.

Another elderly woman clucked and disturbed her. "One science folk in a factory sends his children one by one, all eight, to America every other year or so."

Singing to Todi and tickling with a bird plume on his plump cheeks, gurgling, Todi grabbed it. Robin Hood, Maid Marian, Dumm Hans, Rumpelstilskin, Humpty-Dumpty tales and nursery rhymes and songs were vocalized with him. Later, he tickled his father's nose, and they both chortled.

Onto the rose-purpled midsummer, ex-soldiers explored and prowled the Saxon moors, south into the Harz Mountains; Meta regaled Todi with tiny stuffed bears and metal toy soldiers, war-paupers and soldiers. Harald saw only as their shit fouling up the forest. "It's no better here than their outlandish city behavior."

Back from Berlin to picnic on the colorful Heide they talked. "Men in make-up, women tarts in hordes and men in endless fights," said Liesl, back from Berlin. She was complaining to Meta. She'd come to enjoy country life with Hansi and his quiet little brother.

"There's safety with us together," Tante Lore added. "Otherwise veterans will hoodwink you before capturing you. They'll be chopping down oaks, birches and softwood conifers to awaken Father Time."

"You're going too far, Mother," Liesl said. Lazy and sleep, like Todi, Meta little understood her aunt and cousin.

"Warnings mean little to you," said Tante Lore. "Not the kings' men but foresters scouted the woods to protect us picnickers against the hangers-on. The foresters even rode back with us to Heinrich's farm and Celle."

Sadness jabbed Meta, when her aunt and family left her behind. Eyes moistened her loneliness. An eyelash between her eyeball and socket bothered her into rummaging in her rucksack. A spoon, polished, revealed the lash; better yet, the knife like a mirror located the hair irritating her eye. On the mossy earth thereafter, she and her son curled in her arm and slept in peace.

As time passed, fewer visitors sought out Meta, Harald and wee Teodor in their "new home," in the grand hunting lodge. This huge moribund estate lured curiosity seekers, friends and relatives paying social calls. She'd expected more.

Local folks still brought humble gifts of daisies or planters with violets, heather and mistletoe for love and luck. With his dark brown wavy hair and brooding eyes, Harald smiled and plucked a bright yellow-green mistletoe sprig to place behind her ear and kissed her for her socializing.

☒

Outside two horned Heideschnucke separated from their herd and followed her for lack of a herder. Their wet noses twitched, as she pet them, and their limpid eyes brightened with food.

In married life, she missed Ol' Christoph's ongoing teachings about herding, harvesting, forestry and animal care. Without Nanna, now semi-paralyzed from her stroke, Meta felt lost.

On a marketing trip to town, she and Todi stopped at the local market and struck up an acquaintance with the butcher's young son Alain. When they drove on, turkeys cackled, and Schwabisch-Hall pigs oinked. Little Todi waved at an off-white landrace sow and her consort.

Dazed, she savored her son in a peaceful stop-off. Dried leaves with blued and fallen rusted pine needle underbrush crunched; canopies above camouflaged them. On mosses, green and rusty, Todi enjoyed lying and waving his arms.

A light shafted on a clearing ahead. By crawling away from the sleeping baby, she plucked morels, fascinated by their tiny pockets under their covers. If she was miniaturized, she'd sit under one in this temporary Walden, Waldeinsamkeit. Unless preserved, the morels though supplied food she feared they'd lack at home in the future.

Away from fantasy, Todi's gurgling brought her back to suckling. Afterward, he stayed naked in the day's warmth. Belly down, his head bobbed, his fleshy bottom matched some mushrooms. Re-diapering him, she identified his tiny penis with stalk mushrooms, the stinkmorchel, phallisimpudicus and life.

On the moss, he crawled on his belly flared his arms like a polliwog, fussing and bouncing his head. Lying back, she smelled the pure ancient pine. Could she eat it? Her baby's and the brook's gurgle reflecting shoreline heather with sun gold comforted her beyond thought. In the sky, white was puffing against the deep indigo, its sulfuric acid emerging like Saxon blue, sea-like, for wool to spin from merino yarn on Nanna's old spinning wheel.

Momentarily exhausted from growing, Todi napped. Relieved, she lay back again. Leafy branches swayed like upended ballerinas in green tulle and bark eyes, kohl-darkened ones, watching her.

Metal clanking stirred her. In the clearing beyond, swords or metal sticks fanned like a ceremony and banged like a metalworking shop, only menacing. She crept away from Todi toward the bulls-eye target for bows and arrows. Only two swords began whipping the air and clanking. Lugers and Mausers, recognized from Heinrich's talk about the Walther Werke not far away, were yanked from holsters and out along with rifles posted upright. A deep voice urged target practice with gunshots, instead. Next, as blocked by tickets of birches, these troops formed and marched.

The Stahlhelm was practicing its maneuvers. Or was it the Freicorps with Georg or Heinrich through the trees? She studied the maneuvers. Was this practice for war legal? Doom was pending?

Todi's months passed, directing others to fulfill his wants. At seven pounds, seven ounces at birth, he, a quiet baby cried for breast or soft food. Gradually, he squatted, crawled and sat. From his alphabet, his words spewed out at one year: "Bee," "light," "Mama," "Papa," "Nanna" and "bookkeeper." Manuals that discouraged hovering by mothers and hugging them to spoil them bothered Meta. By four, Todi was energizing the household.

Out of curiosity, aged war survivors and other youthful elders continued to visit to bask near the glowing new being residing in the hunting lodge of the Kaiser, now exiled in Doorn, Holland.

To Harald, she fretted, "All these gifts for Teodor will spoil him." She was referring to a toy plane, glider, U-boat, teddy and elephant bank.

"No one will spoil my son." Harald rebuked her. "You spoil him, take him everywhere and ignore me. Now he'll go with me on my rounds, learn to be a boy, then, a man."

Thereafter, he hoisted Todi to piggyback on rounds of the estate. When Todi became four years old, his father demanded Todi follow him.

Fitful, she'd still played hide-and-seek with Todi, bake sugar cookies in a mammoth back kitchen iron stove oven and tie his shoelaces. But Harald insisted his son tie, his own.

Sometimes, "Mama, mama," heard far away, as if deep underwater, and she'd run after him or swim. The non-life eeriness within life resounded during a blood red-blue sunset, the evening's evening before the dead of night, like the dark of the forest.

To disentangle her worries, she turned to the old carriage house contents. Out came daggers, long swords, Saxes, and old Frankish Scramsax, weaponry and axes that hacked people and the ancient Irminseul, she likened to an antique tree of life, knowledge or wisdom from great oaks the ancients worshipped on the moor. Old tools, scythes, rakes, hoes and spades all familiarly had prepared the earth for planting were dug out from under other junk.

Hardly a mews anymore, doors replaced horse stall gates. Grubby from self-imposed cleaning tasks for reviving her sanity, she welcomed Katia's breezing up, waving her stole out the window and attracting Meta with "I've missed you!" Katia rose out of the white meteor-styled car, customized for the 1920s like sleek car, name unknown, driven for her.

No one's got money these days. "How'd you do it?" Meta blurted out.

"Nobody does. I borrow." She whispered. The car's horizontal and chrome style made Katia elegantly vertical, all legs and languor.

Thrilled by her friend's surprise visit, Meta hugged her and dropped her doubts about their friendship. Katia's makeup enhanced her luminous eyes within her deep hair waves of hair, dappling in sun and shadows, like her burnt sienna dress. Beauteous Katia introduced her to Karl, the presumed beau. Gesturing toward Berlin, Katia's legs ambled within her skirt, like a soft conch shell edge.

Gleefully, Meta walked Katia and Karl around the estate, hoping to find Harald and Todi. Could she, Meta, ask about Georg, without disclosing feelings? What about hidden politics? Everyone was cautious and nasty toward the wrongheaded opinions these days.

"Space here for many buildings, for what? How can you live here? Isn't it creepy?" Katia asked, without pause. "I'm used to crowded streets but not a massive house like this."

"We grow our own food," said Meta, eager to show off her skills against conspicuous housing. "I can, pickle and cook in this house, not ours, but the Kaiser's. He's gone. The buildings stay.

"So, we've heard. Who could afford such a house in this economy?" Square-faced Karl asked, strutting and removing his white wool jacket.

Happy with them, yet shrinking from them, Meta talked about common friends, friends gone, horses, cattle and returnees to the post-war farm life. These warm-blooded horses, about 1500 pounds worth, in sleek gold-brown coats, white face and manes thrilled them, especially seeing saddled Arabians or working Trakehners. Pasturing, two drew up close. One smelled her hand, gobbled hay and nodded his head, though his mate looked away, hurt without getting fodder immediately but rejecting it when offered.

En route from Bremerhaven-Bremen and the Worpswede art colony to Berlin, her guests too worldly to care about animals said, "Come with us. Your family's not around."

"Ya, for sure." Thrill of escape, like four years earlier. Why not? Harald insisted on watching Todi. Accompany them to Berlin. Otherwise, she'd become a mummy or soul wanderer before ever seeing artists' colonies.

"If you can't go now, we'll pick you up on our way back." They drove off, the automobile coughing exhaust and spraying loose gravel.

Next to slender Katia, Meta's body felt heavier. It, so Harald said, ill-suited him. After his fleeting sight of Katia with Karl, meeting them before tea before and sundown, he compared her with Katia. "Too round for a Saxon woman. Walk more. Fat unbecomes you."

Laughingly, she waltzed to Harald and cooed, "You're cranky. I'm pudgy, I am." Dreaming of joy, she danced in time with her humming Swing. She opened to him.

He grinned, "Silly."

Todi needed her less, and she was relieved she was not pregnant again. Working off anger, she grubbed away at junk piles and wandering. Harald began a second face-off. "Cut your wandering. Your uncle, uh, your father, warned me about your rushing about. You're backsliding. You were upright, when we wed."

His cobalt green eyes squinted, and he sniffed the air. "Clean out that old carriage house. You'd like a car, wouldn't you? Buy one with what you earn from what you sell."

Five days later, she threw herself back into the carriage house mess to cope with tangles of rakes, trowels, hoes, and dagger clotted with dried shit and rust. He expected to haul it all away.

Yet no one helped, except at her behest, old fellows on the estate called on Ol' Christoph, now 85, still active and inventive about all these finds stashed away, especially Saxon tangs. Her Uncle-father enjoyed lecturing her on their provenance.

Soon afterward she kicked a planter, its edge split off: another find, Christoph called it, a headpiece. Jolly, she covered her head, until headachy. To enlist Harald, she said, "Junk's the schmaltz we live on. Make some money from it, or we'll sink into poverty."

From a jar, she spread this rendered fat on bread and salted it.

Harald jabbed, "Aren't you fixing a real lunch for us?"

"Want some? I'm working." She gloated over "finds"; he glowered.

Chronicling the goings and comings of folks with tools, her uncle-father who visited, unlike Harald, was enthusiastic. Heinrich dubbed her "a good woman" and crowned her his daughter to one and all. Meta accepted that role, warily. Father-Uncle Heinrich bear-hugged Meta within his ale and pipe tobacco breath. She shrank within herself.

Previously hauling items for the local historian to examine, she'd jumped out of the car Harald let her drive to visit Heinrich. He'd called up to Ol' Christoph, repairing thatch on an outbuilding. "Did those grass huts come from your time in South-West Africa?" The lively octogenarian grinned showing two missing front teeth.

One sword's scabbard, brought along, looked scripted: Irmenseul. She interpreted its holiness with human meanness. Was it soaring through he spheres to the outer worlds?

"Only ceremonial only, too modern for anything significant, other than like a souvenir." Heinrich dismissed. "In olden days, they stuck ones like them into farmhouse dirt floors with good faith, fortune against attack for a good harvest."

Also brought with her were helmets, conoid, which protected warrior brains. In the tedium of Saxon group, obsessive chitchat about the gear she'd driven over in, scratched and tarnished metal, escaped meaning.

Ol' Christoph sidled over and said, "All them types went everywhere."

After Heinrich's cheered her finds, she encountered Harald, who'd followed her to the farmhouse of granduncle and father Heinrich. Shooing him away from having seen Georg on the premises, she sought to escape. Heinrich despised Georg might have to allow his visiting his sister and her aunt Lore and ailing Nanna.

Alone for a moment, Meta dolled herself up with makeup from the forbidden bedroom, unlocked—not enough to call notice to herself—and brushed her hair. To woo him would reek of sin; some would say but not matter to her. If only Harald would leave. Heinrich now did not like her husband, at this point, anymore than Georg.

Her beat-up, muddy shoes, knee-thinned knickers, wrinkled smocks or odd dirndls smacked of natural country vigor, Heinrich liked as folksy, however off-putting. Quarreling with herself, ah so, if she improved, Harald could believe Heinrich or Georg nor was influencing her.

"If I wear stylish clothes, who'll do the dirty work here?" She taunted Harald, when he appeared. He shrugged. She'd daubed on red-pink rouge. So, Harald asked, "How come you dress up to clean the barn and go see Heinrich?" She never did find Georg, nor would she on Heinrich's lands.

Observing her animal husbandry gifts, such as, healing sheep, calves or colts and rearing them for market, Harald gave her two sheep. They tantalized and comforted her and their coats, if dyed, could adorn their wool. Catalogues helped evaluate the benefits of new Moorland sheep, Skudde, Frisian, merino or Heideschucke. Elder herders pastured them. Harald let her hire a part-time shepherd pair.

Her flock benefited from their care and enlarged. Four grown moorland sheep and nine small ones to shear spin their wool, dye it into rich primeval medieval colours for weaving the Grete's designs and Katia's.

Measur and Metod necessitated a mob of placid black faces with white puffy backs, stretching into the horizon. Occasionally, one or two sheep separated themselves out from the herd and followed her.

Daydreaming about a less loveless life, better for her son, Meta began stashing money away, until events interrupted her thoughts. Some men were inciting small farmers to take certain stands.

Hurrahs knocked her eardrums without understanding their field language. She questioned, "Who're you? What're you doing?" Gazing at withered faces agitated her. Here stood no eye-less ones, but dark-eyed or blue-eyed and blondish men. The sun emblazoned their spades and plows, backbones of the nation.

Area farmers were accusing the government in the late 1920s of betraying them by assisting banks in reclaiming unpaid mortgaged family farms. Unprotected families sought to distribute produce with tariff protection. Incomprehensibly, one whiskery codger shook his fist at her. She crept away, mystified.

From their temporary mansion home, Harald traveled north to Osnabruck to discuss the excess pig invasion. This was his first trip away from her since their wedding. Someone must stay with Todi. She must. Harald gave no details. She must not pry.

He never invited her along. Were they still husband and wife? Was another woman vying for him? Meta feigned caring little, however much she depended on him.

Beneath her work blouse, she fingered her sapphire, diamond and pearl drop lavaliere for hope against loss. Sharing friends was impossible; not doing so struck her as odd; Harald's never introducing her to others was heartless. She grieved for what she lacked, a buoyant social circle, a golden norm or Althing.

To find out the problem, she turned toward von Knigge's Getting on with Others, behavior, as she'd consulted old folks and catalogues to figure out sheep rearing. Aunt Lore favored the Sheriff of the 1700s Bremen who wrote this guide to behavior on how to get along with others of all walks of life. Such a theatre and culture lover pressed for respect for all from cottager poor to courtiers. Many he thought ill of, and others he wished to purify. "Do not enslave yourself to others. Keep your cares to yourself when insecure. Talk not about your prosperity. Put yourself in the shoes of others. Let them be responsible for themselves. Speak well. Be firm in conduct and communicative only when necessary. Don't monopolize your marriage partner or excite jealousy.

After months in this new place, she possessed no lasting friends. Never mind, her body yearned to slake her loneliness within warm embraces. Another farm woman, much older than herself, said about her little dog: "It's wonderful to care for a little creature and hug him." She missed Mopsi and tried ignoring Harald's coldness. It mattered little, didn't she know.

Frightening circumstances had boxed from marriage into her self-tunneling. Resentful and wary, she, confused, used her handkerchief to free mucous from her excess hay fever and tears.

After all, even in her most estranged, self-separated or distraught states, she'd curtsied as a young girl and greeted everyone to protect herself. She turned negative, as Harald grew distinguished with his land-lordliness and attractiveness to women. He looked better, as he got older. She'd spied on Katia staring at him. No one noticed her. In his 40s, he filled in his scrawny frame, by physical culture, trekking and hiking.

Guests at their big farmhouse-lodge, she counted on, kissed Harald's cheeks, but most only shook her hand. Some kissed her with detachment. After the post-war period, Harald talked about "reuniting all social units to end individual suffering in this North. About poor farmers, where do they fit?" He didn't answer.

On tiptoes, she asked Harald, "We must remove these blades from the wall and hang wildflower prints there instead?"

"These daggers, swords and pistols have suited this wall for centuries of provenance because a renowned family hung them here. Respect the past and its unchanging Metod."

Skipping one regular market day, she instead removed the moldy table spots. On the next regular, she evaded Harald's haranguing her into going. From her kitchen garden, she gathered enough carrots, potatoes, corn, parsley, cabbage, beets, kohlrabi and turnips without going to the market to feed her family, give some to poor neighbors and sell extras at the town market.

Three weeks later, on foot from marketing, she saw other farms' produce for sale and examined the pickles. Feeling rather fit, strong within herself for a change, and she was laughing with oncoming spring, as she wandered on a lane with flat stones. By the forest, a small blue car drew near her. She said. "N-nice to see you." Its driver Georg waved and drove on.

Dumbfounded, Meta plunged into hated failure. Was he with Mala unseen? Passion for him was semi-acknowledged like hidden, past torment; a new lit bulb sizzled in cold water. Forbidden trust, sexual rollicking and plain warmth twiddled in her.

By dinner time, Harald, attuned, cast his darkened cobalt eyes at her and smiled. "You party with your friends. I'm off to a meeting on real problems such as pigs, tariffs and the farm crisis."

"Guests are your friends, too," she said.

"They care about nothing," he said. "They'll jaw about pigs, chew their fat, puff cigarettes and guzzle ale into a semi-stupor. They are your friends and mine still here, but the world around us we knew has departed.

"Basically, we need to measure what grows best," he continued, "and expand cattle and shepherds." He turned on his heel and departed.

She'd cajole him no longer. No longer could she hide behind a tapestry to watch meetings. Besides she did scoff at listening to anyone.

At about two a.m., he was rummaging in his bedroom, adjacent to hers, and cursing in his Putz. Huddled in her feather-bed, she heard him yell, "Shit." Harald's fussing, crapping and fuming irritated her into wakefulness. "What's wrong?"

"Nothing." He was trying to slam the door between them. "My fucking best hiking sock's caught."

In his little john or cabinet, his best thinking came like Rodin's Thinker, only brooding. Harald overstuffed his dirty clothes in its hamper. His sock was caught somehow in the door crack, so he rattled the knob to release his sock.

A true cleaning woman was unaffordable, one to pick up after him and Todi. Harald maintained their household, but Meta thought they could to pick up their own messes, while she straightened up the carriage house. Her earnings from selling its items to collectors would cover small extra costs paralleled Harald's metal gathering for smelting to cover household food and maintenance.

Gently bringing up expenses only induced his surliness. Finally, he sat on the pot, grunted, relieved himself, wiped himself, got up and grabbed her and pulled her to sit on his lap facing him. He washed his hands, lathered her and stroked her back in circles. He nibbled at her breasts. She sighed and asked, "After I protect myself, can we use your bed or mine?" She gasped, as he suckled her right breast and, then, her left one, while caressing her labia and thrilling her. Annoyance festered arousal and angered her excitement.

How had he become such an exuberant lover, who rarely approached her? "Talking about pigs must have stimulated you." She tried joking later.

"God, I've wanted you like this." He took her right hand to his penis. "Tickle it and rub it, here, not here, here." The instant she touched it, it flared. She remembered reading manuals. He breathed and threw back his shoulders in delight, almost laughing and crying. She too was enjoying herself, as he lifted her up over him to savor their glissando of rising and falling, until swept away.

In two years, the state authorities expected their departure from the estate. High up in the cupboard, the Meissen with the blue onion patterned dishes seemed to demand washing each a year, or rattle at being uncared for. Her log tracked time and place for treasures, defying efforts to catalogue them, as had discovering her mother or at first her uncle-father.

The aged unnamed clock was wound to run; its hands set at the ninth hour and nine minutes. Its face painted in blue forget-me-nots rolled with hands upturned, within. But the clock resisted its rewinding, as if Metod and Mesur had spun out. Wurd had been disappearing.

"Mami, wind the clock." Todi insisted and climbed on a worn milking stool and wound it up, too taut, like an ancient Mesurer. Todi also pulled toys and fixtures apart.

One day, she put him over her knee, took his pants down and whammed his backside with a straight edge, for ruining the antique clock. Only she was ruining him, she despaired later over her act.

Three hours later, Harald whispered to himself and held his head in his hands upon consuming five ales. His dark blue eyes narrowed into slits. Grayed brown hair was losing its coloring. He talked to himself, argued and gesticulated.

She crept close to him to hear his words. He honed his inner wounds; she only guessed at, until he said, "I detest work here now that my responsibility is all but over."

Todi patted him on the back. Meta hugged Harald's hunched shoulders. Both squeezed him from opposite sides. No matter how much she sought to comfort him, he hunkered into his sadness. Meta asked, "Why? What do we do now? Will you see a doctor or go to a sanitarium?" Nothing worked, she feared. The ale, wine and slivovitz bottles lay around him in dullness and sadness.

He vied with her to finish their removal from the house by growling at her. As she packed, she groaned. He messed up her packages and added bundles with old cans, guns and whatever that rattled.

As Harald began to slide, she tolerated him as if someone else. Her brain sang of another gold graybeard with a minute harelip. Sometimes, his shirttail frayed, caught sight of, flapping with the wind. She was stricken by Harald's decline though distracted by Georg's reappearance.

With an oompah band, Georg exuded oomph and tri-umph. He cheered and toasted her, when Harald was out in the fields. They could get lost in the massive hunting lodge. He suggested though his trips in the night and hideouts by day served aims other than hidden love.

As for her son, no matter how often Meta his mother or the part-time British nursemaid Trish, who taught him En-glish, admired him and admonished him, Todi roved away and climbed up to remove the Misericorde and other blades from the wall.

Meanwhile, as a family, Meta, Harald and Todi were to go to a get-together. Mother and son yelled down the cellar, garage and barn looking for Harald. There was no reply. Todi prowled under and around small enclosures looking for Harald.

Eventually, the five-year-old came upon him dangling from a ceiling beam with the Scramasax, an Old Saxon hunting knife. It was jabbed into his chest between his bones to his heart.

In his earliest recorded self-willed act, Todi screamed his father was lying there. Blood was flowing across his chest for whom and for what. Meta, sobbed. "Todi found the body." Later on, she asked, "Where is the valor in staying alive here?"

18.

Already in their second summer, they'd sat around expecting to die. Often in those dog days of August, that she and Harald were still alive surprised her. She bolted upright, while suffocating a little in the airless room that once belonged to the attic, where she'd gone for safekeeping. Opening any vents for more air was not enough. An old fan was better but rattled like her anxiety. She could not nail it nor bind the noise of her thoughts.

So she shut off the metal fan. The overheated air was better, though she breathed with difficulty. A weight on her chest like an extinct flying reptile, cold and scaly, pterodactyl, not dactylic, sought to fly off. No, the archaeopterteryx lifted off, lift her, dragged her.

Once upon a time, they, not the flying dinosaur-reptile, as imagined, set out with the "all clear" over an air stream, as live falcons do. Her great-uncle used to value falcons.

At first, at the first, other pressures came to pass. By accident in a pavilion, she dreamed he'd asked her to dance to a ballade. He preferred not to whirl his Mala, instead herself.

Sitting here on the chair edge with her bags packed to go from the great moor to go for a dig in a far off tell off and under, he began to stay behind with another woman. Those two, Harald and Georg were larking in the cellar locker she assumed they now lived in, like a coffin. It must rattle like panes in the wind, not unlike her grains in the dessert.

Months later, she found Georg or someone like him by chance in a booth. The other he called Mala he was no longer with, as far as could be seen. He commented, "My love, our country." They intoned to one another from among the graves of old loves. When he had left the locker mansion lodge for another, second place with him in a double deck-chair on which they slept by open windows for air and views of the skyline: the incisors of Berlin's skyline.

After all was said and done, their holiday time had served as their honeymoon. They both flew to another zone, where the air around them chilled them.

Over and over, Todi sensed Harald with him, dreamt of piggybacking with him and traveling by cart and horse. Sometimes tears dribbled down his face. If seen, her hanky daubed them. Often his father's face was imagined in others' faces and in mirrors.

The older man blocked out the faces of others for Todi, or features merged with another older man's face. The intense, bright cobalt eyes dimmed in time and blended with long faces and mounted noses. Todi's eyes were lighter. Only Harald's chin jutted less than most chins in this land of jutting chins.

In morning for someone she never cared much for, time little quelled how noteworthy Harald was when young, almost a gentleman, part old school and part new. From extra post-World War extra cash, he could afford a wife and son and live a quasi-squire's life, while caring for the ex-Kaiser's lands. He'd specialized in selling airplane wings and cockpits. Some pieces were strewn on lands, still belonging to Harald's small gentry's family, and stored until saleable; their lands abutted the ex-king's hunting lodge. So read Harald's local obituary, including his widow and son.

Not only in his domicile, but scattered elsewhere, shrapnel remained in barns, cellars and carriage houses. Neither Meta nor Todi, both sad, knew about the boxes of bullets, until he discovered stamped on wooden boxes with "Prize Bullets," rather than empty rifles. The trade Harald had chanced on brought on Todi's upbringing within metal parts and recent and ancient weapons.

His running and racing stage of boyhood at five toward eight galvanized exploring on his own. To his mother, nothing seemed amiss, though she'd see what came next.

At this age, he could go to a country boarding school, a step his father had partly consented to. His mother obtained an extra two-year lease from the estate authorities to stay on plus a warning they must move then.

Thus far, she planted a garden, and Todi played with the metal biplane parts, wheels, landing gear and auto parts with gusto. Enticing his mother's older cousin's sons, he cried out, "Look at these wings. We can fly!!"

Play disguised his disquiet. So distracted was he by playing and imagining his father everywhere, his teacher, mother, Meta, and grandfather little realized at first and, then, worried about the boy's distress. No helmet could protect his head.

His tutor reminded Todi of his father. That Todi spaced out, the older white-bearded teacher noted he focused on classwork and homework with "No, I won't." Life would never be as hoped for.

Familiar faces merged into his father; Harald, lived in his teacher's role and his face blurred into his father. Eventually, Meta caught onto this changeover, but did nothing to measure it.

Instead, the growth of her herd occupied her and necessitated scouting markets for selling her flock's new fleece. But their coats earned only about five pence each. Anyway, she pulled her dark reddish-sunned blonde hair back with a scarlet headband and set out to visit friends she missed: first, Angela the pastor's daughter, Meissen blue-eyed ideal countrywoman with a city glint, and, next, track down Grete, Angelica and Katia.

Meta trekked through mounds, rocks and around upside down baskets Saxons wove for bees, clustered near small Heide farmhouses. Yellow jackets, drones, queens, bees had worked there, it was said, without stopping, since the eighteenth century. Bee towns would not harm her.

She, a modern mother, dared ask Georg to help her, because he stopped by occasionally nowadays. Todi glowered at him and crept up behind the big armchair where Georg sat and threatened him with a small iron frying pan.

"Todi!" She screamed, mortified and ran to wet a towel to sop the blood from Georg's shoulder gash. The frying pan had just missed the head or did. She tried reaching the doctor.

Todi asserted to Georg: "You murdered my father."

Shaken and confused, he sought to call a doctor.

Eventually, he agreed to drive them both to "head doctors," himself to a neurologist and Todi to a word doctor, disapproved of but tolerated on Meta's pretext. Todi needed a doctor, as much as Georg did. But she would not allow his driving. She would drive.

"He must not!" Katia urged someone else drive them to Hamburg for a Herr Doktor Petersen in Göttingen to consult with. Psychologist, child analyst or juvenile delinquent worker or pedagogical social worker, all categories Katia recommended.

With treatment, believed or insisted, even at Todi's early young age, he could retrieve the embittered bitter parts of self to reconfigure into a better self.

"Absurd," replied Meta. "I can't live this life anymore."

"Not so," said Katia and Grete who visited and later on even Angelica. All said, "Yes, do so."

After Doctor Petersen listened to Meta describe her son's behavior, he told her that the boy had received an unacceptable shock. What the boy was dealing with could only worsen with time. New play treatment could dredge up pieces of the past he could learn to understand through play.

"Try not seeing your lover for a while." Petersen advised. "Your son so young is sensitive the loss of his father."

She was silent without intending to abide by Herr Petersen's advice, sounding distant. "Todi's reliving the hellishness of his father dangling from a beam." Still in childhood, Todi would renew himself with Harald's self-murder as outside, not inside himself.

Katia her friend, concerned about the boy, whispered about Freud and the Berlin Institute. Grumbling at newfangled mind work through easygoing recall, sometimes irrelevant, Meta later probed its origins in Uncle's ethnology and philosophy books. The ancients meditated on one-point and sprang to secret routes beyond rote thinking. The Greeks confronted Psyche and Eros, who confronted each other. Surely, they would bother Todi.

Georg ignored her reading of musty books and clinical treatises, and his eyes glazed at her words, and he chuckled at her pomposity. "The old Greeks could turn a toilet into a postemia," she said, for prayer and calm by reflecting. That's what Freud's basic analysis does."

"You've lost me," he said. His movements and thoughts strummed the facets of Georg's face. He said nothing.

Still his university idea appealed to her. But duty-bound, she dismissed more schooling the goals of which could only pester her. Surmounting exam rules to qualify for degrees posed too many obstacles for her to overcome. But maybe. . .

Said he, "Your ideas dredge up the past. Of course, so do university studies."

At least, he did not strike back at Todi. "Sorry." She tapped his arm, the first touch of calm truth between them in half dozen years to open thoughts he could only fail to understand. She tested this hope though recognized the futility of expecting much help from him. "Well, if I search for my mother, I'd also yearn to bring her back."

"Why not study at the university instead of self-educating, reading always while caring for animals and hunting for antiquarian items?"

"I'm a mother, not a student." Motherhood's psyche circled outside in, pressed on the child, Todi, and disturbed her peace. She nixed his support for her studying.

"You married," he persisted. "You brought forth a son, in your duty. Your father agreed. Ask him to help you: he's the local potentate. You could play a role. This is 1932, not the 1914 crises, when most everyone began losing their livelihoods. Our lives are better now." The light flashed down the split in his mustache within some grey hairs.

"Small farmers are losing out now."

"How would you know?" he asked.

"I must move now to a small farm, one someone lost and get out of the Kaiser's estate. I want my son away from this oversized spook house, where his father killed himself. Otherwise, I'm lost, and he is."

Her words misfired. Georg grasped no hint about helping Todi with his problem harmful to him for life within the ever present reminder of his absent father.

"Maybe." His return to Todi's problem satisfied her, even if he criticized the method of trying to help.

Reviving the past with Herr Petersen meant being disgruntled with psychological humbug, digging the child out from under his unhappiness. Georg asked, "Why bother? Put the boy in a camp to learn healthy Wandervogel habits, the flight of birds?

"Sounds like running away."

"You cannot put your unhappiness ahead of you," he continued. "You showed off your wanderlust, when I first knew you on the road." He tickled her chin. In the back seat, she feared Petersen's warning, Todi might confuse their warm gestures, embraces, lust to confuse Georg's rivaling his father Harald for his mother's love, especially when Georg caressed the inside of her thigh.

"Wait." His slow-moving words, deep-voiced, and broad shoulders to cry on calmed her.

Three weeks later, Georg abided by her wish to take the boy again from the healthy countryside into the unhealthy city, because it suited Georg to please her. Also he was called to a meeting and lost in thought, as he strapped the boy in his coupé's narrow back car rumble seat.

"He's too young to sit alone back there." She objected to Georg's inability to bond with the boy she aimed to protect. If Georg wanted her, and she doubted he did, then would he care for her and her son or oppose them?

Georg opened the front right door for Meta, nibbled at her ear, as she slid past him into the front passenger seat. He slammed the door and sat in his rumpled red-brown tweed jacketed self with knickers. He scratched his beard and tossed his hat over the back. Todi put it on his head. They set off.

After Georg drove them to the child clinic, they waved good-bye to him. The young therapist Petersen, a psychoanalytical disciple, welcomed them. He saw Todi in his office, while she waited outside and worried she'd be criticized for poor care of her son.

At the end of their hour, he gave her some child guidance pamphlets, big in America. Also Meta borrowed a psychoanalytical guidebook.

In due time, after several visits, by bus, train or car with Georg, Todi, slid backward, yearning to be a baby, carried by his father, rather than being cured. He played with blocks and random therapeutic toys he selected, built towers and knocked them over.

On a new projective measure, used by new psychologists, Todi expanded and played with a puppet. Todi wiggled its hands and body and made it speak. "The boy's in the door and looks at his stepfather's rock." The psychologist determined that the rock equaled a cemetery marker. But his stepfather stayed alive."

Next time with the puppet, he said "the day was the boy's birthday. Everyone was excited, but I wasn't. Everyone stole my whole birthday cake. No pieces were left for me." Meta could hear him talking with Herr P. He also imitated him in play alone.

Near his birthday time, Todi saw his grandfather's jar, called Heinrich "grandfather" and called it "Beauty." Others termed it a "vase."

Thereafter, his therapist relayed details on Todi's giftedness with spatial links. This positive turn pleased Meta who struggled with hers.

After several clinical visits over a year's time, the boy revealed more that outraged her. On the negative side, he belittled Meta. In his fantasies, she arranged for his father to be shot. Herr Petersen felt compelled to consult with her on the truth of the matter. Had she connived to kill her husband? Meta was shocked, confused and discouraged at rank acceptance of a child's words.

With boy hand puppets, he knocked down the father doll. That figure popped back up to Todi who asserted, "I am the father."

Eventually, Todi no longer piled up blocks to knock them down. From among the frog, cow, horse, dragon, sheep and elephant puppets, he chose a red dragon over his fist. Upon removing it, his fingers inside the pig's snout, "Oink, I'm the father," and the pig knocked down the tower Todi had just built.

Over several more therapy visits, Todi repeated this method with different animals, as self-fulfilling and calming. Todi told his live German shepherd puppy, found by her, "Dad's mad with me. He's gone now. So don't you run away?" She missed her aged little Mopsi, if alive, who stayed with grandfather Heinrich.

One day back at "home," at the corner of the Kaisers' mansion, she was growing determined to leave. Here Todi expressed new awareness of Harald, as the therapist pointed this all out to Meta.

From his puppets, Todi had selected a male. In its sleeves, his thumb and forefinger hugged and caressed the baby puppet. Todi murmured, "We'll care for you and keep you safe from Mami."

The later Hamburg trips seemed to toughen mother and son, if only to learn the way there. They toured the vast harbor, one of the biggest in Europe. Enticed by ships, Todi wanted a toy ship to float to America.

"Vati sailed away on it," he said. "He'll come back." His therapist encouraged such trips and outings with his mother for his emotional re-education. But when Todi drew his fantasies on paper about such trips, he launched a new fantasy to replace reality. In one, dark suited men stalked back and forth with briefcases. Even darker, black navy ones stayed inside buildings, owned by the former, lighter ones who grabbed briefcases from the gloomiest puppets.

His fantasies extended his immaturity and wearied her, a thoroughly modern woman, by taking him to the city. Thus, by refusing to go anymore, she was sure he'd curtailed his fantasies with time swallowing memory.

"No," she prevaricated with Todi who wanted to continue seeing Herr Doktor Petersen. "We'll not return to your friend, who listens and plays with you. We, Georg and I, will do so."

Todi stomped his foot, cried and whined. She tried gripping his little shoulders and kissing off his tears. He ran out and hid. She rushed around to find him, fearing he might endanger himself.

Her own tears dribbled on her face. "We're lonely, aren't we?"

Out of a closet, he nodded and played with model biplane pieces, smashed them only to paste them together with flour, powdering the floor, and water. For now, he'd given up on boats and ships.

For her tears, she grabbed a towel for dusting books she was packing up. Todi continued sniffling, sobbing and sucking in from the next room. He was irritating her.

"You are, she said, "a big boy who will go to school full-time next year. You won't cry there." With his model plane pasted together, he zoomed several rooms away from his tears.

The crusty books that opened secrets to her were packed with a Goethe set. No Kaiser would care about them. "The

Kaiser's not returning; who's next?" she asked aloud. Heinrich used to prefer monarchs.

Todi asked, "What?"

"You, your dog, Fraxi, and I are leaving."

Her tears dropped on a letter inside a book and smeared into an inkblot, a ghostly figure. Unread, it came from Nanna, kilometers away and months ago with no date. Meta clutched it to decipher the old script like that inside a book, such as v's into w's or the reverse. Glasses might help read the words, just as selling the books she was boxing up could pay for some of Todi's medical expenses and her search for her mother.

Thoughts of frail states marred the balancing ordinary thoughts. Only understanding mattered.

Now, though, Meta picked up the black ear part with its long phone neck attached to the wall. "I can't hear you," each shouted. Go see your great-aunt and grand-great-aunt, she told herself, someone's calling about Nanna. The telephone rang again. A voice yelled in the improved connection. "It's me, Grete."

"I hear you." Meta laughed. "How are you? Where are you, with your father?"

"I'm seeing "Trixi the Great Aviatrix land." She's one with a tight leather cap and goggles. Come along? You're married, I know, but can you get away?"

"Not married anymore. I'll tell you, when we meet."

In the following months, Georg's visits to her in the Kaiser's lodge enveloped her. Once departed from her niche there, she'd change. The big dark red-brick house of her earlier life, and its quatrefoils, might overwhelm her again. Next from the hunting lodge, she lifted two other items, a Meissen soup tureen with blue onions and silver ladle. She packed.

Watchful of Todi's loss of Harald, she took him to country meetings. Everywhere small farmers were gathering against foreclosures of mortgaged properties. Each feared losses of soul and soil.

Angelica with her grandmother, Frau Bauer the dying woman, lived a few kilometers away and pressed her to visit them. Meta had not seen Angelica, Grete or Katia for months but could hike or hitch an old horse to a cart to carry her to see them.

This black horse Todi called "Fritz II," the Great War survivor, accepted harnessing. More sluggish than old Fritz, now dead, Fritz ll clogged along, jingling his bells.

One Saturday, a note invited Todi to play with two boys his age, Harald's distant cousins, excited him. Such family knots Meta likened to thistles on wool. But if Todi was left behind, she nagged herself over what she owed Harald. Pity she struggled to push away. But Georg's indifference affected her; he failed to respond to her passion for him. Her neck stretched from anxiety into tension: was he seeing Mala still? The beauteous dark-haired woman had appeared to hibernate.

Escaping from worry, Meta set out to deliver Todi and visit Angelica and Frau Bauer. As Meta's cart jaunted along, the journey seemed to release her tight neck and head.

After tapping Fritz II's neck with the riding whip, they clipped along. In a glade, hepatica grew beyond the sea land of violets with green heart leaves. After dropping Todi off, she rubbed her temples, placed her hand on the reins and looked around. On the roadside grew crocuses, blue and white cups, sucking the wet ground. On the other side, a red berry bush flickered, and at a burnt-green hummock, nature grew red-orange Fireprick.

"Come back." voiced at a crying boy lead Meta to ask, "Who's there?" Because of the screeching child and whinnying horse, a farm laborer tch-tched at the young mother thought ignoring her child. Had Fritz II been a bronco, he might have reared in the racket. But age-sluggishness calmed him, as the boy sniffled.

Arms flailing, Lili called out, "My boy's hurt," meaning her nephew. Lili's dark sleek hair tangled on one side with burrs, like thistles.

"The days I'm with him, he gets into trouble." Meta, startled, recognized Lili Ula. "Lili Ursula," she termed herself. Lili hugged Meta.

Meta asked, "Ula, uh, Lili, you're with your brothers and father?"

"We're caring for our nephew and Landvolk. But my Karl must attend the meetings.

"I've never met your Karl," Meta said. This Ernest boy-child-nephew must be more a younger ruffian than Todi. "Who's Karl?"

"Oh, he came into my life." Agitated, Lili, hands in blue jumper pockets over maroon jersey top, said, "He's political." Hands out, she gesticulated. "So am I. Karl took over his grandfather's farm, where I help. We sow, we reap. We speak for Landvolk. Everyone's apt to lose small farms we try saving from banks' repossessing, because of unpaid mortgages to prevent sell-outs. But he's lost his horse, so we trek and hitch rides from others.

So this Karl had also hitched a ride from Katia, Meta recalled.

"To the Reichstag in Berlin we push for help. None so far, Communists, Nazis are there and Social Democrats. All of them all over North Germany. You know them?"

"I bumbled into a local meeting," Meta said, "once or twice. I'd heard noise and tried to investigate what was happening."

"Meetings spread." Lili's hand waved northward. "Come, one's minutes away. See little hammers, sickles like swastikas, ancient sun symbols." The mystical and bizarre carried her away, and she attacked it. "The president of the republic, the devil incarnate."

"Tell me, if there's another meeting," said Meta, ignoring Lili's certainty. "I'm seeing if Angelica and her grandmother and must get back before dark." She handed Lili her phone number, maybe non-working.

"Your Georg might be there?"

Not persuaded, Meta said that Harald she'd married had died. Lili made no response. Meta said, "Good-bye" and "giddy-up" to Fritz II. Elated with friendships with Georg, Angelica, Grete and Lili, Meta, freer than earlier, with the workhorse clomped away.

Meta brooded. Loneliness was torn from the soul and assuaged by warmth from social circles. But not political circles men and Lili were drawn toward.

Daylight sparked on the stream and silvery birch leaves. Evergreens beyond furred against the sky, and birds, robins, blue jays and phoebes clucked or sang. Spring was rising into Summer. Inhale possible osmanthus, an evergreen.

On this country stretch, she felt watched.

A charioteer sun goddess of the north, he'd told her she was, in dark red hair, too long for the popular Louise Brooks style. When Georg caught up, she barely glanced up, when he said, "See you later back here."

Meta floated under the clouds in the countryside. She had landed, when coerced, into her marriage, treated it as half- or non-existent. With looking back, she felt he watched her drive away. She could have aimed for the stable, as she masked her feelings. Restless for the future, she was fearful, he'd bridge her way to another life.

Nearly swooning on the soft green, embracing country-side, she spot-checked life and ruminated. To Berlin and back to the rural life, she, like a poor squire with honor lost, savored Bremen with its small city artistic crafts, its Hanseatic sea harbor for international trade. Less Berlin-like with centrifugal music and hell-raising government, the moor stayed the same without king or statesman; some landed gentry downgraded into some thieving and thumping hollow logs. Most survive.

She had little money. Money enough would erupt if she lived with her uncle-father. His land might serve her and Todi. Her modern ways, Todi spelling and relentless search for the latest, jazz or analysis, jarred Heinrich's preferred scholarship. On the other hand, she could swerve away from Heinrich.

Better yet, Georg could involve her on his farm? On edge, he'd listen to speeches and poke around the outer circle of political huddles, seek his role and let folkish types guide him, until he turned on them. Less volkisch or folkish, than Hein-rich, Georg could build his following and show off "my young woman beauty," as he called her.

On a whim, she turned the horse onto a hillock and stood in the cart to see Georg, but not that he could see her behind some bushes. He was smoking cigarettes, throwing away butts and nodding at familiar faces. She could beguile his guests at his farm.

One broken off crescent moon cusp outside a dilapidated chapel-sized church Georg picked up, while seeking his old uncle's marble grave marker to refurbish. Because his uncle had no heirs for an old land grant, aha, this marker, if found, could settle Georg's land claim.

The war had ruptured such efforts to settle land rights. Now's the moment. She stayed watching.

The church sexton or another fellow shuffled over, unsure whether to speak to a superior. Georg detested sniveling. The old countryman hesitated, his baggy work pants below his Sunday tweed jacket and might have said, she imagined something like, "Heh, sir, what'd you'd think about this meeting?"

Georg shrugged and shook hands, swept his hair back and scratched his chin. She waved again without his seeing her and drove off to meet Grete.

On the Pavilion grounds, a youngish woman hovered above the crowd on boxes or solid tabletops. Little of her speech was audible, while the klieg-like sun filtered through the high oaks, two or three stories high, spotlighting the click-clacking people, especially a group in red-glorious brown fox and mink fur stoles. Styled for 1928, the women nearest the podium defined the combustible and glamorous group, dressed in knee-length hemlines of the day below luminous hair and shoulder fur wraps.

Someone resembling a Katia was hooting against the furred women. Why at this gathering? This wayside inn, open on a mellow spring day, served at one end like a big pub for ale or wine, while at the other, it offered tea or coffee frothy with cream and berry tortes. Meta had never stopped here before, where Jazz was played in the countryside for now.

On the grounds, some mangy women clustered in reds and greens compared with the tall women in spectacular furs.

Maybe this event was meant to display them. But why here, not far from Lüneberg, Bremen, Hamburg or Berlin, where more fashionable women lived?

True, Lore complained that no one dressed, except this 1928 season was prospering more than in the previous five or postwar ten years. Yes, a Berlin show, must be, Grete's mother?

Her skirt panels flaring, an ultra-lean woman bent toward the certain women cluster, evidently awaiting Trixi. Was it to photograph them? They little noticed her, so lithe was she and subtle in her smooth acts. No standing in two or three lines posed smiles or none here for her. With her brief snub nose camera-close to her subjects, the woman photographer smiled one corner down and one up after her catch or grab-shots. She looked familiar.

Meta half-expected to find Grete's mother couturier behind the overall show or some furrier. But no, not so. Yes, here were Grete and her aunt! Grete and Meta squealed; her aunt shook hands with Grete.

Not yet hungry for noon dinner, they sat. They smelled the kitchen nearby: potatoes, fenichel, yes, cauliflower, roots and onions for a beef stew.

Suddenly, above the trees a tiny biplane soared. Fragile, constructed from two straight wings with toothpicks, as if glued like toy ones Hansi and Todi pieced together or metal pieces, collected by Harald. Observers jumped on one wooden bench to see the one-person cockpit braced with wings land. One fell off. The photography girl Ada, so Grete said, was still there in her jaunty green cloche known to the latter's mother for models. Meta wished for binoculars, when Grete handed over hers. They jumped up and down. She helped pull Grete in her shapely legs and sculpted heels on the table. Aunt Ulrike, evidently her father's sister, disapproved of the gathering. "Meta's okay as wife and mother, not a single girl like you."

Whatever it was, it dealt with no motherhood or marriage Meta knew. When the excitement of Trixi's landing died off momentarily, Meta whispered in Grete's ear. "Harald's gone, and Todi found him dead." She didn't want the aunt querying her for details.

"What happened?"

"He was cranky, overworking, slipping and getting sick. I didn't know what to do." Her eyes watered over whether she explained too much.

"Well, you didn't want him to start with, remember?" Grete whispered out of her aunt's hearing in the talking crowd.

"What did you say I said?"

"Nothing," Grete replied, "Just business between Meta and me."

"Is that courtesy?" her aunt queried. A combo was tuning up and testing rhythms for the dance floor in late afternoon with romantic promises for girls tapping toes on the floor and fingers on the wooden tabletops.

Meta wrote out, "Harald's killing himself upset Todi." The combo drummer was rolling out beats dah dUH, dah dUH.

"You must have died over him and your son's upset."

"What? Well, yes, I died for stability. Georg drove us to a child therapist you and Katia recommended."

"Oh, but you wanted Georg anyway."

What could Meta say or write. Could words describe the coldness or warmth of fantasy and ectasy?

"You like where you live, don't you?" Grete asked, her floppy twisted flower bounced to the combo's rehearsing and her words.

"The novelty's gone." The Kaiser's lodge, one of many truths easing and complicating life, now that she, Meta, was dislodged into the unknown world.

"I don't know, if I ever did. There's more than one problem. Come and visit us."

"This would be my only palace invitation. How could you not be there? Did Harald know about Georg?"

"Too many questions. How could he? There was nothing to know. Harald was never around. Nor Georg." God, she was perceptive and provocative.

"I think Harald worried about our living quarters we had to leave. I've extended our stay, but the authorities are ousting us. Where to live is the problem. Should I go to Bremen or Berlin or back to Uncle's farm or America?"

"Take me, take me with you, please, please." She grabbed Meta's hand, squeezed it and pulled it.

"I don't know how. Just apply."

"Why beg?" Aunt Ulrike asked. The combo was tuning up.

"We'll dance, so we can talk," said Grete to Meta. Grete's silk flowered shoes danced beneath her flaring skirt in her portrait of grace, unlike unsmiling Meta, within her pinafore-like dress. "Spiff up your dress a bit, as you used to?" said Grete.

Meta knew not what to say about her folk outfit.

"Now I'm free," Grete said, changing the subject, "from my chaperone, set upon me by my father, when he doesn't know where else to put me. She's Calvinist Dutch, a bit severe, you see, and her children are grown. The two friends danced and spotted Ulrike smiling and bouncing with a mustached gentleman.

Surrounding them, when seated, others settled down at round tables. They conjectured, "What's this get-together for?" asked Meta.

"Mami asked me to look in on the furs and Trixi for style setting," Grete said.

"On this end, but maybe a Landvolk social fundraiser at the other end." Meta speculated. Grete shrugged.

Another person overheard was irate: two speakers, she'd insisted on, but the arrangers had put them last on the list. Of this bickering within a nearby group, one, who wrapped her neck in her slipping coppery scarf, charged with irritants. "You didn't back me, when I tried to move them to the top of program. Now, I'm the fool for inviting them, and they'll blame me for taking up their time." Words whizzed out of control within the femme fatales and farmwomen.

"They won't mind," a countrywoman reassured her, her braid wound in a bun, homey, attractive, not chic, like the deep waved, marceled hairstyle of in-the-know women.

Small groups argued within themselves. In fact, one said, "Trixi's the key speaker who's buzzing overhead," another declared. Trixi demonstrated her aviatrix prowess in this age of transatlantic journeys and universal sky riding. Circling round and round, she flew, swooped and rose up.

"Just think, she's joined the heavens," said the elfin young photographer said with her Leica and Graphix, small and large cameras. Meta nodded to her. Ada waylaid her. "I'm working for your mother. I'm happy when I'm working." Grete nodded. One who accompanied a very critical entourage? Only here she was on her own without one. NOAKES

"No angry protesters here," Meta said. The photographer nodded back.

The copper-scarfed woman disputed. "Read the newspapers? They all say the same thing in different words: We're struggling for the countryside. Bankers buy and big marketeers, like your father," the woman said, "Grab everything." Meta wondered if she meant Men like Heinrich were buying all possible land. "Your type's men serve the German landowners."

"How does she know to say such stupidities?" Grete asked.

"What?" Bewildered inside, unsure which pavilion end she belonged to, Meta almost spoke: But my father/great uncle's selling off land to pay his taxes. To intercede struck her—go pay his taxes in Lüneberg. No, no protesters here though.

Trixi now landed to cheers, approached the knots of supporters and stood at the podium, like the lectern of a restaurant maitre d'. The crowd quieted down. Most women stood or sat up. Some men stayed in the back—Meta looked for Georg—with elbows akimbo. More arriving women with some men folk grouped in the back, some with arms crossed.

Stillness allowed in the sound of the wind. Close by, the local brook's piddling over rocks lulled Meta. The speaker could be Trixi, or someone else with the Ventriloquist in the trench coat. Were the groups intermixed or mixed up about their locale."

Only thing for sure was Trixi who had landed and arisen out of the cockpit as if dismounting from her flying silvery horse. Gradually, Trixi projected her voice.

Everyone applauded. Meta believed Trixi said. "We women support the country people and the right of its women to own property, if necessary. Or for some to combine to supply food for all." Everyone crowded around and muffled words.

Trixi derided the reddish-fur coated women in mink, bear or fox, for the animals should graze in peace here on the protected heath dazzling in beauty. Her close-fitting leather cap hung by its strap around her neck above her snug body suit, fit for a firm torso. Her curled hair fell helter-skelter around her bare eyes, free of her goggles.

"Did you hear about animals?" asked Grete.

"Not quite. Let them pasture or stay in the woods, not lose their fur, unless sheep for wool."

Meta was confused about what she was seeing.

"Certainly, Trixi would favor animals."

"Harald never was. He only wanted army metal."

"Wasn't he earning a living for you by re-selling it?"

"You do what you have to do?" Grete didn't understand that Meta earned money too.

"What happened to you two?"

Delving into her five-year marriage and loneliness, except for Teodor, her beloved Todi she must rush back to.

Ah, friendship is happiness. Talking here to someone who at least half-understands her, she felt momentary peace, while they nibbled treats and sipped tea. "Harald never loved me; I never loved Harald. But we survived in leftover splendor and more or less got along. When Todi grew into a little boy— Harald claimed his duty to direct Teodor's development.

"He took him to meetings about land use changes he could not control and refused to introduce me to his friends. Then he lost his way. He killed himself or got caught in his military equipment accident. "He provided well for us in these dire times.

"My son blamed himself at times and me at other times for the death. We fought, child against mother. Surprisingly, Grete wasn't quite listening with all the noises around them.

"I saw that fellow there." Grete asked. "Isn't he your type?"

"You mean the one from my big church? Paul?" He's city-type, not from my other small church, where I was married, no."

"He's agreeable and good-looking."

"He and Georg infuriate granduncle-father, who infuriates me. He favored only Harald, acceptable without an old-fashioned dowry. At least, I know so. He dislikes Georg somehow for his politics. Heinrich prefers Völkisch, nationalism folk-like, less elitist. I'm trying to figure this out.

"Paul's a good man."

Grete was delicate, for sure. So then, Meta said, "You pursue him!"

"But he's with the Christian social democrats or with social democratic non-believers. My father-uncle despises both, says they're fewer everyday, about to be overtaken by the NSDAP.

"Onkel-Vater wants fit all together without rights or conflict—in between agricultural labourers and landowners. Georg, his newer opponent, unknown, favors heritage, customs, Fachwerk with straw roofs and squashed roof points, opposing Bauhaus starkness. Don't know for sure. I can't quite tell. I want to get out of here."

Grete nodded. "But for your happiness, consider Paul."

"You consider him yourself."

Paul, Meta knew, belonged to the quasi-correct human way. She gleaned Grete was becoming an outcaste and nagged herself. How to know truth? Meta tried ignoring anxiety she sought to trek away from, however much she'd been hating country viewpoints. After all, only Georg matters," for he was drawing her toward him. "Georg helps take him to Berlin for therapy."

"Let's go together," Grete said. 1928

"I don't know where I'm going. Often Uncle treats me like the enemy. How can I go back to his farm?" Questions lead to more questions. I want to get out of here."

Meanwhile in the pavilion, the models fawned over the audience and swarmed around the runway. Wherever from, the audience was forced to sit on the side from some mix-up over space use by style watchers and land rights women. Meta was puzzling over such complexity.

Next, the woman, coppery silk scarfed, groused. "The Ventriloquist, if here, would straighten our troubles out." Women thought her style-oriented, not political, as she whispered his sacred name.

19.

Aunt Ulrike noted "no one helps us," to her new smiling gentleman companion. "Grete, did you see?"

"We should leave," Grete replied. "My father wants us back earlier than usual."

"Stay awhile," Meta said.

"Dance more," Grete told her aunt. "We might not be here soon again." Grete was tense.

"Meta, find me the Lüneberg autobus for escape, please." She disappeared into the toilet. Mete waited outside.

"The country's downhill. Not enough food, kerosene or electricity" was overheard in the women's toilet line; Meta looked behind to see who was speaking: all women were mum.

The silence was gruesome.

Their faces burned in the sunset. Short nosed and pursed-lipped stout woman in blue puffy-sleeved housedress was ordered by the coppery scarfed woman. "Partake."

"No, everybody's going to hell."

After sipping ale, Meta guessed the Ventriloquist was—the one with the small oblong mustache and trimmed black shock of hair—who harangued audiences.

Weary, she asked for Weisswurst. Noticing the time, she hesitated. Someone ordered, "Sit for a minute."

He gripped a chair about to heave it.

Surprised, she smiled up at Georg, "I figured you were over here." Disarmingly, he cocked his head and watched the double self-made gathering of women.

"Just passing through." Meta said, "To visit Frau Bauer and granddaughter."

Ale for both, he gulped his dark gold in both steins. She sipped in between and tried to like the taste.

He said, "You see, I follow you."

"I'd assumed you'd gone for good." She tried adopting his playful tone for serious words.

"We need music and dancing," he said, "not haranguing."

She shrugged. "Before I get where I am going and return, hours will pass."

"Stop back for music we'll dance to."

Surprised he'd noticed the dance programme, she ran away to the toilet to change into riding clothes from her ruck-sack and see how wrinkled her rolled forest green straight dress was.

On her way out, she waved to him and rushed toward Grete but wished to avoid being seen with him or him to see her with Grete. Grete was less cordial than when greeted, while departing with her Aunt Ulrike and new friend. Did Grete disapprove of Meta's lost marriage and son, Todi, left behind?

Grete's Aunt Ulrike's dance partner was eying her sashaying, as if in some rare new cinema. Oh-well, somewhat dignified in English-Indian style jodhpurs, Meta strode onward. Gently, she hugged the horse's neck. Her riding stick prodded Whoa-Fritzi II, now resting, onward.

Yearning for Georg skittered willy-nilly among guesses about Grete, the Bauers' whereabouts and Todi's fretfulness within Meta's cold dread. Still, the horse's clip-clopping monotony calmed her. In this last trip lap, a partridge skirred from the bushes, honoring spring.

Pine inhaled soothed her within familiarity, though most giant pines had been cut for paneling. On the hillcrest stood the indestructible oak, mammoth and solitary, Irmenseul forever. The tower of principle: the great tree was between human earth and human paradise. Above, no clouds roved across the sky and sun, not even Trixi. Some inhabitants were gone for good, some said: another war's looming, dispiriting.

An hour's travel later, "Meta, meta," a slim figure waved. The one-way horse was bent on the home way, even if whacked and fed to go the other way.

"Through the trees," Angela said, "I saw you singing and riding past our lonely rented farmhouse room?"

"Angela, I'm so happy to see you." Meta's hand reached down from the horseback to her hand, squeezed it. She dismounted and bussed Angela's cheek.

"Grandma's dying. . . ."

Meta, nervous about Nanna, said, "Leaving the Kaiser's lodge with my son without knowing what I'm doing next scares me."

"What do I do," said Angela, "except wait for grandma to die? Next, I'll go with you to Berlin or America. I'm afraid. God is good and will care for me."

They two sat on small rocks folks called "wandering ships," believed to have rolled downriver from the ice cap's melting eons ago.

"I'm unsure about going back to Heinrich's farm." Fritz lapped water, while they caught up with each other. Heinrich arranged for improvements in home and outbuildings. Still he preferred the past to the future, old peasant ways to anything newfangled.

Inside the rental farmhouse, smoke passed up the chimney, and through roof thatch, dried up, dark beetles, drying up, fell on the dirt floor. Angela's grandmother began calling out. The kettle was also boiling over the low fire in the fireplace.

Angela went inside and checked on her Grandmother Bauer, and they returned outside. Angela had told Meta life tales earlier. "When young, she and friends married farm boys in fall harvest times when most farm marriages took place. No farm for me. Now I'm young," said Angela, "Who's old enough here or young for me to marry?" She pulled her ash blonde hair tightly back under her yellow band.

"Marry anyone and stay as long as you can. Then leave."

"Oh, I could never do that. That's what my mother did. She's happy in America. We're miserable here."

In her grandmother's youth, even parish records chided a girl with her infant's birth and marriage afterward. "But," Angela continued, "A boy does benefit the farm community." True German blooded females, as twisted in from old inheritance practices could inherit some farms, if no workable males existed. Extra hands, extra babies were welcome.

Angela's handsome pastor father, seen in photos, married her mother who tired soon of Christian ladies coming to see her Danish-Saxon husband, assigned to their area by the church. "People expected prayer and comfort from his pastoral care."

"Who comforted her?" asked Meta, who observed Angela's limbs were bones, just.

"My mother strengthened her own backbone somehow? I guess. Without pregnancies, she talked my father into adopting war orphans, see." Another photo inside displayed a baby, tulle lace flounced and blond curled. "Two years later, my older sister was born."

Failing in school, her sister, Helene, grew up to chose motherhood. "Believe this? My sister had two lovers, one rich enough for marriage. But she loved her poor lover more."

"How do you know?" asked Meta.

"She told mother her rich would-be husband fathered her son.

"Who knows?"

Angela puffed up her flattened right sleeve.

"At first, Mama planted vegetables to feed the family, annuals and cultivated perennials, like roses and blue flax. Gardens save people, you know. That's all we've got here with rental rooms.

"My wayward sister begat five children to feed. They and war distressed our mother. They'd all go to war.

"And my father was stretching his parish as far as Africa. . . ."

Diagramming these family details was exhausting for Meta. Angela was getting a lot off her chest.

"Along came another baby orphan boy for my parents. This toddler ran and howled without stopping, so they returned him to the orphanage. Sadly too, some said he should be done away with."

Meta said, "I know problems from my son."

Angela went on. Consulting psychologists intrigued her reverend father into trying psychoanalysis in Berlin.

On her deathbed or couch, her grandmother must be disclosing family secrets and semi-secrets to Angela. "Your father, my son, wishes only for success. Happily ignorant about rendering unhappiness in others, my father urged watching for sadness in others."

"When at last, he traveled to Southwest Africa," Angela said, "my mother was about to give birth to me. Her breasts dried up. With no milky substitute, I withered and almost died. She could have just let me go. Still her joy of joys arrived, me"

"He'd tell her," Angela continued, "'You have no profession! What does a woman do these days? She'd studied kindergarten pedagogy in Switzerland, but I could not argue with him. Anyway, her "joy of joys" arrived—me.

Three years ago, my mother decided to leave, settle down and send for me, her only birth child later.

"Mama said though in a recent letter that she should have followed him to Africa or Berlin but stayed at home for us. I'm afraid caring for grandmama. But what happens happens. God is good."

"Your mother left for America. Your grandmother," Meta continued, "lost her farm.

"Well, Landbund or Landvolk are saving farms for farmers. Maybe they'll help."

"No. Angela in spite of weakness and pallor was able to snap back at Meta.

"When father left mother for another surnamed "von," mama asked, 'Who needs me?' After all, this is the 1928. Grandmama says people do things like that nowadays. If mama went to America. I can too."

"Mine went off maybe to die there."

"Who told you?"

"No one, I know."

"You can't be sure!"

Inside, Frau Bauer snored and gagged before the expected death rattle. Because Meta had not yet witnessed dying except for Harald after death, she wished to flee. Nanna was hanging on though.

Said Angela's grandmother earlier about her son, "Your father's modern world. He's 'psychological,' I'm social with the community."

"And your mother?"

Now she writes from America," Angela said, "telling me—cope and study."

"I wrote Mama back. You won't have to care for Papi on his deathbed, as expected, like his mother, my grandmother, did.'

"You went off to America, so will I." Angela wrote back.

"Yes," Meta said, "When I was a baby, they say I saw my mother. My uncle-father tells me, 'Forget your mother.' Study to overcome evil. I try; I do."

While Angela tucked in her grandmother, hanging onto life and flailing, she threw off her featherbed, Meta tried out their spinning wheel.

"Was your grandmother happy?" asked Meta.

"She knew no other life."

"My so-called father would dote on your völkisch grandmother. You should hear him argue with his sister Lore over old and new!"

Angela begged her grandmother to swallow liquid; the old woman refused. Hands in pockets, Angela sat close to Meta in a rocker by the fireplace, big enough to walk into.

After pleasantries about Katia, they snickered about Lili Ula and her brothers turned hicks from the east and wondered about Grete the sophisticate, just seen by Meta near the pavilion.

Meta worried about Grete and Todi. "I must go find my son. Soon let's go to Berlin!"

"When? An outing's improper, when grandmama's sick. When I was gone before, grandma got sicker."

"After your grandmother dies, let's go to America. But I prefer Berlin, weird Berlin, America."

"You still live in that creepy palace?" asked Angela.

"In the hunting lodge. I'll finish the drudgery of packing, leave for the creepier house of my uncle-father."

"Can I iron this dress in my bag?"

"We don't have an iron. Not one that does not need a fire to get hot."

Powerful knuckles pounded on the door. They jumped. Her finger at her lips, Angela tiptoed on the packed dirt floor to peek out a high window. Meta comprehended neither her Sorbisch nor German. They waited without speaking.

"Sorry, I must go." Relieved to flee this death house, she hugged Angela and was preoccupied with a stranger at the door.

Outside, no one stood at the door, and her horse was gone. Next time, Meta would ride a young sleek bronze horse, hide it or fasten it to the door handle wherever she entered. But the old horse ridden here from the lodge was gone. Along the road back, she passed wildflowers, rosy Glocken-heide and blue harvest of time, as she fretted over what path she'd veered off and Fritz II's losing his way. Unable to find the horse nicknamed Whoa, she struggled up a monolith to scan the heathland.

20.

An hour later, frantic without this horse and lost in nowhere, she found its halter by the road with semi-legible marker from the old Herrenhaus lodge. This chocolate horse, "Whoa," was lured with hay if needed. She'd reminded herself from Katia's directives, "Don't hurry."

Meta, beholden to no one, would have angered no one by riding him. Some rogue stole Whoa. All persons waved down told her they'd seen neither horse nor rider.

The Pavilion ahead where she'd observed Trixi, her supporters and opponents was destiny. Meta was hungry and lacked sterling, Italian, Czech money or marks. Others were vying for money to pay for food.

If with Georg, she'd obtain a meal. Otherwise, the more she counted her pence, the less she counted on these days.

Oddly, Georg appeared and waved. "Your horse's untied." She heard words though restrained her tongue. Up closer, her eyes crossed, meeting his look and Whoa who'd stolen back along the long road home, as far as the Pavilion.

Georg gripped her hand with a stiffened arm for her mounting and kissed her hand, though in daytime. Saxons did not kiss, they shook hands.

"How's the horse?" he asked.

"I avoided megaliths and rocks."

"They've never stopped you before."

That she'd lost Whoa she could not acknowledge without anger.

"I sent the horse you rode back to you."

"Whoa never arrived." She did not retort, for this time with Georg might be her last. To protect herself, she'd already, while in the water closet, tabulated how many days would pass, before seeing him again, or when next they'd dine and dance, if ever.

The pavilion managed in these mean times a menu: beans, rutabagas, celery and cabbage from its garden and duck, chicken, rabbit and pheasant from nearby woods or fish from the not far Elbe or Llemenau Rivers.

Diners feasted. Everyone more or less was celebrating the First of May. His arm whirled from his back with a tiny wildflower bouquet. She smiled. He kissed her forehead, nose, cheeks and lips, repeating his touches. His free hand stroked her back. She kissed him back. She laughed. "Walpurgis Nacht, are you bewitching me?"

"Eat and dance away the witches this May eve or morning."

Candles illuminated the enclosed porch. Other couples and a family huddled nearby. Georg held the chair for her to sit again, never done before, and crowned her with a tiny roses circle, its thorns cut or bound. "May Queen."

Expecting thorns for a May bride, she was not emboldened, except to thank him and squeeze him.

Suddenly, outside local great need fires were killing off contaminants, befouling smells and sights like decompressed memories, until the midsummer fragrance arose once more.

Here with him yearned for and given up on, he was tweaking her chin with an oak leaf twig before placing it on his ear. "Caesar," she named.

"My Queen of May's here, the Kaiserin's gone forever. Till we'll invite back with old customs, we'll make do." He poured a goblets of May wine, tipping it into her mouth and she his.

Toast or sip in the pleasure: overcome shyness and accept semi-delirium. His indifference for months had incited her to bind herself to him. "Now," he said, "you've recovered from widowhood, let's go."

She nodded but fretted about forgetting her son. "I must rush to him and the residence. Otherwise, do I live anywhere?"

Dowdy in her wrinkly smock, as seen the water closet mirror, blue over rosy blouse, soiled for two days, Meta'd dabbed her face with soap, water and brushed her cheeks with rouge and her curls to shine in the candlelight. By contrast, she thought she'd seen Grete still dancing on the floor.

"A mourning year's passed," he said. "You've noticed? I encouraged your observing your church calendar? Your son's fine now?" His candor wrought anxiety in her. With her first glass of wine she wiggled in her seat, and her eyes blurred. Her second excited her and her third dribbled on her bosom he tasted.

Unluckily, tasteless potato soup, vichyssoise, within the serving dipper shook when she served him. Luckily, the Baltic perch was tastier with herbed tiny potatoes.

"Be serious," she said, aghast. "Where've you been?"

"Chasing a horse for you. Now I'm with you." His face handsome in spite of his upper lip zigzag through his mustache, a wound from war or heredity, blending with his sometime black eye patch.

Sitting in this atmosphere with him dizzied her. Candle flames on table wriggled, when a window opened to the piney aroma and cool outer air. The finished oak paneling and polished dance floor reflected candles. "Makin Whoopee" music welcomed her feet. Could this moment freeze like a frieze? After forever yearning for this man, being with him elated her.

Background piano music tinkling slightly out of tune suited him. Their medley began. "You're driving me crazy. . . The Jews, the Germans," hard-to catch words, part-English. "Stormy Weather" followed with ordinary words. Hazily, she saw Grete here, away from her aunt?

"Happy?" he asked.

"I suppose, yes, yes." If only happiness suppressed danger. "Why ask a witch in the night air. I'm happy. I've known no happiness before." Did he hear? She sipped her May Rhine wine again. "Are you?"

"Yes."

"More happiness will come, as the world shifts, wait and see." He poured more wine and asked for another bottle.

After the jazzy pieces, they danced slow waltzes and surprisingly a mazurka, she could change skirts for each dance step. Because the piano player and combo played Benny Goodman, Georg was offish. American music contaminated the atmosphere for him. Still they shimmied and fox-trotted more or less. Where did he learn steps she was picking up? Mala? Her arm rounded him and stroked his upper back muscles, until her hand rested at the nape of his neck, where a bump under his collar was a swastika her fingertips deciphered.

Pretending herself an UFA movie actress, sultry-voiced, and dressing in a slinky wine-colored bias-cut satin slip gown with a low back, risqué, she ought to have studied theatre with Max Reinhardt, after all, as Aunt Lore recommended. Then she wouldn't be with her lover her, but in Berlin. Here she was swooping, singing, swinging, gasping, kissing and being kissed, swooning in an unreal life whooping in a tinderbox world. She nestled in. Giddy, throwing back her head, she laughed.

"I knew." More uniformed men arrived and circulated.

"Hm-m-m."

"Come to the meadow with me."

"Meadow?"

Rolling up his sleeve, he looked at his watch. "Almost midnight." Now comes our May Solstice." His fingers ran down her spine, where she was succumbing. He nudged her off the mini-dance floor into the out-of-doors.

"Let's drink some dew for our gaiety and the earth. We'll love more here."

Into the human cradle, like olden times, his mouth wandered to her belly button, like the moon's phases over wild oat and clover fields to the meadow, until they sank back until dawn.

"Georg, they'll see us."

"No one cares. We'll stay in our meadow." He rolled over to cuddle her. "It's our tradition."

"Leave we must. The hourglass insists I go for my son. His father's cousin will think me lost. Todi'll fear my disappearing. I must go."

"You must. But this area here is free. No judging here. You're free, Meta Freya. I adore you." He hummed to her and tickled her under her arms and her belly, until she released herself, and they attained their joy.

Like Natur printed, Meta saw herself semi-obligated, strolling hand in hand with her nude partner, caressing her palm, as he drove her home in his old lorry with the horse tied behind.

21.

The next day, Fritzi II-Whoa nibbled grass though was less hungry than earlier en route toward Angela and back to the pavilion. Meta dismounted and tied his reins to a birch tree, as he was gobbling cold oats from the pail below. When he finished, she untied and loosened him.

Suddenly, maneuvers occurred. Swords clanked and rifles were shot. She ducked her head and put Whoa's pail over her head.

No mayhem would drive her wholly away. She'd go at her own pace, if possible, cantering away in fact and thought. Would Georg ever reappear?

Back at the Kaiser Lodge's apartment, the long streaky mirror with mercuric cracklings revealed her tousled, hairy self. For almost 24 hours, no comb had combed her hair. Her jumper creased into folds drooping like that of a poor caryatid. She must iron her wrinkled dress to cease being a mess. Tipping with hands on hips, she tried to shake off herself from herself and slip into another self. After rubbing her temples to relieve her headache and trying to find aspirin, she chose items from closets, but each bore only nineteenth century designs, not twentieth century ones.

To reassure herself, no matter her garb, she'd try clamping down on her inner bitter guesses. Georg would never return, her mother would never get found, she'd never aid Grete in a getaway, and she'd alienate her son. She fell asleep, still tingly over Georg.

Once awake and somewhat energetic, she was packing again to move back from castle-lodge to uncle-father's place.

Every love has its lineage. This Lore once told her above her wimpled neck and chin line with grace and smiles against outrage, as she was about to welcome one of her circles of friends, whether the Trixi kind, Nannas, Metas or strangers.

Because her uncle-father cranked out his views on local politics regarding country life its decline, including excessive taxes and poor crops, she might be stopped on foot by country people she always stopped to chat with, if possible with them about his issues, as they knew of her link to him. Above them on Whoa, she could avoid them. Great-uncle, she struggled to call "father," was loving the land within his righteousness toward people. Heinrich knew country people respected him. These views were as far as she could go in her regard for him. She was also trying to depart from them and him.

Still out everywhere, Heinrich doddered with a cane. Nanna sat more now than puttered. Lore fretted about war coming again and wished Liesl and Hansi would leave Berlin to come home. Unwilling to detail her cousin's, her aunt's only daughter and child, Meta said little of whatever she knew about Liesl. Because Meta thrived on city drama, she needed to forsake this soothing outdoor life. Turbulent within, Meta plotted to depart for the city. Glimmers of a momentous shift were encasing her. She needed money.

"Leave it to love," she'd murmured to Georg, indulging her. Already, he was elsewhere and elusive about his whereabouts.

"Go, if you must." She vowed to herself to go opposite the compass point from him.

Biding time in September, she poked down a road kilometer to an impromptu play area, where earlier with her cart and workhorse, she'd almost run into a boy. Indeed the boy was running and testing Lili Ula at this time.

With him, a big man, once seen with Katia, frayed in a dress shirt with sleeves rolled up his powerful arms, was pushing the boy on a swing from a high branch in an excess of energy. "Enough," said the man with an iron cross face on his squared head that smiled when speaking.

Meta asked, "Are you Lili's husband?"

"You could say that," said Karl. If only someone easygoing, more available, came forward, she'd be set for life; instead Georg as distanced from Georg, she miniaturized him.

Beyond Lili's husband, the Hanoverian palaces of cousins of the English Queen Victoria and Consort Albert stood across the channel from Niedersachen house-farms. They dominated the landscape of former Kaiser's territory, still Prussian.

Within this land framework, timberwork braced many roofs and walls. Outside, the nearest timberwork house, the crossbeam above the wooden front door scripted: The wind blows wherever it wishes; you hear its sound but you know, not where it comes from or where it is going. It is like that with everyone, born of the Spirit. John 2:8.

With a thick rope improvised from a high oak tree into a swing, Lili's Karl pushed the boy higher and higher longer, until he said. "I'm exhausted."

Lili spoke. "Unite farmers against their losses."

Meta's eyes filmed over.

"Enough," he told the boy, and shook hands with her. "I'm Karl." His exuberance surprised her. "Party tonight!"

"Georg might not go."

"Bring him," Lili said. The sun highlighted Karl's hair wisps. Petite and erect, she said, "Come alone." Her walking stick pounded the earth.

Karl urged Meta. "He'll meet people he knows."

Life was passing. Georg appeared at times. When distant from her, she ached in premonitory loss.

Would Heinrich or Georg object to partying? Why dither over riding Whoa through white birch columns lighting up the country road?

At the party, she alit from her glowing horse and laced the reins around the pole within bushes near the door and strode in. Her image detached from her silken horse presence shone in a full-length hall mirror here. About her husband, boyfriend or father, no one asked. Maybe they knew nothing.

Partygoers nodded like neighbors from childhood. Fleetingly, she thought to withdraw, but who was better for joining fun than she? She watched. Guests were giggling. Two were tickling each other, a man and a woman, balancing glasses of wine. Three men spoke in a corner of this house with many rooms.

The main ones were cream stucco within beams, marking the room like dripped bitter chocolate on off-white frosting. Overhead, a candelabrum lit with candles for a tallow smell. To the room requiring no electricity, they gave luster.

The hostess with kiss curls, a coquette in webs of overlapping yellow lace to her knees bobbed in and out. Pausing, she drew in her cigarette holder, puffed smoke like myths whirling any way and jutted out her arm to draw others toward her allure. Someone had alluded to her wish to be crowned Queen of the Heather in the upcoming summer festival.

After a rush from wine, Trixi of all people with a fringy satin maroon dress and her leather cap and goggles arrived. She began whooping, "Dawnce, everyone. Life's wunderful without war." Whoops of complaints roared, yet they allowed her to stay. She must have joined up with the crowd she'd opposed seemingly the other day.

Grinding out from the Victrola gramophone, the Charleston, foxtrot and swing looped out, as the party givers hooted at everyone to dance. Some groaned but joined the hoopla.

A woman with Grecian profile and deep marceled waves caught the candlelight on her body outline. One jock, hair centre-parted introduced himself as "Rolland." Another, Hans, an inventor-engineer of the nearby electric works dandled a girl on his knee. Most men wore dark suits and gabbed with girls in dressy colors.

Rolland could have been sculpted from a statue to life from Bremen. Armin an interloper stuck his chin outward though carried no upright sword. Thanes and Kriegers abounded. When Rolland, the biggest, tallest man, stood to go, the front door vacuumed in lilac fragrance. Thomas Arminius strode in and shook hands with him on the way out.

Victrola music yearned in Nostalgia. "Beginnings, beginnings," someone sang, "when is the beginning going to begin a rhythm to dance to." Benny Goodman and Louie Armstrong awed and wowed them, as partygoers stole dances, more than their share of hooch and kisses, until the serious talk began about war, especially World War I repayments, cusses, love, sex, trampling on others' land, whatever, and nasty tenants' refusals to pay rent or taxes.

Whirling with the music with second and fourth beat, wine, and ale turned into Trixi's American mambo.

"Such dances and music steal our Schottisches." Then someone croaked and laughed. "Do something about this jazz in-at-the-door."

"Ban it," Rolland called out.

Someone stopped the Victrola midway in a Goodman record and replaced it with more homegrown words with Swing. All present could ill-understand them, as rhythm with clarity. "Here's Winston Churchill: Yes, the Germans are driving me crazy. . . .The Jews. . . "sung in Englisch with German accent heard at the pavilion.

Hot grog with rum was circulated. "Voelkisch, isn't it?" Lili called out. Tiny sausages, served by a slender nondescript woman, fit into the partygoers' mouth to mouth tasting of tubes within a semi-secret, new Kultur.

One sobered up enough to change the Churchill record to Swing. Another asked Meta to dance. Instead of improvising on impromptu themes, everyone wanted to join the decorous set. Never having quite learned the parlor arts, she laughed at her clumsiness, almost sidelining her. "Teach me this step?"

"Easy, follow me," a man named Roy said, dipping. A tap on her shoulder wound her into Karl's arms. Lili waved her conductor's hand at them and danced with big Rolland. Roy stroked Meta's upper arms and the soft of her satiny green back to the split between her buttocks. Overheated, she wished to disrobe into nakedness.

Georg tapped her on her shoulder. "No swing here!" He bellowed against jazz. Once his rant subsided, she kissed the bottom of his nose and pouted. "Where have you been?" Kissing his lower lip, she noticed its pinkness.

Others watched his three-step, until she departed for the toilet. In the Mirror: she needed the right hair color, blonde blond, the blonder chromium white, off-yellow, the more platinum the better, the more in style of leading women these days. Hers in this light was too bright dark reddish.

She walked out. Two fellows off to the side were extending their hands to Georg.

"Meetings, meetings, drives, practices, forms to ready," he said, etherealizing activity beyond ordinary life. That he beguiled her she knew, but he did not quite know her.

"Georg, the Stahlhelm, former war officers where's it going?" Armin asked. The Kriegers were self- and group-made, not governmental, erupting ground up, not top down. What did this phenomenon mean?

"Excuse me." Georg bolted for another room. No dance partner now, whereas before she'd had too many.

To grasp this party scene, she leaned against the wall. A cigarette was lit and handed to her in passing. She inhaled. Someone had done that in Berlin, male-to-male goodwill not allowed with females, until nowadays. She coughed. "What do you do in such troubles?"

Out of the Freicorps, the old vets, the Stahlhelm a young-older one, more established and ensconced in society's middle that fought old battles and open new wounds to deal with, according to Heinrich and Harald, when living. The Stahlhelm was marching at dawn. Those partying all night would go participate or watch. The midnight sun would arise over North Sleswig-Holstein, not here. In the old Saxon and Danish territories fought over for centuries, now farmers were facing skirmishes.

Placing her palms backward on her hips, Lili accosted her. "Today Germany's ours, tomorrow the world belongs to us."

Her puffy red lips pursed and opened, singing to Meta, who preferred to escape from Lili. Her right arm tapped an unseen podium and cracked the air, as she again sang the song about Churchill and the Jews.

Lili's gibberish began whirling with her knee-high flared black skirt, displaying her knees and thighs—odd sounds with strange ideas in combos. "Georg possesses fish-eyes, all-seeing, too nationalistic. Why stay with him?"

"For the same reason, you stay with Karl." She must do something about foul labeling, but what. Her qualms began shaking.

"Choose sides, rather than objectivity, Sachlichtkeit." Lili squinted at Meta. "Learn what each stands for, what everyone says. Your father's still more the nationalist than the Nazis—that's why he and Georg clash. Both ignore the big picture."

"How so, how do you know so? Meta asked. Father, once a force, was deteriorating.

"Why think about how your parents coped?"

Meta seethed against Lili's self-assurance, willpower and glibness. Was there anyone else to talk with?

"You're a baby." Daring to, Lili asked, "Who fills one's mind with truth?"

"Lili, you cower before the soldiers, and your husband never served."

"You," Lili, her dark eyes blinking, shouted above the party din. "You should favor the farmers and tenants altogether! They'll grow together. Take a stand to work together with us."

Meta wrenched inside over what to do. Landvolk was demonstrating on the street, as seen in town. But she must pay Heinrich's taxes.

Her thoughts reverberated now off the walls within soft jazz. Which side was hers? The hardliners forbidding jazz must have left already. Two men staying on spoke chin to chin in the corner. Three others, dark-suited with light brown hair tufted on their heads, cooed near her, unaware of her though aware of Lili who asked, "What're the Reds up to?"

"Around the Landvolk," someone replied. "Where there's trouble, you can count on reds like horseflies."

"And the NSDAP?" Lili's dark shiny hair was flickering in the candlelight.

"Their gains spill out from the university, Göttingen."

Meta shirked from Lili's words, unaware of their exact beliefs. She favored a good time without thinking about Lili. Favoring a political fight, Lili, smart, had attended the university and fled her family lands with her brothers, who'd feared war with the Reds, so she was organizing and speaking about Landvolk. Suddenly, she disappeared without Karl.

Where was Trixi, the aviatrix known to speak out?

Meta's raced ahead—pay Heinrich's taxes. Should war start again—such talk was everywhere—anger was mounting against the Imperial Empire of the Prussian State as if it still existed within the Weimar Republic. Heinrich said all this and was missing out on the fervor. Was he losing his place? Was he being left behind?

Postponing her move to Berlin, she'd mulch the dirt. Gauzy air moisturized surfaces and clung to her eyes, and could help seedlings' rooting. Plant in the small troughs and sprinkle with prepared dirt. So the peace of spading and hoeing a garden against scarcity comforted her in a life of caution.

After dragging herself to church, what next? Enjoy the hymns. Disassociating from this party rattled her, she mouthed,

"Lamb of God, take away the sin of the world, and have mercy on us." What happens with such words?

"Sing," "Sing no more," a voice said. Life was falling over her perch within a huge semi-whirling kaleidoscope, like a spinning swastika, outfitted within stained glass pieces of medieval garnet, ambers, yellows, greens, blues and royal blue-purple, outlined in black to brace them. Flickering like candle flames, the pieces settled, then flew away, until the tube stopped for a musically colored rosette, ancient sign, a stay-put.

Part of Psalm 74 memorized for church school. Lift up thy feet unto the perpetual desolation: even all that the enemy hath done wickedly in the sanctuary. . . .

A man was famous: as he had lifted up axes upon the thick trees.

But now they break down the carved work thereof: at once with axes and hammers.

They have cast fire into thy sanctuary: they have defiled by casting down the dwelling place of thy Name to the ground.

She leaned against the wall of her thoughts. She was interrupted. "What's a young beauty like you doing here, not in Berlin or Vienna," a tall dark blond, alcohol booting him up, asked. Flashing a smile, "I'm Otto Swering." Others not recognizing him shook hands with him, passed by, and others seemed awed.

"Meta." A live oompah band whooped in. Raucous brassy and booming sounds brought everyone out of side rooms and toilets to dance or listen. Everyone hooted.

They stopped the political talk. Better times are here, others declared. Not yet, some few said but would be soon.

Even Georg, older than the twenty, thirty year olds, and Meta, younger than many, jumped in with polkas, jigs and local folk steps. In shadows, even the help and older farm labourers were allowed to dance to the live music, by swaying in the hallway and outer entryway.

"Who are you talking to?" Georg asked. "Be ultra-careful what you say in these times. Otherwise, you'll say too much to someone who'll soon be passing your comments on to the authorities. You'll pay."

She and Georg slipped out through halls of antlers and horns, where Reebok and Waterbock saluted them like up-raised arms.

"I keep my mouth shut."

"New types here I never much liked." He grumped about a certain local landowners' advantages. "They don't know struggle yet."

"How could they?" she asked. They're too young.

After scurrying away from that party, she climbed into her bed.

With no real home, a homeland to rest in, she sank into her trundle bed. Strange with Georg and insecure. Her feath-erbed though welcomed her.

She slept. To start a plan, her broom of straw whirred of its own accord. All was lazing along, Nature oozed in endless time. Work continued, but nothing was ever done.

To clean the corners of sparking jewel colored objects, Meta doubted what she could do. A blond helper sat down, as she rested from endless tasks and waited for the whirring broom to stop. The man pulled off his cap from his brushy hair, shook it and put it back on. He'd also helped to sweep but said this. "I'm knocking off for the night."

Another man crept up beside her. His hair, also blond, but longer than that of the first one, familiarized himself with her plight. They'd met in daylight fog. This second, Otto, wore a wider brimmed straw hat fraying but no glasses. "Fölen! Fölen!"

This eyeless one offered to sweep toward the glittery objects, slipping away.

Georg approved, she knew, of her household arts, her skill in locating missing foods and fodder. That was her essential role, if ever measured. Her mending skills from Nanna fit with baking and roasting learned from the old cook, now dead and cleaning from Lore. Rearranging artifacts satisfied Heinrich. But Georg little involved her in his household, a fact disturbing her. What he did while ignoring her disturbed her. Whatever she did to please him he took for granted.

Dancing in the countryside to swing music displeased him. "Sinisterly beautiful and sensual in the moonlight," he said, "disturbs my peace." Half-awakening to him, she sighed, shook and writhed to his tasting her nipples and her small barrow of wonder. No tall warrior could win her, if he secured her forever.

"You'd like to replace me, wouldn't you?" He teased her, or she thought he was. He tickled her by blowing into her belly.

With the dawn, she rolled over to push herself to stand up. He pulled her back down and hugged her. Released, she climbed upright. He did. "I must," she said, "feed the old horse and see Todi and see the sheep."

"Me?" he asked.

"Fodder, groats?"

"You are," he continued, "mine." Standing up, they hugged. "I will see you soon and my son." Meta shook.

Startled at how much she must love him, after leaving him behind. Yet he dissolved before saying what he meant, or she. Through the clear window, unlike the old medieval bubbled panes above, like a Ministeriale of the Middle Ages as if with double-edged sword at his side he traveled down the drive.

22.

Today because Georg reappeared, they'd drive to see the troubles farther North. Inside the car, Todi whined in a high grating voice, insisting on sitting in the very back. "Stop whinging," said his mother, "or get whacked." He refused, though lowered his tone, as if Mopsi wanting food scraps or bones. "All right for you, you'll go in the back outside all by yourself!"

Gleeful, he was when lifted him into the bumper seat but mad when strapped him in for safety in the dark blue coupe open back. Back in the auto cab, she, annoyed, often turned to check on him. He waved, as Georg started up the motor.

On an incline, they paused within a Hufen, strange country, patched feudalistic still, where blood relatives might divvy up land for lifetimes but never pass it to outsiders. Changes were a-coming though. In Holstein, they crafted brick public and private buildings, such as wood beamed manger house-barns with folded down roof end points, like Lower Saxon ones.

"Like home," Georg said. Its peasants like Ol' Christoph, thatched rooftops, nowadays sometimes redone with shingling or tiling, a change Heinrich abhorred for blending less with the moors and hayfields.

Exactitude reigned. Dithmarschen, according to Georg, within North Saxon folkways, was more than astir. Riled up,

Georg drove through the marshland to scan its upheaval. "Not much to see."

Warrior bands had long before nailed their brotherhoods onto the countryside, according to their old guidebook. Each brother or cousin family could have been holding the same sandy ground, sour Heide, for a thousand years. Its baked earth bricked up walls, its plots of land inter-linked with growing, harvesting and beekeeping, while underground salt could bubble up to preserve cabbage, beets and cucumbers in this area of anxiety and enrich some cross-pathed towns. This trio of onlookers sought men on maneuvers or protestors in land wars everyone whispered about.

Meanwhile along the fields, Georg and Meta were pointing out dragonflies, blue with clear wings, to their little boy son, while on the ground. There also, long insects were masking as tiny sticks exciting to him, as was a grasshopper jumping. Slightly higher, bees were commonplace. "Look at the green tortrix!" Looking flat on the ground, Todi squealed Georg and Meta were almost like devoted parents watching him. In his small circle, Todi scouted caterpillars, one gripping a twig near ants below and more bees above. Eyes on butterflies and moth wings intrigued him. All these land and higher up creatures would later on encourage Todi to value outdoor hiking and soon enable him to be able handle a kilometer on the flatland. In a couple of years, they believed he'd know survival skills.

They poked along the forest edge and meadows toward the church. Placing her hand on Todi's shoulder, she chuckled and hummed, "A Mighty Fortress is Our God," linking with Georg's arm and shivering.

Because of tiredness, Todi piggybacked on Georg, who let the boy, too heavy for such ongoing play, slide off his back. Meta and Georg wended their way forward, holding Todi's hands. Hoisting the tall little boy in between and swinging him, the kindergartner-soon-to-be giggled. When they stopped, he begged. "Again."

Others might deride them as undignified for Evensong. The little boy's pestering with "Again," would annoy some. Meta let go of Todi's hand and said, "I'll be back."

"For God's sake, why?" asked Georg. "You're going into the church with him, not me."

"But you said you'd care for him."

"I did not; I said we."

"I must go to the graves."

"Why now, for God's sake?"

"Hold Todi's hand, button him up, please, so he's warm. I'll return soon from the cemetery."

"You take him in, and I'll watch from outside."

"I must go, must go into the cemetery," said Meta.

"You only go to cemeteries, never to churches," said her son.

"That's where the answers to my quest are. Sounds a little screwy, doesn't it?"

Todi added, "You watch sheep and cows and say you'll find father's and grandmother's graves. But you never do."

"Give up," Georg said. "You know where Harald is buried. Your mother's not here. Maybe she could be preserved in salt."

Within the portal with sacred bas-reliefs, she said. "To the cemetery, Todi, darling, be good. I'll be back. We may not return to this churchyard soon."

Georg gripped Todi's hand, and he said to her, "You baby him."

"THAT's why you should take him in now, so I do not baby him." Into the sanctuary, they strode, the boy running to keep up with his father...

Pale rose, greens, blues and yellow faceted the stained glass windows. Meta prayed to find the stones of her mother with other relatives. Todi and Georg sat down. They were all right. She could leave the sanctuary to search.

She paused. Harald, if not buried here, still marked for her with an unseen arsenal of guilt, in which both parents also wracked her thoughts. Now infirm, her father-uncle was beginning to preside from his great bed. Here she'd been longing for Georg. Here too, he appeared. As for Annike there was no name on a grave, Meta propelled herself toward probing and maybe digging for the unknown.

Up above, medieval insignia banners hung within the church and modern ones with crosses within angles, blue, white, amber and red with fesses. A few bore the ancient stylized eagles, as if having flown in from Babylon, Assyria or Scythia. Elongated lions appeared to leap off banners with. Monumental eagles of the empire also mounted up there.

Words as read were scripted, incised in the wooden beam across the nave and gilded. "I am come that thou might have life and have it more abundantly." Farmers and others hereabouts grappled with or ignored scripture. "Where there are two or three gathered in my name, there I am also." Rote known verses licked consciences. "Come unto me all ye who are heavy laden." What about the food growers hereabouts: why had she and Georg come here? The thought fell away from her.

"I am come that thou might have life. . ." vexed her most from these word ribbons around living skulls and souls inscribed on beams. How could you act freely for others or for yourself? "If you have done unto the least these my brethren, you have done it unto me," haunted her.

The breeze through the church doorway shook the imperial eagle. Also, it blew her skirt up from her calves to her thighs and strands of hair in her face.

Her head was jammed, chilled, and indecisive. "Wherever there are the sick, wounded. . . there I am also." Confusion from these words lifted and fell away. Stepping farther back, she bumped into someone, who turned and scowled at her going the wrong way.

Lightening stabbed her outside the sanctuary portal. So, she thought. The sunlight zigzag at sunset blew outward like a fire wheel.

Into the day's pallor, she slipped backward through stragglers in their bluish, navy or mauve dresses and some in double-breasted suits, with a few though in work clothes. Who could afford church these days? Not many.

Awareness crackled within the lightening. Her skin shivered in its thinness, stretched like hosiery. Dashing from the church and feeling skinless, her bloodied and scratched legs tried to distance her from guilt.

Her footpath below was barely visible, but near the highway and seemingly far from the church, it followed the cemetery edge along two or three-square kilometers of fencing, spiked rows of swords or spears tipped by gold arrows. On the gate's metal crest, a skeleton danced against a red line.

"Yes, I am with you till the end of flame time," angled to abreact the skeleton. She was hunting for the markers not of Harald—not here—her mother who might be; Meta crept and scanned row by row.

Next, she noticed what she'd omitted from her earlier awareness. Boxy letters seized her.

After bending, standing, feeling dizzy, she plopped on a marble grave, a sacrilegious act. Spirits could haunt the area. Lore had told her so as a child, when she'd sat in another cemetery on the alabaster odalisque angel, where the unknown was buried.

No one approved her stepping on it to see its words. If on marshy ground, mud now sucked her footprints. An upside down bowl of earth covered a new coffin. Could this one have contained her mother in the fatherland?

One foot ahead of the other, she dragged herself and her feet, heaviness overcoming her from having plunked not on someone's casket but on someone. On from that point, a weight drew her down.

The darkening sky eliminated seeing markers with endless surnames chiseled in small print. Whole Hufen, small farm communities, must now live below ground.

Lightening zigzagged from the sky into the ground, and clouds did crowd each other out, while light peeked from behind them. Jittering, they soared across the sky. Below, within the storm, trees batted one another. Her stomach churned. Fall colors glowed in the dark. One tree grayed against the shadow of the next. From ancient fir to elm, from ash, oak spruce, they swept apart and battled.

In the battening among them, Meta felt out of herself and beheld a strange being. Someone intact cropped up out of a coffin though the mud earth. Gazing aslant at this phenomenon, for a direct stare could destroy the site and sighting. Careful. Harald was haunting her. Or someone else. Before she could be sure, another being spewed out of a coach or cart. Her ancestors were rising out of the crotch of the earth and were emerging like folks blinking their eyes, even in dim light and glaring at her.

In this pale light, three so far were local types. Before naming them, others piped up through the ground, mostly bent, they were arising like skeletons, and their bones were rubbed with red. They smiled like skeletons and dragon bones. Otherworldly or nether-worldly, some recently dead, were shading into maroon though restoring life. Perhaps from deep burials, the root dye had stained them. Many figures appeared skinned and skeletal, colored red or tinted ochre, some tawny and maroon. They withdrew unto each other, circled and huddled, as still others erupted out of the loess. Others stills came from sheer topsoil.

For reality, after evidently fainting and failing to find her Mother, she began searching for Georg and Todi. Nowhere could she see them. Even known features, Harald's cobalt-green eyes and her mother's reddened hair and heart lips melted into fields of faces.

To shake free of them to be able to see them, her heart pummeled. Her feet slogged through a washed land, the moor famed for salting the food eaten by the dead. Instead of dissolving into the earth, they themselves were preserved. Men, women and children then grew up like shoots.

Men wore spikes of armor; a plaque here, a shin guard there, an elbow shaped pleat against an endangered funny bone, humerus. A mesh mask was worn against a jab in the face. A silver rib cage protected the dead heart. Even heel spurs pointed out from boots to rev up beasts of burden were moving on the trail.

Sideways, heads were shaped like breasts or beaks or helmets, resting their visors in the nose area. Others resembled eyes; some oval heads tipped sideways and balanced into ancient Sakiz birds of prey.

As more bodies sprang from the ground, their features reconfigured with large hazel, blue or green single eyes. Some creature-cadavers started to see her, until all eyes were upon her.

Squirming, Meta looked down at herself standing nude. No leaf covered her, no gossamer. Her belly breathed hard and fast. She crossed her arms over her breasts. Ashamed, she shrank back into childhood.

Odd people scrutinized her but did not see her. She despaired of escaping them. All the dead who had ever lived were returning to earth to judge the living.

Within a streak of lightening, she could see the Volk in the light that dissolved them temporarily.

As she groped back again along the cemetery fence, spear-by-spear, spike-by-spike toward the gate, within weak light, these night wanderers, a whole cemetery or county of them, rushed to people the earth with the past to crowd out the living.

Somehow, they needed thrusting back down underground once more. Such judgment singed her. Their presence also embarrassed her and lead away from bad thoughts, such as the death of Harald, loss of her mother and the rise of the worst evil not yet known.

Crows or vultures circled overhead and cawed. No one helped Meta. Once she latched on to the gate, words came again: "I am come, so that you may have life and have it more abundantly."

To the church she flew. Seen from the entrance were old banners and new grand flags with swastikas, fire wheels, signs of darkness, were spreading from above and flying. Slipping back into the church next to Georg and Todi, she whispered, "The dead are coming back to life to show us how to live!!"

"Sh-sh-shush." His tiny harelip scar without hair caught light and reflected like lightening. "You're out of your mind. Listen to the reading. Look around, everyone thinks all's right with the world. It's true." Two hooked crosses rippled overhead in the inside wind.

Below the church ceiling these dark gammadions, "hooked crosses," on banners ruffled in the breeze. Someone's voice, hers maybe disguised unto herself, whispered to no one in particular. "This House of God stands for the House of Lucifer!"

23.

"Not as beautiful, as she once was," Ol' Christoph's oldest daughter, Johanna, commented on Meta's dark reddish-blonde shaggy hair and stained work pinafore. Wizened and white-bearded, he smiled at his daughter.

Back from Berlin, where no one was hiring, Johanna had lost her childcare job. With Nanna failing and Todi growing up, they needed her help.

By 1926, great palaces had been expropriated. Uprisings in Berlin, Hamburg, Bremen, Munich a decade or so earlier, stirred an ongoing national frenzy, sensed and sweated over but little spoken about as recent history in Heinrich's presence. In all, the Kaiser and all the Kaisers' men were gone from Prussia, as was the Tsar was from Russia.

Now in 1930, Meta dreaded that tough old Heinrich would find more work for her upon her return. He'd sent over trusty Johanna, unmarried and clean, to finalize Meta's packing. Contents included a spiral auger, old-fashioned blue work shirtwaists for garden and fieldwork and tarnished helmet for Georg or Heinrich, and Prussian helmets. She laughed at herself in one a mirror. From years earlier, her trunks held childhood dolls, butterflies, agates and amber collections. They packed dowry gifts, passed through family generators. Runners, cutwork tablecloths, linen and damask, appliquéd bedclothes and brocade drapes were taken, not that she cared for them to inventory them for trunks with bentwood strips over pressed leather.

Driving away from the oblong stone mansion, Todi's birthplace, she'd gazed back at her life. Clutching the tufted front seat of the car sent for them, they approached the Cherusche farm through the rain.

Nanna now hovered between health and death. Meta yearned for another reality: music, lovemaking, spa holiday, freewheeling life or day-to-day activities. Berlin, Bremen or America, New York lured her—could she just go—like her imagined mother who beckoned her to begin again.

At the farm, Christoph was leaning on his wooden cane, sculpted with faces, from Africa. As a steward, he tried supervising labourers, and bantered with them, Meta swooped up the drive. Others took the baggage and boxes inside.

But once stored, leaning on his black cane, Heinrich spoke, "Sweet to see you here again, Meta." She was flabbergasted.

"And Todi, how are you? Glad you're here." In his short khakis and striped blue and white shirt, Todi grimaced and, then, managed to smile at the gruff white-haired man, barely known, already planning Todi's life.

Also entering the grounds, Lore rode up high on a young trotter, gleaming and strutting with mane flaring. Her updated style dramatized the matron of better times.

Christoph said, "More beauty, that Marianna riper now, like her mother." Their lips pursed against words about the mother. Johanna was spiteful about his comparing her with Meta who disliked being measured against any farmwoman and said so under her breath.

Heinrich, puffing his meerschaum, always could read local folks. He shushed Johanna. "Women must talk less. With work to do, Meta asks too much of others." At once, he half-hugged and again patted her and Todi.

The spread of his land, barns, and outbuildings, flat though elegant, depending on one's artistic eye, pleased Heinrich, who'd sold land for cash to improve the central farm. The grand lad, Todi, Heinich had often said he'd groom for a grand future on the farm. "Not a Dumm Hans, he'll learn the ropes with me, study for his Arbitur and university technical agricultural degree."

After the war, farmers, tenant farmers and labourers, former soldiers were fleeing the land for the city. The half-deaf Christoph agreed with Heinrich's expressed wariness of parties, splinters and enlarged ones uniting under one agricultural banner. Believing his fellow farmers would lose authority in uniting to dissolve local groups into larger ones, he grumbled that landowners, big or small, got hooked on city sleaze and parliamentary organizations. Neither Harald, nor Georg reluctantly, had done so, thank god, nor had Todi. Some defectors claimed the land protected Saxon Germans with agricultural laborers also into the same fold.

Heinrich, the country squire, withering, cranked out his opinions. "Parties are program, not complaint." Not doubting the future, he favored tough military-mindedness from World War I whose veterans gave way to the newer Stalhelm, higher types he felt had been left out were finally being let in to lead in the local NASDAQ.

"Outwitting the Russians, they are. If I were young like Todi, I'd be more involved. I will teach him." The small old political parties of landowners were mingling and regrouping with those that supported small merchants against the big

Jewish merchants, he whispered to Meta's squirming. "DVP, DNVP, DHP, DVFP, of these small groups which do you favor? D stands for Deutsche, not democracy."

She was quiet. The world was shifting, beyond what even he gloated about. Nationalist regulars were losing out to racist nationalists.

The future was unknown, but the Ventriloquist howled about the future. Once the Ventriloquist stalked with his Putsch, the authorities threw him and his gang into prison, he cast his voice far, up here in the North Saxony, Neidersachsen. Gauleiter-organizer-like Reverend Munchmayer's preaching favored the Ventriloquist.

"I listen to Trixi, the Aviatrix," She held her breath.

"Damned woman? After hearing Munchmayer, how could you?"

Meta walked into the house.

"More like Lore and Annike everyday," he said to Christoph. "Lore, at least, continues life's responsibilities. Would Meta dare pursue her mother's path?"

Less and less could Meta disguise her contempt. Her mother's and Nanna's Geest people would disallow climbing on her high horse.

"Watch out, or get caught," he growled, as if reading her thoughts. "Times look better with false wealth and worsen with inflation." But he warned that by mid-decade and on both debt and inflated costs of necessities, like food, would endanger the Fatherland.

His sister's hair still lustrous in the sun, gray-blue tinted and gold-streaked lead him to ask, "Going dancing later?" as she clip-clopped up on horseback. He offered her his hand to dismount.

"Hope to. Your hand's more steadfast than your views. You're gallant today. Want to hear Ab Reinhardt or see The

Chocolate Soldiers?" She bussed him on the cheek. "How's Frau von Handler? Let's go dance the tango. "I want one more fling before late middle age drops me into this era's bottomless crevice of old age, high costs and more war.

When he didn't answer, Lore said, "Politics interferes with life. You used to go round to the poor, remember? If Christoph's wife was recovering from the flu or worse, you'd see her. Is cook's daughter's broken ankle healing, and whatever happened to Harald's sickly parents? You've changed, unless you want to dance. We'll gather Meta and Frau von Handler to enjoy ourselves before another catastrophe assails us. You're the last gentleman in the middle distance going on down the road." She pointed to his portrait by the wall of the stairwell.

"We used to consult with and joke about von Krigge, an out-of date 1700's Lower Saxon unpopular neighbor who guided our behavior, manipulated it and became the Sheriff of Bremen to great success. Remember him." She laughed. "Downhill, we've gone. You've been withdrawn."

"You're too cheery," he said. "What'd you eat and drink? Georg's the one gone down the road, though his Meta doesn't know that yet." Meta agreed though said nothing.

"Thought I'd pay you a call, as we used to go visiting, dropping in on the weekend afternoons." Lore said, "I want to see if we're still related and nudge Georg into marrying your daughter. After all, he's Todi's father."

"He's the last one willing to marry her. He's won her, and she him, without marrying. In fact, they were married by capture or captivating each other, an old, medieval tradition."

"A wild streak's in her, hard to see, but there." Lore planned to pry his plans from him for Todi, and relay them to Meta, who only pressed for her mother's whereabouts, if, indeed,

Heinrich knew. "Meta's still a young palomino, headstrong." Meta grinned with hands on hips.

"Her son needs watching, though her heart's with him. She's caged, so Johanna will assist her with him and Nanna. They'll plant and cook. I'll urge Meta to earn a teaching certificate, maybe kindergarten, for extra income, to keep her busy. She placed her arms across her chest.

"She's practical, now over from the Kaiser lodge to help with the rye, wheat, cranberries and cattle—better than her mother—and preserving, canning and pickling with old cook. Soon she'll go pay the taxes for me. She'll surprise you with her homemade soap. We'll be clean and fed in hard times." She began walking away.

"She's the almost perfect daughter," Lore echoed. "Wish mine were like yours."

"Where's Meta now?" Tears dribbled down to his trimmed gray beard. His head was hunched into his shoulders. He lit his pipe, sucked it. Because of Meta's work, he defended her against Lore and even now against himself. "New growths pop up from her seeds. Where is she?"

Meta was listening inside the open door. "None of us is the same."

Rising early, Meta spaded to loosen the earth for new plantings. Night mist dampened the soil enough for seeding cabbages, turnips and carrots. Prepared cucumber seedlings transplanted to the garden would issue more cucumbers to pickle later. In hard times or war, the family would eat.

They would also see her peddle away down the road lane opposite from her aunt's trip in. To pay the taxes, long avoided. He'd told Lore and Meta not to risk any takeover of the farm over bank notes. The cash in a laundry bag might prevent authorities from troubling him about non-payment and take over his estate.

24.

Without hinting at its true intent, she'd finesse the Berlin move. Heinrich would authorize her visit to her cousin Liesl, a once-upon-a-time a friend. At least, she hoped so. If work was found, funds earned and sent back would help educateTodi and pay for her journey.

If Heinrich objected, little could he harm her plans on the smoky horizon? To begin, Liesl was scouting a clerical job for her cousin, salaried work entailing learning by doing. By running into Alain in Berlin, the only pedestrian visible through his dark glasses, this Pomeranian treated her like a lost neighbor-lodger, which she was, from the Kaiser's lodge and urged her to try for a post in his Berlin office. She interviewed knowing not what she was doing. She waited.

Meanwhile Berlin parks, churches and cinema attracted her, though auto headlights, like eyes, glared at her, as she crossed from sidewalks to trolleys. Ahead, buildings, frosted in whirling décor, and the big church like mocha cake that held Seals of Solomon or Stars of David protruding from its steeple base in four-sided bas-reliefs. Other buildings nearby stood like gingerbread. Like the Lüneberg churches, rose windows flowered in the Berlin church, Kaiser-Wilhelm-Gedachtniskirche, she scurried into. Instead of reading sidewalk news headlines, she dissolved into Bach measures and especially the Bach Evensong. Unready for communion, she watched others and measured her worth by scrutinizing her soul, wherever it wafted?

Back outside, tiny shops and theatres with marquees gushed out working people who clambered around one another or were swept into limousines to roll above and beyond the waves of Berlin poor, where the jobless, masses of them, shuffled along or fought.

To stay above on the Berlin flatlands, Meta raced to her new job. Hand on cloche over her bob, dark mauve coat overlay her brown skirt clinging to her curves, above high heels. She tried imitating Grete's mother Renate's salon flourishes wished for but too costly for salaried clerks.

Walking stickpins of Tiergarten, Berliners animated the parkland outside. Peopling it and the Mitte, open promenade, they welcomed all to the clamor and flora of the city with its tiny vegetable gardens and big separate trees, like the giant beech or Eiche, oak with massive trunks. There Berliners thrived and passed through the Brandenburger Tor ominously pinnacled with Victory on her Chariot. Can she topple? The swastika was flying overhead.

Once hired for her typing job, a tall solid man eyed her. Sad, his blued pupils and demeanor also brooded.

Once semi-established at her first kneehole desk, she was also told how Alex cloaked and comforted new subordinates. A longstanding regular, Nina wore clothes for hips and derriere low slung, as if in a hammock, as she rushed toward her co-worker friend and stressed how well Alex did. Bent slightly, she flew between projects. "Beware." Meta told herself.

That Nina and Neva were separate, not one, Meta hoped her newly learned steno reflected. Meta left off note taking for her new Ministry of Health boss. Impatient for this meeting to re-start, she passed her time by drawing his upper forehead lines. She felt he eyed her tracings but said nothing.

When he left, she slipped her notebook to Lani, assuming their new friendship was real. Lani wrote back. "Me? Who? Oh, him." Meta glowered.

Neva spotted the drawing and intruded. "I work for him. I don't follow him around."

Piqued without details, Meta felt over-confident and ambivalent.

Sketching again to remember details of her surroundings to orient herself in an altered psyche, Meta drew Lani's sleek rolled hair and recalled the Mala portrait to draw next, utilizing anxiety for energy versus Georg who did not write to her.

"Not me," said Lana. Losing the pose, Meta next passed the time by drawing Alain, who ignored her, and next Alex whose hazel eyes paralleled the sides of his mustache and sleeves rolled to his biceps. His dark blue tie curved over his chest, swelling at times in laughter. Suddenly, he announced, "Meta Cherushe go to this week's conference." She nodded at the order.

The woman at the front was training employees in administrative loyalty, method and know-how resumed their conference with ". . . Meet them where they are. Reach customers or patients in their crises over 'personal interest.'" Training trainers to train in Berlin, the trainer, copper bobbed and mentored by the desciple of the management specialist, crossed the floor, as she spoke. "They'll work to attain their dream with our purpose." This time management specialist, disciple of a famed one, drilled the staff.

Once grown used to life in Berlin, Meta figured she must find new work.

After two hours, this trainer recommended stretching. Alex stared at Meta's side bang caught on her eyelash, as someone sneezed. At eleven a.m., many appeared dazed. She heaved to breathe.

Dark-eyed and black-haired, this Armenian, professional in longish beige suit, asked the trainees to match her words. "Organization."

Someone replied, "Form." New management science efficiency experts now reigned. "Order." The Armenian-German asked, "Opposite?"

Alex said, "Chaos." Everyone laughed.

Meta breathed, as doors opened to fresh, cool air gusted into her nostrils, while two men talked about children and gazed down at the courtyard, a natural living room with oaks and bushes. Unlike others with shirts, ties and jackets, Artur unbuttoned his tan shirt in this hot fall, his blond waved hair must grow dense and darken near his belly button. She was uneasy very uneasy about Berlin. How could he not be?

"No kids. Not in Berlin. Maybe in the country. Would have them, if the economy improves, and I marry, not yet though. We're in the Health Ministry of Health, aren't we, for healthy babies, or none."

"Ah so." Peter said. "We're doing what the government expects."

"Some question this," said the third, a former soldier, not yet a father.

During rare trips to see Todi, Heinrich urged Meta to return to the farm. She confronted her need to flee with Todi to America.

Here and now though, Alex strolled out for air. She followed the air. He turned his head with Viking blond-reddish-dark and graying threads of hair. Neva asked. "Any at home?"

"No," he pushed the swinging doorway.

Julie said, "Call from Main."

Alex paused. "I'll follow up later."

"I defer to you," Julie squeezed Alex's arm. His flesh tautened around his eyes above his trimmed ruddy beard.

"You can't pass through that door." Neva's skirt pillowed over her backside for hard church pews. Backing away, Alex eyed Meta.

"Alex's staying," Meta whispered.

"Because he's dead," Neva replied.

Slip away, Meta told herself, from Neva's eerie, screech owl antennae.

Weeks later, their office group escaped to the arched courtyard. Before the seminary of memory, winter cold bonded them. For some hot lunch outside their health ministry child saving work, they dashed beneath the dome and along walls with portraits of modern forebears. Their fathers were not attached to the wall. Although hers was the gentleman in the middle distance next to his horse at that time in the upstairs hallway loggia, not downstairs, why so.

Toward the seminary dining room, co-workers scattered to pick up their vinegary potato salad, weisswursts and barley soup, only to reconnoiter a few minutes later over their meal. How long would their camaraderie hold up and their food supply to last?

"Let's hold services," Alain said at their long table. His opaque-blond hair matched his scalp, and his tongue must poke out his cheek.

"Find Protestant clergy." The gothic church block was located near a synagogue and Jewish Seminary, fenced in with joined high iron pokers for safety.

"No seminarians here. Two or three ex-soldiers," Meta noted, "for war. In our office, one's a cantor." Under her marine blue cloche, she tried sorting out words, coming as she did from her country solitude.

"Soldiers by the thousands in Berlin on the streets without home or food," the man on her right said, while voices ricocheted among banging food trays.

"You're the cantor," Alain said.

"I'm secular, high-voiced," someone said.

"You could be a castrato."

"Join their chorus, conduct it."

"Hymns I know. Does she?" Meta asked about the Quaker newcomer Ellen.

"She'll inspire us." Alain scratched his bald spot. All relished the barley soup with chicken and beets like their last supper before an oncoming famine. Affordable food was chancy these times, Meta agreed with Peter, ex-soldier and ex-novice. Met up with in their work nook, he obsessed over "wars people ignore." His Kassel in-laws visited battlefield memorials, where he, lo and behold, they'd met Heinrich.

On alternate days, Peter and Meta shared one office desk. Berlin real estate prices cramped work space. Leaving news clips and messages and not entering each others' drawers, they befriended one another. This weekend, he and his wife would see a friend's third son at Hamburg off to America. His friend, a pacifist, informed them about wars. As the latter's six children reached gymnasium age, year by year, one by one he relayed them to America, for quarantine.

Of the saints' days' calendar, Peter hung over their common desk, only St. Francis was familiar. Protestants knew scriptures, and Catholics relied on saints' days like horoscopes, though she lacked the heart to tell Peter about her wavering beliefs.

Omens, Tante Lore once warned her, render people too lazy to think; her brother Heinrich she emphasized, liked omens and gods.

Here at lunch, Neva was saying to Alain, "You hinted you were bi-sexual." Meta froze. He'd told her the office transvestite, Mathilde, frizzy-haired receptionist whose Pomeranian grand-mother had crocheted a fan stitch shawl for her, had just made him an Afghan.

The Quaker asked, "You know Julius's cousin's kindness?" "What? Julie's two-faced," Neva said.

"Alex checks my work," Alain said.

"Herr Schmidt," referring to Alex, Meta said, "said he's not my boss. If Mr.

Rosenberg isn't, the reason is he's returning to the gym-nasium for work as a teacher, and Mr. Schmidt isn't, so who is my boss?"

"Alex's a gentleman," Harry a mid-level administrator and rabbi said. "He finds what's needed for us and cares for his ill mother," reminding Meta of hers in America. The Quaker, Friend, agreed.

"Frederic's lover," Alain commented, "followed him to his French university and here." They covered for each other in their office. On a cabaret stage, they also mimicked their former boss in free time and clowned like poor women imi-tating the ex-Kaiser and ex-Kaiserin. So too, Alain imitated Mr. Bingelbein, the wheeler-dealer. At the weekend, half the staff had trooped off to watch these characters.

"No one listens to German tyrants go on about the Treaty of Versailles," Alain said.

"What?!" hooted someone. "Everybody does. It's a Set-up for another war?"

"Shush, we're in a seminary." Alain asked, "Where'll we be next year?"

Peter slipped away from their table.

"He's secretive." Words sallied among them en route back to work.

Meta sped before Neva so as not to botch chances with Alex. Despise him, she told herself, and pretend not to be a clerk or a friendly-visitor-in-training, for she was trying now read social pedagogy and psychoanalysis before scouting a university diploma to advance herself.

Back in their conference room, Alex's greeting conferees led her to wonder about his transfer in? Middle age softened his face, blue-eye above a stalwart chin, a well-beloved.

Two hours later, he entered where Meta stood in the doorway. Eye to eye, she asked, "In that conference room earlier, could you breathe?"

"That's why I left" were their first real words. Thereafter, folding in and out of their office maze, he crept up to her, height fluctuating by standing or leaning. Usually, she reached his chest.

"Where's Regina?" He the efficiency specialist whitened, recognizing few names yet. Wary, her new office mates gleaned he'd improve their output and root out extras for efficiency.

"No Regina yet." Nor did he know Alain or Neva, the Bohemian in the bureaucracy, for whom office conflict was her personal warship. Meta sidled back to her nook.

Regina, so petite she might be missed, was located, and this wavy dark-haired woman asked, "Who's Alex Schmidt? The attractive one who told Meta and her to push cases, without quite reading them for examiners. When he loomed to check their work, Meta stiffened aware of her brown nondescript dress with brass earrings on her ears beneath her red cloche. Worse than dull costuming because of no money or leisure for stores, her feet rested on another chair.

He objected to cases piled in their airless room and urged their move to his to breathe its open window air. For one month, in there she typed his words on their key campaign for unsuspecting postwar mothers, giving birth to extra babies. Without having discovered her own mother, Meta at 24 and Todi at twelve would find her, an unwed mother, rumored in America.

This man, bearded-calico over lantern chin, leaned above her. She looked sad. She hugged him, shocked herself at how unabashed she was. Or he hugged her, and the hug lasted hours.

Regina and Neva set work without her on the campaign and were miffed. Her dress white and black, they did tell her, was striking.

Unclasping, he gripped her hand in his large chamois hand, he led her down a back stairway to the Hotel Eden, where they danced, sipped May wine and rented a room. They went to dine at Josephine Baker's place in the former Pavilion Mascotte, where the hostess dressed in a silken blue cape dress to the knees, covered with white silk stockings dipped in gold slippers. Everyone tippled while Baker sang and danced. Never before had Meta seen a dark-skinned beauty, a woman, playing the saxophone, singing and dancing with her own orchestra. "Americanism," the club goers decried and loved. She tried to enclose herself in onyx skin, and imagined people staring at herself.

In the day's light, "Enough is too much. I'm leaving for the Wehrmacht." His spoke from blubber inside and solidity outside.

Her words seemed too out-of- date to speak. Besides it was her time to depart: no advancing here above her paltry salary and petty status.

"After I leave," he said, embracing her, "take my office." She shook herself, to rid herself of this experience.

25.

To America with Bildungreise, a learning journey, Meta day-dreamed of was devouring her. After all, her uncle-father had journeyed east; now she preferred to float west.

Before going, conscience demanded another trip from Berlin to the Lüneburger-Heide. Brooding about the Berlin attacks on her young cousin Hansi, Lore's nephew, preoccupied Meta. Witness: Berlin street battles for hours among groups: right against left, right against right: left against left, unarmed and armed. Leaders were assassinated in hot blood, President of the Republic, Rathenau, Jewish. All this haunted her without much understanding, and Todi's stay in Lower Saxony, moving faster into strife than elsewhere.

Returning to the big farm stirred her into a walkabout over its hectares with crotch houses. Their thatch roofs matched the grassy moor, Heide and some old Hanse towns. Women agricultural laborers newly wore dirndls and blousy, peasant tops puffing the by nationalized rural life renewal with old styles. Was there a festival going on?

Inner vaulting originated from the one tree houses she walked by and seen on their outer walls, beneath roofing meeting flattened roof points. Within them and beneath crossed horse heads, inward signifying family proprietorship, the crossbeam was incised, "All the best in the world comes from the plow."

I must get out of here, she thought. Down the road back home, she hugged and kissed an ever taller Todi, wrenching away from her womanishness, embarrassed about kisses, feeling like cows' wet noses.

As a child, when told to hug strange relative's good-bye, she shook hands.

"A general," Todi said, "visiting grandfather told me I could join the youth group, if I wanted to, to make one big greater world."

"What else?" The boy did not answer. He'd been tutored and attended a Volkschule by age six and now a Grammar school by age ten.

He was pursuing biology, horticulture, agriculture, drawing and mapping. His tutors, arranged for his future with his grandfather. Because of Heinrich's muscular flaccidity, he motivated his grandson's heavy lifting and planting in the rich loamy moraine with some agricultural laborers.

Ach, she must to stay here ongoing to supervise her son's studies and life.

She'd not separated from Todi, as her mother had from her, leaving her to her fascist uncle-father, planning to unify everyone. Thrilled with his grandson and heir, he opposed the boys' departure and hers. Knowing such, she must thus wrest Todi away, while the Ventriloquist, was spawning endless wooden dummies.

Grandfather and grandson might seal themselves off via Freicorps' practicing and Stalhelm working out. Or Todi might advance in self-worth.

Lost in half-thoughts, she was stuffing old lingerie and folding two fluffy dresses, one blue taffeta and green crepe for dancing into tissue silk garment bags from the forbidden room, even if romance was gone from her life. With stealth, she gained entry to her son's room. There she grabbed practical items, like knickers and undershirts to pack in her most to-go bags (others readied for long-term cheaper ship cargo) with Todi.

Besides hoping to slip Todi away from his grandfather, lately fading and whitening to reveal veins and arteries, pulsating like the Elbe and Weser, she yearned for others' approval of their passage and Nanna's and Lore's blessings that would encourage her to embark by ship on the great sea. Or swipe him and go?

The ghost of ambiguity and indecisiveness is shape shifting.

For her hoped for passage to a new land, her stored walnuts and hazelnuts, were packed in a ready-to-go bag, to eat anytime. Good old usable clothes meant stuffing unzipped slim skirts for hemming later, according to the rise and fall of hemlines, and shirt tops with embroidery into old, emptied footlockers. While she was hoping no one, especially Heinrich, would see her, she mooched seeds, jams and pickles from the old house cellar rather than from the Kaiser's lodge to tide her over during her escape to America.

Hopefully, Mrs. von Handler also would not catch on to her packing and inform Heinrich or Todi jumpy from noises. Nanna with lessening sight and hearing could still sniff out food or secret moves. But then, she'd boom out disapproval.

Win Lore over into helping her travel to the Bremen at Bremerhaven ship for America, occurred to her again, she must.

For now with Lore and Nanna in her small rose wallpapered sitting room, Meta's skin parched from expected their slamming the door against her, as she approached. Yet Nanna the elder asked, "Something's going on, isn't it?" She chuckled to convey all was really well.

Todi appeared at her door and looked Meta in the eye. "Why didn't you ask me, if you were taking my clothes to wear? I need them. You can't steal them."

Shaken, his mother asked, "What? Why not? If you go to visit her, you need clothes.

"Didn't I tell you?" Lore asked, "About those brazen Neanderthal youths hereabouts Nanna guessed at? They're back to gangs' lives, like those attacking Liesl's boys? You must prepare for every gangster, even ones close a hand."

For backdrop after his doctorate, Lore's daughter's Liesl's husband, the chemist, Lore regaled in their little huddle, pursued germs and poisonous flowers for a living before death. In depressed times, he'd lost his university posts though bettered himself in clinical research as a Kruss manager for the industrial chemical giant Kruss. From his research, he wrote many research papers. Lore recalled that he'd advanced so far as to be able to do away with the reality of want.

By adding a poisonous tincture to mocha cake, for example, he eliminated it, upon demonstrating the feat to his son. Hansi, then a preschooler, cried over his lost birthday cake.

Chemistry was magic. "The darling boy," who'd been taught strengthening through early calisthenics, wanted his mocha back. When his father could not restore it, Hansi began whinging. His father finally walked him to the bakery for a new birthday cake.

Many weeks later, in fact months, after his papa abruptly died, Hansi believed his father had dissolved himself. In time though, the child also believed, his father would reappear. Todi, listening to grown-ups, said, "No, he won't. My father didn't. My own mother believed she would bring my father here. She did."

"You know about," Lore tried continuing, "his war injuries?" Meta hadn't known about her uncle's injuries in the Great War 1914-1918. "My husband suffered," Lore said, "maybe your Georg and my son-in-law suffer from wounds and were 'shell-shocked.'

"So doctors say that some recover, don't they?" asked Nanna.

"We were also living too fast, back then, remember, from within some economic recovery in 1923-24. My receipts tell me so. "With the downturn, the party's consolidated; Heinrich gloats, over its jumping onto us." Aunt Lore had not bothered to mend a run in her finely knit dark blue dress.

She was gloomy, Meta was gloomy.

"Liesl's rarely home. Her boys will be all right in Berlin, won't they?" Meta and Nanna nodded to Lore's words and in time to the Bach record Meta had placed on the Victrola.

"After my son-in-law's death," Lore murmured, "another grandson was born." She paused, suddenly attuned to a factor not thought of before. . . . Liesl tried hanging on to their home. "But her partial widow's benefit, you see, necessitated moving to a run-down neighborhood, near Wedding of all places, until she found work."

Within this family static, anxiety surged in Meta toward her getaway by stowaway plan to America. Erect, Todi stood listening. Also, if understanding her aunt's words, Mopsi the busybody little old pug, stared at her through his bubble eyes with beginning cataracts. Todi did the same and hid from her with in himself. "I'm staying here," determined to stay on the farm.

She'd deal with him later and return for now to Berlin.

Lore asked, "Visit Liesl, please, and her boys in Berlin, and write me about them?"

"But how? Meta whispered back to Lore. "I'm not their father or grandmother who can push them back."

"You push them, and I will go after Heinrich to let go of Todi for his passage to America."

"I will, if you get me to a ship at Bremerhaven to America to see your sister."

"We'll see. But you can't leave your son. I'd forbid you to, if I had any authority over you. Wait and see. He'll disappear."

Almost instantly, Meta began trying to assemble her required emigration documents: birth certificate, marriage certificate if she'd had one to enable her getting a police certificate and the Affidavit of Support from Lore's sister. This sister deemed Meta's other aunt, had been met as a child. Why had little Meta not been more hospitable to her when bringing Heinrich kerchiefs or cowboy hat to impress him on her knowledge about America and hard work. Meta sighed over needing "a financial worth statement" to emigrate.

Did she possess money enough to avoid becoming a public charge? Would her aunt in America support her? Not belonging in the refugee category with signs from the persecutor stalling her packing, she asked, what if she, the applicant, could not own up to on an official formal demands. Could she go as a childless widow? She'd never received a dowry from Heinrich for Harald, so far as she knew.

Her papers were supplied in duplicate, in case the government lost papers. Apply she would from the farm to qualify for the "skilled agriculturalist" category.

She must do a quadruple set with the double for Todi.

He wondered up into her rooms one day, as she sorted and double checked both sets of papers. "You're going with me to a new life in America. I'm applying."

The boy stood breathing

Steal away she must, especially if Heinrich intercepted her forms and gave them to someone else? More importantly, she was contending with Heinrich over Todi, both happy enough within their present arrangement. Could German-Saxonists capture her boy child for his army future?

Here was her life breath embodied as an infant cradled and much cuddled and now boy growing so fast she could hardly measure him.

Herr Paul Fleischer, the smart young man Grete urged her onto, who'd tried to befriend her in their church from childhood on might know how to expedite a permit to leave one country and a visa to enter the other, America within its quota. But someone else could have precedence, because of its 1924 law restricting emigration into America.

Grete, again contacted, informed her she was unable go to her school for her Abitur. "So let's go to America." They could dance away on shipboard.

Two days later in the here and now, Meta set off back to work and visit her cousin in Wedding, a Red working class part of Berlin with small factories, where conflict was rife. Everybody knew it was so. Why did Liesl go there to work? "Lie" in the Norwegian way of her name that many used, could wait at her flat, Meta surmised. Lie's boys would return there from school. But Lie preferred she and Meta meet in her manager's office.

To get there, which side of the paved boulevard islands should she stand to jump onto the streetcar or be lost? Finally, she reached the correct trolley stop.

Not far down the street, for the National Socialist Workers Party, NSDAP, with swastikas, SPD, Social Democratic Party and KPD, Communist Party with hammer and S rippled in the breeze and whipped in the wind. These hammers, axes and scythes cut the air, to close in on opposites.

There stood a small window paned factory, seven stories dark-bricked and fortified around its courtyard, where she centered herself on lookout below where Liesl worked as a secretary within a constant thump and metallic clank.

Soldering crackled to prevent anyone from yelling up to her. Drills screeched with sparks, like fireflies, iron bits to magnets from welding by masked workmen.

Why Liesl descended from the factory above was mysterious. Upstairs in its office, this white-silked-bloused tall woman reigned, as others glanced up to offer her bits of glory. Liesl introduced co-workers and managers to Meta, until one bald-headed and dark hair-winged shook Meta's hand, though his eyes tubed unto Liesl's. For Meta, Lie puffed up to sense good fortune. After dictating his letter to Lie to type, she could leave. "But could you wait for me to finish this desk work? Or go and come back," said Lie.

Meta could leave for the Adlon or Bristol, whichever, and try not to lose her way back in the dark.

Whether they were a couple, his right hand wedding ring brushed Lie's shoulder; her finger bore the band of a widow. As she worked, he removed a shiny hair strand from her cheek. Lovers? Her husband had died nine months earlier. Was her manager a family man? He fetched water for them. After Lie snapped her purse shut, she received a sly kiss from him.

Smiles from his minx, this stocky man, Sebastian, with a dark wavy hairline retreating from laughter in his eyes, contrasted with her deceased husband, serious and ascetic.

Who knew the future from the present? Color high, Lie was enraptured, prospecting for happiness. Who could blame this widow, ten years Meta's senior, neither friend nor confidante, like her mother, Lore?

Lie helped lug her leather bag back down three flights to the courtyard and waved to her manager friend. Naked together, Lie with her light blonde hair might not mind that he also inserted himself in his wife, or others. When asked, Lie flushed and winked.

Arm in arm, Lie led Meta to tea. "Tomorrow evening, we'll go out with Sebastian and his friends." In from the countryside with her urbane cousin out with a male for the evening, was exciting to her as if she'd never before stayed or lived in Berlin.

Next day, Lie pointed Meta toward the school, before returning to work. As if not working, Meta waited for Hansi and Erik to report on them to Aunt Lore. Erect, Meta crossed the schoolyard. Unlike her Todi, though like poorer schoolboys, they wore hand-me-downs, tight or big. Fear of the known arrived subliminally before awareness.

Two bigger shaggy haired louts hovered near her little cousins. They socked and, then, kicked Hansi. The tallest pretended to Max Shelling fists, swinging and slugging, sliced the air with hollow gusts bashing Hansi and Erik. Meta gasped and raced with tall Hansi to the gate, when little Erik lost his shoe. With their snotty hankies, she daubed his blood. She screamed at thugs, "Headless monsters."

"We're many," an onlooker said. "Many of us, ninny. You don't belong here, and won't find us again. We'll return all together." On his collar, Meta spotted the tiny hooked cross button.

Off to the bus, Hansi found one boy's shoe and heaved it over a fence into a ditch. "Be careful!" Meta said, "He'll pursue us."

Larking in Wedding in northeast Berlin was risky, unlike the countryside. Lie's boys must be vigilant and rip off to home to skirt trouble. She could hardly safeguard them.

26.

Six weeks later, back in the land of low slung thatched houses crouching on the land, she reported on Lie's happiness and safety in Berlin without the part about her unlikely return to farm, Luneberg, Celle or Bremen. With her aunt's advancing years, Nanna's deteriorating health, the family net and lines were thinning into a cobweb. Meta reassured Lore the boys were safe.

Friendship's mesh was also loosening. Grete's father dropped her off without seeing Heinrich. The latter though launched a low key commentary grow into a tirade. "Take her around the grounds. Not inside."

"If she cannot be inside," Meta said, "I'll leave forever with Todi." Hearing declining, Heinrich left Meta and Grete alone for the time being.

In the meantime, Todi went off to hear the speakers, who were trekking or biking throughout Lower Saxon countryside. Such as she knew, Nanna huffed about these gathering, engulfing, encompassing crowds, including the Freicorps and those younger. "They do not belong her. Wandering speakers were founding study groups. Heinrich had developed one for a long time. Nanna said, "Those folks aren't us, don't you know. They come up from the south."

"Came from the south?" Meta bit her lip and asked Grete, "How are you?"

"My father refuses to leave me alone," Grete said, "or allow me to see my boy friend. Says I'm too young to be alone with him. The truth is I no longer warm toward my father. He threatens me. If he catches me going dancing in my little feathery dress to the pavilion or halls you and I danced in, he will act. Erik's picking me up tomorrow for one in Berlin near my mother's salon. She's too busy to notice. Now, thank heavens, I'm working for my mother in Berlin," Grete continued, "behind the scenes, designing, ironing just so and hoping she doesn't send me back to my father. She threatens me: my father's household in a small city is dangerous.

"See, I can't go into your father's house either! He won't let you let me. I can't go to my father's house. He says, "Berlin's too dangerous." Because my mother is Jewish, I can't go anywhere.

"How can I go to America?

"Remember how life used to be. We chased butterflies. We danced with joy

"Now we collect boys to rescue us." Meta laughed. Grete did not.

"The last time," she said, "my boy friend took me to a dance hall, my good father slapped me so many times I thought I had welts, and he yelled. 'Nazis go to your dance halls. You go there for thrills and danger.'

"Good God, we all do. But I go there mostly to learn new dance steps."

"We'll leave together for America." Meta vowed. "We will!"

Grete choked. "Only my aunt backs me, not the screwy one you met, but the other one who says we must scram. She packs money into her bra cups, belly and thighs and slips away to Switzerland to her bank account. Then she whispers to us to do the same.

"No one bothers to listen to her. Others think she's becoming as crazy as the first aunt."

Next, in small print, Grete wrote out her aunt's views on a small pad of paper print. Suddenly, Grete ripped off the note. "What if someone finds this?"

"I'll burn the paper."

"Keep it, read it to learn by heart. But what if someone hears us!?"

"We should talk only in a noisy beer garden. Never mind, nothing will happen to us. Nobody believes anything will happen." Meta patted Grete's upper arm.

Only Grete knew her secrets. Hints of others as enemy—however probed—were disturbing like scars from feuds with Heinrich over her departed mother and skittishness about Georg.

Grete's worries jabbed Meta, little understanding what was happening. Still, they chatted for two hours on the porch, where the breezes carried their words away.

"Take me." Grete again begged. "Take me. I can't and won't return here ever again."

On his way back, her father picked her up to pack her off to Berlin for safety, away from this local epidemic of sluttishness and paramilitary acts with street fights.

27.

From her bed-sitter, a dollhouse sized studio, Meta rode the trolley it stopped at the underground S-Bahn stop, where she hopped off tipsy on her pointy toes and heels to dash into the circus underpass to the transport system, the pride of Berliners. She was determined the train would keep going and wind up in America.

On the tube, women, sat in their slim biased skirts on bench seats like one long ruffle. She'd propped herself next to a window, when a passenger sat next to her and jammed her elbows into Meta's ribs, "Every morning I've ridden in this very seat, until you sat down in it."

"Get help." The woman streamed out at the next stop.

Overhead cigarette ads enticed riders to smoke with the big Camel. Beer ads drew in ale drinkers: St. Pauli Madchen girl folk, low-necked and puffed cleavage above cinched vests and dirndle, and pretty girl Odol Mundwasser swim-suited or gowned would please Heinrich.

Up on the sidewalk, women in shifts, crisscrossed in satin ribbons, dressy crepe, or light mauve or beige muslin tiers moved en masse. These newly salaried women lubricated the chains of command and brightened new Bauhaus-like offices, as men in suits and ties pushed ahead to their offices.

Blocks away, men gathered on street corners, and workless ones massed for soup ladled out to an unbroken line of men. Fights broke out and spread. Sometimes they fell like strings of beads snapping apart. Taken aback by crowds, Meta sought to govern herself. Stand tall. Ignore catcalls and wolf whistles and striking limbs. Stay in your own tube. Don't tarry. Read the Sermon on the Mount to show sinfulness or the way forward against the worst deaths. God was speaking only fitfully.

The church obeyed state authority, stated in sermons. To improve her mind, she read newspapers business listings. Headlines differed from party newspaper to party newspaper, rivaling the NASDAQ Ventriloquist vs. the Social Democrats Party. She opposed the upstart as a loser with tar pit hair. No one she knew talked about him or politics out loud. No one much warned anyone else or even seemed to notice

In any warning, human denial lead to the human certainty of death.

Her Arbitur and some teaching credentials enabled new post, thanks to Lie and "her boss." Earlier, at the job advice center, her Gestalt tests, know-how and aptitude tests were reported as high. The graphologist's findings were withheld. Evidently, she was stable enough and neat enough to be seen like the vamp, Lie told her, unable to win a job. A lower manager though studied her head to foot and passed her on for hire. Thereupon, she sat so long in the high chief's office that her crepe everyday dress got worn down into tissue.

In time, she was offered further training, though her veterinary half-practice with horticultural arts was useless in this salaried workaday world, remote from gardening and farming.

Instead, she learned punch card efficiency: recordkeeping, bookkeeping and shorthand, resembling Arabic or Hindi in Heinrich's philology books little served her office work.

Berlin was a foreign country though freer than in the countryside, where her aching heart stayed on. Her city status could not fill its void. Mobility up was impossible. Going down expressed female work, a growing few labored in offices. Most females were streetwalkers.

Smooth skin and finger waved hair above her dresses with artful top-stitching on her satin attire to attend opera houses. Moiré-like sweaters offered warmth in late summer or early fall evenings. Concerts by chamber music artists allowed escape. Jazz was alive, moody sad, spirited and laughing. Xylophones or marimbas pitched out their joy and razzmatazz.

Straining to hold on to her job, while looking for another, Meta's restlessness ballooned up. Urban air possessed its elixir of chance.

His craftiness screened acts and words in the office, though buoyancy here included who lunched with whom, who walked out on his wife for his mistress? In the quietest of all: Who was slyly political with a swastika on the lining of his jacket? His office workers talked through curtains, screens and mirrors.

Man-about-town, or a Mirki Loki, trickster, Bernie Bingelbein, the office manager marked her up and down profile as satisfying. Let his friend, an Ulstein photographer or one with Associated Press, "Do head shots" for you to show to UFA film directors."

Meta knew only one UFA building, dark brick walled and flat pitched roofed cinema theater. People noticed her, he said. Hopefully, he expected only photographs from her.

For the Adlon Hotel studio headshots, her hair sun was streaked gold and curled with a hot iron, though she burned her crown red the first time she practiced for the shots.

The woman photographer waved her to sit under lights and tilted reflectors. "The Ada," as her assistant referred to her, "examines photos here." She ignored him and ordered Meta to sit. "Head down, stand, muss your hair, tousle your dress, straighten herself out, muss up. Hope for cinema stardom?" asked Ada. Meta recognized her as the self-confident photographer at Trixi's landing near the landing.

"Not exactly." Meta, cautious, knew not what to ask for.

"Everyone dreams," said Ada. Everything happens in Berlin. Connect with people. Evidently, I do. Of course, my sister's a photographer who helped me obtain a post with Heinzmann. You'll learn?"

Why comment, Meta recalled the Armenian-German trainer had emphasized objectivity, Sachleichkeit toward other persons, not self-disclosure or frankness toward others, like a nobody like herself. Besides, Ada seemed ready to pop off to an event with her dusty rose dress a flaring around her knees (no street dresses too short nowadays) and bonnet-cloche. Meta flinched within her own inadequacy; she'd never worn such an outfit. But try on new outfits.

All business in manner, never mind style, this slim elfin woman gusted and evidently teased Meta about her allure to goad her into returning. In mauve felt cloche, Ada slouched and put down her light camera, she rearranged the silvery umbrellas and light reflectors and darted back to her large format camera on wheels.

Without name dropping, sly reminders of renowned portraits spiked newspapers. Her photos were shot from her Leica, Hasselblad and Graphex with floodlights and flashes for

Heinz," as if the cameras acted on their own. "Do you have an older brother or sister," Ada wondered.

This favored photographer and family struck Meta's ganglia much later. She was anxious to be on her way.

To pay, Meta pawed her bag to pay the chic wavy-haired photographer. "I need to get on my way to work. I'm here with you only because my assistants are lunching and Bingelbein was urging me to shoot you.

"I told you so. Come back for your photographs and pay in advance for more shots. Happiness is paying bills on time and doing creative work. Find yours."

On her way out, the photographs stared out at Meta from their drying screens, display racks or from hanging lines, Before leaving studio premises, she surmised Ada's dark room assistant was touching up portraits' languid eyes, filling sunken cheeks, covering moles or flaws, such as, over-exposure to light and heightening contrast with photographic chemicals, before official use. One stern face with microscopic eyes and official military hat stared out with another bull-shouldered, squinty eyed man, semi-secretive.

Downstairs en route through another door outside the Bristol, Meta shook herself off and shimmied one step before another. Everyday these photos like hers upstairs or hers stared at the public from newsprint, hawked on her street on her way to work. They bore names Meta barely knew, but Ada did: Goering, Goebbels, Heyrich . . . . von Schirach known for his vast youth groups, including one her Todi might belong to.

Off down the street she walked to eat her creamed dried beef on toast for lunch in a diner. From the chair she sat in, she could see the soup kitchen lineup.

Inside herself she flagellated herself. Her Kultur Klub would have danced on the boulevards, oblivious to sightings of transvestites, prostitutes and drunks, familiar to her in her twenties.

No names existed for denatured people with bullying shoulders and telescopic eyes above mouths haranguing rallies. Someday, science would pump up knowledge, Bildung, self-cultivation with originality and expressiveness, from roving outside one's community, according to reading in depth and breadth, and seeing.

In parkland, birches had clasped the ground from medieval times; silver was mined in the Harz Mountains enriching Barbarossa and Berlin. Gloating, this city prized its status, rivaling Paris, Rome and New York. The whitened bark of birches spaced their branch marks, spiraling around trunks. Marks from fallen branches stamped their eyes.

Nearby, the prossies, most prostituting of women and men arranged working the street in cahoots with pimps. Read the city: porn city society, unlike rural life cleanliness family most women preferred the government's law the Smut and Port Act. She'd heard of it, hardly read about it and tested herself against tarts with necklines plunging to their outer frizzy vagina.

By contrast, Meta thought herself prim in a flared blocky print skirt below a billowy shirtwaist and hair rolled over a rat of hair around her head in a new style pseudo hat of hair. Suddenly, at a narrow angle outward, sparks pivoted and, a man shouted. Others watched. Must be the rowdy area or a red light district, where women came out at night and people. "Butch, no, no." The pimp was throwing her into oncoming traffic.

At the moment, men thrived on porn and women on romance with little or nothing between.

Into the store to beg for a call police came a couple with trim hair. Behind the counter stood a clerk blank-faced with the phone off the hook. He refused to call the Polizei about the bully.

"Coppers are around." Someone complained. "When you don't need them, they're here, and disappear when you do. For police, news sellers or prossies?"

Someone grabbed Meta and pulled her back. She yanked back.

The proprietor was impassive to gawkers. "Streetwalkers here day after day."

Feeling glass-protected, Meta strolled into the beloved parkland birches, where silver and green leaves danced above old Freicorps, Stahlhelm and odd surviving elements added to and sunned in the park hurly-burly. As if she could not feel what she saw, others existed in a diorama panorama of the park. From nature lovers hiking, bathing and singing like the turn-of the-century Wandervogel, wandering birds, now political youth groups, gathered here under trees as well as in far mountains of the country. They flew, split and metamorphosed through The Ventriloquist, throwing his voice through young and younger ventriloquists. These wooden dummies joined the old tin soldiers, World War I vets within the Volk.

Most pedestrians rushed into their personal destinies. Time flew. Big public clock hands turned like knives to slice people off, if late.

A small statue came to mind for all seers: Jesus to doubting Thomas: if you cannot believe, put your fingers in my wound.

Enlarging swastikas ever marched on the outer city streets and military men in quarry-colored uniforms jumped off the barge-like trucks at any point to demonstrate. Some removed guns, swords or daggers, filed steel buckteeth or already carried them.

Days later, the newspaper headlines screamed. The gun toting men won their very first election in Germany Meta's home Lander, Neidersachsen. Heinrich must be elated.

Her stomach dropped at the armbands, stamped in black on the universal red sun sign, the swastika, emboldened the masses into a high. And so many public guns. Their celebratory mood prevailed.

"Left. RIGHT!" Banners with swastikas were hooked inside and onto fences with metal teeth. For group maneuvers, their armbands with black whirling blades menaced and began swinging to drum beats. Torsos aligned themselves and arms saluted. Roused to act, they slugged it out with those with red flags, until captured.

28.

After one year, she returned to the farm and wait. Her little old black Mopsi barked with joy, stood on hind legs, hugged her leg, and welcomed her with three staccato barks. After him, came Todi from marketing with his grandfather Heinrich in his old Daimler. She hugged the boy. For once, he hugged back. Heinrich said, "I thought you'd gone for good."

Other than this greeting, her family truths unknowable were still buried in hill graves and under recent markers. Truths could resurface like people on the ancient low flat rock seats in a semi-circular theatre for debate and talk, some scratchy rough and others more polished.

Trips to town were getaways from talking or more likely perpetual farming, canning, pickling or goading others to work, a release from the unreal lodge of the former king or from Berlin's speed.

Peddling her bicycle here allowed reflecting on rural activities, like making soap with Nanna's favored methods Heinrich propounded. Homemade soap signified the Volk, more than the store bought kind. By watching the process, Metod und Mesur, she'd learned the homemade way: combine two cans size nine and a half to ten and a half of lye with cold water. Strain the fat. Cool it to the correct warm temperature. Pour the lye mixture into a stone crock, and stir until honey-like consistency to pour onto a paper and wet cloth lined box.

By accident, her two thumbs pressed from its barrel rim into the liquid soap. She squealed, as the lye stung under her fingernails no matter how much washed and rubbed.

Tending bees and collecting honey was sweeter than soap making, though both endangered the soap maker as beekeeper. A bee sting's pain did absorb fears of great dangers. Not so the lye.

Back inside, she raved within herself, slumped on a lounge chair, prayed and slept. Got up, did chores, sat down. Smoked a Camel.

Longing for succor, love, comfort, as she was, she studied her dirty, semi-stinging fingernails. She helped busy Todi with his chicks, rabbits and schoolwork, and tutors, whenever available for history and citizenship. Showing most promise in botany for his future Arbitur and university degree studies, Todi was gleeful with potted seedlings and measured their growth.

Notes she scribbled notes for seed packets of Targetes, orange and yellow, stashed with others for America. Flowers like Wicke needed planting there a year before flowering and Ringelblum for improving its blooms with time.

The growing season meant hoeing and spading the soil before dusk lowered under the moonlight like a cameo. Night insects buzzed until the morning tune-up of the birdsongs.

A mound of earth stood for morning garden layering and re-molding. Stomping her boots free of dirt and animal matter, she greeted a vehicle driving up with bundled hay and seeds. Ol' Christoph's mutt snarled.

Girded for months to go the local tax office on behalf of Heinrich, she was lifted off from ordinary urban work during the growing season. Trees were budding. Low buildings earthen bricked like huge wide-angled tents were dreaming back toward Eurasia's infinity.

Great ancient bonfires of May announced spring. Instead of her usual natural self, she wished to doll up with color. Again, she realized she preferred urban work.

Now though, she parked her bicycle and climbed the stairs to the tax office, where she the long winding line requiring hours to wait to haggle with the tax clerks. The tax bill's accuracy roiled Heinrich and overwhelmed her. Her irate reacting within herself burst in inexpressible anger, so much so that she might bludgeon someone. Other farmers, like her, paced between two legs back and forth beneath the wooden rafters. No one familiar or unfamiliar chatted on the waiting line, only seethed.

Abruptly, the fireball envelopes them. Ten thousand fusees whoosh over them. The extreme bright rolling flame encompasses them. Plaster walls crumble into dust. The firebomb results in screeching, coughing and gagging.

Handkerchief covering her mouth, she groped toward exits, down two flights. Fearing a hole to fall through, must she stay put? She lowered her head to protect her eyesight clogged by smoke rising in the stairwell. White shirts and work clothes, barely noticed earlier, were bloodied and torn.

Her hair was singed, crisped or broken, when touched. Caught on a wire, her skirt ripped and revealed gashed red legs.

A siren cart, battery charged, swung up. White-coated men jumped out and pulled out stretchers for the dead or wounded. Her eyes teared at the carnage. What to do? One man bothered to ask, "You all right?"

After the bombing, her head throbbed. A crown of thorns, lopsided, rotated inside her brain, Go or stay?

"Wall of bricks blew out," someone boasted, as a survivor to newcomers outside. A newcomer was cheering himself as if one. Holes, where rods pronged through brick or blocks for stability, were exposed and bent in the crush. The bomb had split two walls, like crimson Saxafraga.

Someone's lost jacket was hanging through rough, broken bricks.

"Those guys better rush victims to the hospital, or they'll die," an observer claimed. "I was in munitions in the war. That bomb was meant to kill."

In the chaos, Meta lost her right shoe and hobbled around the building with its buckling wall to look for it, as random words rattled. "Looks bombed. It's happened in the Geest too. Holstein."

"Good thing the bricks aren't wood that burns in fire-bombing. Brick just melts."

"Russians tricked us," someone said, "into fighting tax authorities."

"Your eyelashes burned," someone noticed. She rubbed her eyes. One lay on her forefinger.

"What're you doing here?" Patting her back was big taking-care-of-children Karl, more solicitous than his wife, nowhere to be seen. She daubed a tear away. "What should I do?"

"Go home."

Where's that? Where's my bicycle?

Paul appeared. His height surpassed the crowd's. "Can I walk you home?" Vaguely too, the Heinrich belligerence would come out, if she allowed him to. She couldn't think why. His father negated Heinrich somehow.

"Oh, well, I'd better go on my own." Otherwise there'd be no leeway, no forgiveness. "My father will scout for me on the way and catch on."

"Walk with me part of the way. If he comes along, I'll duck out into the woods."

Others were biking or walking up toward survey the bombed tax office mess. The crowd still lumbered around the half-fallen building. An authority urged leaving, in case the three remaining walls fell.

Individuals crowed about hows and whys of this bombing in their community. People feared and relished catastrophes.

29.

Reaching the house on foot, Meta expected some approval for paying the taxes. Alas, before the blast, the payment was never registered, unless the money belts and bags of money survived with records. Free money from tenants was allocated for plantings, new bricks and some farfetched new car. All right, she'd fix the finances of the family, she'd leave for good.

Scratching her drying leg drew new blood that dribbled and stained her skirt. To remind her of this day, she kept it. "Don't waste a drop we can donate." Her Aunt Lore clucked over Meta and dabbed her bloody leg and sweaty forehead.

"Who came up with you to the gate? Heinrich asked. "I saw the shadow. Someone familiar."

"Someone from the crowd saw me limping."

"You must know him."

"Sundays only."

"Worse, someone from Church?"

"You should know him."

"By sight."

"Who?"

Grete's father. She lied. He'd favor him over Paul.

"Ignore Heinrich. You'll feel better," Aunt Lore said, "fox-trotting at the pavilion. Forget the accident."

In the long mirror, Meta saw her bloodied and black-and-blue face, like the dark half of the moon, the western hemisphere. "I'm wiped out. My head's split. Go without me." Dazed, she swallowed two aspirins Heinrich managed to find, in spite of shortages. He patted her right shoulder.

"Where's Todi, number one?" She asked. Owly bastard Heinrich.

"With Johanna. See him in the morning."

"He's not to be with her. He's supposed to be with me. Number two, where's my mother?"

"What? We, an old family, care for you, feed you, shelter and comfort you. You need her not at all. She gave you up."

"I'll find her." Meta's head throbbed. Nothing more could harm her. Mortared, brick walls could collapse and a firebomb explode. She was on her way.

"Go west," Lore whispered.

Still thinking of Karl or Paul or anyone who could have brought her home, Meta was downcast. She belonged to a ghostly enemy, the once powerful or powerless. Karl was no help, certainly not Georg, and definitely not Heinrich. Only Paul who was barely known. Meta the loner sagged on the couch and slept.

In due time, when she awakened, the bunch would to see her off. What choice had she but to go? Heinrich, Nanna even hobbled around her, *Todi* with his five pence and Christoph visited to hear about this bombing event. Would they be relieved at her planning to go? Could she oppose the gloomy or ghostly powers-to-be? She was so weak.

Surprisingly, Mrs. von Handler and Grete occupied her during convalescence. Most came visiting, reviving this custom these days. Grete paled next to Mrs. von Handler with rouge, lipstick and mascara. Meta worried about Grete. Where was

Heinrich? Because of the area cattle sale, her father dropped Grete off. "Put me in your trunk, won't you?"

Katia wrote to confide her departure for America.

Tante Lore rode over several times from Celle and wept to see Meta, head and legs bandaged. She was no longer hiding her departure. When she could stand, she packed. Surprisingly, other farther off neighbors materialized to talk about Meta's survival.

Delighted to entertain them, Heinrich the Saxonist held forth. On warm days, from his canvas brown armchair in the porch-like room with windows, screened and opened to the heat and breeze, he rasped on. "Who came up this far North, except Eskimos, Norse, Lapps and us along the Ice Cap trail? World Trees at Merseberg, Verdon and Geismar survived. "We kept our straw hats on through it all. In spite of such attacks, the Saxons never became a mixed race."

"How would you know?" Meta covered her ears though still heard. Lore sighed and laughed.

He droned on. "You belong to a long struggle, Meta. Now we fight Leftists and Jews to the death."

Meta closed her eyes. Did Grete, coming from the water closet, hear him? Lore said, "You've said as much."

Meta piped up. "Don't forget St. Walpurga," the female saint who converted the Saxons. Meta and her aunt suppressed giggles. The latter said, "The saint opposed the pagans. Some must have viewed her like a pagan."

Georg was heading north toward the Baltic Sea, near where they'd driven not long ago. His Saxon Heimat, his Balticom, Lore's summer onshore playground, farm battle scene, where people, Heinrich noted, were the most nationalistic, the Stamme. Meta shivered like her Mopsi.

Spring chilled upon his return, Geog less attached to her said, "Now's my last chance for a high career." Beneath his raincoat, in his uniform with runes, two lightening strikes, he kissed her goodbye. "Right behavior serves the Volk." He kissed her again.

"You're going for good this time?"

"To Dachau for training. . . ."

Feeling as through her Mopsi's wrinkled brow, slanting indented, and eyes popping soulful, she scouted going far west. Leaving her elderly white bearded black dog and young son could break her heart. Tears dribbled. On this day, Todi cried over Georg's leaving. "Be Strong," she said to him. Todi seemed to tear at him with his young hands.

Practically, she aimed for Bremen. Work in Berlin prepared her for New York. Reportedly, Katia was staying longer in Berlin at the Technical University. She'd met Ada, cocky and aloof granddaughter of the famed composer Brahms. Grete knows her, Katia wrote, Meta must knew her. She did.

As for Todi, Georg and Heinrich engrossed themselves in the Fatherland and hooked cross, not fatherhood.

An inner arrow spiked her in endless self-reprisal, guilt and shame. She squirmed to deaden prickliness erupting in her. She also dithered.

The authorities had released the Great Ventriloquist from prison in 1924. Yet no one listened to Meta spoke about him or Berlin. He'd passed by in a swanky white Buick car snaking throughout their region on the road to Hamburg. What to say? No one she knew talk about him, except Heinrich, so busy were they all planting seeds for winter meals before hard times, Lore warned about, ransacked their lives.

No one of course knows what would happen, but some few people guess. The one who could throw his voice through anyone else's or any groups popped up here and there. Quivers threw darts containing hints, and silences floated everywhere.

Had the cemetery forebears arisen? Cursed awake from her nap on the sagging leathery dark-brown porch couch, she stood up. Then, sundown exploded on the horizon like a massive plane whose wings spread across the horizon. Pieces of sunlight glowed from a vase here, windowpanes there, a polished leaf, a tile inlaid in the fireplace.

In this the sad time of day, suited to preparing soil, she chopped it for seedlings anyway. Heinrich was pressing her for more food in case of attacks and war.

From his monthly bath given black Mopsi with Todi, the dog when dried off shone in the sunset, as he nibbled the edge of the wooded compost, decayed matter, delightedly snorting.

"Lost in thought?" Christoph asked, "Your maternal grandfather on your mother's side. . ." Blip, he clamped down and walked on.

She begged. "Go on." Both had mocked family secrecy, in the past, half-joking when he removed fish and fowl scales, feathers and insides outside on his cleaning board within the elm tree V branches. The bent man now crossed the horizon and waved to her. She signaled to him. He threw himself over the fence, now swifter than Heinrich.

"Christoph, who left for America? Plaggan lead to my great-grandfather leaving for America?"

"Forget it, nothing." She refused to back down. Doffing his squashed brown hat, Christoph squinted. "You're old enough."

With vast forests cut down resulted in Plaggan, no more needing foresters. Prussia swallowed the Saxonies. Heinrich had reviled the battle won though lost, when everyone in Lower Saxony, North Germany became Prussian.

One forebear who'd worked for the deposed king as chief forester joined a 450 person emigrant group to the New World. Heinrich though would have meant to have kept Meta here.

The squint of his eyes told her so.

After her brief sojourn in the forest remainder, she smelled the cooking and saw many who visited Heinrich, one man in particular was outlined against the sunset, burnishing in brass in a peculiar yellow light. In full regalia, Georg stood in formal, official dress; the hooked cross on his armband jarred her. Ought she to bow, curtsey in a Knex? Salute, yes, like another soldier or agricultural laborer.

"Georg, you're leaving for good?" She held her breath.

He nodded. "Do not to expect me for a while. I am going north."

"You're always going north. Where else would you go?" She never dared ask her full enquiries, such as, whatever happened to Mala.

Georg embraced her. He's gone. She thought, I'll never see him again, I too am going. West. He will die going. East.

Through blown medieval amber bubble panels next to the main door, she gazed at his retreating down the road to his lorry. Sadness covered her, like a big old dark umbrella tent, open but sinking within her own inhaling without escape. His aftershave smell lingered. To sit in the sun within summer fragrance and sip May wine with him would not soon happen again.

30.

Ocean travel daunted Meta, as she gripped the railing of the boat and set off on the darkening river Weser onto the sea, kilometers from home. She transferred at last to the Nord Deutscher Lloyd ship launched from Bremerhaven.

She dreaded U-boats blowing up the ship. Childhood memories selected her like gulls around the ship pulling on her with invisible strings to and fro.

No one listened, not even the gulls. Nor did anyone seek to oppose her voyaging, from the Old World to the New. No one believed her leaving on the ship of fate.

Below the gigantic landing pier, built in staged platforms, connected by stairs, from which passengers were setting off for the ship. If U-boats preyed on them, she could little prevent its sinking. "Aha, there's the Bremen, in 1929 billed as the world's fastest liner with 2200 people. Six hundred floated three years later inside the ship bottom.

Earlier, her father-uncle had been stomping and uttering dire words about American or British U boats, off his beloved country. "Not now."

Actually, his old brick factory consumed him more, now than torpedoes for the new Reich Volkland. Brick use could build a "beating camp." He'd been measuring bricks, and was now dressed to go out. She stood there. "Father!"

"Powerful." He'd gloated. Titanic. A U-boat had torpedoed the Lusitania in German military success, didn't it? Weren't these great sea liner treasures on the sea bottom, floating beneath her on this sea liner now? But her father was concerned himself about losses of pleasure liners, nor did he implore her not to leave as "a defector," like her aunt, his other sister. "We'll all be stronger," he commented, "together now."

Heinrich was brushing off his coat lint, when Meta informed him she was leaving. But she did not tell him. He found out.

For that fear, when leaving, she might or might not see her friends again, or worse, Todi, now Todd. Both tore at her. He'd remain at the home farm with Heinrich. Fetch Todi for to America; she must snatch him. Really, she wanted to make her life new for her son, far beyond being the household drudge on peasants' lands. Her uncle-father's rising and downing all but himself in praising them. Her aunt from America on that one visit had said Americans called this phenomenon, "Making name for yourself." Her journey would be to go first to the ship itself.

When she told Grete, her face knotted, said, "Put me in a trunk. I have one."

Whoa could haul it like a burial cortege for Bremerhaven. Already, she mourned the departure onto the sea. She wept. They both wept.

Johanna would report back on Meta's departure. Good riddance. The others like waving flags, summer yellow, orange, periwinkle and chartreuse dresses blew in the sea breezes. Lore, who'd hired a car for the day with Liesl, Katia and Grete drove them to see her off at the Bremerhaven pier.

Grete maneuvered to be allowed out for the day. "I plead to go with you. Take me. Her tears clouded her eyes, as they did Meta's. Meet me in New York." She'd begged again for parental approval, their financing based on meager savings. Governmental papers critical for departure and arrival in New York delayed her. So here she was, desperate to go. Down there was Grete down there, pumping her arm up and down up at Meta.

Martine, her curls bounced around her face like squiggles, must contend with the same fears as Grete, according to Katia, who promised to follow later. None knew where Lili was. Once Angela's grandmother died, she too might get to New York, where her mother reputedly lived, as Meta guessed, in America, like many German speakers in America Central.

Her friends had told her how sad they'd be at the dock to see her off. Even the semi-sullen Johanna, glad to see Meta go, waved above her drawstring white peasant blouse.

No friends where she was going.

As the ship disembarked, they drew away like specks. The group feathered away like dust on the ocean. When would she see her friends and son again, if ever, and Mopsi alive?

The quashed house points, flying horses' heads like dragons and old ritual fire wheels, restyled, were everywhere at a distance, and words were still leaping along the wooden beams like worlds scripted on them above cows and horses and persons grouped on the ground? When would she revisit the land of fairy god-tales, gneiss, slaty quartz with mica like glyphs with figures or rocks broken by flowers, like saxifrage, with sighs and fretfulness? Her eyes watered, while the ship's motors blasted and ground its motor awake.

White gulls, winging hankies and white hands waved at the Elbe's mouth, on this high oasis afloat on the Atlantic. Meta snuffled into her man's big white handkerchief, lifted from Georg. The gulls hovered around the deck, white batting against the blue sky, until most flew back to shore.

Spiraling down the narrow stairwell to her cabin and stowed luggage, she tunneled through unknown doors. Retracing her steps, she bumped into someone and counted numbers backward to her cabin. There her ticket reserved her third class upper bunk, hardly the dreamed about stateroom; instead she was in a tiny cottage in the pit of the ship on the water.

Her cabin mates, emigrants, students or those less well off hid in these bunks, or they swelled up on deck, more like rich or better off passengers from cabins still higher up. Evidently, she was sharing with four others, according to chartreuse, violet and scarlet dresses hung against wrinkling for dancing this evening to Henry Kasper's Band.

Her two cabin mates burst in laughing, so Meta sought to joke but couldn't follow the English-German mix, humor or mood. Two young travelers, German-American teachers prattled on their joy to be going home to America the merciful and carefree. They giggled over their high jinx, like "short-sheeting" their group leader's bed.

Their cabin possessed no porthole, so Meta's ear to the cabin wall heard water sloshing. Communicating best with gesture, she studied English grammar and tried minding her manners, as haphazard as growing up with them had been, she sensed not to probe others about leaving Germany for America. "Why are you leaving Germany?" sounded hollow.

But her cabin-mate teachers were actually stepmother and stepdaughter, living with her husband or father part-time.

However closemouthed, they seemed to like each other. With Meta, they froze.

Still Meta tagged along with them for supper: Krebs Suppe, with Konigin Pastetchen, creamed chicken in timbals and tomatoes, English roast beef with Blumenkohnm, creamed cauliflower and potatoes. Ice cream on fresh fruit dessert, tasted over-creamy for the mother figure.

Asked about leaving Germany, nearby passengers said, "Free trade lets in too many pigs, cheapening their price." Everyone ate Lower Saxon pork. "Too much pork everywhere but not here on board."

On sea, the ship rolled, as English blurred in sound. An older man said, "A crying shame, those horrors in Germany."

Meta asked, "What?"

"Wine drinkers are mellow," he said, "ale or beer drinkers support war." She shrugged.

The following noon, those who drank too much slept late. Some awoke very early from hangovers. Which kind was she?

Mornings at seven, the cabin boy roused the cabin mates. But not their fourth cabin mate who wanted to sleep off her night before. Wearing only a bra, she howled. "Get out," "Shit," "Omygod" and other unknown words.

Next morning, he came still earlier to scout other pretty women as night bed partners. The stepmother cabin mate, Joyce, swooned over his lieder in his natural tenor. Elaine, the stepdaughter, rolled her eyes.

Americans loved pranks. Elaine's ringlets bounced when talking about the cabin boy. Two nights out, the sunrise roused them to view the Atlantic moonlit highway back to the Old World. Meta re-invoked Georg; Elaine remembered Ralph. The night of the full moon pushed away from past hellishness and toward the romance of America the future.

Everyone danced the Swing and Tango, passengers spoke and danced in French, English, Spanish, Italian, Swedish or Norwegian. As her German thoughts stabbed her that evening, she puffed a cigarette at the railing and gazed at the moon.

"Can I light your next one?" an urbane tall male with black sideburns, a New Yorker First Class, eventually revealed. She nodded. She'd been hoofing solo on the edge of the dance floor, until chancing on this suave partner, Peter his name. They smiled and nodded. He wrote his name on all her dance partner card entries. They admired the moon's pathway to eternity on the sea.

On their fourth day on the Bremen, the dinner menu featured Tomatensuppe/ Fleishchbruhe in Tasse, third class first course choice. Tomato soup for color with roast chicken, fried potatoes and lettuce, never eaten on the farm nor was Bacalao Madrilena, the Spanish national dish, tomatoey. Cherry compote and lemon ice cream with cornet wafers completed the meal. From the dining room, now she could not glimpse the New York approaching, as if sweeping in passengers.

Across the long table, she heard, "Will we arrive in New York soon?" She sneezed as she'd heard. "Is someone Jewish meeting us?" an older girl child asked, "Will a bad person take us away?" Oh My God, where was Grete?

Someone answered, "Shush." Meta coughed from Camel cigarette smoke.

In the harbor, Diana, small at home, enlarged in the New York harbor. Gothic cathedrals spikes enlarged as "skyscrapers." Meta disembarked down the ramp within scores who blurred in colors into this new reality within the ship's horns' blare at arrival. The sound used to thrill her when she'd watched ship departures with Harald now stirred anxiety. When she landed, would she find where to go or be lost? Would she cope?

People began thundering down the Nord Deutscher Lloyd Bremen gangplank. They called out to people specks waiting for them.

On the landing, she scanned the gangplank signs, to mark her way forward. She dug into her rucksack for a mirror to flash at those below waiting for their loved ones, though no one would be waiting for her. Before immigration and customs but knowing not what line to stand in or documents to show, she was trudging along and trying to strike up talk with anyone ahead or behind her or across from her in parallel lines. No one bothered.

Passport stamped and documents cleared, she cast about for the landlady also known to Lore but was unsure of this person. Spotting a Traveler's Aid sign, Meta dragged her luggage into the agency, where the volunteer told her, "Someone was just here looking for someone, maybe you.

There are more of you than we can possibility count."

31.

Sigh and expect to die. How often in those dog days that she and others were alive surprised her. She'd bolted upright in her first night she paid for in the Y in New York, suffocating in an airless room. The side window locked shut looked out on the roof. Opening the vents in the wall, still allowed no easy breathing. An old fan placed in front of the vent helped her sleep. But its rattle matched her anxiety, rattling without end.

An extinct flying reptile, cold and scaly Archaeopteryx, weighed on her chest. Or was it a pterosaurusdactyl or winged dragon that again sought to fly off from her chest?

Her uncle-father's old volumes taught her that the ancients built their kurgans, death vaults within wooden frames, and grave pits on steppes. They also used their tools for arrowheads, sleek enough stones to glide like eagles and vultures.

Saxons, Sacae, Saka, Sazonkin, Niedersachsen, Anglo-Saxons, Sakka, Kshaitrya, Sakha, Sakya. The women wore beads of crystal and amber, garnet rings and spoons were strewn around them in death, with an occasional short knife and used arrowheads.

The their forebear swords bore animal lacing, incised designs on spoons, mirrors and battle-axes called pickaxes, narrow with blades and points.

Her thoughts bated her and batted each other. She dreamed of forested Ural steppe nomads converted into warrior nobles forever on the verge of war, though in peacetime, they built steeples like seagoing boats inside upright. Cows mooed, and sheep bleated and moseyed around these buildings. She missed her old flock within these skyscrapers.

From beakers, the ancients poured communion wine by their portable altars, while traveling. They kept their artifacts of peace and war within their grave homes, along with hand or palm-sized stones with finger-sized holes and censers for incense.

Over and over, she tried to escape from her non-alcoholic hangover into sleep. Shut off the metal fan for overheated air, better than noise. Crouching on her bed to inhale, she raised and lowered her arms to wear herself out to fall asleep again.

Once up a time, they two, not the dinosaur-reptile or imagined bird-dragon, they received the "all clear" signal over an air stream, like live falcons. Heinrich used to scan and hunt for them with Christoph.

Other events came to pass. By accident in a pavilion, Georg asked her to dance to a ballad. He preferred not to whirl his wife or other lover. They lost each other in the banality of everyday. While she was off and under, he stayed behind with another woman in their would-be locker that must rattle like panes in the wind, not unlike grains of the desert.

Months later, she found him again by chance in a booth. "My wife, my husband, my country." They intoned. They did, when he left their house-locker for another's, hers. They slept on in front of open windows for air.

They yearned for cloud nine. After all had been said and done, their holiday had served as their honeymoon and blew them to another zone, where the air was chilled.

On shipboard, awake now, she had written Todi that his father might have fallen. They might never reclaim his body. She would mail the letter back to Todi, once she'd landed.

Awake now whereabouts of her mother was unclear, though an older woman, presumably her treasonable aunt had vouched for and later introduced her as witness and sponsor who possessed enough farming and wartime assembly line job income to vow to sustain Meta in this new country. Lore had written to her. Did this Annike know about the truth of Meta's would-be husband or father as divining rods for hell on earth?

Everyone needs a nurturing core. Silence. The receiver closed off. She pivoted between failure and victory.

Still his curved block face interrupted her thought stream. Sometimes, his nose blued, eyelids reddened, while the air blanched. The solidity of his long body still beguiled her memory.

Ignorance of the present though was asphyxiating her. A degree forthright though, she'd believed any problem could be resolvable though unable to solve her worst problems. At least, she denied little, and weakened in countering Uncle-Father's active support for the Fuehrer by diehard Nazis and Aunt Lore's semi-acquiescence.

The Saxonies had long disappeared into Prussia, now most of Germany expanded eastward into Poland, so raved the headlines. Such drive could snap backwards. Not understood is that what is thrust outward is apt to wham back. In a darkening sky, the ones moving on poked holes up there to gain light. Wherever they journeyed, they were also streaming their stars across the sky.

Pulling up her boot socks, mukluks comforted her on her chair edge for a summer on the plains. She'd arrived in the land of skyscrapers plains.

32.

With chalk, pastels or sharp stones, Meta scratched secrets on stones or paper about the worst of times. Expressiveness gave life to thoughts.

Her path of stealth had carried her from the North of Europe to Bremerhaven and across the water to freedom in New York harbor with the huge Statue of Liberty.

Necessity meant any job to survive on and travel with enough to her mother, and back to rescue Todi. Thwart she must the hatreds felt.

How could she, when so weak? Could she reach the heartland, the midland, for her mother, aunt or cousin? Mothers knew what to do. Others reacted as if nothing was going on. Denial was holy, and they all were surviving Death.

Family trees crossed the globe. Irminsuls posted banners to crouch under during worry about Todi whose family at home included Lore, Heinrich and maybe Liesl and sons. Would Todi remember her, during her absence? Great-aunt Lore had promised to call Meta to report on him, if the squat black phones worked there. Meta would also try.

Battle lines slashed across front page news maps hawked on the streets. He'd be killed. But could he travel alone to America? Should she, a horrible mother for leaving him behind, go back?

On Broadway, the marquee lit up Chocolate Soldiers. It necessitated saving for standing room only, in this gorgeous release from real life. Now though, a gigantic dark umbrella was opened, spokes broken, fallen and enveloped her and others.

The void sucked in material: everyone inhaled. Everyone exhaled: all was alive in this best of all possible worlds.

At least, she'd flourished at the new job desperately sought. Before Christmas, Mr. G., a florist, offered to pay her for ten to twelve hours a week in this low economy. Hour by hour, she walked the streets looking for bulletin boards and tossed away day old newspaper classified ads, to click into job possibilities. Finally, a neighborhood bulletin board posted work possibilities with children. A newly formed public school unit, according to a neighbor on their apartment building stairway landing, could interest.

Needing to leave her expensive Y room, Meta scouted a tiny studio, to be paid for by her school clerical job with little speaking.

At the florist, escorts ordered corsages for their dates for proms. She swept the floor and learned the lingo. To suit Mr. Gennatos, her new boss, she wore a white blouse and dark navy blue skirt to work in; she unpacked his new gift line for shop windows to catch women's eyes. Mr. G.'s enthusiasm for his flowers induced women to gaze into his eyes to remember their "sweethearts." His gifts and flowers lured them to buy. Americans were so romantic.

Penny by penny, she worked more hours during the Christmas rush, though the country stayed in the world Depression with lines of unemployed. "Respectfully, I need more hours of work??"

"Why ask for more, when I have less now than when you arrived here. You weren't even born here. Why expect so much? You walked by some unemployed on park benches, just to get here."

Mr. G. not only refused her more work hours, but when he asked her to leave early, she refused to lose promised hours of work. "I close early for the Sabbath, didn't you know?

"I brought in men and boys to buy your flowers for their wives, mothers or girl friends, adding to your profits."

"No, I bring them in through their wives and sweethearts."

"No, you know I do. I wave to the men, flirting from the front window. You owe me more."

He grumped and handed her some extra coins. I know your kind from your country."

Weekly, she retreated into books and magazines during rare free time in free libraries, none like them in Niedersachsen, to learn new words. On their few open days, librarians welcomed checking out popular novels like Little Women and The Great Gatsby. Often she spoke only to them, books and clerks, so alone was she.

A 1937 issue of LIFE pictured Hitler with children. They clamored to give him flowers or take his picture with them. Study this shot of Marienburg Castle of the Teutonic knights, Hitler Youth in Berlin with a magnifying glass. Scrutinizing the photograph for Todi, she spotted him, surely. She gagged and wrote him.

Dearest Todi,

I miss you! Be a good boy, and find a seagoing liner to America and ride your horse to the harbor.

We will find a way to live in New York City. I work hard in a flower shop, like city gardening.

I dream this letter reaches you. I am missing you.

I love you. Mama

Her written German sounded like beginning English. But she must see to his learning English. If only she could compose music to impress him and sweep him up into her hopes and arms. His thin body would not fit into military drills and thundering trumpets. He likes flowers and horses. She fretted and writhed over his pitifully and wrenchingly demanding life he could never match up with. The authorities and manuals did not want her or other mothers to sop the fears of male children. Tender, he would be marked "incorrigible" by the regime. Aha, Heinrich would protect him, if he did not send the boy to the authorities. Life's greatest love was mother's child. She despaired.

Hopefully, the authorities would allow her letter into Germany to her son. If only. . . . Going over his presumed life, she'd lived through days of turbulence.

Mostly, she toiled to make ends meet and rescue Todi. At the florist, she cut ends off to preserve stems before wrapping the narcissuses, daffodils and blue-purple irises in stiff paper cones. Gradually, with Mr.G.'s trust, she arranged flowers for luncheons and swept plant leavings from the floor.

At her clerical job, she winced over her accented English, though tried her best to show only competence during calls set up in-person interviews and group meetings. To protect mothers with truants and delinquents, it was mandatory for social workers to expand their workloads to hold onto their positions, jeopardized in the low economy.

Her work phone rang again. No one spoke. Faint cross talking could be heard. She hung up the phone and resumed her clerical work.

After twenty weeks, making café curtains for her tiny flat's windows was feasible to block anyone seeing her disrobe or drip nude from across the U-shaped apartment building insert space. Also barely affordable, her telephone might ring with this or that "dreamboat," as American girls called their wished-for boyfriends or possible "sweethearts." Many strange words to learn: most girls lined up their fiancés or "dreamboats" before they joined the Pacific theatre or Atlantic wars. She dared not to disclose that her people were the enemy, and clammed up, but they probably already knew.

On Saturdays, she rushed to reserve books and study the latest periodicals. LIFE magazine shocked her. Christmas in "Naziland," as LIFE called Germany.

Presents displayed were tankers and machine guns. Candles, okay. But an object that ornamented a Noël tree flattened her.

Hanging there two vultures gripped the shoulders of a Jewish man in a big black hat from a virtual gallows tree, a Christmas tree.

Mr. G., portly and bald with hair patches above his temples, listened to her distress.

"My country Greece is under Nazi attack, too. I left Salonika, also in Naziland." Mr. G. pounded his fist on the worktable.

"Democracy there rose and fell in just 15 years." His handlebar mustache bobbed in time to his pounding. "Watch out!"

Depression was everywhere, the economic kind and the psychical kind. More than ever, phones failed to work, and users could not pay tabs for flowers. They tried plucking buds and getting away with them under their coats. Food was rare; often, dried beef in milk on toast was her cheapest best meal. On the streets, beggars lurked asking for money and sought out food lines.

In another LIFE photo, violence to Diana: a low life sought to tear her eyes out and attack her twice with a dagger. Would the war topple her? Notice a whispering presence. . . .

33.

Fantasy obscures hope and denial. Anon. II

Excited by the hoped-for Todi voyage, her fingers hugged Stefan's arm. He was interpreting her new clerical work in child guidance. Well trained in Berlin, Mr. Bingelbein, her dapper manager, had taught her to calm her façade into glamor and cheer up everyone possible, but this Depression, economic downturn with high food costs everywhere. Because she'd acted her entire life, she could perhaps now pursue the New York City stage.

"Are you all right?" dark-bearded Stefan asked.

Ignoring him because of ammonia from the closet nearby, she noted, "You Europeans have your troubles." His arrival ten years earlier meant he was still European.

"You're already acting. Why say you want to act?"

His eyes ran over her body. Was he thinking her clothes unstylish?

Shrugging, she noted that in spare time, she looked for amateur plays and loved dances, "The Big Apple" and "The Little Apple," performed close to the floor. The

"Charleston" and "Truckin" were more upright. Shake woes via Fred Astaire and Ginger Rogers' movies and George Gershwin's Rhapsody in B.

Little understanding her, Stefan would come to her door with a corsage.

And she'd supply him with a boutonnière.

Through gauzes of disguise, the slightly older Max distanced himself more than Stefan did.

Only Fleur, her older work friend, nails polished deep-red, like lipstick, told her Max called her an "untutored North German girl." Just like that. Max the commander belonged to categories: tweedy man, intellectual, wit, sport, woe-is-me hunk or aging has-been.

"Stable," he'd spoken about his mother to Meta, Fleur reported. "She's on less medicine now in that hotel that passes for a nursing home. She needs it." The big reddish-brown-haired man's hovering over a tiny, shy wizened mother, appealed to Meta.

"She dangles her feet, slides off and says, 'Shit, I want to go home.' My mother's old self orders me home."

"I should think so," Fleur told Meta.

Meta brooded. Max signaled to her, while attaching himself to self-possessed Fleur. In a many paneled skirt and bolero jacket, she cared for him at work.

Her phone rang. "What?" Silence from a new client perhaps suicidal. Careful, she informed her new receptionist. "I'm no good alone in this job with deciding what to decide."

"Don't hang up," she said. Hurt me not by doing so. Static ensued and sounded underwater.

She was dry-mouthed. "After years in solitude, everyone needs a nurturing core."

No one hung up. No one replied out loud. Was Todi calling? This idea pinged.

Whether Grete or Todi or a troubled student or parent called, she must arrange for Todi and Grete to break out of Germany, like son and sister or mother and son. She reeled off pairs. Katia could take care of herself.

Meta berated herself for failing professionalism by not drawing out the silent caller.

Remember speak in German; Todi calls in German. Softening her tone, she said. "Don't worry. I'll not reveal you to anyone. Can I help you? You will speak." No speaking or breathing.

"Wrong number?" Must be, she hung up. The mind replayed its pieces, flying in her, sealing old scores and trying to heal old wounds. She must not speak in German at work. Did Max speak in German?

Between failure and victory, Max's square face blued with sad eyes of St. Bernard within his short brindle-red hair. Max lacked a beard and the solidity of long, curved body like Georg's.

The next day, Max's office oak desk, rock-like, was free for work. On it, a picture of a girl-woman stared back, a soft-edged dressy old-young woman and boy with trim sideburns.

Rolling her new word, "peers," Meta worried if the photo belonged to his peer or mother. Then too, if a peer was a nobleman, as Heinrich could have been in olden, feudal times, when men took oaths to men above in power, and women swore allegiance to their husbands.

Twisting in her oaken chair during lunch, she half-secretively studied her School of Philanthropy coursework.

Her Arbitur degree was useless. Transferring from the Soziale Frauenschule in Berlin was impossible during wartime. Because of limited English, stressing a point in class was almost impossible; doing so in the enemy's German was impossible.

Later back in her studio apartment, her new radio offered a backdrop: Benny Goodman played his One O'Clock Jump and Jumpin at the Savoy with Lionel Hampton.

Men also intruded—Georg—not that he mattered, or that this Karl had asked her to a party, because his wife, Lili put him up to it, and Meta weakened into "Yes." Her beige gown clung like a nightie at that party, bought from Grete's mother's Berlin shop in Berlin would not shake free out of her body or brain.

In tweed knickers with leather flat shoes and brown leather golf hat, all Englishy, Georg burst into the party. He'd clutched her mauve silkiness and was offended by it, on horseback at that. "Why the hell are you here?" Did she know?

Django Reinhardt guitar music stayed on her head, an odd stuck thought. Still, the quasi-jazzy party atmosphere had confounded Georg in his countryside purity. From there he'd was off "to serve my country with all my heart against the Bolsheviks." He'd managed to write her. She cringed at her belated awareness of the sun drill of the swastika.

Now at last, she caught on–Django was Gypsy French both of which Georg abhored. When he and Meta returned to her front door, his scorn and desire turn palpable. If he closed in on her, a gag might well up in her, as if Nanna's black beaded rosary was choking her. At work, she also raced once in a while to the toilet to wretch, when inner nightmares from the old country flew over her here in New York like dark vultures against her composure.

Within the greenish and off-white scaly walls, here English improved her interviewing poor children and parents, sifted data and applied principles of self-respect toward social therapeutic practice. Around the corner, someone galumphed. Max's step was measured.

"Who's there?" she asked. "Frederic?"

"No."

"Time's racing."

"Passing, I hope." What does he mean?

Rising from his desk for him, she'd tried nailing down endless paperwork and said, "I'm crazy over forms?!" Immediately, she was self-recriminating over her nonprofessional comment.

"Do you know Lili?"

"Who?"

As he walked on, his fingers waved over his shoulder like minute teasing puppets.

In their offices, clients and staff meetings dulled hopes for chance contact. Sliding into his office though, his breath was close enough for her to be able to smell his smoky breath and Old Spice.

Five hours later, his number, scatted from his phone list was dialed. A man answered, she jumped and said nothing. He hung up; her home phone rang, and when she answered, it clicked off. Another German spied on her fear.

Need she live within deceit? A sheep was a sheep, a cow a cow, a lover a lover, a dog a dog, death, death, life, life. Thwart what widens hurt and helplessness?

34.

Nothing more would happen. On the window sill, ultra-green rhododendrons furled dry leaves. After the secretary presented a letter, Meta braced against the emergency stretcher to read, "You failed to arrive in our main office yesterday on time and. . . call in your absence last week."

Blocks away from the main office, a nondescript green medical office, Max was reading a newspaper. On its front page, two photos white and black showed militarists of Lili's men's type, for sure, only jacketed with epaulettes, standing before semi-rolled out American and Nazi bund flags. In one, speaker Kuhn presided. The scene flabbergasted Meta.

Max closed his paper into his briefcase clonked on the oaken desk. "Something sold on Broadway." His red bowtie crooked below his whiskery chin, he half-bowed, removed his tweedy overcoat. "I'm working here today."

"Should I leave?"

"Stay. I leave at noon." He called numbers to leave messages. Between calls, she appealed to him with light talk about absence and travel escape. She added this. "My last visit to mother was not-peaceful, in an unknown land. How can I drive there with gas pricey or rationed?"

Not quite listening, he rid his foot, argyle sock-covered, of a shoe pebble. Because their office secretary knit argyles, during lunch, Meta asked, "Did she make yours?"

"H-m-m."

"Ask her to mend them." Initially, she'd befriended Meta, until recently promoted.

"Your mother," Max asked, "brought you here from the old country?"

"I myself came here on shipboard."

"Orphaned?"

"No, she left me behind."

"I too," said Max. "We mother ourselves. See her anyway. I see mine once a day.

Everyone needs a mother."

"Some have none. I didn't for years," said Meta. "Some of my friends knew theirs only from afar." He must be smoking her out, while sitting on a folding chair, like an open scissors. He slouched against the black medical cot that knew suffering indigent New York truants or sick students. If their mothers do not grant them hope, who can? Students must find hope elsewhere.

Fathers go to war.

"Otherwise, like the old country, they'll. Grab them, or without jobs, fathers will proliferate without jobs and plot against fellow citizens and government. His memory exploded. "In her prime, my kind mother never criticized me. When old though, she cursed and cussed. "Asshole."

"Shit.""

Like aged Nanna, Meta chuckled. "Grossmutter might be dead now." Nanna, hair poufy like a lantern with tousled strands, fluffing around her ears, in Plattdeutsch or German.

"Your mother's dead?" he asked.

"My grandmother may be, but mother's not.

"Should I have stayed?"

"Understand anyone awake who could leave, did. Most who stayed are more dead in Germany than alive. The Germans started the wars. Those assholes were already soul-dead, while killing off the Jews, the weak political types and the disabled, even themselves off. Your grandmother though must have died by aging." If you speak against ostracizing of the vulnerable, you're squeezed out, ridiculed, ostracized.

"What about the Ventriloquist in the raincoat?" according to the newspaper Max had been reading, who could stir people to slaughter? She mourned Grete. But no one was halting the zealotry.

"He's organized, evil is organized. It's not ordinary. It's not a big puppet with a man's hand inside or strings attached. Some think he'll pass. Some say he will. No.

"He will. He must."

"He's not an everyday fool, nor a lowlife."

"Let's travel by ferry to Jersey and back."

"I must stay." But the idea enticed her. "You'll turn me in for work failure."

"Suit yourself."

Already suited in red and blue, high padded shoulders, she must stay.

"I'll be back here for you in two hours."

"But the letter said, 'Failure in duty.'"

"O, hell." He left.

Next, a mother and daughter with scoliosis arrived for her interview. Rheena and sat in shadowy humility. How did these old shtetl country Jewish people get here and live on? The whole village settlement was already wiped out in pogroms.

The apple faced six year old daughter of the grandfatherly father, came next with time away from his Canal Street hardware store with tiny drawers up the walls for screws, and nails. Go see them on Featherbed Lane.

On the fog-clouded barge, at their mutual corner, he asked. "Why so down?" he asked, "Worrying?"

She left to buy a ham sandwich and tea, while he bought her a Daiquiri, his favorite drink.

Unsure of its sour contents for taste but thanked him. At their big table's end, older men were playing poker and women beyond then slapped cards down in bridge. Their red-brown polished fingernails danced to laughter. Exasperated watching them and not knowing game strategy.

Unlucky in poker, lucky in love, or lucky in love, lucky in poker, one or in both?

Max watched her munch her sandwich, and she his drinking his Daiquiri. He offered her another. She declined. He said, "I'm tapering off work."

Their meal finished, they strolled off the gangplank from the ferry at Dyckman Street, and walked back to their office. "Thanks." The mist is lifting.

A week later, Monica promoted her from assistant visitor to social worker, because of study advance.

"Testing the intercom. We must go to a meeting because of your progress. You'll take notes.

We must stay organized."

Did he know about her advancement? "Monica feels newcomers," Meta said, "displace citizens."

"But I'm not one yet. You are?" Meta tensed and froze over her direct query.

Once Max left, she, over-warm, propped open the fire door. From above, visible trees spiraled into chartreuse fan tops she could see, as she called parents for appointments.

The bell from return calls reminded her of sing-along cartoon ball with bounces in time to her inner unease.

The fire door slammed. She jumped from accents: "Shut the door against fire. It's the rule—shut. No air!"

Meta ran out of her office, as did others, hearing, "Achtung," for warning. The cleaning woman, brown-haired, pitched her blue eyes at their rubbernecking toward her screaming. Her right hand was waving a floor rag mop and left gesticulating, accusing Meta.

Life fractured. Adopting New York via her marriage, Sol watched this outburst. In the office talent show at a nearby bar, in cinematic style, she mimed Carmen Miranda's singing, her turban balanced waxy bananas and oranges. Puertoriquena, Sol taught Meta salsa in her avant-garde New York dressiness and told her, "For a German, you dress well lately. Want to go shopping?"

They discussed sons. Sol brooded about losing hers. "The army's a profession for life."

Meta's son must be fighting Sol's.

"More South Americans, especially Puerto Ricans," Monica said, "are filtering into New York."

Joan Brantley, more artful in her off-gold Charnel suit than other women present, entered their suite, where Monica, Sol and Max worked. They eyed her glamor. "Glamorous." Miss Brantley thanked them and avoided shopping with Sol and Meta. "Psychologist here," Monica whispered, "colored, at that."

"Gorgeous," Sol asked, "So does she sing? Many are overcoming their problems."

"Look at Max, handsome, but. . ." Sol crossed her dark eyes and made a sign of the cross. "He doesn't overcome his."

Reeling off remarks, Sol said, "You dislike his friend Abby's Jewish challenging authority?" Her red mouth pouted and black eyes squinted inward above high cheek bones.

Meta squirmed, when Sol noted, "Max's ashen like his pants," and cocked her head to her right. "Smart, but his eyes have red accents and cheeks from tiny popping tubes—capillaries." Her Spanish was accented over another tongue. Meta hated this betrayal of him by Sol he so liked.

Monica, buxom, short and brassy haired entered their suite, away from Max' office.

Their oaken desks abutted each other enough to quarrel. "His problem's taken him into the caring professions."

Meta said. "We're all in them because of personal troubles. Six to 12 million people in this country is a heavy drinker, LIFE says."

Sol left and burst in with folders. "Americans, one and all. Soy. Soy, Peudo, I am. I can.

Do." They scrutinized names and categorized folders.

Sol asked, "Does he have any friends?"

Meta swiveled. "Who?"

"Max. Forget him. Everyone falls for him."

Meta felt left out and lost. The school clock face noted that it was the time to return to her neighborhood apartment building with German, Jewish and Spanish nationalities. This very Saturday night, Ileana's brother alternated semi-scratchy records of swing and merengue on his Victrola. Meta swayed miserably with nowhere to go on Saturday night. Lili's BUND?

German apartment dwellers complained. A crooner vocalized across the cul-de-sac, her stomach lessened its acid. Ileana's brother played on. Meta trying out steps: tango with head pulling left, head right, female follows the imagined male with responsibility to lead and whirl. The Viennese waltz sweeping from side to side with natural turn and verse, swinging and gliding, slow foxtrot in many tempos with feather steps gliding and floating, quick step, hop, skip, and jump; cha cha cha in separate turns, shakes, twirls and hips wiggling; and rhumba slower than some others. Try the three-quarter rhumba step close step, lean weight back and forth to music through a window.

A door slammed, and Spanish and English was screamed. Metal banged, and men's voices yelled. Meta cracked open her apartment door to see other neighbors peeking at the hullabaloo.

On the stairwell, Ileana's brother wielded a long sword against an unknown's machete. Their metal whipped the air and cracked, weapon against weapon. The two men pointed weapons upward, growled, jabbed each other. Neighbors came out and screeched in German and Spanish. The police arrived.

"Family dispute," one said. Unwilling to intervene, another leaned against the wall, as Ileana screamed, "Stop them."

Neighbors vied to get the tale straight. Ileana's brother accused her boy friend of fathering the baby. Neighbors gawk. Ileana's brother yelled at her boy friend, "You dishonor my family."

Ileana said to her brother, "Mind your own life." Neighbors disperse.

Next day in the library, Meta paged back through another LIFE issue to a photo. Thousands of Hitler Youth cram into the old Teutonic Knights' Marienburg Castle.

Her dime store magnifying glass enlarged Todi's face with Georg? On her last trip West, her mother had chewed her out. "Go back there, snatch our Todi."

"Alex vowed to reach him," she'd replied. Her ears boiled at her memory. "No Ma'am, I won't go back. I entrusted him with money, saved pence by pence for 1300 Marks for him." Searching for the remainder, he'd slipped her marks and coins out from under the damask tablecloth doubled over in her flat's table with pad. He'd made off with the sum.

Tippy-toeing up to Alex, she'd feared losing his embraces, but she was desperate for that money and loathed herself for not stashing it wholly away. If she had what it took to do what she must, he knew nothing about it. He'd be remote, castigating her.

From her wobbly stance, she'd confronted him. He'd pooh-poohed her. "You lost the money, just like you've lost people; you said so yourself." He'd walked off.

Out of Niedersachsen, into Ouisconsin, Annike her mother said, "O, don't trust anyone in wartime. If you do, he'll steal all you have. Her knotted fingers combed her graying strawberry blond waves. "Find your son, the boy, yourself."

Who's trustworthy enough to help? Not Heinrich. Harald's dead. Nanna's fading and dying. Not Lore, who worries about her own child and grandchildren? Not her son's father, Georg's the officer for war and Todi's the Youth soldier, like grandfather, like father or both.

Annike noted, "Rescue your little son! Willpower counts."

"He's not little! He's tall. I can spot him. I can sneak back in, I did so before. Besides, what's it to you; you never rescued me."

After replaying their argument, her stomach churned, like a fool alone without any will in any city.

Back in the New York City world, her cases outside herself, persons with problems, absorbed her. Still, the world of Todi engulfed her. How to win him from loss and heal him from wounding preoccupied her? How to wrest him from an angry world? Heal one's self first, lecturers taught, meaning that no one could rescue someone else. Rescue yourself first. Hm-m-m.

Ignore office gossip. "I didn't work Friday," Max was saying over her thoughts, "because the ambulance drove Mother to the hospital. She refuses meds from the head nurse for congestive heart failure and opposes any transfer. She's crazier than ever, says I'll kill her in my war."

At work, Max's care for his mother comforted Meta, and made long distance listening easier.

"For days," she'd say, "I couldn't reach you." Meta studied her mother's photo, taken with her box Kodak with her loose gray-reddish wavy bun that might cascade down.

"Were you on the town?" asked Annike. Static on their line meant a poor line. To see her mother in person meant traveling long distance by bus, more affordable than driving in her imagined car. Her bills paid, her bank account stood at $10.

Max said nothing more here and now in the clinic. Still, Meta paced her words, and thought to touch her toes 200 times in the bathroom. Drink black coffee, while he occupies the phone.

She'd then say, "Are you okay?" He agonizes over his supervisory load, claims he's phasing out, because his mother's dying. Hold his arm in his wretchedness, so he'll find her irresistible.

"Everyone's leaving," she said, as Max harrumphed.

"Richard also wants out. No depth in these people." Max cleared his throat. "Dull folks trouble themselves little beyond their abilities. I used to care. Now, I rubberstamp whatever they want me to do."

"Will I ever see you again?" She held her breath and patted her dark reddish new pompadour. "You don't advance here." The office manager, Monica, with her unacceptably enlarging belly in these days introduced Sharon Anderson as her administrative replacement.

At day's end, Meta collided again with Max. "Why leave us?" Her arm squeezed his, as they revolved in the revolving door to exit.

Outside, he hugged her hard and long, as if never to unwrap from her, even if others watched. His mound was heightening. "I've been called to serve our democracy." Donning his army cap, he saluted her good-bye.

35.

Fleur with peach glass skin entered the cooling tree-canopied park to attend the public band shell concert featuring *Semper Fidelis, Stars and Stripes Forever* and *Hands across the Sea*. Such music was drenching Meta's sour mood, as she grew livelier when back from the country's midland.

Now in New York City, while marching home, they chatted until they parted, while shopkeepers lock up for the night.

On stilts unseen, from one still-open dress emporium, some mannequins watch passersby. The nippleless breasts and torsos light up hanging in the windows: some few in chic stripes, some naked.

To restore equilibrium in this late evening daydream, she hurried on 15 blocks from the park, where Indians still lived up above in the caves. The evening darkens, and small businesses close.

Behind her, a woman's heels snap on the pavement; she rushes across the cobblestone near the river toward her apartment and hopes to lose the steps behind her. Heartbeats pump through her to her toes. Breathlessness has overcome her, she slows, and the click-clacking lessens, as the public light dims, and night darkens in wartime with bombing fears.

The street crosses Broadway, a diagonal across Manhattan, busy by daylight with pedestrians and by evening with cars. On weekends, tulle and taffeta partygoers and their men in black stroll to the Hudson ferry dock or nearby supper club to dance to a combo. There she and Alex had escaped from work.

At this moment, steps reverberate. On the incline toward her apartment house door, steps pursued her, spurring her in heels that almost trip on sidewalk cracks.

Her biggest key she clutches for her front door. A phantom hovers, unnerving her.

She struggles to shut it. A big foot between the door and frame impedes her grappling for the second inner door key, she pushes into the keyhole and slams the door or tries to against him. But the door valve's air pressure tube slowed its closing. In her frenzy, she squeezed his hand and jammed his foot.

An unknown neighbor nodded. "Anything wrong? Bad night out there—storm's coming."

The truth struck here in 1940. Georg attacked her, didn't he? Wild flower bouquet weakened her? Her mind slowed: Monkshood, deadly in a few hours; Oleander or Foxglove, rosy decorative though sought for headaches, nausea, light-headedness; Castor or worse or Hogweed, lacy, still more toward deadly.

The flowers interlaced problems, not Harald, who never attacked her. Unsure though words came back. "Slip back in carefully," voiced conquest.

To restore her mellow evening daydream with Max, she blinked.

Instead, a flashback haunts her dreams. Semen and blood runs down her legs. Pulling down her petticoat and skirt, she'd been self-recriminating. "I'll get you." But he'd been sleeping. Half- waking from a stupor, she was regressing into daytime nightmares. She locked the doors against her own escape and attacks on someone else. She knew it was so.

Hours later, on Saturday speaking long distance meant time later for escaping into the public library for the latest LIFE. On Sunday, before her mother awakened her by phone on Sunday.

Meta called Annike who'd answer, "I need sleep before going to the government factory."

After trying dutifully for two years to get acquainted, her mother dutifully urged another visit. "God knows how time passes."

Sleepy like her mother just spoken to, Meta felt drained. The bedroom door was shut against the cat, meowing her awake. She slept and dreamt.

The huge bed shared years back with her "husband" in the Kaiser's hunting lodge revived.

With so many bedrooms, they'd hardly shared one. A bathroom linked two. Hot water pipes beneath floor tiles warmed the rooms. Fired-up blue tiled heaters also warmed the bedrooms, as did lit fireplaces.

"Warm my bed." Charged up, she dreamt of Georg. "Don't stay on here." So Meta told him, I won't, unless you arise and carry me home.

Away from city pavement, the countryside in 1940 was re-vivifying her Lower Saxony, flatlands and inclines. This New World area flourished along rivers with the same fish underneath, while birch, oak and beech trees grew above against sunsets and birds at sunrise, all except the cardinal. Maybe, she edged toward belonging within the Mississippi's valley within America's Great Lakes and geese-land of the Ohio, Missouri and Wisconsin rives in the land.

Local folks were little familiar with geology, unlike ardent hikers like Meta and Annike.

Trekking along the unmarked ridge, they sought to rappel down the rocks along the river or try climbing standing rocks, which only Indians in ceremonies seemed able to Now back in the cottage, her mother's ivory hair was matching her skin. Her eyes, focused afar. Across her five acres, quarter acre by quarter, she'd purchased, near the overgrown Ice Age ridge and the river edge, they joked about purchasing land from a fellow who'd got it from the Natives. Meta felt she walked in a Karl May book.

Annike jested. "On the move, we Saxons were for ordinary life here, not where I came from. Signs said —I was crazy—"danger" along the river. Heimat lures, wherever they go. Call Lower Saxony home or Holstein against the Slavs. Or here against the Indians."

"You sound like Heinrich," Meta said.

"Nowadays, against others' lands, everyone's going someplace anyway."

"Couldn't you stay put?" Meta asked.

Annike referred to Heinrich, "I had to leave. He stayed. You can't bargain with a fanatic.

Hopefully, you undermine fanatics, and they run their course. They fade from women who are free to find work, comfort babies, forests otherwise left untouched nurture good land for food and cull already fallen logs. As if Meta couldn't hear, Annike repeated each point.

"That Old *Hund* forbade such ideas. So I called him *Hund* to his face and swore to myself to leave." She swallowed water from her glass.

LAST GENTLEMAN IN THE MIDDLE DISTANCE

Meta agreed, "He called you fanatical. He said I was stupid, unserious."

Annike said, "I produced a daughter—you. He was furious."

Meta said, "When I produced a son, he was happy."

"Why, for God's sake, did you leave your son, our *Todi*, behind?"

"My son's captive there." Meta sank into the wing-like wooden rocking chair and shrank. "But a friend might retrieve *Todi* for me.

"But why'd you leave me?" Meta's eyes pooled.

Referring to Heinrich, Annike said, "He hid you. I tried keeping my mind on the Lamb of God. Was I the Lamb, or were you?

"I was outside searching so often, I always carried an umbrella in case of rain." She lifted an imaginary one. "I looked in barns, sheds, neighbors' houses for you. Lore swore to support my search. I stole around and groveled before laborers to find you. Perhaps Mrs. von Handler snatched you for him. Young fillies and beauties with the von names captivated him. She was already married, why did she need another one, him. She helped him with the horses and cattle less than I did."

Meta shivered, as rain fell through screened windows. She began reaching upward to unhook the windows from their hooks. Annike napped. Meta dozed.

Annike hummed and picked up. "Truths and fantasies are trouble."

"Hooked crosses are worse, like drill bits fired from the universal sun, the *Hakenkrauz,* as it explodes out of the cobalt sky. "Go to war," they drilled.

"Conquer. Or we could lose.

"Speak not, and then lose speech. See nothing, and then lose sight. Breathe not, we suffocate.

Hate closes in."

"I know," Meta said, "Grete only wanted to sing. The *Kapellmeister* told her that only Christians could sing songs by masters Bach and Mozart. She's Jewish, not Christian, so she wasn't allowed to sing them.

"Where is she now?" Meta said.

Geese and gulls flew. Defying fear within stars and headlights, while going downhill whether followed or not, she confessed to herself that morning doves saddened her and roosters' cackling cheered her. Mother Annike awakened with the Cock-a-doodle-do; Meta calmed by doves stirred to her mother's saying. "Meta, I cannot believe you're here."

"I can. For years, I looked for your grave. No one revealed anything about you. You didn't care!"

Across the Mississippi tributary from them, fields contoured with gravel passes begin shifting in the area. On this side, new castaways arrived; groups differ and clustered. Roots are cut by war. More Europeans appeared in the area during the war: war brides, refugees, exiles, escapees, Displaced Persons arrived. DPs spoke German, Polish, Yiddish or Czech, an infinity of tongues added onto English and Native ones, unknown to Europeans.

Doubting an early return to New York was feasible, Meta gabbed with anyone to slake the ache of loneliness. Rural life with trees, grass and a sprinkling of people lessened crankiness.

Wind stirs the cowbells near their modified bungalow the previous owner built upland to better admire the river and see the road. The front loader shoved the earth to extend their dirt lane. Sounds changed, as vistas did. Sand and dirt with pebbles gave way to blacktop, while cowbells surrendered to the golf course.

In wintertime, the Scottish curling game flourished in this area. Annike and Meta stared open-mouthed at the big stones teammates threw, and their brooms swept the ice to suction their stones sliding ahead. In movements, their tams, plaid beribboned tabbed, never fell off players' heads.

Not far away, parishioners' offerings built the architect's model with a pointy triangular church. Pipes and bells started broadcasting ancient ceremonies lead by the monsignor with scepter. Outside this modern Romanesque church a long walk from their cottage, Annike and Meta, wary together, watched its processional.

Kerosene lit up lanterns on dark days in area cottages, when they might stop to visit neighbors by Vera's and Hank's fireplace. The mason had interspersed collected artifacts with stone chunks for chimneys, some mica-flecked, and fireplaces nestled volcanic glass with petrified forest and cave stalactites or stalagmites, which could polish knives. He mortared rocks in rough overall diagonals. Squint and blur one's eyes: the rocks looked tossed into the fireplace's squared frame, suspended in flight.

Unlike the old country German kitchen-living rooms, no working animals rested there nor pots hung in this fireplace. By it up high, out their little window, Vera craned for her husband's homecoming. A young war-bride, Vera had met Hank just out of the Merchant Marine, also playing Biederbecke's *That's my weakness now.*

Annike suggested Meta, experienced with boys, watch over them. Their sisters would stay with friends. Annike said, "Hank, Joan and her parents will eat out. We'll bring food back to you. I disapprove of their boys, but you need good terms with our neighbors."

Meta bit her tongue. "I don't need more boys."

"But you left yours in Berlin."

"Who said?"

"Lore did by letter."

"A loyal aunt blames me? Her grandsons live with a married Nazi."

"Your son does too."

Before Meta thought her next thought, Vera's oldest son, James, ice-pale haired, flew in before the grown-ups left for dinner. Vera screamed. "Stay here!" He flew out.

"At least, James avoids war, so far," his mother, Vera, said, as he swooped back in and buttoned his dark cape raincoat, choke-neck buttoned, and left again.

Gloomy, Meta read the just delivered newspaper war accounts. If here, Grete would escape war by work, and Todi might behave like James. She paced the floor over what to do and strolled on down the road.

Later, Vera's father, Edward, saw Meta in the backyard. "Young woman, as a German, your studying English vocabulary pleases me." What? Mind the kids, she thought, felt sad, a bit furious.

His goatee and hair white around his spectacles above his sweater with epaulette vestiges, indicating Canadian Royal Air Force. "Better your outlook," he said, "with minion, authority, enigma, power, violence and bivouac?"

"Words thrust war forward," her mother would say, if present. "If one listens. Dare ask him about words for democracy. Or against it. He's military." Jolted, Meta asked them in for Lord Grey tea. She'd noticed the respect for soldiers on this side of the Atlantic, but knew little about the British custom of serving it.

"His grandfather's having 'sessions' with James, his grandmother Joan, noted, as she entered Annike's and now Meta's place. "He has demonstrated a fine mind worth saving." Edward the grandfather pressed tobacco into his meerschaum, and his wife, Joan reposed her coiffed head on a wingback chair side. Their Vera also came in for afternoon tea. Seeing her cream silk gold-circled honeymoon dress that harmonized with pallor, her mother leaned forward. "Buy a maternity wardrobe to replace your wedding dress." Hennaed and French-roll-coiffed, Joan dabbed on lipstick.

Vera craned her Venus body toward the window high up, as two waking Cupids toddled near her calves. One clutched her right hand, as Vera bent to kiss them. "Henry comes," referring to her spouse, "later and makes less."

"No more children," her father said.

"Children are luxuries," Annike, Meta's mother, added. "If you're pregnant continuously, more will overwhelm you."

"Make good soldiers. And lose," he added, "their elders' wisdom."

"You have plenty to go around, father," Vera said.

Meanwhile, someone called through the screen door. "You who? Anyone there!?" Vera's puffed face tensed to joy. Passers-by distracted her on this dead-end road community. The door opened sucked in air and shook windowpanes.

Because Annike knew not the American-British custom of cocktails, she was urging, Edward "to do the honors." He left and re-entered the front room minutes later with cocktails for arrivals Jo Bloch and her mother Leah. She kissed the toddlers' cheeks; they grabbed her topknot with her red silk poppy.

RAF Commander Edward, retired, a Whitehead-ad look-alike, tray in hand and towel on arm, noted, "Here's the younger set with more coming."

"To our grandbabies!" Leah raised her glass. "But no puppets today." Her singing and bouncing them yielded their giggles. "Everyman's a carpenter, cabinetmaker, locksmith, mason, cobbler, sawyer, tailor or watchmaker, like my father. Everywoman was a doll maker, hat maker or dressmaker, like her mother and aunt."

After chitchatting, Ed urged Leah on. "When the war started, the Germans sped across the border occupied Bedzin, three rail stops from home."

One toddler grabbed and loosened her topknot. The poppy fell. The other curly-top pulled out its petals.

"With my devout father's go-ahead," Leah continued, "I was the first in my family to cross the Atlantic to my uncle, in 1914, alone."

In America, in her aunt's hat workshop, another woman directed her tacking ribbons on wide brims. Leah's rounds of ribbon wholesalers for deals earned her three dollars a week. Opportunity arose, as she ate lunch alone, when other girls went outside. The head curler taught her to curl feathers into plumes. From a poor shop to a richer one, Leah dampened ostrich feathers on grand Lillian Russell style hats.

Meanwhile, her sister wrote from Bedzin: a "schmo" asked her for marriage she opposed and her parents favored. Leah sent money for her sister's arranged marriage, while her New York girl friend goaded her going to the Catskills. There Leah met a waiter earning enough to study in London. They became sweethearts, "kissing outside, nothing more."

Alas! Leah's friend snatched him. Guilty later about winning him, she urged Leah to go to the Concord Passover in the mountains.

"Oh," Meta piped up from dolor. "My friends Grete and Lili taught me from the Haggadah," We were slaves in Egypt under Pharaoh . . . ." Leah nodded. "Still are . . . my friend Grete."

Meta asked no one in particular. "Where are my friends?

Anyway a few years ago, Leah's aunt introduced her to kin cousin. "Keep him away from me." Leah ordered and wandered free on a Catskill mount. Lo and behold, a new beau joined her climb. She teased him. "If I jump off this hill, will you catch me?"

"Jump!" She jumped. He broke her jump.

A month later, Leah married her beau at City Hall "without the faith." The justice of the peace called in the floor mopping woman and elevator man as witnesses. Glad to be married but miffed at such little ceremony, Leah exuded happiness.

Leah brought forth her new husband, Sam the druggist, to her uncle, who said, "Sam's better looking than you, Leah."

"He's a good-looking nice guy who cares for me."

His extra 1928 speakeasy money, Leah continued, promised a bountiful life. Yet just before spending "his bundle of gold, he died"—before the Ventriloquist, Hitler was designated German chancellor in 1933.

Her right knuckles were knocking her left palm, as its third finger diamond flecked light. "We'd hoped for the best though ignored reality. Who knew about this coming horror?"

"You did," said Jo.

From around the inner fireplace within pine-paneled walls, they moved onto the porch for some breeziness. While still listening to Leah, fanning herself and one cherub, huddled by her, each grownup was slouching on stuffed or rocking chairs or couches within the walled in porch. Within its three-sided walls of storm windows, their bottoms were hooked up to the ceiling, from where they mirrored the listeners below.

She'd taken her Jo in 1932 to visit Paris first and on to Bedzin Poland relatives. Expected to visit around and help out, she entrusted Jo to a Polish girl to watch her. "You left me alone with the Polish nursemaid, new to me, and my new friend. But the Polish girl refused by saying, "No Jewish children, I care only for American children."

"Who are we?" Jo then twelve years old asked.

The girl replied, "You're Americans. I'm the proudest girl in town, caring for American girls." The babysitter paraded Jo and her cousin in General Pilsudski's parade."

"Mother! We only watched him. The poor loved him, and the Jews appreciated his opposing anti-Semitism. But when two Jewish boys marched by, two Polish youths on the side began stoned them. Jo, taller and blonder than the stone throwers, grabbed and throttled the shorter one's neck. Her mother decided to stay on for two years. Jo's bold native ability enabled her to enter a Polish school. Now Jo asked the stone throwers in Polish. "Who orders you to cast stones? Take me to your priest."

"Jo courts fate, she does," Leah noted, "like Rebekah my sister the teacher who desired the only Jewish lawyer in town over the young doctor in the next town. Both families opposed their marrying a mere teacher from a poor family."

Better than her military junk dealer, Meta thought, who'd been living in a onetime Junker hunting manor, intended for a king, Meta thought. "Better to collect silver items from forebears and scratch around for gold."

Jo nodded. Back in New York City, her grandmother wrote to Leah still in Bedzin. "Send Rebekah a dowry to qualify for marriage to the lawyer."

Meta though must have qualified for Harald without a dowry from Heinrich.

Leah and Jo escaped in 1932 just in time before the 1933 Nazi onslaught, they raced back to Paris, New York and finally Chicago, thanks to the friendly uncle who'd brought them up to the lake in summertime. "We knew troubles. But how can you foretell the future? Only catch onto it. Others simply organized for it.

"What if we jump into canoes here on the river because of fire in the woods?" Jo gestured toward a couple paddling by just before dusk.

"See the white caps rocking them." said Ed, "A storm's coming. The rowers are trying for shore, but undertows could overturn them. I saw the river engulf one pair in a boat."

Jo, hair bobbed, continued her mother's tale. The Polish army commissioned Rebekah's new lawyer husband hated Russians. But her family approved of them. "For the moment, Jo said, the Jews had evaded pogroms in Poland."

On the floor, the latest available newspaper headlined: German planes and tanks blitz Poland to end the decade. 1939. "Rebekah's lawyer-soldier husband rushed to the next Polish town to head them off, but the Germans conquered, her aunt managed to write, "and killed him."

This awareness punched Meta in the belly.

Annike waylaid Jo and Leah... "Stay for our vegetables for a meal. Henry plays saxophone at the supper club." Hank evaded in-laws with his music.

Edward served yet another round of cordials. "Come to think of it, the Canadian RAF with the Brits and Americans shall fly missions over Bedzin. Watch us win this damn war."

"Nothing's known about my aunt. We won't, till the war is over," Jo said. Her mother Leah dropped a pearl tear on her right cheek

Leah and Jo took a rain check for food and thanked him for the cordials and left.

Because of rumors along the dead-end road, they called on neighbors and visited. Annike with her heart pain, diagnosed as heartburn by a country doctor. Meta fell to reflecting, she wasn't there with her mother when needed but got here eventually.

Outside, beyond their dirt road, five miles parallel ran a state highway blacktopped for military jeep and trucks between the munitions factory and all-out war effort developed on bases north and south.

Her mother, Annike said, "We're, Meta and I and others are the ventriloquist's dummies who help drum up these problems, war too. We're numbskulls and knuckleheads." Wavy graying hairs trickled from her bun, while Annike was displaying her English vocabulary. She was going to work in an ordinance works; she'd volunteer there, if she had to.

What if Todd was sent to work in the Volkswagen factory on the Dütter River in northwest Germany? Over there, now Germans might capture him into forced labor in Firmen Werkes, munitions factory, glimpsed from the road and conjectured on from memory, ticking out time.

36.

The small emissary goddess statue Diana, protector of mothers, centered the city-town and crowned it with a moon crescent. With her bow, arrow and quiver, she stood alongside her deer.

How could anyone seek out truth from falsity? In her passage back to Todi, she was also on her other mission to find Grete. The mother Meta commissioned her to go. Jo her American friend urged her push ahead?

Here in Niedersachsen, camps whispered about did not sound like the camps Meta and Liesl attended as children. Nor Katia and briefly Grete in Wandervogel camps, nor their children play within temporary campsites.

Eventually, Meta gleaned that Grete tried coding about other hidden predatory ones, where authorities starved fathers, mothers and children as well as imprisoning them. America was devoid of critical details. From her experience with Todi, Meta gathered that no letter could pass through the censors. Meta's letter somehow passed through them disguised bits for Grete, probably already known.

From her earlier visit, rose fragrance breezed around unlike duress now. Now with faint smokiness in the spring air, the leaves scratched in the overhead fall coloring.

At the window, like Vermeer's portrait, sat Grete with a scarf pulled forward. She did not wave back. At the Van Relke front door upstairs, Meta hugged Grete, who re-introduced herself as "Greetje," amusing herself. They hugged again and spilled out words too fast to communicate in. Free to go or disappear, she played with "Greetje Elysse," for her new identity; trying out Dutch she'd pestered her father to teach her.

White curtains billowed within sage green ceiling-to-floor brocade drapes. "Don't part them," her grandmother said. "From the street, wicked strangers can see you."

"I need air." Gusts blew the filmy curtains at the open window.

"See now your friend visits you here inside." Her two hands took Meta's and squeezed them.

From Meta's last visit here was a windy spring day, when even the heavy drapes blew open freely.

"Instantly, people must dash out for their food before prices rise again and rush to stash it at home." Butchers displayed few steaks, roasts and shanks windows; bakers offered less strudel and hid the Purim Hamantashen. Because she'd learned pastry making, thanks to Aunty Ruth, Grete could knead bread like a baker for pocket change, while here with her father.

For morale, her Dutch Protestant father prevailed. Today they'd draw together for Grete's birthday. Typically, they celebrated birthdays and holidays with mocha cake frosted with Black Forest chocolate. He'd go find one. Bad times required good times with sweets.

In good old times, at family gatherings, he promoted music with simple percussive instruments: Triangles, little drums, pianos; recorders into flutes, or violins and cellos in combos or singles. They would play Sevçik and start early Mozart, Beethovan, Chopin, and Mendelsohn. Her father urged advancing on to their later works. "Practice the classics. Tonality soothes listeners, but atonal music's hard on the ears.

Cousins, all fifteen, were prodded to practice behind closed doors and windows, so not to rile the neighbors. For piano, her father moved it into a big closet without windows for playing against the salted cold sweat of fear and rehearsed for their best against the worst of times.

A neighbor knocked on the door to complain about the clamor. "Sorry, Sorry," the grandmother said.

"Try silencing me, totally," said Grete to Meta, "Father does. I desire more than birthdays and dressy lunches on the sly, I desire work and my boy friend. I find none. See below for many unemployed men stranded around the Diana or down the street.

"Does any of this matter anyway?"

The statue tiny from the window and tinier still with big Luneburger, surrounding her semi-nude statue, unlike the big military heroes or state leaders, immortalized before public buildings.

"Greetje" noted while she'd been staying in Berlin with her mother, now supporting their family, Grete fashioned lily and orchid corsages for elegant Berlin women selecting gowns in her mother's salon.

"You could do the same," Meta said, "in New York. I do corsages part-time." She bit her lip.

"If I could only be with you in America, but father holds me back. Here I cannot meet anyone. He sees his friends though forbid them or my friends seeing me here or in Berlin. My mother warns me to stay invisible."

On the wall, a photograph profiled her mother, Renate, from her back with head toward the viewer, Ada maybe the photographer? Hair glowed black and clipped to the nape point. A high style designer for Nazi ladies, Renate offered sleek dresses in her salon with hair styling. For her daughter's little party, Renate black-velvet gown contrasted with the white silk with tine red roses.

Besides, her mother had wrought a career from her needle and designs here in Lüneberg. Her studio and salon expanded to Berlin near Hausvogteiplatz, where she and her assistants styled gowns, raiment in peach, blue, or other favored colors to suit their male partners in khaki or iron blue. Rather than sewing, she preferred draping the nineteen-thirty's sloping calf-length crepe dresses.

What could Grete do, but stay home? Working less now, her mother also came home from Berlin to lift her daughter's spirits for her birthday. Hope was sought. Her mother slipped out the front door.

"In America, we'd laugh, Meta, but not here. No one's here, except me, and now you, so I cannot leave. I'm protected, they tell me, against leaving. I dare not talk on the telephone. "Whether my mother's in Berlin or father's here in Lüneburg, I'm confined."

Where did this disjointedness start?

Their old Hanse trading town, Lüneberg, unlike harbor towns, acquired abundance and wealth inland during mercantile times based on salt, preservative from the earth. So, too, citizens nourished their bodies in its mineral baths. Grete and Meta yearned to soak and splash around in an old bathhouse, like Bevensen's.

Coming in her father said, "Be careful what you say to your aunt." Grete had not told him to expect Meta. "Oh." He nodded without engaging her.

"Don't ask for changes in plans. Don't go out" he told Grete. "You have no papers to go anywhere."

"Three years ago," Grete said, "after Georg left for war, Meta departed from Heinrich's for Berlin. I know her plight, necessitating her going to America."

Herr van Relke said, "Don't talk with her father." Meta thought he meant Grete not to talk with her.

"I do. I did. Her uncle-father said so."

"I don't believe you!" Perplexed, his eyes twitched, as if for his focus. "I've done business with him for twenty years." He needed little reminder of rounds to sell cattle to Heinrich and his like. Now his business was slowing, and his trips outside lessened. "I should, have found a way to let you leave."

"I care for myself. I could go now. I'm older. Yes."

"You have. . ." his voice choked, "your identification card won't allow you out."

She squinted at the card's stamp, "Jewish. Why?" He warned her. "Keep the card with you. Don't lose it, ever."

Her father the cattle dealer, now dressed in knickers, light wool brown jacket and golf hat, objected to his laundry basket full of Marks, hoarded from lost value, to buy a shirt. His fraying ones her mother, sorrowful, joked about. "He only knows how to spend money at the cleaners." Renate sounded like a far-off creature.

Greetje was annoyed, when he added that this small city would protect her more than in the countryside or Berlin.

She replied, "You won't let me out, so how would I know?"

"There's no one to rely on inside home or outside.

"The maid's a Nazi to be paid off."

Besides the van Relke family was too poor to employ her or any helper. Nowadays, every family member did chores for themselves, sewing, cooking and cleaning. For background, the radio was snapped onto Mozart, too much from the south Meta's father say from his preference for Bach. Meta nodded to it, and wished for swing just now.

"Don't question him." Grete ordered herself aloud. "I cannot challenge or change my identity. Others dream lives outside."

Her identity card was not for struggling to know her self. Others marked her and rolled her into her tube of destiny.

"Don't go out," He paced away from and returned into the Stube, visitors' room with modern Biedermeier. He said, "Authorities check cards regularly. Mine too. Watch yourself."

He left out the front door.

"Quick, let's rush out the back door and around the corner to my aunt's bakery." They scrammed without sweaters in the cool September air. Entering, Meta saw display cases with stacks of cookies and few small cakes. Apparently supervising from the back, a man with a yarmulke waved Grete into the back. Meta could hear, "You're not to be here, you know, your father and mother do not want you outside." See from there, he removed his skullcap and nudged the two outdoors and gave them a small bag of cookies. Grete and Meta re-entered the apartment building by the back way.

At Grete's birthday party, her mother reminisced. "At your birth, no one had expected her to live to age 18 now. As a two German pound and a half preemie with Das Welt Water, water on the brain, they heard Renate say, "You're lucky to be here!""

Looking backward and forward comforted. Some at the party directed words to Meta, as if entering an unknown world. Uncle Hermann, a World War I veteran, related his exploits,

"A sniper shot me.' Lousy shot.' Later, I hoisted the peace flag for surrender."

"Repression's unhealthy" Uncle Louie, Grete's mother Renate's white-bearded older brother replied. "We've been assuming our freedom existed as really free."

Everyone nodded. From the post-world-war government, he'd received the Iron Cross, First Class for war service. "Three in our family were then imprisoned then in Russia." No one asked why.

Acorns cracked against the windows in the thunderstorm were distracting.

For Grete's hearing only, through her fair cup-cropped and deep waved hair like her mother's, he whispered about Meta's great-uncle. She heard what she knew. "The new Stahlhelm ex-serviceman's uniform replaced his old Freicorps one from the old Imperial Army."

He and Grete's uncle both wore in the war they remembered, hearing and whispering about the overturn of the Sparticists' Rising. . . . "No one celebrates the first great war's end. Everyone scorns its treaty," said Uncle Louis.

Changing the topic from the military to the economy at her birthday gathering, Grete's papa was griping "Agreed but excessive taxes and inflation are the problems. They've pushed us downward from the 1920s on." His eyes tightened at their corners.

"That's why, Grete," he said, "I'm sending you back to Berlin now. Schools there are more cosmopolitan than local ones, wallowing less in anti-Semitism. You might still find your way into university there."

Meta could maybe counter anti-Semitism there, but how? She howled within herself: soon do something. Here and now her little know-how squeaked out. Stealth was essential, quiet watchfulness. Everyone attending Grete's birthday party was quiet, though Meta gathered the following.

At Grete's mother's atelier, they disguised their identities with masques and drapes and lived in its back rooms, while Christian assistants fronted in her shop. Christian customers valued Grete's mother's latest designs as raiment. "'Oh, the Jewish designer isn't still here?'" No was the answer. "'Gut'" answered the answer to the answerer.

Grete's father worried with his brothers-in-law about bad times and hard times. Nazi headmasters were ejecting Jewish teachers and forcing Jewish children out. Her school must have been among the first to do so, though she'd progressed ahead just about ready for her Arbitur. "You're lucky to have gone to the gymnasium."

He left for the day, and they asked what he meant, and they chatted until sundown and overnight. "I don't bother anyone. And I'm not little anymore." Her card did not say, Greetje Alysse. Grete's paternal surname, van Relke, misspelled from some Dutch town.

Some forebears reared and were said to export Haflinger work horses north in the Low Countries. "The Dutch excel," her father always said, "in work, moneymaking and great paintings, like Rembrandt and Van Gogh, though not music. While Germans specialize in sweeping music, engineering methods (except dikes) and science, and they hate politics.'" He chanted foreign names to rouse curiosity, critical for knowing or inveighing against issues. He'd followed his curiosity from Amsterdam to Hamburg, Lüneburg and Berlin, where he'd met her mother.

"Your security troubles me." Grete's father emphasized again, loud enough for Meta to overhear. He worried with his brothers-in-law about bad times and hard times. "Nazi headmasters eject Jewish teachers and force Jewish children out. Your school must have been among the first to oust the Jews."

"That's not so. I finished. I don't go there. Our headmaster told students and especially teachers to leave their Nazi buttons at home. Some did, and some didn't.

"Then comes sadness and shame of losing our favorite teacher, Dr Rosenstein. So you said this yourself. Our headmaster called us all together to tell him we do not want you to leave, and welcomed him back when he could.

She'd progressed and was just about ready for her Arbitur. "You're lucky," he said, "to have gone to the gymnasium." Grete was grimacing.

Such words gave Meta "the willies," a strange new Americanish word. She wrapped herself in her mother's old, she believed, not-yet moth-eaten cashmere pale green shawl to warm herself and to cover her ears.

In the early autumn chill through the crack between the window and its sill, Meta felt she must leave and placed the shawl across her mouth to prevent her speaking out. She must listen only.

Next Grete's father began pacing up and down the long hall. "Remember, you have. . ." his voice choked. "An identification card holds you in, it won't let you out." His eyes twitched to focus. "Unlike vines crawling up through stones or up bricks crack their hard surfaces. You cannot."

"You've been here three months. When your mother returns to Berlin, and I go see her in Berlin, I'll take you there."

Again, Grete squinted at the card stamped: Juden. Why?"

In the morning, he came in. "Keep your with you at all times. Be honest, study and work hard. And be my good little Jewish girl."

Short notes had been filtering in from their friends on going to America. Yet they seemed unaware of goings-on in many cities.

Her Uncles Hermann and Louie, Grete revealed, were rushed off two weeks later to "beating camps." Her birthday was the last time she saw ever saw her two uncles. Therein began the momentum of iniquity.

Meta left after breakfast.

37.

Hopefully, she or someone would gauge how to slip Todd a ticket from Bremen to New York. Horseman he was, so he could race to the Bremen, the world's fastest diesel-run ship in the shimmering harbor. So far, no promises wrenched from Heinrich and his cronies were fulfilled.

Maddeningly, she'd been pursuing her mother first, like the rock of the sun, if such, and mulling over leaving her mother, which is what her mother wished for her to do—Return to northwest Germany to rescue Todd and avenge them both against Heinrich, before it was too late.

For Todd, any trip was affordable by scavenging, begging from his grandfather Heinrich or nagging him for Marks. Sadness overwhelmed her warmth toward Todi and morosity over Heinrich.

Shabby up close, the George Washington would have allowed his sailing in steerage in its last civilian 1931 journey, like Annike's 1921 one from New York to Bremen. This ship was now being revamped for sale, so Todi could not travel on it.

Heinrich would say this. "Earn your own ticket. You deserve what you earn. Remember, first obligated to fight for your country land."

Who knew whether her son, would leave? So on her way she was.

Meta's chosen ship flowed, thought backward, toward Bremen. Waves thundered against its sides, and accompanied her pulsating temples, seen in a mirror. Would she make the whole journey long against expected, known wartime torpedoes?

To prepare to starve in North Germany, she ate on board five meals a day: breakfast, Fruhstuck with crusty roll with marmalade, cheese, salami or egg sliced; midmorning treat, Zweites Fruhstuck,; lunch; dinner, Mittagessen, primary meal with her favorite oxtail soup, fried noodles or next favorite Kloss dumplings and cauliflower, peas, cabbage, asparagus, peas, onion or mushroom choices—barf the asparagus with Schwein, pork—else Rind, beef with potatoes, cauliflower, cabbage and peas; then came the favored night snack, Abendbrot.

Gemutlich distracted her for moments, when the claxon sounded. Enemy ships sighted. Lights out. Below deck, water level, she climbed down for safety to third class of 452 steerage or possibly 1200 people, wondering if Americans, English, somehow Russians and German enemies, whoever the volunteers were, hustled passengers off the deck. Was the enemy on board, on or in the sea?

Gradually though, the ocean liner steamed into Bremerhaven. Only seagulls began massing again to welcome her and other passengers. Few were awaiting them in wartime.

Nausea over her about Todd and her thoughts filled her belly more than morsels from the five meals a day. Todi, now Todd, must be lured to America. If only, she could do so with a neighbor girl back there near Annike. There maybe he'd eye the young buxom Saxon woman, a flaxen-haired Balt.

By now here, the Nazi swastika flags waved like menacing windmills everywhere, and targeted like augurs or drills with punches that set off tocsins over the whole German country-side, especially Lower Saxony.

Was Todi being used by this new regime? Adapting to it? For sure, he'd care for himself, though she was frantic to find him.

Once the passenger ship docked at the Bremerhaven, no one met her at the gangplank, like her New Yorker friend. At least, she could wend her way from Bremen into the Nieder-sachsen countryside, over gravelly roads by catching buses and lorries.

When finally reunited with Todi, he asked, "Why, in hell, did you come here, it's dangerous. His face had already grown whiskery, and his blue eyes were blazing to emphasize his words. "You got out of this jail land; you came back, fool, when you didn't take me the first time?"

Miraculously, he'd been hiding from a Labor Service work camp. "You preferred Grandfather Heinrich and farm animals to me, botany and agriculture." Wrong response. Her unease accelerated. She tried to stifle her words, as von Knigge would have preferred.

"You like animals too, cows, sheep, dogs, you told me so." he said. "You taught me. Then, you left me with him and, then, you skipped out for Berlin."

"Flee or stay! They keep coming up from the South! Over-coming us, they were, and they are." Forces crushed her insides. Rescue or stay. "F__ck, I must leave."

Much later he spoke with his mother with trouble regarding her as his mother known first at her nipples. While trying to sleep under the boathouse roof, breathing startled him before dawn, as someone rustled the bushes. If he breathed, the other breather was breathing in the same rhythm. That sameness was rife within Nazism in Lower Saxony.

Though uneasy and unreal, like the bas-relief gold woman god flying with her gold sword length, in Bremen, he'd fled on his own by steerage on the ship Bremen, from Bremerhaven, to arrive exhausted, dirty and sickly. In this new strange United States, he must have been sleeping in his Grandmother Annike's boathouse enclosed room on top.

From the vaulting oaks and elms with narrow trunks, unlike those in Lower Saxony, a woodpecker flew across to a metal roof point strip; his wracking sound was echoing across the water and hole-drilling into the wood trunk awakened Todi more than the breathing. Did anyone else hear the rooster's' "Cock-a-doodle-doo," like a homing sound?

Minutes later, his cross-breed dog, up to human knees in height, Grant sniffed animal scents like any pointer. This reddish gold dog was blending in, yet standing out in his lean shiny magnificence.

All this he told Meta later. Within the Black Earth area, Sun Prairie and Spring Green and Portage he welcomed such names, like and unlike farm clusters near Barum, Natendorf, Vinstedt and Roenstedt, near Bevensen, south of Lüneburg, triangular with Hamburg and Bremen, carried him back in thought to Saxonland near the Elbe to finish growing up.

Born two score years earlier, he ate, nurtured by his grand-mother and mother. He also reminded her of this. "You ignore my grandmother and me." Hopelessly distanced, Meta despaired. Some great thinker would someday parse out and differentiate forms of filial love.

In this Heartland, walking and hiking, this country kind bounded over barbed wire fences newly dam-electrified on Elbe and Mississippi tributaries. Barriers organized must be overcome.

Neighbors complained to Meta about Grant on the loose to father too many pups, "Todd," as he was often called in his new country, ended his trips for the time being through yards and fields.

For morning dips, Todd and Grant took to swimming free with or against the current. Naked bellies and torsos, still taut, cut across the waves riled the river through the old territory. Into deeper cold water, his toes pointed downward toward bottom sand mush.

Enameling an old canoe red, his grandmother asked, "Why red, for notice?" Both Annike and Meta worried about alienating him by telling him to cover himself and not swim naked in the river, what you could do where he came from. When their gumption allowed them to speak, he asked, "What about the girl down the road in her all-but-nothing, scant bikini?"

When dry, Todd paddled it, onto the mid-river sandbar to fish. Through field glasses, Meta, loving Natur, screamed through a homemade corrugated bullhorn. "Watch out!" Deer rose and fell in leaps downhill to swim in the spiny and silvery river, known for undertow.

Todd yelled back. "Too late. You should have warned me years ago!

Along their dirt road, parallel to the river, slogans were spicing unfamiliar tongues, flying out of cottages, hand-built and authentic though not manger houses. Todd paused at the screen before the Dutch door with Norwegian rosemaling. Lene, the one in the scant suit, there unnerved him. In her cap-sleeved dress over her tan, his mother watched him watch her and, then, both canoe across this body of water: no Baltic, Lake Geneva, Great Lake or Atlantic, though passable for reverie.

Alone without moving, this now older Annike was likened to Nanna. Meta had left the once laughing Nanna months earlier with tender good-byes. Lore's whereabouts though had remained unknown.

All the same, Lene's grandmother asked her point-blank at the Dutch door was her only granddaughter was in love with pesky Todi.

Her mother ignored him though possessed enough English to lace into Mrs. Hasserack whose ducks up and down was the favorite topic on the dead-end road: her fowl littered the shoreline and road with feathers and shit, outraging even the sleepiest people or those most bored with local affairs. She even tended a swan flotilla staying over at the river bend.

Permanent residents did favor two peacocks, who after escaping from a game farm, dwelled all summer in and around the gulley, promenading into yards and heightening the land décor with their grand eye-tail fans and jeweled combs like natural exotica.

The Joneses rolled off their bluff from their lodge, above the riverbed. White Russians descended from their paneled cottages on knolls to view the elegant peacocks.

Ferns also feathered the shady landscape along with poison ivy, oak shoots and locusts with cotton blossoms tufts below which the noisy fowl strutted.

After weighing the matter in their parlors or privies, out-houses, or studios, even irregular summer laborers or fishers gabbed, while catching pan fish at the grade across the grand water pane, edged by green algae, like tiny shamrocks, and yellow lilies.

As issues defined themselves, people sided pro or con: summer regulars though Mrs. Hasserack breached the code of quiet. This short white-haired Eastern European imposed herself on others. Full-time residents hoped she would redeem herself by restoring her earlier fleet of swans, however peevish they might be.

So Oscar, older than Todd and Meta's neighbor, acted. Some said his colonel father egged him on. Others reacted to Oscar; they insisted, like Todd, he should join up before called up. Oscar's pot-shots at her ducks indicated such. Some joked. "Stuff the ducks, and serve them to us."

Mr. Kisofsky, never working, strolled over to Mr. Goldman, another manager retiree, both unlike most retirees and refugees with modest camp-like lives. An informal circle organized to rid the neighborhood of Mrs. Hasserack and her littering fowl.

This group also initiated another aspect of their clean-up campaign by interrogating lodge owners or cottagers to ward off potential tavern owners, other riffraff and feathered folks.

The two longtime permanent residents, antagonists usu-ally, allied with the nature seekers and fishermen. Coming and going, Todd grinned, as he awaited Lene in her khaki shorts. "Foreigners, the whole mess of them, whether Chicagoans or Eurasians," as his grandmother and others newcomers derided them. Some chuckled. "Mrs. H. was cooking her goose." In flowery apron, blood spotted, she plucked and sold the bodies for roasting and feathers for featherbeds.

Todd, Meta and Annike, attuned especially the or-ange-gold orioles' glory high in elm and oak trees, heard only Mrs. H's shrill, "Here ducky, ducky, ducky, ducky. Here ducky, ducky, ducky." Todd, once weak from hiding out and fleeing Europe grew healthy, delighted in ducks, robins, blue jays, sparrows and orioles, secluded himself, except for Lene.

Veiled by dense willows onshore, his gazing on Lene was blocked from Meta's view.

1933 elections had just thrust the Nazis into Niedersachsen, Lower Saxony, for the first electoral success of its program in the whole of Germany. "They came from the South," Nanna had always said. "They came from the South. You saw their swastikas on the sides of trains and in their flags."

38.

When Todd at 18 first landed in this area, his grandmother and mother feared that he foreign-speaking would fall in with bad types. But he'd studied English and other subjects, when able to do so. Fishing he continued from the Llemenau, Weser and Elbe on the Mississippi branch outside their front door.

In time, engrossed in photography, nature, art and women's bodies, he stayed fit and prepared for mountain climbing without any local mountains by climbing the high standing rocks along the rivers off and on the Mississippi.

Thankfully, he'd never fallen in with the negative types down the road. Enough of them existed in Meta's family and hoped-for former country. Hopefully too, her new chosen land would not fall into a similar desperado status.

Herding and growing were practiced again in local farm jobs, where he learned to supervise migrants all the way up north from the West Indies and Mexico. They plucked cucumbers, "pickles," from the ground or apples from trees or work in canneries. A Mr. Meyer hired him to keep an eye on his workers in the Del Monte canning factory in town, meant to scrutinize them and prevent any acts deemed insubordinate or treasonable. By that Mr. Meyer referred to those local folks called "foreigners."

Todd assumed at first that Mr. Meyer distrusted the whole pack of them. But uneasily Todd figured out he could press one against the other, if necessary, especially those of different races.

After the governmental agricultural unit authorized local canneries to utilize laborers from the enemy, Mr. Mayer charged his prime worker, Todd, with checking for shaky fences and those prisoners of war. Deliberately, Mr. Meyer directed him to scrutinize the newcomers on the cannery floors, in assembly lines in canned corn and other vegetables.

How it developed was this. Governmental personnel called on Mr. Meyer to determine how many workers he'd use for the harvesting time of anticipated bushels of cucumbers, apples, cabbage or corn from fields into cans. Totals known for needs, government offices arranged for the workers' bussing north.

But a new element sprang out of a bus. Todd and the newest ones spoke the same language. Not surprisingly, Mr. Meyer assigned him watch over them.

The first time face to face, once the migrants climbed down from their buses, shocks flashed throughout his body. Mr. Meyer was noncommittal about their arrival; he let it happen. Todd let them spread out on the floor, wherever there existed uncovered posts on the assembly line. So far, so good, tow-headed or brown-haired men, straight black haired ones and black-tight haired interspersed. At his order, Todd, free thinker, prayed for peace. Also, his mother did.

At first, Mr. Meyer said all was going well: a daily rhythm occurred, a hum in the productivity. Todd held his breath. Tension mounted. From greater experience than Todd's, Mr. Meyer re-arranged some workers. Could they sing? The newcomers could, as Todd soon discovered. They baited each other.

The indigenous Mexicanos called the African-Blacks from Jamaica called the latter, "Tom-Toms". They named the former "Tomatoes." Both pointed to the Krauts as cabbage heads.

They saw nothing; he anticipated nothing. One day, an inmate from the war prisoners camp group jumped on a pyramid of tomatoes, jumped on them like a pestle and yelled, "Heil Hitler! Heil Hitler!"

Todd's stomach, he told his mother, Meta, bottomed out. Nausea overtook him. The air stank. The tomatoes mashed and squirted.

39.

Driving East six months later from staying with his grandmother in the West was slow. Soon due at NYPD headquarters, he drove the winding narrow turnpike through the dark
green mountainy hills of Pennsylvania. Mist and fog clouded
the valleys. Rain gusted, so he languished in the roadside park.
Swing music and classics sounded through radio static, as rain
slashed his windshield.

He whiled away a Howard Johnson lunch, with mint
julep ice cream. Starting again, he drove at a crawl, so Meta
never awakened, until the rain dribbled, when he began
gunning the motor, then stop-starting his car. "Shouldn't we
stop?"

Mugginess brought on sweat, as he was pulling off a sleeve
at a time and stretching his old hounds-tooth sports jacket
caught in his seat hinge. He wanted to rip it out. "It's hot,"
She said.

Caught in traffic and with his mother, needing delivery,
he might not make the appointment with Brid and other victims, much less the Chinese feast with his co-workers. He
slowed his Chevie on the freeway, and drummed his fingers
outside the door window. ing," he said, "two ways at once to
get where you're going. Traffic's so slow, you could walk on this

damn turnpike faster than drive it." Drivers watched backward, while going forward.

The cars in sight of New York's spikes lined up the side view mirrors. To distract himself, in these mirrors, he examined faces and parts, while cars traveled five-ten m.p.h.

Ahead, the driver was chatting to someone unseen, a short woman, child or midget, maybe with no one else to talk to. "Cars are houses." His mother nodded.

Two cars ahead, the driver chewed gum, reminding Todd to stick into cinnamon tang into his mouth subbing for a cigarette for ten-twenty minutes. Roosevelt used a holder, like his great aunt. Another driver behind, dark-skinned, threw away his gum or cigarette stub out the window.

The third barely visible driver rotated his head and adjusted the car side view mirror, revealing bare skin below his glasses' rims and above his dark beard. "Doesn't that head remind of Georg?" Meta, sleepy, asked.

Its shape did remind him of his dead father's. As cars lurched, the already semi-broken tube of mirrors wobbled. In this reconfigured tube with stopped cars shaped itself out of reflected jaws, chins and eyes. In the angle of the sun and highway incline, light flashed along this periodical tunnel that approached the highway exit. He continued on and was about to deliver his mother to her upper Manhattan apartment.

Inching toward the police center, Todd swore he'd seen the guy who'd bashed in the doors to burglarize his Brid's apartment and others. The burglar had pistol-whipped each victim and raped some, not Brid, thank God, and rifled homes.

Halfway up the stairwell to her place, Todd in an instant spotted the attacker's dirty white sneakers flying by at eye level and the criminal's face in that light, he'd have to account for him with the cop artist. Only a glimpsed face, true. He'd welcome Brid's and others' describing the criminal. He didn't have to, did he? At the NYPD, wrangling inside himself, he'd help identify that bastard. Do it and escape to Chinatown.

Finally there, in the big pressed tin high-ceilinged, ivory room with a dozen desks, the group was standing around on one foot or the other, unbalanced, and kibitzing among themselves, until something happened in a cubicle.

Within the victim cluster, he found Brid and squeezed her arm. She responded, "What took you so long?"

"Traffic and letting off my mother. I should've walked here."

"A yellow cab, driven by a cop, brought me here. "One of the fleet parked below this building."

This fact intrigued him more than the endless talk about the alleged criminal's features. While the police artist was sketching the attacker's face, his victims were kyboshing his drawing.

Brid, Todd and a tall woman runner from the neighborhood thought that they'd seen the attacker. She pressed the artist, "Change the criminal's nose or ear." Brid heard and he perceived the ears as pointed and devilish.

He said, "The hair should be bushier."

The tall woman disagreed. "The hair was flattened."

"His hair was bushy."

"What's seen depends, Todd said, "view angle, time of day, amount or slant of light."

No one listened. Face down, the artist, bearded in silver-needled, was re-sketching features for a composite agreed on, a likeness, for a WANTED poster.

Todd was disgusted at this endless process and stayed more the onlooker than witness, much less a victim. This artist guy should use an abacus as a palate. To get to the mug shot, give each a try for the frontal head they'd each seen, he grumped to anyone who'd listen, and draw their views. The victims bickered.

Todd brooded. Was he was blowing away his last best friend? Or else, he had none left. The elder grandmother he'd left, flown from, in the mid-country, out West. She'd fret, strut and drift into sadness. Ramrod though, his mother, Meta, sat by the window or in a shadow in her maroon lounge chair. A-tilt, her bearing resembled youthful jauntiness. She, like her mother, his grandmother tucked her heels in the front ledge of her chair to bring her knees up to her breasts. Her posture looked that way. Only her high blown bust, not her knees, puffed out. Her knee-ed bosom and trifle upper crust dignity had protected her, from cowing by his grandfather's ravings.

"What's on your mind? Meta his mother asked

His grandmother's and great grandmother's joyful pre-tense safeguarded him from her fears and his. As viewed, they, like those of his great grandmamma risked dementia, madness from governmental dementia. Forget, forgotten. Yet muddles clear, and candor returns.

They could leave Annike on her beloved little farm, even if her state of mind fluctuated and, then, stabilized. Meta told him that he gathered the neighbors regarded him as careless, when in fact he was care-ridden about whether to uproot her. Nanna would have opposed leaving the v. Cherusch home-stead. To think her own thoughts belonged in her place on earth. Annike's too.

As for Meta, her lucidity struck down their anxiety some-times. Inaction and disorganization stymied her and enraged her.

Here in the police lab, he sat and later told Meta in dutiful ways, the two would-be criminals' indistinctness played on his mind and harped there. Another accused prisoner he'd visit next. He could little leave the two alone. The drawn face, agreed on by the victims, was looming up at him from the drawing board and wound into his father the generic indistinct criminal he'd rid himself of.

Re-attuning to the most recent attacker, not his father, who made off with Brid's jade jewelry, car keys with its glow in the dark color coded rubber orange, red and green circles. The robber stole a portable record player, three buzzer alarm clocks, two radios and an ultrasonic insect exterminator she'd borrowed from him.

Around the police artist, the victims ranged from squat to stately. The shapely woman to his left planned her life as a photographer. Her trim beige felt sombrero was fringed below in light brown long hair to her buxom self, as her pants tightened on her butt above her boots. What boots! Bas-relief cherry inlaid cordovan!

In their semi-circle, the tallest dark-haired woman beat against the attacker from above him on the stairwell, by swinging her bag and screaming. After her standoff account, a tall odd duck with lank mouse colored hair leaned her flat backside on one of the desks and said nothing.

In the circle came three more women. A youngish matronly black teacher in a daisy print dress worried about her husband's finding out about the rape itself. Others were preoccupied with stolen goods. Next to Brid, another tall reddish-blonde stood hoaxed by the mess she found herself in. Only Lia the Philippina remained poised by saying nothing.

Finally, they agreed on the attacker's wanted poster. Their wretchedness concluded at that moment by defining this looks. Until they met at a future lineup to identify him in person, they said good-bye.

Todd gazed up out the window, at the Manhattan Bridge and Brid, when he bid her, "So long," and kissed her good-bye.

Outside en route to the Chinese restaurant, near police headquarters, the bridge soared across the East River. Between little Poland of Williamsburg and Chinatown, the structure lit up at dusk like a dragon.

Two months after the break-in and composite drawing meeting, Todd visited a buddy in Philadelphia that familiarized him with a live prisoner, the third so-called criminal who preoccupied him. The burglar the first and the second Michael and his father was the last-first. The second met through Mack, known in grad school five years earlier.

Mack's stepfamily and he stayed on under one roof. Todd believed his mother came from a stepfamily. Considering family comfort, security and street solidity, psh, he countered his wish for easygoingness. His family, if any stayed on in Niedersachsen or dispersed. Who cares? Who curses? Did it matter? He survived. The heroic Saxon must gave birth to the Individual, not that anyone cared.

Mack returned to the Philly house. He referred to his father's stepchildren, as "brother and sister," and asked, "Want to see the house?" Not really. Checking the 1700s' home top down, they his father's woodwork staining and the family pet.

Early modern pin pillow style chair and sofa fit the antique Seth Thomas, clock and Chippendale. Todd would like to flop there.

In the kitchen, he could enter the colonial fireplace. Down from there, cellar stairs top, Mack lit up. In this household, Todd felt calmer than in his mother's. All was order, though on the last step, the bottled cobra daunted him. Due its daily mouse, it uncurled and sissed.

When the snake wiggled, Todd shivered. "No snakes in Ireland," Todd said, "You taking it to there?"

"Kidding? Snakes live on the continent." In Ireland without original sin, they were all sacrificed to appease some god or goddess, who carried them over the Great Unknown, land of eternal youth.

Back upstairs, Mack asked his father, "Are you returning to Europe and Mom," Rowena, "or staying here with Tina?" Gill was noncommittal.

To Todd, Mack said, "Gill's spending time here with a maternal woman on leave from her husband. She caters to all his needs and cooks."

"Your father's a lover," Todd said, "Mine's a killer."

Brid, less staid over time, was letting down her long flaxen hair, draping it over her body, Godiva-like. When clothed, she hid her low round breasts just above her blouse or under her see-through jersey. Her low round buns to her calves tapered to long feet with high arches and to stubby, wiggly toes.

She demanded nothing from their emerging bond. Since the incident in her building, she vibrated her body less. The break-in and burglary in her apartment rendered their lives form-less. Loss of her large and small gizmos lessened her confidence.

To escape chaos and see the Old World, they'd seek clarity in the bracing green desert, where peaks fell into the ocean, where Michael had sailed. They would avoid the German continent.

He imagined Michael's color WANTED poster for the second criminal, hair waved and sun-bleached, so that his eyes averted into an inward light toward his own thoughts--instead of away, like most eyes. Transferring his focus to others, he heartened his listeners, as a star leader, not a criminal.

Michael's beliefs victimized him. Todd struggled with what they were and sought his principles, as he strolled along the corrugated prison wall. He noticed a plaque that honored the first Sunday school conference here on this spot. Picture the building forerunner now housing a government agency at one end and a prison at the other.

Now its planners ridged the grey, concrete walls like bars with spaces between. To look up, he leaned back, a would-be architect, at iron wedges into the concrete windows, like castle or fortress.

Inside the waiting room, two guards did duty in their navy blue. He waited for the procedure. "What do you want?" Todd asked. Reality is what we argue about.

"Apply to get in," he said and filled out the blue form, name, address Meta's, age twenty-five. He sat. Moments later, he stood to get a soft drink, walked the corridor and gazed through the prison's street-level steel windows.

Yellow cabs whizzed by outside. The authorities, he conjectured, used one in their surveillance to capture Michael.

In this dying day, he stayed put in the lobby of inner tinted glass and concrete walls. Its steel beams overhead resembled a hangar.

A helicopter on its roof here could rescue Michael who could not get out. Usually, prisoners awaiting their federal offense appealed. Todd tried to let others think of himself as inoffensive, a viewer rather than detector, shaker or pusher. In wash pants and blue-black jacket, his fingers combed through two inches of hair to his neck fuzz. Now his guilt was imprisoning him.

After each entrant, the metal door clank-locked. The sound reinforced how pissed off he was having wasted three hours to get through it. Worse, Michael's defense lawyer had yet to arrive to accompany Todd inside. The door's glass' shaking left him shaken and gloomy. Before it fell shut, he'd expected to get into prison and out fast.

Living nearby, he could leave without seeing M... When all the area city buildings locked up for the night, dusk was cheerless.

Nearby outside, the dragon's mouth opened to grandeur in disrepair and barely lit in wartime. The monument, a triumphal war memorial arch, opened to the causeway or bridge, like the serpent biting Manhattan and disgorging chariots.

Meanwhile, opposite the prison waiting area, plate glass stood at right angles refracting and reflecting images, such as, blue guard uniforms over visitors' red, green, black clothes. They riled in movement, as the door rattled and clanked. One living color flesh blotted over green.

To while away the time, he read magazines. In the margins, he doodled. Brid told him his doodles embedded phalluses in a network like tattoos or wire constraints. That's what happened in Germany: the garbage of human nature took over and combined.

Surly inside over waiting to get into the prison, he snarled. Many are called, few admitted, thank god.

Just then, an African-American guard called, "Over here." He jerked his head. Reaching for his package, he hesitated, as she called out again. He'd leave it under his chair and doubted he'd get it in without the lawyer. Clay rounded its head, club foot shape or shoulder for tailoring fit, such as his mother used in fine woven business suits, made though out of soft Saxon wool imported in her avocation until she flew back to the Midwest to farm. He was at the prison's door.

"Fill out the form again! Doublecheck for mistakes. For one, your hair's gray-brown, not dark brown." His hair was graying by twenty-five. Now he was thirty-eight, going on ninety-nine, like his mother. Next the guard let stand his blue eyes and six feet and two and a half inches as facts. "You've got Michel for Michael." He never could spell.

Vexed. Fascist type in the making, though changed his mind, when she waved him on in. "It's too soon," He protested. "I-I'm waiting for the lawyer."

"Go in. If you don't, you lose your bench place to someone else. She buzzed the door open. "No packages. You apply to take in packages."

A gong sounded. Five guards dove to confiscate his clay. While he rose in the elevator, they disappeared from his view. So much effort to find the clay, and they snatched it from him and Michael.

He likened this elevator to A&S or Macy's. The prison needed an escalator. At the sixth floor, bars along the inside glass marked the place a prison. He stepped off that locked behind him. Within vault-like in thickness, his spine stiffened into a rod. A prisoner bounded over. The blue uniform set off intense inward eyes assessing the stranger on the bench.

Todd gathered, was expecting to see the lawyer.

"He didn't show," he said. Anyway, they shook hands close to the locked entrance.

"I tried bringing in your clay."

Last seen five years ago, girls vied with his wife for this fellow. Now his hair clipped, sun yellowed and skin burnt-darkened around his face. The weather-beaten, salted eye lines and stubby though his straight nose dented deeper than when seen last. His gaze hawked Todd. Weight surrounded Michael's torso, extra girth from all the arms who'd hugged this prisoner, now hunched over on the bench. Clammed up, he looked calm, when Michael found him. They might have been meeting at a gallery for the new man sculpture.

Abruptly clouded, Todd designed his father's mug shot with his pen or from guides with dozens of feature shapes; he might arrive at the truth. He sweated. He wished to sit down. Todd was transposing his own father's head onto the so-called fluid criminal.

The police sketch compelled Todd to turn away from how agitated he remained over his old man ad Meta too. He'd told her so. Long before the break-in and attack, dealt with right here by the cops, that Georg old son of a gun with his poses and sodden views died. He'd fallen on the sidewalk, didn't he, around the corner from his mother's house?

Of ears and eyes, as if jellied, sights could mold them and the ear from memory: he'd had even talked with some men about his old man.

Todd dared not talk too much. No one would believe him. They might abhor him. With pen, ink and paint, he tried, he told his mother, with some therapy with no outcome.

Talking friend to friend, Brid, about his father would overwhelm her. With his mother, he might speak about him. He'd preferred to wipe him out, altogether. To say this to his mother would only weaken her and enfeeble his grandmother, now gone anyway, though ever present.

The man dead, Todd could smite memories of him into oblivion. Paternal criminality still dominated his life. He thought back unendingly.

Named Theodor, nickname and botched into Todi, until his mother mispronounced "Todd," he could be Ted for new life, new man.

Resembling his mother, others said, at times more than the father he barely knew and grandfather, he paused here in the police room on the way out.

To Mack, he'd choke and say, "My father would prefer to kill your Jewish father."

40.

Hansi, Erik and their mother still lived in Berlin, not far from Grete's mother's former design studio, staffed by others. Liesl wrote, "By the way, another youth attacked him. He's a target for bullies and has been staying at home to recover. Now he's afraid, but his new stepfather will see to protect him. Hoodlums will go to the prison camps or the army."

Greete, now back to Grete her real name or sometimes Greetje, more Dutch sometimes than German, not so Jewish, re-interpreted her name first but not yet in the vicious circumstances referred to in a letter to Meta that might never have reached her, had it not been for Liesl's relaying it from Grete's mother.

Grete's confinement document, Meta knew from earlier visits, was preventing departure, obscuring her deepest wishes and muzzling her. Shame in Meta about this crisis was set in unease that began dizzying, in fact, over figuring out how to get Grete out, Grete who'd listened to Meta. If she had been listening, would she have known what was happening?

Meanwhile, Felix disappeared. He was Grete's favorite uncle. Originally, to aid the family family-wellbeing, Felix had put her father into business. Later he did so with her mother, his sister.

He and his brothers were shipped off to Oranienburg, a castle out of routine public sight. Still anyone, Meta, Grete or Katia, might have been sightseeing or wandering and found it a place to walk around in and see inside. Except that in1933, local NSDAP party officials kept inmates of sight and whipped them before release. The camp belonged to clusters with central names in and around Berlin.

Even so, none of them could trace Felix. Moreover, other party members, conservative or liberal, could not appeal to the now master party new to tracking lost family keystones, like Felix. Neither the Polizei nor the courts follow up on these SS wildfire campsites. The court and police could not produce the camper bodies anyway. The local security units too were in flux.

New authorities seized other brothers of Renate, uncles of Greta were abducted. One wound up in Teitz's model Columbia House, the Berlin Polizei jail.

They ordered her mother's cousins to dig a canal from the Elbe to the sea. Also in the Sachsenhausen orbit was Neuengamme with 90 sub-camps all posted on the North Sea and near Hamburg. Near there, Grete's older cousin was railroaded to a Wentdorf, transit center by way of Hamburg.

Thank heavens, Klaus her younger cousin aged 13, got packed off to London by Kindertransport. There Bleak House laid bed side for him.

Later on, her mother said her father was imprisoned in "the Dutch quota." Her mother worried about him out loud. Sh-h-h. Eventually, they heard he was working in the Wine Mountains, near Bordeaux. After French disbelieved his ethnicity, he was rerouted north to Todt, doing forced autobahn labor.

Because of Judischverszipt, her parents' mixed marriage, her Jewish mother confided bad news, she slipped out words. "Your father's imprisoned in the new system." Karin Goering might have revealed its nature within Renate's art deco salon clientele.

Art Deco seen as geometric zigzag, but to Grete was mostly a bull's-eye style with gold target embellishing the elevator door or etching on the glass door window.

"Where'll he stay?" Her throat ultra-dry, Grete asked her mother, Renate, who no longer dressed up much at home and slouched more than was in style.

"He sleeps on the stone floor in a place, a, a–prison camp for criminals."

"Why?"

"Don't ask." Quiet! Be rational. Don't be rational.

"You're father's head injury was stitched twenty-one times. He hides in his armpit a Star of David inside a heart locket with a cross outside for luck. He told me he would."

Why did a Star of David adorn the church steeple on the edge of this jeweled city Lüneberg? Meta wondered and once asked her uncle father. En route away from it toward Berlin, looking back, she noticed it.

Eventually and disdainfully, Father Heinrich explained to Meta that Christianity contained the Talmud, maybe as the Bible enclosed it. So too the steeple dramatized the Star. All the same, it was called a star fort.

Meta imagined what Grete knew. Where her mother wept though to suppress her tears in, their cousins cowered. "Mutual support in the camp might help. That's what we kids knew at home."

Their Berlin once considered elegant, contained poor people, poor Jews, others now poor. Jewish lawyers and businessmen were becoming more poor. The Jews were stoned in both cities and mauled and were about to be hauled away forever, in gallows injustice.

Could they have known?

Years later, Angela the avenging angel told Meta: "My grandmother and I watched the Kristalnacht destroying all the Jewish –owned shops by daylight and night moonlight."

Her uncle was becoming the district Gauleiter.

So Grete's Uncle Hermann tried a flight to Cuba via Bremerhaven. Uncle Ralph did so too, though no one knew where. Two other uncles fled to wooded areas to work as farriers on horses going off to war.

If they did, she told Meta, why could she Grete also stow away on a ship? She plotted to do so.

Now the aunts and women in general, considered irrelevant to the regime at first, were trying to lie low. They were endangered. Ultimately, Aunty Ruth hid in a water pipe but was caught and sent off to Zamosch, near Lublin. Aunt Edith did hard labor only in her underwear. These facts were learned only later helter-skelter at first, when someone somehow got let out and told. Most aunts and cousins dissolved, never seen to leave.

Upon hearing this account, Meta blanched. Why the horror beyond words? What happened?

On Good Friday, fifty women and four children escaped from a forced labor camp–just as they were lined up for shipping to Thieriesenstadt.

"I'm surviving," said Greta thought to herself. "I'm still alive." Much later on, she tried speaking. Insisted they listen; her eyes were sparking out of her eye sockets within her pert face, dappled through her straw hat in sunlight, as she spoke. Reality shimmered, as she was cold and exhausted.

All in the family ruminated in half-phrases. Her leg was broken in two, like a stick, rendering her lame with a peg-leg at best.

"Some Poles, part-Jewish," her mother said later, "helped us get away for awhile. But the Nazis chopped down the oak and elm woods for firewood, so no one could hide.

But they were terrified of revenge.

"Even the camp cook, who'd made us cabbage water soup with bread crusts for our daily meal got away. But he was the only Nazi the newest authorities found at first.

"What you are matters little now. How you do everything does."

41.

In her New York interim, Meta layered herself in sweaters and winter jacket and bounded into the spring snow on a rare free late Saturday afternoon and loped toward the river. Globs were splashing her, and more refined swastikas as snowflakes were cascading. Humming and half-singing an aria from La Rondine by Puccini from Berlin opera memories, she danced toward the Hudson, as a barge drifted by.

A new life across this river and farther west awaited her in the larger Mississippi valley, where she'd planted corn, groats and grains, potatoes and strawberries. Making new friends, she'd inured herself against self-mockery for now also by circulating flyers for Jo's campaign.

Walking along blocks of brick stacks high up, she ruminated about present horrors from newspaper headlines. The ventriloquist Hitler had ordered his troops to march east. What could knowledge do?

Upon her New York arrival two years earlier, 3000 miles away from Niedersachsen, she'd worked in the flower shop, picking up wilted flowers and clipping stems helped pay rent and buy food. Daydreaming about the future lessened worrying about the past while picking at a hangnail over the future.

Her unwillingness to stay in New York overcame her. Should she let go of this man of her new office, or go with him. Not that he wanted her to, nor did she expect his anger, much less his irritability when his money ran out, he'd returned to the office. Playfulness soothed his crotchetiness. Behind Max, Georg flew and was ignored.

Thoughts of her grandmother, Nanna, ever spinning, crocheting and tatting, saddened her. "If anyone's handing out blessings, take them," Nanna once told Meta. "Don't let them go." Aunt Lore wrote: the demoniac warhead countered all hope and blessings to sustain them. Her mother, Annike, was still beckoning her toward the Mississippi.

Like snow, her thoughts floated with new American English word meanings, such as, "smash hit," on a Broadway theater marquee and billboards, "The Wizard of Oz." Thoughts ran onto "heartbreak."

In the conference room, Max lined up employees to lecture on work habits. Then, he'd guffaw.

Max was manifestly safer with Abby than with herself. Abby's stone face was stoical, how odd. When he left, wide-browed, placid, Abby noted with Meta, "You're enjoying your work." Together in child guidance, Meta pretended to happiness pursued in her new country. Matched with a devout red-haired man, Abby was happily married.

The child guidance movement struggled in 1920s' and 1930s New York and was still. Money was funneled in the 1930s for dire necessities, like food and this Central Bureau annex, "school behavior clinic for "truants, retardates, and de-linquents." Such clinics had been tried out in Berlin. Here psychiatrists, social workers and some psychologists teamed up to diagnose troubled kids. Their family members confided in these professionals to thwart criminality.

In 1930s Berlin, it hadn't work. Berlin. She scrutinized Aichhorn for leads here and now.

Mostly new in Manhattan, Viola, Abby and Meta chimed in about their skills and eagerness to assist black agricultural laborers' children, Central European refugees and even new Americanos Latinos—desperate to survive, Jewish children also trickled in now.

"We and they're up against the odds," Viola, her black hair trim and skirt deftly hemmed by hand, said. "Look at me growing up shit dirt floor Hungary, the winter earth. Here I lived on Rivington Street and now in Riverdale. If you've ever been dirt shit poor, you don't want to go back." Jane Brantley nodded her understanding.

During lunch, Abby withdrew into Talmudic study. Once she mused on her spouse who daily bussed into the City from their Catskills bungalow across the river valley. En route and back, he prayed.

Fleeing Germany early on for Cuba, she thanked her father's acumen. But their flight wholly re-possessed her every dark season. Her grim affect lead her husband to devise a lamp board with bulbs, like udders, to brighten her, as if in summer.

Could Meta find his Christian counterpart, though more secular than Abby's Jewish husband, to line up rose-colored bulbs to uplift her own sour wartime mood?

Her protestant Aunt Lore once whispered, "Jewish men make good husbands." How would she have known? Meta would not disclose this view to her Orthodox Jewish co-worker friend. Perhaps some good man would materialize, though LIFE reported little possibility with America's divorce rate the highest in the world, and its veterans dead from war. Not missing her deceased spouse, German lover turned soldier, whichever, she did miss warm beings. They included Todi, Mopsi, Georg, and nursed a ballooning grievance, hidden or disguised, from all out loss.

Abby had married into a Jewish winemaker lineage, her daughter into a shoemaker one and her son into one of doctors. Her husband thrived as a structural engineer, "the finest man who never lets himself be known to me. I wish only for my husband to tell me I am the most special woman. Otherwise, he's as perfect a man and father as known in the universe. If only, he told me he loved me.

"Nevertheless my cruel, imperfect father accuses me of speaking street Spanish and ordered me as a child, off the street to study only the highest culture."

"Mine, too. Mine is much worse." Meta cowered at her thought. Not quite, "Far more than yours." She could not speak about his unspeakable violence and views.

"But I wanted friends," said Abby, "in any culture. If we could get on board, we chose Cuba, for she was granted instant citizenship. Compartments on the way over were never clean on rough seas. Once we reached Havana, my father ordered us around. 'No street Spanish.'"

Of the child guidance movement, organized by social workers across the U.S., this particular office maze offered minimal light and no frivolity during the Depression.

Abby and Meta returned to work. Humility met infinity. German hardly mattered to Abby. Winter and war sadness overwhelmed everyone. At times, Max and Abby spoke Yiddish, his acquired "Piggin-Yiddish," and in their

Hebrew-German, they seemed to understand each other. Was she intrigued by him?

Safe though, devout, married and truthful, Abby worked with her husband's consent on her "City College degree," though her father pressed her away from CCNY toward Barnard College, Columbia University. "Too old to change," she told him, and was matching her daughters for marriage, when with fewer shoemakers and winemakers existed.

Three hours later, Max's office door was closed. Meta did overhear him say, "Thank God for Abby and Meta."

The next day on the fire escape, his inhaling his cigarette and exhaling scratched her throat. She whispered to his back, you're photogenic.

Once Jane Brantley stepped onto the fire escape, everyone noticed. The elegant woman, ebony, leaned on the railing jutting out allowing extra room, poised, she noted, "It' close in there."

Also out for air, Thomas chuckled and puffed between eye blinks in their smoky shroud. He puzzled over his brand's wrapper, newly from blue to white, "Camels."

"My father," Jane said, squeezing farther onto the fire escape. "Mine foisted Camels on me."

Fred also eased onto the fire escape and asked, "Max, dinner tonight?"

Nausea fit paranoia in Meta, as they dispersed back into their offices. She could ask Jane to lunch with her, she would but could not at this time.

Isolated by a temporary duo, her own parents barely known, subjected her to attack.

Rippling thoughts of Max let her down. Her face, mirrored in the bathroom, tipped and pale like the moon.

A recent folded circle fortune cookie read: "The greatest joy in life is doing what others say you must not do." Meta's tummy scrunched up. She'd ask Jane soon to lunch.

One week later, when Meta asked Max, "Could we ride to the meeting in my new old jalopy Chevie." Max agreed. Now, he might think she wanted to seduce him. She did, but did not know how. His friend Thomas might advise him to get rid of her. The frightening ambiguity of life offered no certainty. Any overture from her would swamp him.

Up the ramp, he said, "I've had some bad luck here, can you tell?"

She was struggling to comprehend the exit sign. The highway authority had switched the highway ramp sign from left to right.

"Sorry about bad luck. But from where I'm from, my aunt writes and hints about how the war is horrifying there. Women must end this war. No one else is,"

"We must do something about this war, mustn't we? But what?"

Helplessness overcame hopelessness. "We should. But what?" She snapped out and got out from under the driver's wheel and stood downhill from him.

He stepped uphill. "I'm getting a sandwich."

"I'm eating Chinese," she replied. Her last fortune cookie's message, "Be more outgoing."

Why her sonority with Max? Ducks quacked in thick cold rains and were stopping the thought.

At her shared desk. He was at his down and around the hall. In honor of Nanna, she'd bought and paged through her saints' calendar for St. Rita, saint of lost causes, a little similar to St. Anthony's role with lost items.

In the afternoon, Max avoided eye contact and chuckled over headlines about embezzlers and war profiteers. Up closer than newspapers, his wrinkles were ridges, and Sol's cheek pores were holes. Nervously, on her first day after a six week leave, Sol ordered Meta to search papers.

At E building office, heat even penetrated the thick walls. Sol and Abby were somewhere

Before Meta answered phone receiver, the caller clicked off. She was thrilled, as if discovering gold, though she was afraid Todi would know only the war and was about to be called up. Meta prayed, "End this hell soon."

Rounding the maze, Max sputtered. "Hell, Can't people write, so I can understand congestive heart failure or hardening of the arteries? She's crrrazy, says I'm trying to kill her in the war."

Sorry for him, Meta remembered her grandmother and mother's shaky health.

Six months in their office, he said, "Maybe I'll meet someone, if I leave here." He ducked into the men's toilet. She'd fled into the women's. Now his partings in a few days lead her skin to separate from her body.

Opening a window the next day, Max smashed its pane, sliced his forefinger and jumped in pain. She raced to wet paper toweling to staunch his finger's blood.

Biding time with Abby excused Meta's worry and not working. Going back to Germany was a possible impossibility, because birthright and custom dropped her and Todi, for sure?

42.

Meta's summertime away from the city school to see her mother was impossible without extreme scrimping for the trip. Her mother, a bit frail, had begun to hug her upon her arrival in the most recent of her three visits, as someone other than a stranger. They spoke about relatives, including her mother Nanna, her mother's others unknown. Nanna was long absorbed into Heinrich's estate. Mother and daughter mourned her, while they ignored Heinrich for the moment.

Settling in, Meta wore shorts or pedal pushers with a flowery halter and her mother plaid Bermuda shorts or jeans for gardening, farming, canning or working in munitions. Now dressed for gardening, they checked on Targetas, marigolds, sprouting without yet blooming, yellow Ringelblum and the new Wicke row to bloom in a year.

Her next task was to see to her mother's health and Todi's well-being out of war. Her arteries own felt scooped out, her mother's sagged and wanted stiffening to feel natural. Everyone commented on hardening of the arteries, whatever that was. Todd looked well. But Meta felt weary.

Throughout the river valley and hollows, glass panes and dishes rattled and startled the defenseless. Some men, wrinkled inside and out from age or half-disabled little qualified for direct war, and some women, like Annike, kerchiefed in yellow, carried their lunch buckets with sandwiches to work in the American war effort.

A week later, mist spritzed her. Her new acquaintance, one of several area including "von" surnamed people, meaningless here, though meaningful in the old Saxon territories invited her to a casual party. A von married to a non-von, was giving this party for "J.T.," someone unknown.

Attending friends would create home gifts; anything plucked like berries, knit, crocheted, built small items or fished from the river, because most people lacked cash. Handmade or handcrafted were regarded as quality, more so than ones bought. Crocheting, knitting or wood carving would most of all cut down on general boredom. Waiting or waiting for the war to begin or to end.

In silent wait, she swam in the river that changed her skin into a coppery shade, if underwater. After hosing herself off behind the cottage, she lay on the bed spread-eagled, half-awake in humidity.

In her worry dream, Georg smiled at her, wrinkling with interlacing fine wires and hairs from his beard for a mask to seize. Her head became feverishly paranoiac. Once he'd owned up about the daughter of Sarah, Mala and his mistress. To know what's going on in the world, ask the mistresses and prostitutes, her bon vivant distant spouse and her work buddy in crochet from Pomeranians once said. Where did he or she land in the war? Odd bits about Georg, Heinrich, Karl or Conrad, never thought about, crept into her sleep. They must gathered together forces and follow the swarm at the war fronts in Germany.

Where was Grete now? Angela? Mala dead or sent off, mustn't she be? Was Grete, oh God?

Awake on the bedstead edge, she tried drying off the ever renewing humidity from her skin, and breathed in homey bread, suffusing the cottage from an electric oven, unlike the once familiar old walk-in fireplace, where kneaded rising bread had risen and baked in the old country. Would bread suit the party, called a pot-luck picnic?

Lise, mother of Erika was baking the birthday cake for J.T., America's new army recruiter in their area. Meta was scouting potential loves and hates to blot out her Georg perplexity with its anxiety. Upon hearing musical razzamatazz from a distant radio, she swooned and imagined the curve down hiss spine. God knows, Georg could have been ambling toward the same party.

At the actual party, the most beautiful girl in the world with split curls greeted her on the front porch in German. Was she the fabled Mala, when young? Possibly, both she and Meta, who froze, were angling toward the same fellow in this world at war with fewer men. The greeter's natural ebony shiny curls, dandling rococo around her wide dark brown eyes. Her skirt ruffles gathered in tiers and flared rose-colored at the knees. She held onto it, so as not to trip, as she showed Meta the way in.

J.T. handsome youth watched beauteous girl. Neither spoke though nodded, for they lacked common tongues. She did smile, as Meta handed warm bread to her.

In the living room, some hovered over nuts with a nut-cracker, homemade cheese and pumpernickel crackers, and two older women spoke incomprehensible English mixed with German.

"The family she came with put her in the kitchen. She's changing families now. She perfects her English, but she refuses to speak." The women, all solidity and no-nonsense, wore aprons with appliqués of apples.

"No?! Here she must not speak German."

"We're just back. She's our distant relative."

"You heard about the camps thereabouts and now hereabouts?"

"You mean the Jew camps with political types over there are here!?"

"No, Prisoners of War, POWs from Deutschland right here?!"

Meta lingered no longer. As she tried to mingle, she recognized no one. Ferns swathed over an iron planter within the window light through tiny-leaved vinery, and silhouetted it and people. French doors and screened windows muted their sounds.

Because of the party's lack of a center, the party givers and goers wandered onto the veranda around a rare huge trunk oak, almost within the house. Mist warmed the haze. Everything touched was clammy, and everyone seemed chummy, except that no one spoke to her.

"Has anyone run into newcomers?" a voice asked.

"What newcomers?" Voices lowered, as if among inmates. Everyone knew an actual prison with guards and heavy fencing topped by heavy spiraling concertina wire, seen from the highway. German prisoners of war! POWs, getting what they deserved, aha! Voices collided and compared notes.

Her German accent rendered her suspect regarding the pro-ventriloquist Bund. Sweat ran off her face and chest, while rain tapered into dripping from the leaves, bringing later arrivals into shelter under the overhanging roof. Some even arrived by canoes or rowboats down or up river. Folks' unseen voices, amplified over the water, though muffled onshore. Instead of pushing herself into the talkers, she sat by the fireplace's blue flames.

Someone began sketching on the stone hearth with chalk and charcoal around the fireplace. Young again: as if the background judged the foreground. The youth presided over the old. This youngish woman, richly pigtailed down her back, stood back from her cartoon drawings to add small logs into the fire and twigs. One blue flame bobbed up, and viewers "oh-h-ed."

Stonemasons had lugged stones in from the woods and quarry and stacked them with lime cement to craft the wall-sized fireplace with small carvings on the flat stoned mantel.

Saxanus the old stonebreaker unknown here could have quarried the stones nearby with his mallet. Actually, two guests in jeans said that in this Depression economy they'd found quarry work near Devil's Lake.

Startled by blasting out here, though miles away, the fire arranger jerked out another wet log. At dusk, did the party-goers hear war sounds, the detonating and splitting rocks?

Of the party goers, one noted that America stayed out of war as long as possible. Now they could not get away from it. Others called the war avoiders in cat-calls, "kraut-symps," "weaklings," or "pacifists," or "isolationists." Sounds came from geese, loons and whippoorwills, when another quarry boom roared.

"At least, our family line knew where our parents came from and were going," someone was saying. "And not get pregnant, until ready."

Meta knew about unwed mothers—she was one of sorts═ the two women voiced, "Ja." Meta guarded her thoughts.

"Ja is not in our language here," this voice said. "It's German—here we speak only English."

Meanwhile, the graceful woman continued to stoke the fire. Frustrated that neither coal nor charcoal would light this fire, she eased back and said, "Too much paper in the fireplace."

Dry chunks age-compressed needed fluid to ignite. Struck and lit, matches fired up shavings an burned out. "No luck," burning up the recent or ancient past.

"Katie!" Somebody else called out. Meta jumped. She and Katia scooped each other into their arms and sang joy in this strange midland place. Katia had arrived here to visit escapees and relatives who'd invited her to this party. Katia was "scraping by," as a book designer. Nothing about her was self-conscious. Smiling between her wide cheeks sweetened her face between her small eyes. Hair braided over her spine, she chuckled within other loose hair waves around her features...

For once, Meta relaxed. But the crowd noised about with four letter words, "shit" and "fuck" heard in Niedersachen, Lower Saxon farmyards. Seen from the sofa floor, four legs in jeans came in from farm or quarry work. Sizing them up, she glanced at her own outfit. One man sank onto the long maroon plush couch before the fire. He admired the flashing green spikes. "Nice Hookers' green light."

"What?"

"A watercolor name the green lantern at the nearby small resort pier end warned boaters, against crashing."

"Not so." She turned toward this jovial Don rotund at his waist. He laughed at her doubts; his belly urged her to hug him, as it jounced like Tante Lore's jolly old silver Buddha incense statue she lit incense in his lap beneath her first pointed radio, back in Celle.

Eyes smarted, throats coughed within the slight haze and smoke. Faces still glowed from by the indoor bonfire.

Another fellow strolled over, but the smoke still bent up out slightly of the chimney. "Watch out. The flue's been clogged for years. Why this fire anyway, when it's warm inside and outside?"

"Not here. Chilly, damp," said one fellow.

"Pour water on the fire," someone ordered.

"Some of us like fire," another said, in a cool spring night, May 1.

"Smoke's okay, without breathing!"

"Sit low. Hot air rises. On the floor you can breathe." Voices disconnected, as everyone was regrouping away from the smoke.

Another man smiled, devastating her. He entranced her. She tracked his words. How are you? She groped for some topic to hold him. Men were instants.

Life here by the fireplace meant sitting around waiting to die or burn.

Under the overhang braced by a pole held onto with her right hand and later a broom in the left, sweeping up ashes from littering newspaper. There was grilling of "hotdogs," "weiners," "marshmallows."

The jolly man swung round and above her at the pole, nearly colliding with her. Both laughed at their impromptu Maypole. How could she dream of and swell over Max, if transported here will such a fellow as Don who was asking how she was.

"Sad?" Meta replied to Don, who thought her oddly unpatriotic.

The Civilian Peace Service camp was the best way through the war, he told someone on her other side. "But I resist war, even 'this good war. I can't shoot people in it.'"

Terribly religious, believes in God, must be pious. She said so aloud.

"I am," he laughed.

Someone handed her another beer, too acid from American hops to swallow, unlike the mellower European ale. Instantly, her mind pleaded for a benign father, who'd cherish her and her son and thrive within the area with good will and leadership, one who'd not driven the mother figure away because of her beliefs.

At such thoughts, a tall bearded man with skin straps on his feet beneath his body sloped around his petite mate, "We've been secretly engaged for a year," he told Don.

Back near the fire, Meta side-glanced at Don.

"Want to go home?" he asked, "As a medic, I'll give you a ride on my stretcher." She ignored him. Americans were so informal. His belly, shirt buttoned down, rose in humor in time to his words and beer and drew her closer.

Her thinking back to a guffawing Heinrich, father-uncle, if here, would be "Henry" or "Hans or Hank." He'd never tolerate such informality, except with enough ale.

"Nice dresses, nice weave," Don said about its texture around muted pink and blue squares. Others here wore jeans like Don here on the long elephant hide couch before the flames, shooting up, "Great blue shades." His living came from copying old masters' portraits and originating painting of old people, some fishing.

"Fishing's an odd subject. Artistic? Realistic?" She asked.

The war interrupted his life, as he earned cash from painting. Due at his base to ship out, this medic Don was painting his models in their homes or old age homes. His buddy photographed, he painted. He little persuaded her of the worthiness of his elder portraits.

"Why start this fire anyway? It's warm outside and in," Don asked. He must be hosting this gathering. In his spotless blue work shirt, after throwing a log on the fire, he moved adjacent to her on the couch arm with his arm back against where Meta sat, as though a couple. Hopefully, no one noticed. Leaning away, she heard Don start talking to another girl.

He'd studied pre-med. A conscientious objector (CO), he lived as a believer. "I'm a simple man," overheard to the lean younger girl in a red dress, shrunk, for sure, from its original size.

Swing musicians began setting up their stands and music sheets, as Meta browsed among partygoers. "Oh," Don reintroduced himself, sensing the crowd bewildered her. She was lost in anxiety and startled by his acuity.

On her other side, Meta heard from the engaged tall bearded man, arm still around his fiancée, said, "For the sake of love." He toasted her, as he held his see-through stein of amber beer.

The Chicagoan held forth with Don. Both were CO's, and reminded anyone listening they'd challenge the police. He'd seen a black man banged on the head by one and wrote down the badge number. "Out of nowhere, three plainclothesmen threw me on the concrete and hauled me off. I wasn't dressed for jail." He angled out around from his fiancée.

Backing away from the fire, Katia said, "Sounds like home." Meta tensed and nodded. Don was moving back toward Meta and squeezed next to her. She thought to edge away but listened. Die or live.

Don said. "I'm the fool. He's one. For people here, I'm their arts and crafts peace fool. In fact, they ate me."

The other C.O. said, "In the cells, we waited for orders to turn over all our things. An inmate explained: remove your shoes and hand over your wallet. That's a search. If this black guy didn't tell me about the routine, I wouldn't have known it, shut up as I was for 24 hours without food."

Don was standing closer to her, while finishing talking on his other side.

Bother with someone who submitted to authority only to resist it instead of joining up with authority? Men as men stood tall shoulder to shoulder. Accept this new kind?

"Want a ride home?" he asked, "on my stretcher." She nodded yes.

43.

Now back in New York, Katia promised to meet her at the silvery new diner. Coming out of the subway, Meta scolded herself for neglecting her mother and Todi. Was Todi making friends? Was her mother ill? Where's Grete? What about the almost late Katia? And that Ada.

To update her knowledge, Meta, while she waited reading a social work journal to compare her exit from Germany with the trials of those still trapped in "greater Germany," struggling toward America. Over two million Germans leaped the hurdles to get in just before the 1930s Depression. To win acceptance, the article said, immigrants must prove ideal citizens with family support through any troubles and with employability. How had the Hamburg consul determined she was? Aha, Todi's visa must also have granted him "agricultural worker" status.

Here waiting for Katia in the chrome diner, citizens blissfully sipped coffee and chattered. Could they know the German concentration camps began smoking in 1939-40?

Social work periodicals wrote about the Germans applying to the consuls to enter America. No visa would await her, if she'd tried coming in now.

Incarnadine the sky was enveloping them before dawn within the shadow fort, an embrasure, where if well armed, human arms grabbed them, and revealed their faces in turmoil. Their voices begged the world: Listen, what do you see, really see? The sky has turns to blood.

"In waves, we crept against messengers biking with messages. So our sleuths moved in on tiptoe against these under-miners rising out of the earth center and exploding.

"Do you know that to the north and east, the middle and west," Meta's mother, Annike, said, "They've returned to life all their stalwarts, and we're all tyrants?"

Studying for her American citizenship, Meta sweated out the truth from her random thoughts about democracy. *Treason to gather together in Germany, where even the stalwarts kept silent or if they spoke, they were provocateurs or malefactors. All who speak out are lined up to meet the hangman.*

After whispering to Katia about encountering Lili, Meta also tried campaigning for a newcomer for the City Council in the 1950s. Jo the candidate had lived for ten years on Smith Street and was running on behalf of refugees, immigrants, displaced persons and especially ordinary citizen folk. Working folks, how Meta saw herself as a citizen. Her longish jacket, forest green, with high wide shoulders above knee length flared skirt was stylish enough.

But her voice betrayed her. "No one believes you," her mother told her. Katia agreed, "With your accent and no formal citizenship training, you lack credibility."

"But Jo has my accent."

"Barely so. But she and her mother were born in America. We weren't."

Meta loathed canvassing. "Yes, they'll believe me with my accent," but liked planting trees or making Red Cross bandages more than educating voters. "They will accept Jo's American-Norwegian-German regional inflected accent, but not her ethnicity. The clergy will forbid it and topple her."

The mission of Meta continued: her candidate should win. By will, Meta knocked door by door, house by house, district by district, and person by person. Good streets and their people were organized, just as evil ones turned evil; they did not just happen, for sure. Annike, now Anne, tried handing out election pamphlets with her, but was sickly. They were organized. Such were Meta's thoughts that sank inside her, while waiting for Katia.

Both, Katia and Meta had met each other's fathers though hardly ever spoken with each others' mothers. Nor had Meta ever met Lili, though she'd longed for an elegant mother, like Grete's. Meta had only met Grete's mother and father, mostly her father.

Katia's gold hairs, some pewter, glinted in the window sunlight, as she spoke. "My brother left and returned home, as un known. By the way, he failed his Arbitur studies.

Instead, he enrolled into the military, surprising my father, who'd said nothing to him in front of us, mother, or aunts. Without pushing him to lose face, father had goaded my brother to learn Greek and trigonometry. In time, my brother vowed to follow the Free Corps to salute to sing and march. "With real men," he said, "we're renewing the past."

He'd believed in affiliating with a party union. His father, mine too haunted the galleries and raved about orchestras. "So his son, my brother, says, 'War debt's gutting us. Versailles Treaty extorts more debt from us. My father agreed. My brother promoted himself as Man of the air, invincible, ready to fly, ready to kill.

"The first sons begin to sound like losers, and women like weaklings." So declared Katia.

"I never saw your father or brother," noted Meta, "with you in your home or with you when you visited, or we went to Berlin,"

"You did," reply Katia, "But you never noticed. You saw them ordinary looking and quiet.

"The maid though watched both and was coy with them. Were they, one or both secretly involved? Katia thought her father had been with her once, when her mother seemed inattentive.

In time, as the brother's new self emerged from learning auto and plane mechanics. "Also, he began angling for their maid-wench voluptuary, who sought to better herself. He sought further to improve himself by joining with the Nazis and the party for aeronautical engineering and pinned the ancient sign of the sun, the swastika, on his lapel. But no armband, not at first.

"'Not here in our home!'" Katia's father renounced such insignias.

What difference would that make?" Katia asked him. "The Nazi insignia prevailed. Then, our maid leaked her pro-Nazi views. She quit us to expose us. 'You are not a true Nazi family,' she said.'"

"I came to America, as soon as possible. Why didn't we come out together?"

"Why," Meta asked, "didn't we catch on fast enough to swift-work against the regime?"

Hunching shoulders around her head, Katia, saddened. "I miss father and mother. Long ago, they grew apart. We parted from our Fatherland."

Meta feared aloud about the motherland—"What if my real mother was Mrs. von Handler?" She'd excavated for her real mother in the Hanover or Holstein cemeteries. "Instead, how was I to understand that I, a child, had already met her as my other aunt; Heinrich bellyached about her like a Saxon deserter the New World. Lo and behold, I'd met my mother in a childhood instant with Tante Lore. Remember her?"

"I couldn't really know for sure," replied Katia. "Besides, I barely knew mine so busy she was with volunteering and traveling with my father, so I was often left with the nanny, housekeeper and governess. You seemed even more on your own."

"Abruptly, everything shifted. Ugh.

"We went round to see the tenants, and sometimes to attend church, until he wanted the church out of his way.

"The military and the party scooped them all up into lowlife status," Katia said.

"It did. Who knew? We didn't expect soldiers to war against us civilians, especially females, and pivot against the Jews. We complied with Hitler's war and regime by leaving. I left, instead of hiding and struggling against it."

Three weeks later, Meta was again expecting to meet up with Katia in another restaurant. Instead, Lili sat down in her diner booth. Shiny ebony and silvery, hair around her eyes and behind her ears curved to her voice box to resemble a dark-haired Veronica Lake.

Meta felt within a broken umbrella, spokes collapsed and black material enshrouding them.

"You don't know me, do you?" Lili asked.

Meta jumped. "How could I want to?" She lowered her voice for civility.

Lili continued, "I'm here. In fact, I'm everywhere I can go. Most war zones I have survived in, Poland, Germany, America. Come with me to the Bund, around the corner. The group unifies against the enemy and speaks German together."

Seeing Lili, Meta, awkward, asked, "How do you win Americans by speaking only German?"

"They're not all German."

Curious about—whirling umbrella on fire—the insignia-wearing Swastika group repelled Meta, the whole idea, but curiosity ruled. Be invisible to Bund members. Observe, but ignore. Her mother would fume. Lili was sucking her in. Should she be lured into it and confront it?

"Come with me! It's an organizing meeting. You don't have to join."

"They'll never make it here. Too crude. She looked at her watch. "Where's Katia? She was to meet us, wasn't she?"

"She's coming with us, isn't she?"

44.

Because of Annike's delicate health, Meta bussed from New York through Chicago's loop and up to the northern midwest. Illness did not stop her mother from welcoming Meta. At present, two clerics opposed Jo's possible candidacy for the city council, so that Meta and her semi-ailing mother Annike drove from the river edge into the college town, where Jo lived. They would attend a mass one Sunday and a protestant service the next to get acquainted with attendees. What the clergy would say, as their Adam's apples rose and fell above their clerical collars, from their pulpits, mother and daughter would take note of.

How to support Jo was unclear. Nor did they discuss the matter community of semi-exiles by the river. Meta and Annike seesawed over what to do and whether to continue ringing doorbells to urge others how to vote. They scolded themselves.

Annike scolded. "Going door to door benefited the NSDAP rise in Lower Saxony.

Magazines and newspapers, as you know, helped their campaign."

"Communists also stuffed their literature inside dailies or weeklies."

"I know." said Meta.

Fine letters on vellum, as if personally addressed won over Heinrich, who felt honored at the acclaim for his local role as leader. Meta recalled too well his Thing, rural men's circle who sat on rocks to agree usually with him or on chairs by his fireside. "Nazi enrollees went into club by club, church by church, government agency by agency, unit by unit, pressured, squeezed and threw out opponents and enemies." The powers- that-be rammed any resisters. Rallies with Nazi speakers enthralled most.

"If we're silent here, we'll discourage votes for Jo."

But Meta and Annike belonged to the "foreigner group," more so as Germans. So they two renamed themselves, "Margaret and Anne," nicknamed "Peggy and Annie." Abruptly, Meta said, "What kind of guardians of the public good are we, if we disguise ourselves? Or should we?"

They bickered and snapped.

"People will hisss at us." said Anne-Annike. "Because of our accents and lack of knowledge, listeners will avoid us. Endless amounts. They don't want to do anything, until they know more.

"Worse, if anti-Semites in the pulpits speak out, listeners will stay silent. Or they'll whisper."

Anne the mother says, "No, listeners are anti-Semites, and their leader-speakers silence the others. They follow the swarm. It's like whites against blacks."

"What good does ringing doorbells against words do?" She and her mother opposed the rise of more wooden dummies.

"Because of German birth, Jo's a foreigner," one clergyman we heard said. He omitted her Jewish ancestry in America, his first god forsaken words. Another referred to Jo as 'that Jewish woman.'"

"Her mother Leah was born in Poland, remember?" Anne/
Annike said.

Hemming and hawing over their remorse for suffering
hinted at love of faith that life could be better versus the strong
slay the weak.

Pell-mell, Anne and Meta rehashed Jo's campaign yet
again for the town council—but on their dead-end road, many
expressed themselves with accents—Poles, Russians, Byelorus-
sians and "Krauts, and anyone else." White Russians all spoke
accented English or in tongues few on their dirt road understood.

"No." Meta: "Keep quiet, mustn't we? Someone might spit
at us, mightn't they?" Without certainty about electoral boundaries, Anne and Margaret still handed out leaflets to voters to
win them to Jo the candidate.

Without citizenship, one could not vote. Nor especially
could the black fisher-folk who fished on the grade, as it crossed
the recess in from the branching Wisconsin river toward the
Mississippi.

Slipping on new espadrilles, Meta yearned to whirl to dance,
not mull over voting.

After donning these wood-stacked wedgies and tying the
fuchsia ties crisscrossing her shins, she began click-clacking
on the wooden floor. Her tiered gold skirt above her rare new
cotton and straw shoes from Depression and wartime rationing
suited her love of square or folk dancing.

Her vacation ending, she'd relaxed too long in the far
countryside and missed the New York bus from Chicago. If
she didn't hurry enough, her director back in New York would

let her go. She loathed herself, walking along the shore line. To renounce fear, she must return to the New York City. Dancing and canvassing did not help enough. A sign on the shoreline, jutting into the river, as she walked along it, warned, "Undertow." No one knows their time of death. Her mother's recent pallor and frequent need to lie down suggested death.

Later, Meta also browsed the night sky. Ready for the North Star on a break from her mother's red-stained cottage, she climbed the bluff at sunset and looked toward the river. The raging sun on the tributary was flowing toward the Mississippi. Its surface disguised whirlpools.

Her frenzying inside her and outside made her path too risky to climb around during the sundown meltdown in the near dark.

Stormy talk from the night before and ideas flooded her mind this morning. From the all-out crush of death wishes and war, Heinrich must have indoctrinated Todd.

Her mind turned. Was Grete alive? Meta shuddered and slumped and felt nauseous over other issues: Jo's candidacy in memory of Grete?

To find Indians in the area while she hiked and trekked, every face needed scanning. Place names everywhere suggested landed natives in New France.

Late May air chilled all creatures. Birds strutted pecked on the promontory sand, where Blue Herons landed. A sleek blackbird, raven maybe, thumped on an upturned old-fashioned copper washtub not yet green. Wind up wringers in wood, noticeable in two farmyards, like small rolling pins for bread or miniature wooden Irminsuls. Gusting in the wind, a grand oak, giant tall Irminsul branched heavenward and gusting in the wind. A raven, the dark big black, flew off in the name of memory. From its oak branch, its acorns could knock anyone below.

Now here she was hiking again with an old map to seek old Indian mounds along the edge of known Ice Age ledge fragments. In her pants sides, she'd pocketed the hand-sized knife and .22 revolvers, both with opal-like handles from Heinrich's drawer within a drawer. She'd shoot a dying bird.

Unaccountably jittery during her walk, once in the house she answered the phone. "Don't hang up. Speak up." Instead silence.

Silence continued throughout the next night, Friday. Struggling as she was through the New York School of Philanthropy in the old Carnegie mansion was her fate.

Now though next day in the local free library, she studied newspapers, days after issued, arrows knifed the latest front-page map. Nazis attacked one side of the line and the Allies on the other. Thank Gott, war was diminishing in Germany— only women must be left. Russians fought westward, the Allies eastward in 1944.

Back at the house, her mother was recuperating from a minor stroke, and the doctor warned her to handle her work schedule gingerly. "More calls?" she asked Meta. "The line's dead."

The phone rang again. Unhooking the receiver for her ear, Meta in a livid state and on tiptoe spoke into the black horn of the telephone, pretending to hear a wrong number to prevent her mother from hearing. "Who's this!?"

Silently, the caller stayed on the line, as if listening in on their party line, ripe for gossip about war prisoners. Across the local telephone exchange, over on Main Street, the local switchboard operator could plug one household into any other.

Her graying blonde mother, vivacious, was alert with ire. "Was the call from a bill collector?" Her little check cared for food with rationing and against waste. "Your check will help." Her mother's words thudded. Looking after her and working here overwhelmed Meta, kinetic-minded into despair.

"I can't." Thunder and lightening crackled against the dark, and a tree blanched and split into stark naked, like birth or death. Trees stuck out their neck branches at the scowling white sky night.

That night Meta dreamed that he played his organ, as others blew up statues off memorial to warriors. Hidden, they lit up and exploded; statues fell, heaving chips or faceted arrowheads; broken stoneware and china with hairline cracks thrown at him lay at his feet. He asked, "Why throw pieces at my feet?" He was sorry about his ruining her life.

For the time being, the two of them were closer, while farther apart. Sullen about his rising temper, hers was slower but meaner in the long run. Men's feelings were apt to merge into war anger. But nothing happened, not so far.

Many stops along the way rattled her into sitting upright on the bedstead edge, she groped for the kerosene lantern to light up her mother's small house, no manger house this one: no cows, sheep or horses. Only woodchucks and squirrels were heard, and the whippoorwill had been here, and ducks quaked, and woodpeckers knocked holes into trees or pecked the metal strip across the roof peak.

"Sorry," he, Georg or Heinrich or a blurred unknown, repeated within the ruckus, "I never intended to ruin your life." Dazed upon awakening, pieces of her life replayed themselves with many stops along the way, for he was restless, so they'd visited an extinct hermitage with live pines above stones, called pillows. Around them, hermits erected stone houses without roofs.

He was determined to cross the Baltic; she preferred the Atlantic. The last time he was blowing war pipes; his winged elbow squeezed the larger organ. Blow it, he did, and hoisted the bayonet.

True, she herself shunned all soldiers though goaded herself into going with Harald. In the war zone, clanking distracted them. Getting used to the hubbub from the crowd that gave wide berth to tanks, Georg or Harold, said, "If only, they'd used more in the last war, it would have ended sooner to win.'"

She sidestepped the cemetery, gated by spikes with a coat of arms: a dancing skeleton. Along came babies around the tombs, playing hide and go seek and yowling, "Take me, take me."

The babies' hair was still downy, longish or loose. Their words, breathless, were innocent, from having been killed as Jewish babies, thinkers and handicapped ones.

As she and Georg-Harald-Heinrich walked, the summer night lit up, and he proposed rescuing her in their joint life with their to-be baby Todi she would envelope with love.

The day after the night before, they two sat in a public house, where he drank in the hidden warrior's sister, who otherwise looked like everyone in his birthday suit. The beautiful dark-haired woman from years before was still drinkable.

While Meta dreamed, a lost bird a prehistoric moa or crane enlarged to carry a human—a stork bringing forth a son in this makeshift joy. As surfaces were scaled to times lived in, he himself was downy. She was a muff. "My member does not fit in," he said, back in their guesthouse room, away from the night, from tanks, pub, cemetery and unexpected church sanctuary beneath ancient and current battle victory banners.

The morning after her dream-nightmare, she intended to go back to the Protestant church. The sun was rising and broadening its fire wings across the river toward her. Daylight brought the joy of baking fresh cookies for others. Nanna would have approved her going to a rummage sale with Toll House cookies, though Meta possessed only these chocolate chip essentials, but no rummage to take along.

The bell turning, not the phone, had been ringing during her hallucinatory dream. But this bell was real. A shaggy, bearded man stood there, blocking the light and the doorway. Georg or the ghost of Harald, not Max or Alex, as preferred, stood there in refracted light through oak. Oaks seemed as tall here as in Germany but not as massive-trunked. Leaves above the yard were the only shelter in this encounter. Above his silvery bearded threads and his slight upper harelip knot, his eyes still beamed toward her.

Collecting herself, she screamed. "Georg, why are you here?" Hug this man? He started to hug. She froze before shaking his hand, yanked it away from the hand of a killer stranger.

Once he absorbed and obsessed her. Now had she ever been enthralled over him? Her feelings converted into stone.

Still, instant bullets shot through her. "What in hell's name compelled you to come here?

"The war's over. I knew you'd be here? You're my family, and Todi's my son whose mother you are."

She fell back onto her mother's threadbare armchair. That day she'd redone her hair, rouged her cheeks lightly and pressed dark coral lipstick on her lips. Ready to go, dressed in a blue cotton overblouse with fitted chest and high sleeves, she tried shooing Georg away. To bolt the doors, she nudged him outside. She wanted only to go to the rummage sale. She fingered the little revolver in her deep side pocket of the slacks worn for the last few days.

"No, the war's not over! Aren't you exhausted?" Exhuming herself from her fear, she tried calming down; tougher answers need demanding questions. "Where did you come from?" What battle, what camp? One here? How did the Americans or Russians let you go? Newspapers tucked such tales in. She must know his.

On his back and shoulder hung his bomber jacket that fell below his belly, lower in front than his back. His skin coloring, dark reddish tan, sun-stained and roughened, like the living dead recalled from the cemetery. His hair coated his chin below his yellowed teeth.

"Why didn't they keep you!?! "Go back to your country! This one's mine—my future. My mother's here with my son."

Heinrich had disdained her. Now his replacement Georg said, "Our son."

Blurting out the name, "Hund," Meta derided them. "That's you, the cur, the HUND.

"What's the use?" He did not answer.

She pulled out a drawer as if to remove some tissue for her sneezes and cover the trigger. He could overpower her and use it, or she could.

Alone in the cottage, he, if trigger-happy, could stay or leave or do himself in. Her mother was now at work.

No, no, she couldn't leave him for her ailing mother to deal with. She was trying to chew him out as an interloper. Owing him nothing, she twisted her hands. Fear began leaving her. Once she'd offered him love, which he'd violated.

Violation at home reinforces the horror of the Hitler regime. She chokes at the thought. Fear stabs her again. She throws the door open and shuts it on him

Refugees were featured in LIFE; their horrors offered slim hope. How could she communicate with Grete, with Georg here? The two slid past each other. She left him on the couch, grabbed her Toll House cookies and left. She should give him one, shouldn't she? She reached for the gun in her pocket. She'd not forgotten it. It was there. She needed its little bullets. Were they all used in the war?

She ran back and dropped the gun in the doorway in hopes he would use it on himself. What a stupid idea. She grabbed him, his arm, then, fled the house for the church with the spire, humble, plain and unassuming, far smaller than the elegant Lower Saxon churches.

Not one with clerical invective: "How can you vote for a woman, Jewish, for the town council?" She'd enter into this church for the rummage sale. She'd beguile others into passing out literature for Jo.

Into this sanctuary with her cookies, she entered and tried to pray. Words would not form, only facsimiles and distaste for

Georg and guttural sounds. Their son might tell her what to do. Offer hospitality to Grete, once Georg left. Did she owe him anything? Todi, yes, she valued that he was brought forth.

At the rummage sale, she pretended to notice merchandise and sagged at the thought of going back to her temporary home. Oh, she must jump on the bus for New York.

Nevertheless, when she'd returned, he'd left. Where had Georg gone? She'd not understood, maybe to his army POW, Prisoner Of War, camp near here. No wonder German POWs were sent over here—so many German speakers populated the state, in certain German-American towns, with next to other tongues.

Not bothering not to light the lantern or wash in the basin next to the bed, surrounded by marble, she tried absorbing solid facts, known by heart. Exhausted, her slacks fell off onto the floor, and she slept in her small room, her cell, on her one person cot, in this only cottage place, uncontaminated by his arrival.

So many facts were unknown and unwarranted: why Georg was here, and how he'd found her? Turning off her brain with two aspirins, she sought to fall asleep.

Inside a new roadster that swept through the countryside, rounding major and minor curves, from the back seat behind the passenger seat, it was seen that a car such as this swerved, when the highway narrowed, and the car skirred away from the bridge side guard and raced onward. All roadhouses, farmhouses, shops hugged the road. The buildings were blotched red. Eying the way forward, the car she rode drove on its own.

45.

With the steel toe of his old shoe boot, Todd kicked a rock and scoffed. Both he and his mother grumped over worldly chaos. They argued, bickered and silenced each other, as old lives re-intertwined and renewed in this new place.

"To go through life," he told her, "Save right from wrong principles. Stick to them even in catastrophe." Whether the working class slum-like Wedding, the locus where poor and working poor, flag bearers fought armed gangs with fists and guns, which was which. There years back she'd met his Aunt Liesl, her cousin. As time flew, clock hands turned like knives to slice off people ready for conflict.

She had not yet told him that his father had reappeared.

Todi imitated her. "The hand that squeezes principles squeezes us and slams the door. He listened and seemed relaxed. His girl friend was to visit soon. Meta was uneasy about this visit and everyone's, especially Georg's. Where was Don?

Grete survived? But Ada had also, surely, and she did arrive. Meta had run into this once intimidating woman, now sloping over like one who'd just fled to see her uncle by marriage. She did seem a bit shriveled. Not even that. She rambled along and justified herself and her flight with ten dollars to her name. Every immigrant came here with this sum.

"Out west. I'm to visit my uncle, handsome, loveable and humorous. He'd loved my own mother, a concert pianist herself by way of the Frisians, and the great Romantic composer's grandaughter. She had married my father. But I've never lived much with him. My uncle married her sister instead in a loveless marriage.

"Did she care?"

"I don't know. Who? The aunt, my grandfather and the universal grandfather composer is the one referred to as never married at all.

"Any of us, as it happens often. Pairs in war often part. All you can do in war horror is hunker down, go underground or leave."

"You did," said Meta. "If, Good God, if we're not careful, there'll be nowhere to go." She didn't think this other woman heard the remark.

When great economy of Germany had dropped, when Ada was twelve, her mother said, "We'll go to the bank, and rush to an Expressionist art even with Klimt from the south, Vienna or especially here in Berlin, for real art was musical rapture.

"No," she told me, "the next time at thirteen, we rushed to the bank" with murals inside. We scurried there, paramount over any other activity. No straightening or tying my bow on straight. I stumbled. She dragged me on.

"The bank was shut with no sign of life and never opened that day. The closing distressed my mother, needing food money.

"When our grand ventriloquist assumed power from the old President von Hindenburg, I was thirteen. Insiders despise outsiders. Vigilant, that's all you can be in life. She'd hoisted her cameras to record life.

Retracing steps to Berlin's Adlon with its glitzy abandon, harridans on the street who begged and whores male and female, who lavished physicality, once passed them, she'd tiptoed into Ada's studio with its faces, some now well-known. "Sit down," Ada and assistant whispered. "Tell no one who you see here."

With enough to pay for her headshots and go, instead Meta had sat and waited. Dark suited men arrived, insisting she leave. She fled into the water closet, and peeked out a door slightly ajar. A black slather-haired man with inked in mustache was recognizable. She was frantic. Evidently, accompanied in off the street, this medium tall unsmiling mustachioed dignitary scowled. Under mistletoe in the studio doorway, Ada pecked him on the check. He growled, disconcerted while angry at being effusively humiliated.

Start vigilance against violence early on. "The president was the ventriloquist, chancellor too lacking civilizing Bildung or learning. Everyone says this. "Loathsome, he's small fry. He passes us by, disappears." Most dismissed him unimportant, overrated and dissolved in import. Still though the difference between good and evil was also disappearing.

How do you see into hell's chaos? And we welcomed the leader to drive us to communal greatness.

"We all gassed among ourselves about the war starting against Poland: the Poles were out to get us. The Minister of Propaganda harangued us, we people mouthed his words. "Attack the Poles first, our next door neighbors."

"In that last summer before the war against the horizon, ship after ship passed our island in the North Sea. What I left behind, Lore, Lie, Hansi visited; Nanna, Annike and Heinrich used to at Swinemunde that last summer before war in 1939. When did it begin? Is it over?

Ada, her mother, her sister she followed into photography and anyone who came to stay lived in Stettin. "My family was bohemian," she said," musical or mostly so, but we oriented toward our disciplines, practicing and rehearsing. We're susceptible people though, for all our defenses, rock-like."

"We did look up and see. There they go to Danzig! They're going after the Poles, making it Gdansk. We said and realized later.

"First, they'd occupied the Rhine, next the Sudetenland, then Poland. Goebbels roared massive crowds of us. 'Poland hides its danger to us with its weapons. Wait and see." He ranted. "We must march east to stop the Poles and claim our west land back."

"We knew about the camps. Not ones for children, mind you, or camps we kids set up to play in. But the Beating camps, they whispered, for political types, and the work camps the rest of us out of line. Inmates sickened and died. We all do, not thinking of work as health that way. When people the Jews were rounded up for "killing camps," we saw from our windows.

"We heard, but did not listen. We'd viewed but did not see. We refused to understand. But we did not think of "death camps."

"In school, our headmaster had told us to leave the Nazi buttons at home. Politics did not belong in school. We reversed this—politics in school, thought disregarded and viewpoint outlawed. The best was a humiliating slap.

"When the authorities ordered Dr. Ornstein to leave our school, the headmaster called us all together. "We did not want him to go, and if he left, we would welcome him back. He left.

He was said to have to be let go. I knew enough. The Jewish students would follow.

"One day, maybe about fifteen years ago, I expected to see my second best friend. Usually we met on the corner near the newspaper shop, where another girl friend's mother ran the candy and condiments shop.

"Good morning," I said. She replied, dark eyes sombre.

"We'd heard no news on the radio. We'd not yet received it on the BBC. If we'd tried listening, we'd be dragged to the polizei."

Listening to her son's talking and watching him sulking, Meta yearned for the same memory time for his boyhood and for Mopsi, tough little squashed faced dog, cuddly and stubborn. She grasped to find out if he was kicked and locked in a human sized cage. Not even Heinrich could get him released. She discerned that the helmeted heads cover weak brains.

Grete had disappeared. She returned. Her leg was cracked and bent at eighty per cent of one hundred.

We are all trunks, Meta thought. Split apart. A thousand years ago, a couple of trees had grown together though able to bend with the wind. The dual tree in its canopy like a windsock wind rushed through by the wind resisted toppling.

One day, in the postal box, a brazen and ultra white letter lay on its shelf. Her cousin in New York assured the U.S. authorities she would post bond, Meta told Grete, if Grete sought to do anything out of order.

Meanwhile, to mull over the whole still murky tale, Meta rested on her back at the bottom of her favorite tree trunk with its old leaves, seedlings and blown in fallen cones. The longer she laid there, as her mother had in the dirt, the more decay and droppings of birds and other compost evolved from the trees' inhabitants, fell, landing on and around her to build support for the roots, as they grew. Below the ancient and primitive tree, she sought to slither out from under memory.

But every act derived from the previous act. There was no leeway.

Happily out free, Diana-like and stealth-full, Meta with her deer under the fruited tree of life, truw for truth was sprouting closer to the ground than its crown of golden mistletoe, she aligned with it and sprawled her arms and legs spread like an axle between the plus and minus of love and war.

But haplessness supplanted courage in those who only watched and granted no happiness. All she was gather in her once-upon-a-time country thrust Gretes, Katias and Metas away and ensnared and Lilies and Adas. Far worse, caught, no, clawed and trapped Grete in the determining shadow of warrior past and present. The future had already taken place. The past the settlers and time racers sprang to life, but the future chose the wrong Idea.

When other tree and animal compost from squirrels and vermin landed on Meta, she continued believing in the biblical tree of life from the ancient Hebrew and the Saxon German Luther Bible, as she did, and in the Eurasian, of everlasting life and breadth of embrace, even she had slipped out from under the Tree of trees for the sake of memory to go on living, though her mother did not. This was how Annike would die: reentering memory under the trees on a cool day, lying down with the breeze and winds rocking her through the great portal and push her ultimately up through the growing universal tree pillar.

Meanwhile falcons flew overhead, soared in their same sky path over warm streams within the estuaries and rivers, one wingspan apart. She would take one step, then another and another to see that Jo was elected, and another and go door by door, house by house until others came along and knocked on other doors.

Months later, Rudy, the crusty immigrant Saxon farmer, folded his arms across his chest and spoke. "Annike still holds power over this land." Her small acreage lay on the opposite side of the ridge that emerged from the ice age. "You won't believe it, of course. Not many do. I swear it's the truth, the other night I saw her, as I see you right here. I sat up straight in bed. A wise looking though garishly dressed angel with brownish aging skin pressed me to go outside and close the barn door, so the cows would stay inside the door to the south. So I got up and did so. Finally, one day I told another farmer up the road about her."

"I saw her too, I saw your mother, I did," another farmer said, "sitting up there on the ridge studying the land and double-checking how to expand her acreage and see how we're doing."

"You know," Rudy said, "don't you that the July rain never poured on her grain fields? I swear. Whereas ours got drenched, hers was dry and saleable here and abroad. We had to make do, whatever and wherever we could. She harvested her grain for the local market."

"In hunting season, we'd be walking along the road with our rifles pointing to the ground. We'd meet up with her going the other way. She'd ask, 'Hunting in the woods?' We'd nod. She'd yell back, 'Words, not swords.'"

Meta had never quite known that mother, nor had Todd know his grandmother well, when Meta told him about the farmers who had seen her. He laughed at her joke. At the time, a tense calm overtook their music of the spheres. Outside, into the sunrise dipped the sunbow of life.

She laughed a bit. Strolling down the road, crunching on the gravel, she, once the girl with Saxon eyes, someone said, and still reddish-brown hair, not flaxen enough. Seeing not enough, acting too little and needing to try harder, saw Todd and Don coming toward her in the middle distance followed by Grete and Katia on another visit from New York and Mr. Paul Fleisher with his wife from Niedersachsen. They all waved both arms up and around each other in perplexing hope. She cried, he cried, they all cried.

Ultimately, a seasoned organizer, the rare resister observed that the women, the only ones left standing finally stopped the war. Now they would have to help overcome all scars. They were history walking down the avenue. Meta tried pressing on as a social worker, advanced, and one day she walked down the hospital corridor to their unit patient group meeting. The southern pastor in his very high phase was presiding for the Lord, as she found a chair. Abruptly, a sweating woman shrilled and yelled. "Stay away from me? She screamed. "You blasted ogre, you fat horror," to dramatize. Her captor attacking her in the camp as some bastard's trapped mistress. She was Martine.

Much later, she felt crucified in her mind that her cousin herded flocks of women into would be showers for gassing.

In 1996, Paul and his family were released by the German government from criminal status for trying to with stealth to counter the Nazis.

Anna opened the door. Like a child with an old-fashioned May basket, I'd hung the small orchid like flowers on the door, because mice were invading most of our apartments and my sheets, fine and soft at ca 600. Our apartments on the same floor plan differ. Hers is 1930s art deco with dark wood: a sideboard expands across the long wall of the living room with elegant older pieces her mother-in-law sent out from Germany. They include a tea set, a rococo vase, semi-Chinoiserie; a nude art deco sylph woman and fawn, Diana seated and other Old World 1920s pieces behind glass, not unlike that of the woman who fled East Germany. Mine is art deco 2000 fusion: Latino, 1940's overstuffed plush sofa and arm chair.

As always, she is groomed in well combined colors, a blouse iridescent in dark rose and off rose, one of two her son purchased that requires no ironing. "Come in, I show you." She showed me a booklet in German with evidently an account of the Holocaust victims who either fled with their lives, able to enter another country or succumbed to the death camps. All I could decipher was what was pictured, the old synagogue. In the front was the plan for the new one they built in 1932. "They should not have built it," she says, "and given it to the poor people to get out."

How could such as this happen, she asked over and over. It's horrible, beyond words, beyond horror, I say.

"They were my friends; I went to Catholic school with them. Was there G-d, a different God, than mine?"

It was so systemic, so plotted, so planned I try to say. They . . . I hunt for words, as I always have. Today I found a new set of words and remind myself to look in my pocket for the card I scribbled them on. Such words loop up from my unconscious at unlikely moments.

How the mind does bend. Bending, yielding into the coerced and forced by others. I say some say: Hitler was crazy and stupid. He won't last.

Grete pointed to her brother and her friend who lives in Riverdale, north of our building's location. She was teary about him in uniform but in what uniform, that of the First World War? Or was this the U.S. army uniform. Did he die in a concentration camp? I wonder but cannot ask at this moment.

Meta will go tomorrow with her brother and sister-in-law and son by car to L.I. for his grandson's Bar Mitzvah. Meta wanted to comfort her but thought it better to let her thoughts unroll. I placed my hand on her arm. A little later she held my hand.

Grete pointed to friends who'd died in the camp and one a beauty in her 1930s fitted dress.

"I had a dress just like that."

Her sister-in-law was the sharp one in the family. She hid money in her dress and and coat linings and rode the train from near Briland (spelling?) to Switzerland periodically and deposited enough money so by 1934 and so was able to buy a visa into Cuba for about $1000? "I said, but this was difficult to get into Cuba and into the U.S.A.

A week ago, when I asked how she got out, she'd said, "My number came up."

Her mother cried when she left as if never to see her again. Anna told her, "We're just going on vacation. I really thought that. But I was the one who stayed here and got my parents out."

They put my mother in jail. They came to get my father to take him away. But my mother said she didn't know where he was. They answered, he's your husband, you do know where he is.

Eventually, Dr. Kretschmer wrote a letter to the Gestapo about how my father had just had an operation and couldn't walk. Actually, he'd gone to the big city, Hamburg. I went to the jail to get my mother out. DOUBLE-CHECK.

"Last year I had a nervous breakdown and needed a woman to stay with me all the time. I used oxygen machines to breathe . . .

"When you're alone you think of all the people who've died.

It comes over you."

Human rights replaced random human empathy.

Those below lost whole families or at least one member into memory.

Friends are freedom, and trees (truw) are truth.

Acknowledgements

Living memories recombine here, recasting and recreating, experiences in art, wholly fiction. Gratitude is expressed to Susan Arends, Elisabeth Bauch, Irene Beyer, Joseph Cordoba, Markus Hagen who knows about agriculture, Lothar Rindfleisch whose father organized against Hitler, Andrea Hoffman-Simmel and Arnold Simmel for surprises. Mrs. Ruth Dennis, a young German citizen, said, "I'm getting out of here," and married a Greek. Ruth Levy who saw Hitler on her junior year abroad, while staying with monarchists. With his rosy-cheeked grade school daughter, Mr. Meyersohn, a widower, who brought her up in the Bronx and ran his Canal Street hardware store. Edythe Ballentyne and Karin Reynolds conveyed their unsparing views. Irene Beyer, Gertrude Seifert, Anna Spatz, who loves to dance, and Ursula Woodfin especially shared some deep and disturbing experiences in the concentrations camps. Special thanks to Jacqueline Schoenhaus whose great grandfather landed in an Auschwitz elevator and Gary Barnett for sustenance. Memory extends far back to my dentist, Dr. Waldemar Dahlk for lifelong friendship with my father and later my mother and his recall in front of a toddler, me, about his wartime experiences.

Fordham University Prof. Theodore Herskovits and his wife Ethel for what is unsaid and Long Island University Prof. Jeffrey Lambert for conversations about youth group leadership to Auschwitz and questions about Jewish life, and Inge Auerbacher wrote and spoke about hers to me offered much I am grateful to have learned.

Theoretically early on and later, in a live medical student seminar I was fortunate to attend with Anna Freud discerning early child development related to parenting.

Others spoke in passing: Karen Fodor, a gloriously voiced singer, on her family's flight from Hungary, Georg Simmel's grandson, Arnold Simmel on his childhood flight to London where the first book handed him to learn English from was Dickens' Bleak House and Andrea Hoffman-Simmel. Mr. Buchwald was engaging while interviewed on his fleeing away from Eastern Europe and he gave a graphic account of his red-haired grandfather's defiance of Hitler.

Dr. Joan Ecklein was highly informative on differences between East and West German dealing with perpetrators of Nazi atrocities, as was Cecilia Gilardi, who was interviewed sought for Stasi and, then, FBI recruitment; at age six she witnessed Crystal Night with her grandmother.

About the Author

Busing across Afghanistan and Iran led Jean Verthein to write about the wonders of survival. Counseling and teaching as an Adjunct Professor in Public Health and Social Work has been invaluable to her. Two Ragdale Foundation grants and a Sarah Lawrence College encourage publishing in *St. Ann's Review, Downtown Brooklyn, Absaloose, Adelaide, Green Mountains Review, River Press Review, Gival Press* and others.

www.ingramcontent.com/pod-product-compliance
Lightning Source LLC
Chambersburg PA
CBHW022244020726
47496CB00004B/1048